AFTER THE SNOWFALL

By Angela Sweeney

COPYRIGHT

All characters and events in this publication, other than those clearly in the public domain, are fictitious and any resemblance to real persons, living or dead, is purely coincidental.

Copyright © 2024 Angela Sweeney

The moral right of the author has been asserted.

All rights reserved. No part of this publication may be reproduced, stored in a retrieval system, or transmitted, in any form or by any means, without the prior permission in writing of the author or publisher.

ISBN: 9798324459796

Cover design by Jenny Bailey
Cover illustration by Gillian Burrows

For Alan, Jess, Ellie & Ned

You will know the truth,
and the truth will set you free
John 8:32

WINTER 1993

Prologue

I opened my mouth and let the snowflakes fall on to my tongue wondering how many of the thirty-five different shapes of flake I might swallow. Bundled up, shovels in hand, we made our way to the end of the cul-de-sac where the snowplows had added another couple of feet to the densely packed snowbanks.

'C'mon Lizzie, get a move on.' Tommy charged up the slope unaware that I'd sunk chest deep into the snow. I shouted and waved the fluorescent pink arms of my snowsuit until he slid down the mountain to my rescue.

'You alright?' Only feigning concern, a broad smile emerged as he burst out laughing.

'Uh, huh.' I wanted to be mad at him but when he smiled like that, I couldn't help but giggle.

'Grab the shovel handle and I'll pull you out.'

I hung on for dear life as he pulled with the tenacity and strength of a polar explorer dragging me to the summit.

'I think we should call this Everest base camp.'

'Yeah, okay, Tommy.'

Four years older, my big brother was always right.

'Let's get digging. We'll start with one tunnel heading to that blue spruce, then dig across to the old stump and a third tunnel back to base. It'll be an isosceles triangle.'

I nodded and began digging down into the snow despite not knowing the difference between an isosceles triangle and any other sort of triangle. We dug in silence until we'd hollowed out a child sized rabbit warren deep into the snowbank.

Above us a solitary streetlight shone over the pure white landscape. Emerging from the darkness, a figure staggered down the shortcut from the main road in our direction. I recognized the red checked hunting jacket.

'Paddy's coming, Tommy!'

'Get down Lizzie, hide.'

Frozen with fear, my heart was thumping. It was too late. My pink arms had given me away and he was already moving towards us. Only eight years old, but I knew what was coming.

Paddy ruined everything.

SPRING 2014

Chapter 1

Playing the dutiful daughter didn't come naturally to Lizzie, but she had come home and was determined to show them how capable she could be. She watched a familiar black and white Dodge slide down the icy driveway, the New England spring weather as unpredictable as the mother she had been summoned to look after. The officer stepped from the vehicle, adjusted his belt, bent forward to examine himself in the sideview mirror, then crunched along the frosty path to the front door.

At the doorbell's shrill ring Lizzie jumped. 'Geez,' she shook her head. She needed to get a grip.

'Mary Elizabeth! The door!' Her mother barked over the TV from her bed in the living room, her vocal cords the only part of her still functioning independently.

'Yeah, Ma. I've got it.' Lizzie opened the door and faced Officer Joe Moretti. She forced a smile as she watched the heat rise up his neck until his face fully flushed. After all these years she was amazed, she could still have this effect on him. 'Joe Moretti, what a surprise. I didn't think I'd been here long enough to be in trouble with the law,' she laughed. But what else could she say to the high school boyfriend she had abandoned without even a goodbye ten years earlier?

'Oh… Lizzie, I didn't know you were in town. It's your mom I've come to see.'

'Ma, it's Joe Moretti, you decent? Can I bring him through?' she called from the hallway.

'I think you should join us, Lizzie,' Joe said. His voice cracked and he had turned a ghostly shade of white. She worried he might faint as she showed him into the living room. Heavy footed as he crossed the room, his boots hitting the old oak floorboards felt ominous.

'Joe, it's good of you to visit,' her mother said. She had managed to move herself from the hospital bed into a tweed recliner and was picking at a worn patch on its arm with her fingernail. She pulled the lapels of her terry cloth robe across her chest and tightened the belt. A musky scent of L'Air du Temps filled the room and for an instant Lizzie was taken back to her childhood and the memory of being held close in her mother's lap.

'How're your parents? I haven't been to mass since I've been ill. I miss seeing them,' her mother said.

'They're both well, Mrs. O'Donnell.' He rubbed the back of his neck and cleared his throat with a cough. 'I'm sorry. I should've called ahead.'

'What's brought you here if you're not checking up on my poor old Ma?' Lizzie stared at a bead of sweat running down Joe's cheek. Her eyes lowered. 'Your hands are shaking, are you okay?'

'I'm sorry, but…' He put his hands in his pockets. 'But the state police have arrested and charged someone with Paddy's murder. I know this has come out of the blue and will be a shock for you both.'

'Jesus Christ, Joe.' Lizzie couldn't bear to think the torment this news would unleash in her mother. Head bowed, her shoulders shaking gently at first, then rising like a pressure cooker until she could no longer contain her wailing. Maura O'Donnell's grief was unleashed.

Joe pulled a handkerchief from his pocket and wiped his brow. A feeble attempt to hide his panic. Lizzie stood silently like a bystander at this car crash, wondering what Joe would do next.

'As your liaison officer, I'll try to share as much as possible, but this is a criminal case.'

'Well, who is it then?' Maura asked between sobs. 'Who have you arrested?'

'His name's Jason Edwards, from Denton. He was arrested following an allegation of sexual assault.'

'Sexual assault?' Lizzie said. She feared what the connection with Paddy might mean.

'That's all I can tell you. It'll be in the morning's paper. I'm so sorry.' Joe stood and made his way to the front door, Lizzie following behind.

'Seriously, Joe?' She moved right up close to him and folded her arms. 'What's wrong with you?'

'I've…'

'I can't believe you were going to break this news to her when she was alone,' she interrupted. 'What were you thinking?'

Joe stepped back and gripped the doorknob hard, his knuckles whitened. 'I've been trying to reach Tommy since yesterday,' his voice trembled. 'His phone just goes to voicemail. I had to tell her today, couldn't have her seeing it in the paper tomorrow.' He licked his lips and swallowed. 'I'm sorry, I didn't know she was so ill.'

'We buried Paddy twenty-one years ago, Joe. It killed my father. Mom has never recovered. I don't know that she has the strength to go through it all again. She worshipped Paddy – he was her golden boy.' Lizzie wiped a tear from the corner of her eye. She was raging inside.

Joe's brown eyes softened. 'I'm sorry your family has to go through this again, but it's important we get justice for Paddy and this deviant off the streets.' He handed her his card. 'In case you need to reach me at the station.'

Deviant? Cop lingo. Since she had last seen him, he had made the transformation from teenage lifeguard into a proper cop, even the uniform suited his strong lean frame. Once he was out the door, she ran upstairs and grabbed her empty suitcase. Her gut instinct was to run, get away. This was not what she had signed up for. Her agreement with Tommy had been that she would look after their mother for twelve weeks, see her through her recovery, then she'd be off. She'd already signed a new contract with Carson Cruises starting in July.

And her memories of Paddy were scant. As a small child they had protected her from the details of his death. At twenty-nine, she was dreading the prospect of reliving it all as an adult. They never talked about Paddy. She took a deep breath, closed the case, and slid it back under the bed. She couldn't let Tommy down. Remembering the urgency in his voice, the panic and fear when he'd called her, almost unable to utter the 'C' word. 'She says she needs you,' he'd said. Pressing the right buttons. The guilt. How could she say no? She owed him.

*

The previous night's glazed frost lingered covering the trees. The branches bending under the weight of the clear ice created an arch over the road as Lizzie drove toward the center of town. As much as she loathed winter weather, it was magnificent, the trees clattered in the sunlight and long icicles dripped from the roofs of the wooden houses along the route. She drove on auto pilot, remembering each bend and curve in the winding road along the four miles from

Mill House to the center of town.

Nothing seemed to have changed in the ten years since she'd left, which was both comforting and disconcerting at the same time. The place may not have changed, but she had. A decade at sea had transformed her from awkward teenager to Carson Cruises' Assistant Cruise Director. Not that anyone in this town would notice, here she would always be Paddy's little sister.

White clapboard houses dotted along the route, she reminded herself of each house's occupants, imagining what might have become of the children with whom she had grown up. At the junction with the entrance to the high school, a giant blue and gold sign adorned with a wolf announced, Newham High School, Home of the Wolverines, Class S State Champions Wrestling 2013, Class S State Champions Football 2012. She resisted the urge to turn into the parking lot and drove on. There was no point in going back. The only thing more important than high school sports in this town was religion.

As she approached the center of town the spire of the stone Catholic church, Our Lady of Lourdes was visible. The church dominated the town center – the moral social hub of the community. The protestants barely got a look in with their understated white chapel. Anonymity was an impossibility here, the residents had bat ears and long memories. It wouldn't be long before people would be gossiping about her return and the 'arrest'.

She crept slowly down Main Street. Like many small New England towns, it could have been a set in a Hallmark film. It had been shortlisted for the quaintest small town in America several times. Charming. A mixture of 18th and 19th century wooden buildings on the right were home to a variety of small local stores and faced the town hall, fire station, and library opposite. Blink and she'd miss it.

A memorial and welcome sign on the green announced the little town's connection with the Revolutionary War and its current population, 5,984. (5,985 including Lizzie) A permanent memorial honored the half a dozen young men from the local militia who had bravely joined the rebel army at Lexington and Concord to fight off the Redcoats. The local historical society re-enacted the battle each Independence Day. The sound of the muskets and cannon had always been a highlight. Lizzie remembered her father covering his ears and feeling the thud in her chest as the cannon fired.

At the four-way stop, a brown sign with an arrow pointed the way to Lake Wunnumwaonk, four miles. Newham came to life in the summer, with day trippers and city folk renting lakeside cabins, all attracted to the stunning natural beauty and providing a much needed, but resented, injection to the local economy. Lizzie had never understood why the townspeople were so hostile to outsiders. The influx of new faces was exciting. Tagging along behind Tommy she'd spent many a summer's day by the lake, jumping off the rocks into the cool water. He was the one who made her a sling when she had skinned her arm sliding down the rocks. She'd been his shadow, but he never seemed to have minded. He had always had her back. Until he left.

The only real change over the years, aside from a few hundred new residents, had been the arrival of Wegman's supermarket, built on the outskirts of the town on the road to Denton, which had courted controversy with the addition of another set of traffic lights. Her father's firm had won the contract to build the supermarket on the promise that the building would be in keeping with the historic nature of Newham. He had kept his word despite never seeing the project through to fruition. She felt a lump in her throat as she looked at his handiwork.

The lights changed and she drove on another five miles to the 'city' of Denton, pulled into the builder's yard and parked in front of the office below the sign O'Donnell & Sons – General Contractors & Structural Engineers. She'd told her mother that she was headed out to the supermarket and pharmacy to pick up prescriptions. It wasn't a total lie, but she needed time to speak to Tommy alone and he had been avoiding her since her arrival. Doorstepping him was the only way to get his attention and she was not going to be fobbed off. Waiting in the car, she became fixated on the firm's green and white sign complete with shamrock. It hadn't brought their family much protection or luck over the years. Her father had built up the best-known construction firm in the county before his death, but there was no O'Donnell & Sons anymore. There hadn't been for over twenty years, and Tommy had three daughters. It needed updating.

A spotless, silver Cadillac Escalade pulled up next to her car. The driver's door opened and out stepped a pair of steel toed work boots, followed by jeans and a Carhartt jacket. Her brother's resemblance to their father Jim O'Donnell was uncanny. The same broad shoulders, wavy black hair, ivory skin. Lizzie got out of her car and brushed her finger along the hood of his car.

'Fancy set of wheels, business must be good, Tom,' she laughed.

'Lizzie, I've been meaning…,' Tommy replied, eyes down looking sheepish.

'Yeah, I know you've been meaning to stop by all week but have been busy with work, the family, and generally being a pillar of the community.' She reached up and wrapped her arms around his neck landing a wet kiss on his cheek. He wiped his face with the back of his hand. 'You can't avoid me forever.' Following him into the office she sat down on the leather sofa. A smell of stale cigarettes hung in the air. She thought he had quit smoking years ago.

'Sorry to stop by like this. Haven't much time, can't leave Ma on her own for long,' she said.

'You've managed to leave her alone for the last ten years without a problem.' With his back to her, Tommy poured two mugs of coffee. He bent down and handed her the mug. She wrapped her hands around it, warming them and breathed in the nutty, bitter aroma, then took a sip of the sweet dark liquid. He had remembered she liked her coffee black and sweet.

'Are you having a dig, Tom?' She couldn't decide if this was playful teasing or passive aggression. He looked like the same brother she'd always known but seemed like a stranger. Distracted and distant. She hadn't meant to disappear off the face of the earth, but in real terms that is exactly what she had done. The intention to return home had been there, just never delivered upon. And the longer she was away the more distant home seemed. 'Something important has happened and I need to talk to you about Ma.'

'The whole point of you being here is that I get a break from dealing with Ma, Lizzie. You'll have to handle whatever imagined crisis it is this time.' He opened a stick of Nicorette, put it in his mouth and began chewing. 'I can't take much more, and neither can Hannah. She's been back and forth for months, years actually. Ma doesn't want to help herself.'

'It's not what you think,' she butted in, 'Joe Moretti says he left you a bunch of voicemails, but you haven't returned any of his calls.'

'I've been busy. Can't you deal with him?'

'I have. He came to the house this morning.' The fluttering in her chest was almost painful. 'He told us they've caught the guy who killed Paddy. It's going to be in tomorrow's paper.'

Tommy stood ashen faced. His hands shaking, he spilled coffee on to his shirt. 'Shit,' he said. He leaned against the desk, covered his face with his hands and let out a long sigh. Lizzie's big brother had always been her go to man for problem solving. Maybe it was the shock of the news, and he would regain his composure. He wiped his eyes, rummaged in his desk, and pulled out a folded t-shirt. 'But it's been over twenty years,' he said quietly. He stared into the distance, then snapped. 'I've got work to do.' He peeled off his shirt and pulled over a fresh one. 'Tell Ma I'll be over for lunch on Sunday after mass with Hannah and the girls. We can talk about it then.'

'But…' Lizzie said.

He grabbed his jacket and moved toward the door. 'I've got a meeting. And don't let Ma see the paper.'

'Is that it? You could show a bit more concern,' she said, slamming the door behind her.

*

Wandering around the aisles of Wegman's Lizzie became disoriented. It was like being in a foreign country. She didn't know where anything was and there was simply too much choice. Unable to focus on the list and distracted she was still feeling heated up from the interaction with her brother. He'd been dismissive, like she didn't matter. Her chest tightened, she took a deep breath, held back the tears, and pushed her cart in search of the final few items.

The sun had set by the time she pulled up in front of Mill House. She sat for a moment staring at the grey shingled house of her childhood. Her father had taken such pride in having restored the place, including the watermill. He had bought acres of farmland all around it as one of his first big projects and built the Mill Farm sub-division of modest family homes.

Lugging the groceries into the house, the resentment rose in her at the thought of having to cook the Easter meal on Sunday for Tommy after he had been such a prick earlier. She called out to her mother with no response. The bed in the living room was empty, television on at full volume. Strange how a woman who had been unable to get out of bed unassisted for weeks could disappear like this. Perhaps the miraculous medal novena she had been praying was finally paying dividends? Lizzie turned off the television, heard her mother's voice and followed the noise down the hall to Paddy's room. Through the doorway her mother was on her knees slumped over Paddy's bed, reciting the rosary in between sobs.

A candle burned on the desk next to an old photo of her brother. The room untouched since the night he had disappeared, the smell of teenage boy still in the ether. Lizzie shuddered. The shrine gave her the creeps and transported her back to childhood, the memory of standing outside the locked bedroom door listening to her mother pray and wail. She had been terrified by this shell of a person her loving mother had become. When would she get her Ma back? She still asked herself the same question. The craving never went away, each time she was disappointed.

No one had been allowed in his room but her mother. On the fifth anniversary of Paddy's death, she had held a five-day vigil locking herself in. Lizzie remembered her dad pounding on the door pleading, 'Please Maura, we've got to try to move on. You can't go on like this.' All in vain. The morning of day six, she'd unlocked the door and emerged exhausted and dehydrated. Her husband had carried her to the car and driven straight to the Emergency Room where she'd spent two days on a drip and another five days in the psychiatric assessment unit. Why had her father never left? Maybe he would still be alive if he had.

'Hail Holy Queen, Mother of mercy, our life, our sweetness, and our hope. To thee do we cry, poor banished children of Eve, to thee do we send up our sighs, mourning and weeping in this valley of tears…,' Maura recited.

Realizing this was the final prayer of the rosary, Lizzie stood behind her mother and waited to lift her.

'C'mon Ma, let's get you something to eat.' She hadn't appreciated quite how heavy her mother had become.

'I'm not hungry,' she held on tight to Lizzie's arm and patted it with her other hand. 'Thank you.'

'Let's get you comfortable in bed then. You need a good night's sleep. Father Larkin left a message saying he is coming by with communion for you tomorrow morning and Tommy, Hannah and the girls will be over for Easter lunch.'

'Oh good, Tommy's coming. He'll know what to do,' Maura said.

Lizzie tucked her mother into bed, handed her two sleeping tablets and a glass of water then turned out the light. Back in the kitchen she grabbed a tumbler, filled it with ice, then cracked open a bottle of Jack Daniels, poured a generous measure and topped it up with Coke. Why did her mother always think that Tommy had all the answers? Where had he been when Lizzie was doing all the looking after their mom as a teenager? Nowhere. Ma's sexism made her blood boil. She took a big gulp from the tumbler. Just one drink she told herself.

The Denton Times

Keeping the community informed with independent local reporting

COLD CASE SUSPECT CHARGED, 21 YEARS AFTER BODY FOUND

By Tina Chandler
April 20, 2014

DNA database analysis led to the arrest this week of a Denton man accused of killing a teenage boy in 1993, bringing closure to a cold case that has "been a dark cloud over the quiet rural community of Newham for over twenty years," Harewood County Prosecutor Helen Wright told reporters on Friday.

Jason Edwards, 39, was arrested Thursday for the murder of 16-year-old Patrick O'Donnell, who was found dead in Newham in April 1993.

"For over twenty years the O'Donnell family has waited for answers." Resident State Trooper Pete Kominsky said, praising state and local law enforcement. "We would not be here today, 20 years down the road, if it was not for the hard work of the initial investigators who preserved the evidence that will be used

in this case. It may have taken over two decades, but we never gave up hope of finding Patrick's killer."

"To the O'Donnell family we pray this brings you the closure and peace you were denied for so many years," Kominsky added.

Patrick was reported missing on March 15, 1993, after a blizzard - the Storm of Century – which paralyzed the whole of the east coast. His body was found four weeks later less than a mile from his home. He died of asphyxiation with indications of physical and sexual assault, according to the court document. DNA was recovered from his underwear and mouth, but no match was ever found.

Police arrested Jason Edwards on April 15, 2014, following an accusation of sexual assault outside a nightclub in Denton. A routine DNA database search returned a match with DNA recovered from Patrick O'Donnell's body. Edwards was preliminarily charged with murder and sexual assault, the prosecutor's office said. Formal charges will be filed when he appears in court April 22.

The O'Donnell family was not available for comment.

Chapter 2

Lizzie sat for a few moments in a state of shock. This was big news in a place where the last big news had been Paddy's murder. "Never gave up hope of finding Patrick's killer?" she muttered as she ripped out the front-page article, stuffed it into her bathrobe pocket and tossed the paper into the garbage can. Her late-night rendezvous with Jack Daniels was making itself know in the confines of her skull, a pulsing pressure not yet alleviated by painkillers, but at least she had managed to intercept the paper while her mother was still asleep. The police got lucky; nobody had been looking for Paddy's killer for years. She was certain of that.

Reading the details of his cause of death in print sent a shiver down her spine. Her poor parents. Their son, her brother. A horrific death. It felt so cold, matter of fact. How could she not have known? Had no one ever told her that Paddy had been asphyxiated and sexually assaulted or could she have somehow blocked it out, along with everything else from that night? No, they mustn't have told her. The O'Donnell family didn't talk about things, especially something so sordid. Her mother only talked about Paddy in glowing terms, clinging to, and preserving the happy memories of her beloved son. The ugly, the dark, the unwanted filtered and discarded.

Lizzie didn't know what to believe. She wanted the truth; she knew that much. She wanted the man responsible for killing her brother, ruining her family, and taking her mother away to pay. Joe was right, this deviant needed to be taken off the streets. She read the last line of the article again. 'The O'Donnell family was not available for comment.' But this journalist, Tina Chandler, hadn't even contacted them. Could she have spoken to Tommy? That's the kind of thing he would say. No comment, story of his life.

In the kitchen she tried to shake off the feeling of filth and began to prepare her mother's breakfast. She needed to stay focused. She couldn't let her mother see her distress. Stick to the routine. It was just like old times, her waiting on her mom hand and foot hanging on to the hope, that craving for a morsel of love, a sign that she wasn't just her domestic doormat.

'I want you to call Father Larkin and tell him there is no need for him to come with communion for me this morning. I'd like you to take me to mass. And can you get the paper for me?'

'Sure. You a little brighter this morning?' Lizzie went through the motion of walking out to the mailbox, opened it and returned empty handed. 'There's no paper today, they must've forgotten to deliver.' She couldn't deal with any drama this early in the day. It would be enough to get her mother dressed and out the door to mass. 'I'll bring down some outfits for you to try on after you finish eating.' Her mother would want to look good. She had been a stylish dresser and had always made sure Lizzie had a new dress and shoes for Easter when she was little. Their annual outing to buy the Easter outfit had been a special one, just the two of them, mother and daughter.

*

A black car was parked behind the old oak across the street as Lizzie pulled out of the driveway. She noticed the camera lens and had half a mind to stop and give the photographer a mouthful but needed to get her mother to church on time. She hadn't stepped inside the walls of Our Lady of Lourdes since her father's funeral over a decade earlier. Now she found herself at mass on the most important day of the Catholic calendar.

The sound of the organist playing the processional hymn filled the church as they made their way down the aisle, church packed, all eyes upon them. 'Jesus Christ is risen today, Alleluia, our triumphant holy day, Alleluia…' the congregation sang. Maura belted out the hymn with a loud and not entirely tuneful voice as they took their seats in the pew next to Tommy's family. Tommy's eyebrows lifted at the sight of his mother fully dressed. Lizzie covered her mouth to keep her composure. It was as if he had seen Lazarus.

She checked the time on her phone, would Father Larkin manage to keep the service to under an hour? His tendency to be longwinded could be forgiven as he had been supportive of their family over the years and so kind to Lizzie. Though she had given up on religion long ago, she could still recite the whole mass. The repetition was strangely hypnotic, cult-like.

The priest's silvery voice boomed over the microphone. 'Jesus is here, among us, he lives in the present. Victor over sin, evil and death, over everything that crushes life.' His hands clinging to the sides of the lectern to support himself, he looked frailer than Lizzie remembered, but his voice was still strong and soothing. Lizzie caught his eye, he smiled and continued. 'His message, in his resurrection is meant for us all. Do not look for the living amongst the dead. Don't let your problems suffocate you, let sadness or bitterness steal your breath, because that is where death is found.'

Lizzie glanced over at her mother whose eyes were closed, and hoped she was taking this sermon in. It was tailor made for her. The elderly priest hobbled down from his pulpit. Approaching eighty he should have retired years ago, but the parishioners had pleaded with the diocese to let him stay on. He had a way of bringing people together. The community relied on him. The two altar boys in their red cassocks and white surplices fidgeted surrounded by dozens of white lilies. Paddy had worn the same garb as head altar boy. She made a mental note to ask Tommy -why he had never been an altar boy - that might be a safe conversation opener at lunch. As the parishioners made their way up to communion Lizzie looked out for familiar faces, the only part of mass she had ever enjoyed, people watching. The older folk exchanged glances, deferring to her mother as they walked past after having received the sacrament. Maura seemed to relish the attention, resurrecting her role as the 'grieving mother', being in the spotlight.

'Go in peace to love and serve the Lord.' Father Larkin said.

'Thanks be to God, let's get out of here.' Lizzie muttered. It took ages to make their way out of the church. Her mother stopped to introduce her to everyone she recognized, while Lizzie nodded and smiled through gritted teeth.

'People are so kind, Lizzie,' Maura said, unaware they had all seen the front page of the morning paper.

As they stood in line to greet Father Larkin outside the church, Lizzie spotted the black Ford Focus parked, window down, camera lens poking out. She turned to Tommy and whispered in his ear.

'Go see who that is. That same car was parked near the house as we pulled out.' She turned back and grinned at Father Larkin; his arms extended welcoming her in for a hug.

'Welcome home, Lizzie.' He held her tight for a moment, long enough for her to catch the familiar scent of his aftershave, then released her. 'Let's get a look at you. I've been following your adventures at sea through your mother.'

'You have?' she said somewhat bewildered. What could her mother have told him? They barely spoke.

'Don't be a stranger. Come by and see me when you get a chance.'

'Will do, Father.' She took her mother's arm and headed back to the car.

*

Lizzie hadn't cooked a roast lunch since she was a teenager. On ship everything was catered for her, she didn't even have to make a cup of tea. In one sense it was like being permanently on vacation, though she worked long hours with little time off, except a day here and there when in port. She didn't mind the work, six months on, two months off and over the last ten years had amassed considerable savings. There were a lot of upsides to cruise ship life - new places, new people, sunshine, cheap booze. But it was the camaraderie of the crew she appreciated most, living in close quarters for six months at a time, they had become a tight-knit substitute family.

Pressing cloves into the scored fat of the ham, she basted it with mustard and brown sugar, lifted it into the oven and set the timer. Her mother had given her orders, Easter lunch on the table at three o'clock. Maura was back in the living room in her recliner watching Wheel of Fortune, occasionally barking orders at her. 'Remember to peel the potatoes and rinse them before putting them on the stove, Lizzie. And don't forget about the cabbage and carrots.' She was determined to make the perfect meal, aware that she would be under the scrutiny of Ma and Tommy looking for anything to criticize. As a teenager the kitchen had been her domain. After ten years being catered for on board, she was enjoying being back at the helm.

She took out the battered Better Homes cookbook and looked up the recipe for the ambrosia dessert she always enjoyed as a child, a wave of nostalgia came over her as she tried to think back to a happier time. Tommy's daughters would enjoy it too. Like the Greek gods, her offering of long life and immortality to her nieces. She looked out the ingredients: Cool Whip, sour cream, mandarin oranges, crushed pineapple, maraschino cherries, sweetened coconut flakes and miniature marshmallows. Folding the sour cream into the Cool Whip in a large serving bowl as per the instructions, Lizzie drained the fruits and folded them into the mixture. She placed the dessert in the refrigerator to chill and went about setting the table feeling like a 1950s housewife.

The sound of little girls shrieking filled the hallway. The trio, five, six and seven bore little resemblance to the leggy blonde who had given birth to them. Lizzie had been mistaken for their mother on her last fleeting visit, when the youngest was a new-born, much to their mother Hannah's annoyance. Though Lizzie and Hannah had been in the same year at school they were never what one might call friends. She had been sniffing around Tommy from the time they were fourteen when Hannah would only greet Lizzie if she happened to be with Tommy. The rest of the time Lizzie was invisible. She wasn't surprised when Tommy wrote to her to say they had got engaged but was relieved to have the excuse that she'd be at sea on their wedding day. That said, Hannah and Tommy were a good match, both small-town aspirational. A small-town girl, with small-town ambitions, nabs successful local businessman. Together they were Newham's power couple, a perfect family, with three perfect children.

'Smells good, Liz. See you got the deli to do the catering.'

Tommy said with a straight face. He turned on the kitchen faucet, squirted a blob of green soap on his palm and began rhythmically washing his hands.

'Are you baiting me, Tom?' He'd been doing it since they were kids. She didn't know why she still engaged in this inane banter. Old habits. It was a twisted way of showing affection, and she didn't like him getting the upper hand. 'Made a special trip to the 'all you can eat buffet' at the food court in the mall for you. I know how much you adore food that has been touched by many human hands.' Lizzie said. Hannah gave Lizzie a knowing look and they both burst out laughing. Tommy was a germaphobe. 'Help Ma to the table, Tom. And you girls come give your Auntie Lizzie a hand.'

She carried the baked ham to the table, followed by her trio of mini-me's bearing the side dishes. It was a triumph. She knew it. Tommy sat at the head of the table playing the patriarch, said grace, and stood to carve the meat like only a man could. The last of the O'Donnell men in a sea of O'Donnell women.

'I feel so blessed to have you all here today,' Maura said. 'If only your father and Paddy were here.' Lizzie glanced over at Tommy and rolled her eyes, neither one wanting to acknowledge her words, knowing it would be the beginning of a long monologue, one they had heard too many times.

'It's good to see you up and about Ma. We've all missed you, especially the girls,' Tommy said. Good redirection Tommy, Lizzie nodded and smiled.

'Tom, I was looking at the altar boys during mass. How come you were never one?' Lizzie asked.

'Red's not my color.' He strained a laugh and cleared his throat. 'It wasn't for me, that's all.' There was something disconcerting in the way he shifted as he spoke.

'Oh, it would've been too hard for Tommy to follow in Paddy's footsteps. Paddy was like an angel, Father Larkin was always saying so,' Maura reached for another slice of ham, her appetite having returned. 'Everyone was so kind at mass today.'

'Yes, they were all talking about how hard it must be for you Ma, especially after the article in this morning's paper,' Hannah said. Hannah, effortlessly beautiful, but not the brightest spark had put her foot in it. Lizzie looked to Hannah and then back to Tommy. Tommy's face reddened.

'What article?' Maura said.

'Han…' Tommy said. He hadn't raised his voice enough, Hannah kept going.

Lizzie saw through the game now - she wasn't playing dumb, she was shit stirring, attempting to de-rail Lizzie's family lunch. Did she really resent Lizzie that much? She took a deep breath and tried to calm herself before she said something she would regret.

'It was the front page of today's Denton Times, all about the police catching Paddy's killer after all these years. Everyone was talking about it at mass.'

Lizzie's pulse was racing. Hannah, the stupid bitch, didn't seem to know when to stop.

'Hannah!' Tommy shouted.

'You told me there was no paper today Lizzie…' Maura said.

'Uh, well…' Lizzie replied.

'I want to see it! Where is it?' Her body was trembling. This did not bode well. Lizzie looked across to Tommy not knowing what to do. He nodded for her to get the paper. She rose from the table, went to her room, and took the page from her bathrobe pocket. Returning to the table she handed it to her mother.

'I'm going to get the dessert, girls will you give me a hand clearing the table?' Lizzie said. They left Tommy with Ma reading the article. When they returned to the table tears were running down her face.

'What's wrong with Grandma?' Siobhán, the middle child, asked.

'Girls, I have made you the best dessert ever. Grandma used to make this for me when I was a little girl, and it was my favorite. Remember Ma?' Lizzie said. Maura sat in silence. She was going to unravel; it was just a matter of time. Like an earthquake, it would start with small tremors, her body would tremble, followed by sobs, then the earth would open and swallow them up in the blackness of her grief. 'It's called ambrosia, the food of the gods and will make you live forever,' Lizzie wasn't sure her attempt to lighten the mood would make any difference but hoped they could at least get through dessert.

'Nobody lives forever, my poor Paddy was only a child,' Maura said. Eyes glazed, she had that vacant look about her. The children huddled next to their mother. Their grandmother had a great way of terrifying them.

'Hannah, take the girls home now. Grandma's not well,' Tommy said.

'But Aunt Lizzie said…' the girls replied.

'C'mon girls, get your coats. You can play with Aunt Lizzie another day.' Hannah said.

As the children left the table, Maura let loose on Lizzie and Tommy. 'How dare you try to keep things from me! I have a right to know what is going on.'

'Yeah, Ma, you do,' Lizzie said. 'I'm…'

'Listen Ma, digging up all of the past isn't going to bring Paddy back,' Tommy interrupted. How dare he? It was a habit he seemed to cling to knowing full well how much

Lizzie hated it. It left her feeling insignificant and small, silenced.

'Let the police get on with it. It's in their hands now, they caught the guy. Like the state trooper says in the article, catching Paddy's killer should bring you some closure and peace.'

'I'm never going to be at peace, that night ruined my life,' Maura said. Lizzie sensed her mother's eyes upon her.

'Why are you looking at me Ma? I barely remember that night,' Lizzie said.

'If you hadn't…' Maura said.

'If I hadn't…., you mean if I hadn't ended up in the hospital?' The lump in her throat made it difficult to continue until she managed a cough. 'I know the script Ma, Tommy saved my life, I owe my life to Tommy,' she said with a familiar deep-seated rage rising to the surface.

'It's just that…' Maura said.

'It's just that, what? Go on say it.' Were they going to have to play this out again? Her mother was never going to let it go. 'Say it, Ma. You know you're thinking it. It's my fault Paddy's dead.'

'That's enough, Lizzie,' Tommy said.

Lizzie ignored him; she was on a roll. 'I was eight years old Ma.' How could it have been her fault? 'And you all wonder why I left.' She couldn't compete with the memory of Paddy. 'I was always going to be a disappointment.' She drew a breath and looked at the tears streaming down her mother's face.

'I'd like to go to my bed Tommy, get my pills,' Maura said. Tommy helped her into the living room.

Lizzie started loading the dishwasher wanting to smash all the plates. Being at home brought out the worst in her, all the old wounds ripped open.

'You need to learn to bite your tongue,' Tommy said.

'The hell I do! It needed to be said. And it's your wife who needs to learn to keep her damn mouth shut. She knew what she was doing.'

'Leave Hannah out of this, she didn't mean any harm. I don't need you going all paranoid on me, we've got enough with Ma.' He wiped down the counter and changed the subject. 'I spoke to that reporter with the camera in the church parking lot, Tina something. I asked her to respect our privacy, that we don't want our photos in the paper.'

'What did she say?'

'She said we were "news", smiled and closed her window. Promise me you won't speak to her. Let the police handle it.'

'Yeah, Tom, I get it. I'm not one of your kids.' She didn't need to be patronized. 'I guess you'll be needing a ride home?'

*

In the dim evening light, they drove in silence through the center of town and turned left, along the road towards the lake. Lizzie pulled off the main road and climbed the steep private drive to Tommy's house. The fifteen-minute ride had seemed like an eternity, and she couldn't wait to be rid of him. He had built himself a McMansion in the woods, high above the lake with stunning views. A master craftsman, like his father. With the trees still bare, there was a clear view of the lake, large swathes still frozen.

'Bet this view is amazing in the fall,' Lizzie said, breaking the stony silence.

'Yes, it's spectacular. You'll have to come stay with us sometime,' Tommy said. He got out of the car without thanking her or even looking at her and walked towards the house.

'Yeah, sometime…' She wouldn't hold her breath waiting for that invitation. Looking back at the house, she thought it was a fine place for three little girls to grow up, then turned the car around and drove back to the main road. As she came to the crossroads the light shining over the Town Tavern was beckoning her towards it. She needed to unwind, and her mom would be asleep for hours.

*

Not much had changed at the Town Tavern since the last time she had been there at eighteen, waving her fake ID. Not even the clientele. She recognized a group of Lion's Club men, her dad's cohort, deep in conversation at a table in the corner. The owner of the gas station and garage waved at her and smiled. The National Hockey League first round playoffs were being shown on two giant screens. Boston Bruins vs Detroit Red Wings. The bar packed with rowdy men; this was Bruin's territory.

Ice hockey was the one sport Lizzie enjoyed watching, the non-stop action gave her an adrenaline rush. She took a seat at the bar and ordered two double Jack and Cokes figuring it would be hard to get the bartender's attention again with the game underway. Two early twenty-somethings sat down next to her and ordered a round of beers and tequila shots. They were too young for her, she knew that, but didn't stop her from thinking about what it would be like to run her hands through the curly headed guy's hair. She threw back her first drink.

'Impressive,' the curly headed one said. He and his friend slammed their tequila shots and chugged their beers. 'You want another one, Miss?'

'It's Liz. Sure, thanks.'

'Well Liz, let's get this party started.' He signaled to the bartender to bring another round of drinks. The buzzer went, it was the end of the second period and the Bruins were leading 2-0. 'Awesome assist by Bergeron, Dave, eh? He's been the top scorer this season,' the dark-haired one said. His friend nodded in agreement and kept smiling at Lizzie. She could tell he was more interested in her than the game by the way he stared at her as she smoothed her straight dark hair back into a neat bun. She didn't think of herself as pretty, but neither was she plain or ordinary. A sprinkling of freckles below her grey eyes extended from the bridge of her nose across to her high cheek bones. Like a butterfly pattern, almost exotic. She had been told this by many a drunk guy in a bar over the years. Nothing wrong with a bit of admiration and free drinks, as long as the drinks kept flowing. And they did.

As the third period started, all eyes were back on the screens. A fist fight broke out on the ice leaving a crimson trail. The sight of blood on ice made Lizzie queasy, not helped by all the booze, she made her way to the restroom. The curly headed fellow followed her and grabbed her around the waist outside the door. Somewhat unexpected but not unwelcome, she accepted his advance. The hoppy taste of beer on his mouth when he kissed her was not unpleasant. She maneuvered her arm to slide open the door and reversed into the cubicle. The heat rose in her as she slid off her skinny jeans and jumped up on the sink. She hadn't had sex for months and needed the release. No complications, she didn't want anything more, she never did. He closed the cubicle door, locked it, and moved toward her. She watched him undo his belt and unzip his workman's jeans. Reaching out, she grabbed his nylon hockey jersey, and pulled him close. It was over in minutes but gave Lizzie the satisfaction she had been craving.

'Let's get another drink,' she said buttoning her jeans and checking herself in the mirror. As they made their way back to the bar, she spotted Joe Moretti. He was in his civvies, off-duty, talking with a couple of guys she recognized from high school. She couldn't figure out why Joe had stayed in Newham, he was so smart, had so much potential. He could have done anything, why settle for being a small-town cop? She swigged her final drink, got her denim jacket and bag, and stumbled toward the exit. Loud boos came from the bar, Detroit had scored. Standing in the parking lot she fumbled with her keys and dropped them.

'I'll drive you home Lizzie,' Joe's voice appeared out of nowhere. 'The last thing you need is a DUI and I don't want to be the one to arrest you.' He picked up the keys, opened the passenger side door and helped Lizzie into the car. It was only a few miles to the O'Donnell house.

'You're a good guy Joe. Why are you so nice to me? I treated you so badly in high school.' She rolled the window down hoping the fresh air would stop the world spinning. 'I'm sorry. I always liked you; I was just kinda screwed up,' her speech slurred, she had let her guard down.

'I've always had a soft spot for you, Lizzie.' He parked the car in the garage. 'We can talk about this another time.' He pulled her out of the car and put his arm around her. 'Let's get you into the house.'

Chapter 3

Waking in a cold sweat she sat upright and wasn't sure if she had screamed, or if it was inside her nightmare. Outside it was still dark and she was in bed fully dressed. In bed, a heavy weight on her chest, she couldn't breathe. She opened her eyes and saw his ruddy face and curls. He was on top of her, his face twisted and angry. His hand over her mouth, he was saying something, but she couldn't hear him. Then he was gone, and it was dark. She was suffocating. No one could hear her silent screams. She was buried alive in a child-sized coffin, scratching to get out, her nails bleeding. A familiar and unwelcome dream from childhood, it had last visited her during her first six-month tour when her cabin was well below deck with no porthole. She had been so claustrophobic she took to going up on deck in the middle of night to get fresh air. This time she put it down to all the alcohol, talk of Paddy, and the row with Ma. Living with her mother was suffocating her.

Her head pounded and with a mouth full of cotton, she wished she had no recollection of the previous night's activities. She could still feel his bony hips and fingers pulling on her hair. Embarrassment. It was a new low for her. Not good. The old digital alarm clock flashed five am.

The sun would be up soon. She walked down the hall to the bathroom, took some extra strength Tylenol from the medicine cabinet and went downstairs to the kitchen to get a glass of water. Maura's gentle snores filled the air.

The newspaper delivery van pulled up out front and Lizzie went out to the mailbox. The O'Donnell family in full color was splashed across the front page. The photo caption read; Grieving O'Donnell family shows unified front. Tina Chandler must have snapped the photo from a distance, Lizzie hadn't seen her up close. It was a flattering picture of them all. Lizzie had chosen well for her mother, a black A line dress that hid the extra pounds her mom was carrying. In the aftermath of Paddy's death her mother had become almost skeletal, but in the years that followed food seemed to be her one comfort. The article was short, simply recapped the story of the night Paddy went missing with a few quotes from some of the congregation, people praising Maura O'Donnell's courage. Lizzie wasn't sure she agreed with the congregation's take on her mother. Courage was about moving forward, and Maura O'Donnell was trapped.

She set out her mother's breakfast tray, complete with newspaper on top. After the previous day's fiasco, she decided to treat her mother as an adult. Perhaps all this tip toeing around like she was a fragile piece of porcelain was part of the problem. She took the tray through and called out. 'Breakfast, I made you a soft-boiled egg and toast. And here's your paper.' She sat down with her coffee and watched her mother unfold the newspaper.

'We're on the front-page Lizzie. Who took that picture?'

'Dunno, guess it must've been that journalist. She was hanging around the church when we came out.'

'Don't we all look good. Let me get on with eating my breakfast then you can help me get dressed.'

'Okay, just shout when you're ready.' No mention of yesterday's argument, no scolding. Lizzie found this very unsettling, she wanted to talk about it but knew she couldn't force it. It frustrated her that they carried on as if nothing had happened, as was the habit with their family. For once, she wished she could tell her mother how she felt. The sadness and the longing to be close.

'Lizzie, I want to go to court tomorrow. I want to see the man who killed our Paddy.'

'I might need to call Joe to see what the protocol is around this Ma. I'm not sure if we're allowed to attend.'

'Well, call him then. I want to go, it's important for Paddy that I be there.'

Important for Paddy or important for herself? Lizzie walked through to the hallway and dialed the police station from the landline and asked for Joe. He was out on a call, so she left him an urgent message.

Lizzie helped her mother with a sponge bath in the downstairs toilet wondering when Maura had last had a proper shower. It didn't feel right, daughter washing mother and Lizzie hated to think that her body would end up looking like hers. She moved the soapy sponge across her mother's freckly back, then lifted her arm. The flabby skin under her arm shook. Her breasts sagged like empty polythene sacks and merged into the multiple rolls of skin from her belly down to her pubic hair. She handed her mother the sponge. 'You can wipe your privates yourself.' Maybe that's why Hannah resented her, it was an unenviable job looking after a woman who wasn't even her own mother. Must have taken a lot of energy to keep up her perfect daughter-in-law façade.

'You know Ma, how about tomorrow, I help you get upstairs to have a hot shower. What do you think?'

'Oh, well maybe. I'll see how I feel.'

'I was just thinking that if you want to go to court, that you might want to look your best.'

*

Maura had dozed off in front of her daily soap. Lizzie couldn't believe she still watched this show after all these years. Port Charles was full of dysfunctional family dynamics – the wealthy Quartermaine's, the mobster Corinthos family, the Cassadines, such a ridiculous script -

part drama, part action-adventure but at the heart it was all about family and relationships. She was a voyeur in other people's family dramas, maybe it served as a distraction from her own. She knew more about Sonny Corinthos's relationship with Carly than about any relationship Lizzie had ever had, let alone anything important about Lizzie's life. But the soap was addictive and Lizzie found herself being sucked into their world, she feared what she would be like by the end of her twelve-week incarceration. Chained to the recliner, her hand submerged in a family size bag of chips, eyes fixed zombie like on the idiot box having gained ten pounds.

Brenda was about to tell Michael she had a confession to make, when the doorbell rang, rousing Maura from her nap. Lizzie got up to answer the door hoping it was Joe.

'Hi Lizzie, I got a message you needed to speak to me urgently?' Joe removed his hat and slid it under his armpit. 'What's up?'

'Ma saw this morning's paper.'

'Yes, I've just come from Tommy's house. I'm really sorry, I was just doing my job.'

'Your job? I don't understand.'

'I had a complaint from Tina Chandler that Tommy threatened her outside her office this morning. I thought that was what you were calling about.'

'No, I had no idea. My mom wanted information about the court hearing tomorrow, that's what I was calling about. But what the hell has Tommy been up to?'

'He was pretty steamed up about the photo in the paper and the fact that his children were splashed across the front page. I told him I understood that, but that he couldn't go around intimidating journalists.'

'He's pretty stressed by all this and worried about our mother. He's a hot head.'

'I know, that's why I only gave him a verbal caution and told him to keep his distance from her. I hope he will.'

'That'll depend on what she writes next, I think. My mom has some questions for you, but please don't mention what happened with Tommy.' Lizzie was relieved that there was no mention of last night's antics. He was keeping it professional. She wasn't sure if Joe had seen her go to the restroom with the guy whose name she could no longer remember. If he had, he wasn't letting on. She didn't want him to think less of her. 'Come through to the living room.'

Joe took a seat on the recliner next to Maura's. Lizzie stared at his profile, remembering the feel of his soft olive skin, his long Italian nose, and fine lips against hers. She shifted in her seat and felt flushed.

'Mrs. O'Donnell, good to see you again. Lizzie says you have questions about tomorrow's arraignment hearing.'

'I told Ma I wasn't sure that the public could attend,' Lizzie said.

'Well, no, it's an open hearing where Jason Edwards will be formally charged. The public is allowed.'

'See Lizzie, I told you we can be there,' Maura said.

'You can be there Mrs. O'Donnell, but there won't be much to it. He'll enter his plea and make a bail application which is likely to be denied given the severity of the crimes. It won't take but a few minutes,' Joe said.

'Don't see the point of going if it's only going to be a few minutes given how unwell you've been,' Lizzie said.

'I want to be there for Paddy. What time is the hearing, Joe?' Maura said.

'The court opens at ten o'clock, but I've no idea where he'll be on the docket so you may be in for a wait. I'll be there tomorrow if you have questions or need anything.' Joe stood up and made for the door. Lizzie followed.

'Looks like I'll see you at ten o'clock tomorrow. Not sure whether to tell Tommy.'

'It's normal for your mom to want to be there, Lizzie.'

'I know, maybe it's time to stop walking on eggshells with her. And, uh, thanks for driving me home last night. It won't happen again.' Looking at her feet, she hoped he couldn't see her blushing.

'If ever you need to talk, I'm a better listener than Jack

Daniels.' Joe's face flushed. 'See you tomorrow.'

*

The next morning Lizzie woke to her mother's voice calling, a sense of urgency in its tone. It was only seven thirty and she didn't normally wake until after nine o'clock. She rushed downstairs fearing Ma had collapsed on the floor or some other sort of trauma, only to find her sitting up in bed wide awake.

'I want you to help me upstairs to the shower. And can you choose something nice for me to wear to court? Maura said.

'Sure, but it's early still. Don't you want to have some breakfast first?'

'No. And not the same dress I wore to church the other day.' Lizzie hoped her mother was getting better. It was a positive sign at least. The next step would be to get that damn hospital bed out of the living room and her mother back in her own bedroom upstairs. She made a mental note to call the medical appliance company to collect the bed by the end of the week. The rehabilitation of Maura was Lizzie's focus, the sooner her mother was functioning independently, the sooner she could leave and reclaim her own life.

Chapter 4

A small crowd gathered on the steps of the Denton Court house. It was hard to distinguish the criminals from the employees and members of the public. Maura looked elegant. Lizzie had chosen a navy dress and matching jacket for her, complementing her chestnut hair. At seventy she still had few greys. As they made their way through security and up the stairs to court room three, Lizzie spotted Tina Chandler lurking in an alcove. She had no desire to speak to her and had promised Tommy that she wouldn't. She wanted to keep her well out of Maura's way. Joe, in uniform, was standing outside the courtroom door.

'It looks like Jason Edwards is sixth on the docket today, so you may be waiting an hour or so. Do you want to take your mom for a coffee, and I can text you when it's time?' Joe asked.

'Very kind of you Joe, but I'd like to go in and get a good seat if you don't mind,' Maura answered. Lizzie looked at Joe and smiled - her mother was taking charge today.

Lizzie had never been in a courtroom before. It was smaller than on television and nowhere near as grand. The court officer directed them to the public gallery which was nothing more than a few rows of seats toward the back of the room. They took their seats in the first row and watched as the courtroom filled with its cast of characters for the day's business. She focused on the large seal of the Commonwealth of Massachusetts on the wall behind the judge's seat to distract herself from the butterflies swirling around in her belly. The native American holding a bow and arrow on a blue background stared back at her. It was ironic to see it hanging in a court of law. Justice had been elusive for indigenous peoples. The local Nipmuc nation had been fighting for recognition and their land for years.

'All rise! The court is now in session. The Honorable Judge William H. Baxter presiding. All those having business before this honorable court are admonished to draw near, give their attention, and they shall be heard,' the Clerk announced. Judge Baxter brushed his silver moustache as he took his seat at the bench and put on his reading glasses. Lizzie was mildly surprised to see the African American judge. Diversity in these parts usually meant Irish, Polish, Italian and Nipmuc.

They watched as each case was called and a plea entered. The range of offences intrigued Lizzie, until a woman charged with a DUI left her red faced and hot, both ashamed and relieved that Joe had rescued her the other night, otherwise it might have been her in the dock. Joe had been right; they were sitting for just over an hour before

Jason Edwards' case was called.

Jason Edwards was led into the courtroom by two guards and sat down next to his attorney. Lizzie' whole body tensed. She was expecting a Charles Manson, but he was small and weedy, with dirty blonde, slicked back hair. This was the man who had murdered her brother? She was underwhelmed and tried to visualize what Edwards had looked like twenty-one years earlier at age eighteen, probably a pimply boy who got teased for looking younger than his age. He was only two years older than Paddy would have been. What might Paddy have looked like if he had lived to be a thirty-seven-year-old man? Would his red hair have darkened; would he have remained short and stocky? Lizzie looked over at her mother's face drained of color and held her trembling hands. She hoped that Ma had brought some tissues, as it was unlikely she would hold herself together for much longer.

'The case of the Commonwealth of Massachusetts v. Edwards, Criminal Action 04-10014 will now be heard before the Court. Counsel, please identify themselves for the record,' the Clerk announced.

'Good morning your Honor, for the state, Assistant State attorney Matthew Cranston,' the prosecutor said. He wasn't much older than Lizzie but spoke with authority. Either that, or was he cocky, she couldn't decide.

'Good morning your Honor, Eileen Murphy for the defendant,' the public defender said. She looked rough, like she'd spent the night in the cells with her client. Her mousy hair hanging lank, needed a good brushing and there was a greasy stain on her unpressed blouse. She looked more like the defendant in the previous DUI case than a lawyer. Lizzie couldn't imagine Jason Edwards held much hope of being acquitted with this woman defending him.

'Mr. Edwards, you've been charged with two counts of sexual assault and one count of second-degree murder. Specifically, the first charge being that on the night of 8th April 2014 you sexually assaulted Dylan Jones outside the Promises nightclub in Denton,' Judge Baxter said.

Promises nightclub, thought Lizzie, the perfect name for a pick-up joint. She glanced around the courtroom to see if anyone looked like a Dylan Jones. The name sounded familiar; she was sure Paddy had had a friend named Dylan. As she looked over to her left, Tina Chandler was busy jotting notes in her notebook. Lizzie drifted off imagining the next day's headline until the judge's voice brought her back into the room. 'The second charge being that on or around the 13th of March 1993 you sexually assaulted Patrick O'Donnell, aged sixteen.' Lizzie felt Ma's body shaking through her hands and hoped she would keep it together until they left the courtroom. 'The third charge being that on or around the 13th of March 1993 you physically battered and intentionally suffocated Patrick O'Donnell causing his death, thereby committing second degree murder.'

Maura was sobbing, and not so quietly that it went unnoticed by Judge Baxter who motioned to the Court Officer to approach the bench, had a word, then continued. The officer made his way to her and suggested that if she found it all too distressing, she might wish to leave the courtroom. Maura sat bolt upright, lifted her chin, wiped her eyes, and pulled herself together. Indignant. There was no way she was leaving the courtroom. Lizzie glanced left again, Tina Chandler stared at them, like she was taking a mental photograph, then smiled.

'Ms. Murphy, have you had an opportunity to review the indictment with your client such that he's ready to be arraigned?'

'Yes, Your Honor.'

'Mr. Edwards, please rise. You are charged with two counts of sexual assault and one count of second-degree murder. How do you plead, guilty or not guilty?'

'Not-guilty, your honor,' Edwards said.

'Your honor, regarding bail…' Eileen Murphy began.

'Bail is denied. The defendant will be held on remand due to the nature and severity of the crimes. A pre-trial hearing will be set for 15th May 2014 at 10:00am.' Jason Edwards sat expressionless for a moment, then shook his head in disbelief.

'All rise, the court will take a short recess,' the Clerk said.

It was over in five minutes. A lifetime of pain, her mother totally consumed with Paddy's death, reduced to just five minutes. Lizzie helped her up and headed for the door. Fresh air was what they both needed. As they made for the exit, Lizzie noticed a small crowd gathered on the courthouse steps. The security guard held open the door for her mother. As she stepped out into the daylight cameras flashed and a microphone was pushed toward her face. Lizzie put her arm around her mother and moved her past, saying, 'no comment'. They were being filmed! She hadn't expected television coverage, it was all too much.

Joe stood guard by the car, his uniform a deterrent to pretty much everyone. 'You alright, Lizzie?' he asked.

'Just about. I wasn't expecting that. Better get Ma home.'

'I'm off duty this evening if you feel like getting out.' Joe ran his fingers through his hair.

'Sure Joe, maybe, let me see how the day goes with Ma,' she said. He had caught her off guard, but the idea of a night out with him wasn't totally out of the question. Being around him again had reminded her of why she had spent so much time with him in her teens.

'I'll call by around seven anyway, just to see how you both are. You can let me know then. No pressure,' Joe said.

*

By the time they got home, Maura's stomach was rumbling loudly, and she was irritable. She had whimpered most of the way, doing Lizzie's head in. Lizzie rummaged in the pantry. A can of tuna would become a sandwich – toasted on rye, pickle on the side. As she assembled it the memories flooded back. She was nine years old again carrying a tray to her mother's bedroom. Opening the door to the darkened room, the silverware rattled on the shaking tray as she laid it on the bed. Guilty. Tentative. Ma lying on her side, face to the wall pretended to be asleep. Anything to avoid Lizzie. Her mother could barely look at her back then. The weight of the guilt made Lizzie try even harder to please her mother. She was still trying.

'Eat this up and then you can take your pain pills. You look wiped out.'

'He didn't look like what I expected. I thought he'd be bigger,' her mother said. She took a bite from the sandwich. 'It's good Lizzie, can you hand me the clicker please?' Lizzie handed her mother the remote to channel surf and returned to the kitchen. She knew what Maura meant. He didn't look like what Lizzie had expected either. She wanted the man who had robbed her of her mother, of her childhood, of her happy family to have had presence, to look more menacing, she didn't know. That a murderer could look so ordinary seemed to diminish their loss.

She found the bottle of kitchen cleaner and a roll of paper towels under the kitchen sink and cleared the countertop, squirting the liquid and wiping as she went along. Reaching up, she pulled down a glass bowl from the shelf above and wiped. The place hadn't been cleaned for some time judging by the greasy dust on the paper towel. She took a break and made herself a cup of coffee. Sitting down at the table she tipped the contents of the glass bowl on to the surface and wiped inside. Multiple sets of keys, all labelled - spare set of keys to front door, car, back door, garage and a single key on an O'Donnell and Sons shamrock keychain. Holding the plastic shamrock between her fingers she squeezed until it let out a little squeak. She put the key down and ate her sandwich, then attempted the killer Sudoku in the paper, and failed miserably. Checking that her mother was asleep, she picked up the key and went down the hall past the utility room to the bedroom at the back of the house. She turned the key in the lock until she felt it open. Unsettled, but excited, she was entering forbidden territory. Her mother would be livid if she caught her in his room. Maybe there would be a clue that would help unlock her memories? Seeing Jason Edwards – her brother's murderer made her want to remember now more than ever. The thought of him ageing while her brother would never grow older had upset her. Maura was right, Paddy needed justice.

It was like a time warp. Beavis and Butthead, MTV and Nirvana posters lined the walls. The last time she had snooped in his room, Paddy had caught her, pushed her on the bed, put his hands around her neck and squeezed until she released the candy she'd been trying to steal. She had never told her mom. What would have been the point? Ma always took Paddy's side. She remembered another time, her dad pounding on the door shouting at Paddy to turn that 'god damn racket' down. He had been obsessed with Kurt Cobain. Shame, he died the year after Paddy. Another one, forever young. Another one put on a pedestal and worshipped. Lizzie rifled through the pile of CDs on the bookcase and slid one into the CD player. She knew the track, he'd seemed to play it on a continuous loop. Teenage angst. She tapped her finger to the beat on the closet door and slid it open – all Paddy's clothes still hanging, all perfectly pressed by their mother. This was vintage stuff, she could make a tidy sum selling it all on e-Bay. His high school wrestling jacket, with its leather sleeves minus the varsity letter, he hadn't lived long enough to earn that.

Lizzie sang along to the final chorus as she flicked

through the rail of clothes, when suddenly her hands were shaking. She could smell him, his breath, the acrid stench of alcohol and weed. The urge to get out as a wave of nausea came over her was all encompassing. She ran down the hall to the bathroom and was sick in the toilet. Wiping her mouth, she put down the lid and sat on the toilet with her head in her hands.

Chapter 5

When the doorbell rang at seven o'clock, Lizzie was relieved. Instead of being refreshed from her nap, her mother had awoken in a fierce, cranky, and demanding mood. Nothing Lizzie did was good enough and she needed some space. Joe provided a perfect escape route. He was kind to her mother, and she wouldn't be rude in front of him. She couldn't wait to get out of the house and go get a drink. Anything to get away from Maura's moaning, even if she had to face her past with Joe.

'Joe's here,' Lizzie said coming through from the kitchen.

Maura straightened up and grinned.

'We're going out to watch the Bruins game. Won't be back late, here are your pills and a glass of water. The tv remote is on your side table.'

'I'll make sure Lizzie gets back safe Mrs. O'Donnell,' Joe said sticking his head into the living room.

'I know you will Joe.' She sniffled and wiped her nose. 'Will that monster get a life sentence? I need to know.'

'I can't…' Joe started.

'You can't let him get away with it.' She was on the verge of tears again.

'Ma! Stop pestering Joe.' Lizzie bit her tongue before she said anything more. Her mother's attention seeking behavior was infuriating. She grabbed her sweater and left.

Joe opened the passenger side door of his Jeep Cherokee and wiped the seat with a cloth. 'Sorry, I haven't had time to take the jeep to the car wash.' The smell of sweaty sports gear mixed with a fishy odor overpowered her, the culprits being an Adidas sports bag and fishing tackle box occupying the back seat of the car. Lizzie rolled down the window and sat back, getting her hair caught in the rod poking through.

'You really know how to impress a girl,' she laughed trying to free herself. 'Ow,'

'Sorry,' Joe leaned over, lifted the rod, and gently unwound the clump of her hair. His chest on hers, she could feel his heart beating, his scent unchanged, fresh. The heat rose from her chest up to her face.

'My dad used to have one of these Cherokees, what year's this one?' She tried to distract herself from the arousal he had inadvertently evoked in her.

'It's a 2000, the only car I've ever owned. Bought it ten years ago with fifty thousand miles on the clock and she's still running great. Where shall we go?'

'Anywhere except the Town Tavern.' She didn't want to run the risk of seeing what's his name from the other night again.

'There's a new sports bar in Denton that'll be showing the game, does great hot wings.'

'Perfect. Thanks for rescuing me, I really needed to get out. My mother gave me a whole sob story about how she couldn't be left on her own but changed her tune when I said I was going out with you.' She glanced over at him, doe eyed, then looked down. Was she flirting?

'Oh, I've got the O'Donnell seal of approval, must've been my uniform.' He did look good in a uniform, that was Lizzie's first impression that day when he arrived on their doorstep, that he had made a successful transformation from teenager to full blown adult man, still good looking in a rugged sort of way. His thick brown hair was shorter, more styled, than she remembered, with a little bit of wax holding it in place. It suited him. He still wore a suede jacket, but with a button-down shirt underneath now, instead of a concert t-shirt.

The parking lot at PJ's sports bar was already nearly full, everyone wanting to see the Bruins victorious. They grabbed a quiet booth in view of one of the smaller screens away from the packed bar. There was a card on the table: Playoff Special – Pitcher of Bud, dozen buffalo wings and two of PJ's house burgers with fries, $20.

'That's a bargain. How do you like your wings?' Lizzie asked.

'Hot with blue cheese dip.'

'Me too. Guess we've got something in common.' Lizzie motioned to the waitress. 'Two Playoff Specials please.' She was used to taking charge, being in control. It was an essential skill in her job. Joe didn't seem to mind.

'You sticking to beer tonight?'

'Yeah, safer that way. Sorry about the other night, you know, free drinks…' She was getting a flashback, not a pretty sight. 'I got a little carried away, but to be honest, I needed to let my hair down. Living with my mom is even more claustrophobic than living with a full crew on ship.'

'Is it fun, the job?' Joe asked. The waitress placed a pitcher of beer and two plastic cups on the table and walked off. Joe poured the beer carefully into the cups avoiding a huge foamy head and handed one to Lizzie. 'You'd think they could at least give us real glasses.'

'Says a lot about the clientele here,' she laughed then took a sip, a small bit of foam staying on her upper lip. I've been doing it for over ten years, so yeah, I guess it's fun.' She could feel his eyes on her, her cheeks reddening as she gulped back the beer.

'You didn't even say goodbye to me.' He launched right in like he had been rehearsing this moment for the last decade, then took a big swig of beer. She stared at him speechless. He had taken her by surprise and hit a nerve, the old guilt she had suppressed until confronted by him had resurfaced.

'I needed to go.' It was a shitty thing she had done, but she wasn't sorry she had left. 'I saw the ad for a seasonal crew job after my dad died.'

'You could've told me. I wouldn't have stopped you.'

'It all happened so fast. Tommy had come back to take over the family business, I knew he would be around for Ma.'

'You just up and left.' He swirled the beer in the bottom of his cup.

'I know, I'm sorry.' She knew he was hurt, but it was so long ago. Had he not moved on? 'I didn't say goodbye to anyone if that's any consolation.'

'What?'

'I just left a note for my mother.' At the time it seemed the only option, Maura would have put a stop to it. 'I needed to move on with my life.' She had never regretted her decision even when she was curled up with seasickness in her tiny, shared cabin. 'I'd planned to come back after my contract was up, six months was all, except I didn't come back. I didn't want to. I think Tommy still holds a grudge.'

'You didn't even write to me.' Joe's eyes welled up. 'I thought we were friends, well more than friends. You could have trusted me.' His voice cracked.

'It wasn't you I was leaving.' She was choked up with guilt. How could he be this upset so many years on? Had she really been that important to him? 'I'm sorry. I didn't mean to hurt you.' She had been a shit person not to have thought of his feelings. She had been trying to survive, looking out for number one for the first time. He just got caught in the crossfire, collateral damage.

'Was it that bad at home?'

'Yeah, and it got worse after Tommy went off to college, then dad dying so suddenly…

'You never let on.'

What was she supposed to say? When Tommy went to Rensselaer he had escaped, avoided coming back at holidays, always had an excuse that he had studying to do, or a work placement to go to. She had been abandoned. 'I was only fourteen. I ended up being a housewife – all the shopping, cooking, cleaning. Mom was in bed most of the time and when she wasn't in bed, she was at church, praying.' She took a large gulp of beer hoping the lump in her throat would go away. She didn't want to cry. The arrival of the chicken wings saved her. The crispy batter and buttery aroma made her mouth water. 'Smells amazing.'

'Ah, but let's find out if they have an authentic spicy kick.' Joe said. He grabbed a celery stick, dipped it into the blue cheese and took a bite then picked up the hot sticky wing and tucked in. 'Wow, these are great. Try one.' By the time he looked up, she had already sucked all the meat off a wing, tossed the bones on to the plate and was crunching on a stick of celery.

'I haven't had wings like these for years,' she said and poured another glass of beer from the pitcher.

'How long do you think you're gonna stay in Newham?' Joe asked.

'I promised Tommy I'd stay until my new contract starts in July. Mom has four weeks of radiation therapy starting on Monday.' She was dreading this next phase. 'I'm trying to get her to do more for herself. In a strange way, all this stuff with the arrest of Paddy's killer seems to have brought her back to life. But she's hard work.'

'I can see that. How was she after today's hearing?'

'She was exhausted. Jason Edwards wasn't what she expected him to be. He looked ordinary. I don't know, maybe she was looking for a monster.'

'And what about you?'

'Oh, you know me Joe, I was okay.' Even now she couldn't be honest with him.

'I guess it stirs up a lot of things for you all. Your mother lost her son, and you lost your big brother.'

'And I lost my mother.' That lump was returning to her throat. A roar came from the bar. 'Bruins scored,' she said.

'Off to a great start again tonight. I don't know what happened to them in the first game. It was a home crowd, they should've been on fire.' Joe wiped the sticky sauce from his mouth. 'Is it worse being in your mom's house with all those memories around?'

'It is. While she was napping today, I found the key to Paddy's room and had a look. It was like a time warp. She has kept everything in place.'

'I guess your house is full of all kinds of bad memories.'

'I want to know what happened.'

'What do you mean?'

'Nobody talked about what happened after the funeral was over.' She took a sip of beer and wiped the froth from her mouth. 'The night of the snowstorm when Paddy went missing, Tommy and I were tunnelling at the end of the cul-de- sac.'

'Cul-de-sac?' Joe raised his eyebrows.

'It's where we used to make our snow forts.' She licked the sauce from her fingers. 'You really wanna hear all this?'

'Go on.'

'We were tunnelling, Tommy went back to the house to get a flashlight and while he was gone the tunnel collapsed and I was buried in the snow.' Her voice sounded very matter of fact, detached, like she was talking about a stranger. 'He came back, saw my hat poking out of the snow and dug me out.' A chill rose up her spine.

'Jesus, that must have been terrifying. How come you never told me any of this?'

'Because I have no memory of it.' Everything she knew she had been told by other people. It wasn't that she hadn't tried to remember. 'Tommy carried me home and they drove me to the hospital in dad's Cherokee with the plough on the front. It was the only thing that could get through the roads because of the storm.'

'You can see why I'm loathe to part with mine then.' A feeble attempt to lighten the mood but she laughed anyway.

The waitress arrived with their burgers and fries. 'I think we're going to need another pitcher of Bud to wash these down,' Lizzie said.

'Not for me Lizzie, but you go ahead. I'm your driver tonight.'

'But we still have two periods to go!' Lizzie looked at the score, Bruins were up 2-0 at the end of the first.

Joe was distracted by the raucous bar crowd. 'Incredible save! Sorry, what happened when they got you to the hospital?'

'I ended up in the hospital for a week with hypothermia and pneumonia. They said I had dry drowning. I didn't even know there was such a thing.' Her whole body was shivering. This was the first time she had talked about it to anyone other than the useless school counsellor and Father Larkin. He at least had been a sympathetic listener. She had wanted to put it behind her. Knowing without remembering frightened her. She had always played it down, but something deep inside told her that it was important. She just didn't know why.

'How do you know all this if you don't remember anything?' He opened his burger and pulled the pickles off, putting them on the side of the plate. 'Can we have some ketchup, please?' The waitress nodded and grabbed a bottle from the table next to theirs.

'I'll have those.' Lizzie reached across and picked up the pickles and put them on her bun. 'It was all Ma could talk about, how Tommy had saved my life and how grateful I should be to him. How terrible it was for her to almost lose two children.' Lizzie had always loved Tommy, they were close, but things changed and instead of being grateful she had begun to resent him. Sure, he had rescued her that night, but he left her when she needed him most. Lizzie took a bite from her burger. 'God this is delicious. We are catered for well on ship, but since I've been home, I've realized how much I miss local and home-cooked food.'

'Miss it enough to stay on longer?' Joe was looking her in the eye.

'I don't know, it's been so long. Hard to come back. And

there's no way I could live with my mom long term.'

A chorus of cheers went up in the bar. Bergeron's scored. He's on fire, come on Bruins,' Joe said.

'I'm not sure Hannah would like me being nearby for too long either. Do you remember her in high school?'

'Out of my league, always dating guys a few years older. But I've gotten to know her and Tommy since they got married.'

'Yup, she snagged Tommy when he came back after college. I never had a problem at school with her, she moved in a different crowd. But boy does she seem to have a problem with me now.'

'You sure about that?'

'I don't know what Tommy has told her over the years about me, but she seems to resent my presence even though they asked me to come.'

'Maybe she's just stressed. Give her a chance.'

'Whose side you on?' Lizzie stared at him then smiled.

The room had filled up and the crowd was buzzing. Watching the screen Lizzie and Joe got swept up in the game. There was something so exhilarating about hockey, its fast pace, the skill, and the physical violence, like the best and worst of humanity being played out in front of them. Lizzie felt alive. By the end of the second period, she was hoarse from all the cheering. She needed a rest. Joe poured them another round of drinks.

'Did you ever remember what happened? In the snow that night?'

'Not really, sometimes I feel like the memories are there somewhere just out of reach. Nightmares, claustrophobia, anxiety and panic attacks but no real memories.' She laughed and dragged a French fry across the ketchup on her plate. She hadn't even known that Paddy was missing. Maura had been upset with her, but she didn't know why. 'Turns out they hadn't realized that Paddy hadn't come home until three days later. My mother was camped out with me at the hospital, my dad was working all hours. I guess he finally noticed Paddy wasn't home and called around all his friends, then reported him missing.'

'When did they tell you?'

'They didn't. Tommy did.' He was the one who had had filled in the gaps, told her everything from the moment he found her to Paddy being reported missing. 'A few days later when we were back home, I heard Ma and my dad arguing, Ma screaming and crying blaming dad, and blaming me, that if I hadn't been in the hospital, she would have realized Paddy was missing.'

'But you were only a little kid.' Joe leaned across the table and took her hands in his. A little drop of blood smeared on the table, and she pulled her hand away.

Looking down at her hand she realized she had been picking a hangnail until it had bled.

'Maybe you get why I left now.' Lizzie polished off the last of the beer and stood up. 'Looks like it's going to be a Bruins victory tonight. Let's get the check.'

'Don't you want to stay for the third period?'

'I should probably get back to my mother.' She was done talking. She hated feeling churned up. 'The Bruins are gonna win anyway, it's 3-0 already. They're crushing them.'

'Let's hope they take the series.' Joe got his coat and followed Lizzie out.

Lizzie climbed into the jeep, shut the door, and reclined her seat. Her ears were still ringing from the volume in the bar.

'You're not going to fall asleep on me, are you?' Joe started the engine and pulled out of the parking lot. He turned on the radio to the classic rock station he loved.

'I see your taste in music hasn't changed.' She moved her head to the beat of the music. 'I was thinking…'

'Sounds ominous,' He glanced over, then focused on the road ahead.

'Do you feel like driving up to the lookout? She looked over to check Joe's reaction. He was looking straight ahead. Maybe she'd got it wrong?

'I thought you needed to get home?'

'I do, but I'm enjoying being out and your company.' She didn't want to sound too keen. 'Your conversation skills are a step up from my mother's,' she laughed.

'Some compliment!' He looked over at her and smiled. 'Why not? I haven't been up there for ages.'

The jeep's headlights illuminated the dark stretch of road from Denton to Newham. Tiny bright spots appeared in the distance, the headlights reflecting in the eyes of raccoons and opossums further down the road. The creatures often ended up as roadkill from drivers exceeding the speed limit. Lizzie looked out the window and spotted a pair of eyes much closer moving quickly from the woods toward the road.

'Slow down, Joe.' She braced herself as Joe hit the brakes and came to a full stop just before a deer leapt across the road.

'She'd have ruined my front end.' He let out a long sigh and smiled. 'You okay?'

'Yeah, I'm fine. It just happened so quickly.' Her pulse was racing.

'You have no idea how many times I've been called to accidents involving deer. People drive way too fast on these roads. But occasionally we get a bit of venison out of it.'

'Oh, I'm glad there's an upside to it for you.' She shook her head and laughed.

They turned right at the junction and followed the signs toward Lake Wunnumwaonk, climbing high above the lake and passing the turn off for Tommy's house.

'Your brother got himself a prime piece of land.'

'You aren't kidding. And built a humungous house.'

'Have you been inside yet?'

'Nope, waiting to be invited.' It irked her that Tommy hadn't invited her over yet. Too busy, she imagined.

Joe pulled into the dirt parking area at the top of the hill and turned the engine off. They were entirely alone. No teenagers parked up smoking weed or drinking. Joe leaned over and grabbed a flashlight from the glove compartment. 'You remember the way?' He got out and opened the trunk of the car and grabbed a picnic blanket.

'I could do it blindfolded.' She thought she could. It was strange how some felt memories stayed with her and others seemed to have fallen into the void.

'Don't tempt me.' He shone the light along the trail. The branches of the bare trees clattered in the breeze as they walked the short distance down the path and climbed up again to a flat boulder. Joe put out his hand, helped Lizzie up on to the rock and spread the blanket out on the ground. She stood and stared at the glowing yellow moon. It loomed large and lit the water, the ripples flickering like diamonds.

'I'd forgotten how beautiful it is.' She sat down on the

blanket next to Joe and leaned back looking up at the sky searching for Orion's belt. She took a deep breath, then exhaled. 'I love this sky.'

'So big, makes our problems seem insignificant.' He leaned over and kissed her. His lips warm and familiar, she sank into his embrace. His scent, the feel of his body, so comforting. She put the nagging voice telling her this was not a good idea – you can't go back – to the back of her mind. He wanted her, she wanted him. They were adults and could deal with the repercussions later. For now, she wanted her problems to feel insignificant, to feel the warmth of him holding her, kissing her neck gently, 'You okay with this, Lizzie? I can stop.'

'Don't stop.' She unbuttoned his shirt and felt the soft hair on his chest, then unbuckled his belt. He reached into his jacket pocket and pulled out a condom. 'You're prepared.'

'An eagle scout is always prepared.' He brushed the hair off her face and kissed her again. She unzipped her jeans and wriggled out of them then pulled him towards her wanting him more than ever. She remembered how gentle he had always been. That hadn't changed. No longer teenagers, they moved like experienced lovers, slowly satisfying each other.

In Joe's arms she felt safe, like no harm could come to

her. It had been years since she had allowed herself to feel physically and emotionally connected. Real intimacy made her vulnerable. Her body started to shake, and tears streamed down her face. Joe turned his face towards hers.

'Hey, what's this about? Was I that bad?' He smiled and wiped her tears with his sleeve. She cracked a smile.

'I just don't know how I'm going to get through all this Paddy shit.' She sniffled and wriggled back into her jeans.

'I'll be here for you.' He meant it, she knew that, but couldn't escape the feeling of dread in the pit of her stomach. She felt his arm around her. 'You're shivering, it's too cold. Let's get you home.'

The Denton Times

Keeping the community informed with independent local reporting

COLD CASE SUSPECT IN COURT - PLEADS NOT GUILTY
By Tina Chandler
April 23, 2014

Jason James Edwards, the 39-year-old man accused of sexual assault and the second-degree murder of a 16-year-old boy in 1993, made his first court appearance in Denton, MA on 22nd April. Wearing an orange prison jumpsuit and handcuffed, he spoke only briefly to enter a not guilty plea. A request for bail was denied by Judge William H. Baxter and Edwards will remain on remand until the pre-trial hearing scheduled for 15th May. If convicted Edwards will face life imprisonment.

The family of the victim, Patrick O'Donnell, was present in court for the hearing and visibly distressed at the sight of the suspect as the charges were read out.

A native of Denton, Edwards is a graduate of Denton Technical School. Before his arrest he was employed as an auto-mechanic at the branch of Xpress Lube on Prior Street in Denton.

Colleagues expressed surprise at his arrest and described him as a conscientious worker.

According to neighbors in the Wildwood Condominium complex, Edwards largely kept to himself, aside from friends visiting his apartment regularly.

Edwards had also been employed at the Silkwood Speedway track on weekends assisting with oil and tire change. Track manager, John Weston said he was dismissed at the end of the season due to allegations of alcohol and substance misuse.

Outside the courthouse following the hearing Edwards' attorney, Eileen Murphy told reporters, 'Mr. Edwards, just as you and I are, is entitled to the due process of law and to a full defense which I intend to make certain he receives.'

The family of Patrick O'Donnell declined to make any comment to reporters.

Chapter 6

Lizzie expected to see the coverage of the arraignment hearing on the front page. This local hack had been handed the case of a lifetime and was looking to make a name for herself. At least cameras had been banned from the court room, otherwise there would have been multiple photos of them. The article included a solitary photo of the defense attorney, Eileen Murphy standing on the steps of the courthouse. She was surprised the attorney had spoken to the reporters; she came across more confident in the article than when she had appeared in the court room but still looked bedraggled. Someone needed to have a word with her about her clothes and hair if the case was going to continue to be front page news.

'Morning Lizzie, set me a place will you.' Ma caught Lizzie off-guard, she wasn't expecting her to come to the table for breakfast.

'What can I get you?'

'Just some toast, a banana and coffee please.' Lizzie put two slices of bread in the toaster and got out a plate. 'Did you have a good time last night?'

'Yeah, it was a good game, Bruins won. Had some nice chicken wings.'

'Is that all?'

'That's all Ma. Don't get your hopes up, we're just old friends.' The toaster popped up and Lizzie went about preparing her plate.

'We were on the news last night.'

'You mean they covered the hearing?'

'Yes, but WE were on tv, they showed us coming out of the courthouse. My outfit looked stylish, shame you covered me as you helped me down the steps. No one could see my face and hair.' Maura sat reading the Denton Times article. 'Why does this reporter always say the O'Donnell family declined to comment?'

'Because I said no comment as I navigated you through the crowd,' Lizzie said as she spread a smattering of apple butter across the toast. 'Why? Is there something you want to say to Tina Chandler?'

'No, no, it's well, Paddy can't speak for himself.' Maura placed slices of banana on her toast and took a bite. 'It seems a shame that we don't speak for him.'

'You remember what Tommy said, Ma, right? Leave it to the police, it will all come out in court.'

'Yes, okay. I was wondering if you could take me to confession and mass this morning? I want to talk to Father Larkin.'

'I'll drop you at church and pick you up when mass is

over.' There was no way she was sitting through all that family values rhetoric again.

*

While her mother was out of the way at church Lizzie called the medical appliance company and arranged for the hospital bed to be picked up the following morning. She needed to move around more and could manage the stairs if she tried. Lizzie was winning the battle to re-engage her mother with life, tiny steps at a time.

She had just grabbed the key to Paddy's room when her phone rang. It was Tommy, so she declined the call. She wasn't in the mood to be berated for taking their mother to court. He'd have to come in person if he wanted to have a testosterone fueled shouting match. She figured she had about an hour before needing to collect Ma and wanted to have a good look around. Tommy had never told her that Paddy had been sexually assaulted. She had so many questions now, questions she couldn't ask her mother.

Paddy's clothes were neatly folded in his chest of drawers, not much of interest. She sat down on his desk chair and looked at the noticeboard above the desk. His calendar hanging, big X's marking off the final days of his life, though he didn't know it at the time. Peeking out from behind the calendar was a pinned appointment card. Father Peter Larkin spiritual counselling Thursday, 23 March 1993 at 4:00pm. He had been unable to keep that appointment having already joined his maker by then. Or not. Maybe he was rotting in hell and that's why his mother had to pray so much for his soul. Was there something wrong with her? A normal sibling might feel sad or nostalgic for their dead sibling. She was numb. She didn't even know what she was looking for or expecting to find, the police would have already been all through his room all those years ago.

*

As she pulled up at the front entrance of Our Lady of Lourdes, her mother and Father Larkin appeared to be deep in conversation on the steps. He held both of her hands in his and kissed her forehead before noticing Lizzie and scurrying off. Maura sniffled as she got into the car.

'We're so fortunate to have Father Larkin, he has been such a huge support to me over the years.'

'That's good Ma. How was confession, how many Hail Marys did he give you?' At her first confession Lizzie had made up sins to sound more interesting and had been given four Our Fathers and six Hail Marys as her penance. She learned her lesson and toned it down from then on always wondering if the priest recognized her voice when she was in the confessional.

'Oh, stop Lizzie, you know I can't discuss it with you.'

'I'm serious, I always wondered how Father Larkin

decided on the penalty for each sin, like was fighting with your brother equal to lying to your parents?' By the time Lizzie had something meaty worth confessing, she had given up on the church. The last time she had gone to confession was the week before she had given a hand job to a boy in her class, she was fourteen. He proceeded to tell all his friends about it much to her embarrassment, but she survived. Her first proper sin, but she had been far too ashamed to confess it to the priest. What would he have thought of her?

'I'm sure there are guidelines for penance. Perhaps you'd like to come with me next time?'

'You mean when hell freezes over, Ma?' Lizzie glanced at Maura and smiled. Even her mother couldn't resist chuckling.

'You do make me laugh sometimes.' She put her hand on Lizzie's. 'I was thinking I'd like to make us some stew for dinner tonight. If I give you the list, will you go pick up what I need while I have a rest?'

'Sure, if you feel up to it.' Perhaps her mother was tiring of her cooking already, but whatever the reason, it was a good sign, and she wasn't going to argue with her.

*

Lizzie walked down Main St. passing the hardware store and stopped to admire a pair of boots in the window display at the thrift store. The little row of independent locally owned shops gave the town character. A car double parked outside Drew's High-Class Butchers rocked back and forth, its teenage inhabitants blaring head banging music. The bass was still thumping in Lizzie's chest when she pulled a ticket from the machine and took her place in line. As her number was called, she waved the ticket and approached the butcher's counter. A hand tapped on her shoulder. Turning, she saw it was Hannah and forced a smile.

'What are you buying Lizzie?'

'Just some stewing beef for Ma, she's cooking tonight.' She stepped forward and placed her order.

'What? You mean she's out of bed?'

'Yeah, all she needed was a little support and encouragement.' Lizzie knew this was a lie. She had no idea what was motivating her mother, but she knew it would get Hannah's back up.

'I did try, Lizzie.' Hannah's face reddened, but Lizzie didn't feel guilty.

She deserved it after her antics ruined Lizzie's perfect Easter meal. There was little chance of them developing a friendship now and she didn't need a sister.

'I was going to stop by to ask if you'd like to come over tomorrow evening for a bite to eat and watch the play-off game? The girls keep asking when they can see you again.

You really charmed them.'

Lizzie was disappointed Hannah hadn't taken the bait; she was up for a bit of sparring. Now that she'd gone all gushing and friendly, Lizzie felt obliged to accept the invitation.

'Oh, sure, I'd love to get to know my nieces better.' It was all so friendly, so why did she feel like she was being set up? 'What time do you want me?'

'About six, but Tom can pick you up on his way home from work. Will give you time to hang out with the girls and see the house before the game starts.'

'Okay, see you tomorrow.' Lizzie took the bag of beef from the butcher and headed out. He looked familiar. There seemed to be ghosts everywhere she turned in Newham.

*

Maura stood at the stove wearing a floral apron stirring the stew pot, the smell of beef in Guinness wafted through the air. Lizzie hoped there would be dumplings to go with it. She couldn't remember the last time she had had home-made dumplings, or even the last time her mother had cooked a meal for her. She must've been eight, pre-Paddy's death since Ma had stopped cooking after he died. She stopped everything after he died. The counsellor at school had referred to it as 'complicated grief' and told her that some people need longer to process loss, particularly when they'd lost a child. Maybe that was fine for other people, but Lizzie had needed a functioning mother.

'The table is set for three, who else is coming? Tommy?'

'No, I invited Father Larkin. He was so kind to me today and he seemed lonely,' Maura said.

Christ, the Lord does giveth and taketh away. The old priest was kind enough, but the thought of making conversation over a long meal, like a third wheel, was undesirable. She opened a bottle of red wine and poured herself a large glass. She needed numbing.

'I forgot to tell you that the medical appliance company is coming to collect the hospital bed tomorrow morning. Now that you can get up the stairs, you'll be more comfortable in your own double bed. I know how uncomfortable those plastic mattresses can be, they make you sweat.'

'Well, I wish you had asked me first Lizzie, we haven't tested it out yet. I'm not sure, it might be…'

'That must be Father Larkin at the door.' Lizzie took a large gulp of wine and went to greet him. 'Evening Father', come in.'

'Mary Elizabeth, so good to see you again.' He blessed her forehead with the sign of the cross like he'd done when she was a child, then gave her a hug. 'It smells divine,

Maura, so good of you to invite me. I don't get out of the rectory much anymore, and since we lost our cook, I've been eating ready meals most of the time.' Lizzie handed Father Larkin a glass of red wine and showed him through to the dining room.

'Mary Elizabeth, can you help me carry the stew to the table please?' Maura removed her apron and joined Father Larkin. 'And I think I'll have a small glass of wine too please.' Lizzie wasn't sure that mixing wine with a cocktail of drugs her mom was taking was a brilliant idea, but she poured her a glass like an obedient daughter. She sat down with them and was about to start to serve, but caught Ma's eye and put the serving spoon down.

Father Larkin reached out, held both their hands, bowed his head, and began to say grace. 'The day is ending, and, like the disciples on the road to Emmaus, we pause to break bread together. May our eyes be opened, and, in this act of common sharing, may we see the risen Lord in one another…,' he continued on. Loquacious, but mildly entertaining. Lizzie kept her head bowed so he couldn't see her sniggering.

'Amen.' Lizzie looked forward to her eyes being opened by this evening's scintillating conversation. 'Pass your plate Father and let me serve you.' She lifted two fluffy white dumplings from the stew, placing them on the side of the plate then dug down into the pot for the tender beef and gravy. These were perfect dumplings, unlike the claggy lumps the ship's chef made. 'Ma, you're going to have to show me how to make these dumplings.'

'The secret is in using soft margarine rather than lard, simple.'

'Do you remember the last time you made dumplings, Ma? It must be over twenty years ago. You haven't lost your touch.'

'Mary Elizabeth don't be absurd. I make dumplings all the time. You've been away for a long time.' Lizzie was certain this was a lie; her mother just didn't want to lose face in front of Father Larkin.

'It's good to see you back at mass, Maura. The ladies in the Novena group have been asking after you.' Lizzie imagined the desperate women all sitting in a circle praying for miracles. What did her mother pray for other than Paddy, like Lazarus, being brought back from the dead?

'Your sermon Easter Sunday was powerful Father. I wish people understood the sadness and sorrow of those poor women who went to mourn Jesus,' Maura said. Lizzie poured herself another glass of wine and topped up Father Larkin's glass. Maura's glass was almost empty. 'May I have another glass too please Mary Elizabeth?' Maura said. Clearly this was her mother's show tonight. Mary Elizabeth, please this and Mary Elizabeth, please that. All done to impress an eighty-year-old priest. 'Didn't you think so too, Mary Elizabeth?'

'I'm not a Catholic anymore, but wasn't it about moving forward and not being trapped by death? Or did you not want to hear that message Ma…?'

'Of course, you're a Catholic!' Maura went rigid, tight mouthed. 'You were baptized, did your first holy communion and confirmation. How can you say you're not a Catholic, you were raised a Catholic?'

Lizzie had hit a nerve.

'It's alright Maura, sometimes young people need to stray from the flock to find their way back,' Father Larkin said. 'We know what you mean, don't we, Mary Elizabeth?' He put his hand on Lizzie's.

'Sure, Father.' She changed the subject. 'Did Ma tell you about the court hearing today?'

Maura sat stone faced sipping her wine.

'I think it was very courageous of you Maura to attend and see the accused in person. I pray for his darkened soul and hope he repents. Your brother was a most cherished son, and I was very fond of him, Lizzie,' he said. Oh, to have been a cherished daughter. What a difference it would have made if her mother had cherished the living as much as the dead.

'This has been a delicious dinner, don't suppose you might be interested in cooking for me on a more formal basis, Maura?' He was flattering her now and Maura was beaming. Lizzie looked over at her and forced a smile. Maybe it wasn't such a bad idea if it would bring her mother back into the land of the living?

'I'd love to Father, maybe we can discuss it again once I finish my treatment. But you are always welcome to come join us for meals.'

'I may take you up on that, haven't had stew and dumplings like that since I was a boy.' He reached out for their hands again and bowed his head. 'We give Thee thanks, Almighty God, for all thy benefits, Who livest and reignest, world without end. Vouchsafe, O Lord, to reward with eternal life, all those who do us good for Thy name's sake.'

'Amen,' Maura replied.

'Let us bless the Lord.'

'Thanks be to God,' Maura replied.

'May the souls of the faithful departed, through the mercy of God, rest in peace,' Father Larkin said releasing their hands. Lizzie felt a sense of relief that the meal was over until she saw a tear running down her mother's face. A little pang of guilt jabbed her side.

'Amen.' Lizzie said. She would need to have other plans

the next time her mother invited the priest over. Maura was tipsy, her cheeks bright pink, two glasses of wine were two too many for someone on that much medication. Lizzie showed Father Larkin to the door.

'You're a good daughter, Lizzie. I know it's not easy.' He hugged her. 'Your mom will come around, just wait.' He pulled his wool coat off the banister and left. Lizzie started to clear the table and reflected on the priest's words – 'just wait'. How much longer? She'd been waiting over twenty years. She took some solace in the fact that he at least recognized she was doing her best under challenging circumstances and could be an ally.

Maura had already taken herself into the living room, stretched out in her recliner and begun to snore in front of an old episode of LA Law. Lizzie got a pillow and blankets and tucked her in for the night, her mother was in no fit state to get upstairs or even into her nightgown.

Chapter 7

The food court at the Denton Mall was heaving with long lines of people desperate for tacos and pizza. Lizzie cleared a tray from the abandoned table and took a seat resting her bags by her feet. Ripping open a packet of soy sauce with her teeth, she squirted it over the bowl of steaming Chinese fried rice and tucked in, alternating mouthfuls with a swig of coke to combat the saltiness of the soy and ginger. She wasn't used to shopping and the constant droning sound of ambient music and crowds had given her a throbbing headache. Her mother had seemed overly keen to get rid of her, giving Lizzie her credit card and telling her to go 'spruce herself up'. Unheard of. Her phone vibrated in her pocket, a text from Hannah reminding her that Tommy would be picking her up at six. It was already after five o'clock, she needed to get home and her mother sorted before going out.

She had been thinking about her new purchases as she pulled into the driveway. It had been years since she had splurged on anything, always conscious of saving money. The sight of Tina Chandler's car parked in front of the house triggered a wave of panic in her. Arms laden with shopping bags, she struggled to get the key in the front door and called out, 'Ma?'.

'In the kitchen, Mary Elizabeth.' Maura was sitting at the table, almost un-recognizable in full makeup, wearing a white blouse and navy cardigan, her St. Christopher's medal around her neck. 'This is my daughter Mary Elizabeth, Tina. Tina and I have been chatting about Paddy.' Photographs were strewn all over the kitchen table, Paddy as a baby, young child, teenager. Lizzie gave Tina a frosty stare and reached out to shake her hand.

'What are you doing here? You really should have called me before…'

'I invited Tina here, Mary Elizabeth, she didn't just turn up. She is my guest, so don't use that tone.'

'But you know what Tommy said, Ma…'

'Tommy doesn't decide who I can and cannot speak to. It's important that Paddy's story is told and only I can tell it as his mother.' Tina Chandler must have fed her mother that line.

'We've about finished, Maura has been extremely helpful giving background. Such a tragedy for your family,' Tina said. There was a distinct lack of sincerity in her voice, no wonder Tommy had wanted to hit her. 'I'll be off then Maura, will be in touch if I need to clarify any facts and will let you know when the piece will be published.' Lizzie clutched her phone as she stood up. How was she going to tell Tommy about this?

'Mary Elizabeth, load the dishes from the sink into the dishwasher.' Maura rose and saw the reporter to the door.

'This is why you wanted me out of the house today. What were you thinking Ma, you have no idea what she…'?

'Enough Lizzie.'

'Oh, so now that she's gone, I'm Lizzie, not Mary Elizabeth. No need to create a good impression anymore.' Her mother was a loose cannon; God knows what she said to the flunky middle aged journalist. But Lizzie would be the one to pick up the pieces when it all went wrong. A car horn sounded. 'That's Tommy come to pick me up. Hannah invited me over to see the girls and watch the ice hockey.'

'Isn't he going to come in to see me?'

'Guess not.' Lizzie shrugged her shoulders.

'What about me and my dinner?'

Lizzie dropped a takeout bag on the table in front of Maura. 'Here, I got you Chinese. You can heat it up in the microwave.' She grabbed her jacket and left without a goodbye. Inside Tommy's car she let out a long sigh. 'Let's go Tom, want to see those girls of yours.'

What she really wanted was a stiff drink, but that would have to wait.

*

The golden hour sun cast a warm, amber glow over Tommy's house. It was unusual to find a new house built entirely of wood these days, people were too impatient and had no appreciation of craftsmanship, preferring pre-fabs with plastic siding. Lizzie stood and admired the exterior, giving Tommy a nod of approval. By all accounts, Tommy had built their father's business and made a name for himself. He had all the trappings of a successful businessman anyway.

'How long did it take you to build the house Tom?'

'About three years in all, I wanted to do a lot of the work myself and had to fit it in with running the business and other construction jobs. Let's go inside and I'll show you around.'

As they walked up the front steps, the front door opened, Tommy's girls dressed in Bruins hockey shirts poured out all screeching in unison. 'They're here, they're here!'

'You're surrounded Lizzie, no escaping this lot,' Tommy said.

'Girls, girls, take it easy. Give your aunt some space,' Hannah said as she appeared in the doorway, beckoning Lizzie inside.

There was no shortage of space in this house. She looked up and admired the cathedral ceiling. 'Beautiful kitchen, Hannah.'

'I designed it, but Tommy built all the cabinets himself.'

Lizzie put her hand on the marble counter, the coolness of the stone gave her a chill. She shivered, then laughed.

'What's so funny?' Hannah said, her face unamused.

'I was just thinking that your breakfast bar is about the size of my cabin on ship.'

The girls grabbed her arms and pulled her out of the kitchen, guiding her up the wooden staircase for the grand tour starting with their bedrooms. Lizzie couldn't get over the size of the place, even a family of five must rattle around in it. The heating and electric bills alone would bankrupt most families. Claire, Tommy's eldest, guided Lizzie to her bedroom where the trio had set up a beauty parlor. They sat her down on the four-poster bed with floral surround amid a sea of soft toys. All so luxurious, she couldn't quite believe it was a child's room.

'We're going to give you a pamper session Aunt Lizzie, you need to take off your boots and socks.' Claire said. 'Come sit down at my vanity.'

The little one rolled up the legs of Lizzie's jeans, placed her feet in the foot bath and switched it on. Little jets of warm water shot out creating a sea of bubbles.

'You girls are so professional; you could work at the salon on my cruise ship.' She winced as a brush was pulled through her hair.

'You have hair just like ours, but you need to brush it more.' The chubby hand of Martha, the youngest, lifted Lizzie's arm and placed it on a tray. They giggled as they filed her nails and painted them gold, black and white. They lifted her feet from the foot bath and went to work on her toes in the same colors. There was a knock on the door, Tommy handed Claire a shirt which she put over Lizzie's head. 'Bend your arms Aunt Lizzie.' She complied with her niece's order. 'Now stand up and come over to the mirror, look, you're a real Bruins fan like us.' They flashed their gold, black and white nails in unison, pleased with their auntie's transformation. Lizzie gazed at the three of them. They really could be her daughters. She put that thought right out of her mind. She wasn't cut out for motherhood, she knew that.

Tommy called up to the girls to make their way downstairs to the kitchen. 'You're quadruplets.' He laughed at the sight of his sister's feet, then disappeared leaving her alone with Hannah.

'What can I get you to drink Lizzie?' Hannah looked pale but managed to smile.

'A Jack Daniels and Coke please.'

'We don't keep hard liquor in the house, just beer, wine or soft drinks.' Lizzie wasn't sure if Hannah was trying to be patronizing or if she was accusing Lizzie of being an alcoholic. Maybe Tommy had said something to her.

'Oh. Well, a beer would be great, thanks. Is there anything I can give you a hand with?' The blue headlights from Tommy's car shone through the kitchen window almost blinding her.

'No, I'm not cooking. I ordered pizza. Tommy's just leaving to pick them up.' Lizzie stood in an awkward silence with Hannah wondering how she was going to manage twenty minutes of conversation alone with her. They had nothing in common as far as she could remember, nothing except Tommy.

'Tommy did a great job with the house. I love how this is all open plan. You must be the envy of the Newham wives.'

'Actually, I did the interior design. That was my job before I had the girls.'

'Oh…' Before she could finish her sentence, she was rescued by the children. They had taken over a large sofa and were munching on bowls of chips and salsa. Claire beckoned Lizzie over, snuggled up and enveloped her in a cocoon. She wasn't accustomed to being around children, but they were warm, and she was safe from their mother.

Ten minutes into the second period of game four of the series, the Bruins scored. Still behind by a goal but regardless the girls jumped up and down on the sofa, giving each other high fives, spilling chips everywhere. Seduced by their pure joy, Lizzie smiled and laughed along with them. Connecting with any joyful moments from her own childhood was difficult, it was like they had all been erased. She smiled as the littlest one stuffed a tortilla chip into her mouth. Happy family, but they weren't playing, it was the real deal for them.

Tommy came through the door shouting, 'Pizza delivery', just as the Bruins scored for the second time. The girls were all over him like flies and he gently swatted them away, telling them to put the napkins and paper plates on the coffee table. Huddled around in front of the tv eating their slices, the girls pulled the stringy cheese off leaving the base behind, as the second period ended. Tommy handed Lizzie another Bud and a slice of pepperoni on a paper plate.

'Where's Mommy gone, girls?'

'She went to lay down.'

Tommy looked at Lizzie. She shrugged her shoulders, 'Didn't say anything to me.' Maybe this was why Hannah invited her over, she wanted Lizzie to see what a normal, happy family they were, to remind her that she would always be an outsider. Her way of saying Tommy was hers. Lizzie took a big gulp of beer to wash down the salty pepperoni stuck in her throat, then realized it wasn't the pepperoni. She choked back the tears and took another swig. 'Great pizza, Tom.'

'Yes, it is. Hey, listen, once the girls go to bed, I need to talk to you.'

'Sounds ominous.' She tried to laugh it off but felt sick to her stomach. He spoke with a tone not dissimilar to their dad's when he would chastise her for some alleged offence. Had Tommy and Hannah lured her over under false pretenses, each with their own hidden agenda? Hannah had already shown her hand, but what was Tommy up to? Lizzie was trapped, realizing she couldn't run if things got ugly, she didn't have her car.

A great comeback in the third period gave the Bruins another win. Hannah reappeared on the staircase, her face washed, and called bedtime. The girls were ecstatic as Hannah herded them upstairs to bed. 'Can Aunt Lizzie read us a bedtime story?'

'I'd love…,' Lizzie said.

'She can do that another time, it's late you need to get to sleep now,' Hannah seemed short tempered. Lizzie saw the disappointment on their faces and blew them a kiss.

'Does she have a problem with me? I could've read them a quick story.'

'I think you're creating problems where there are none. She's just tired.' He took the last mouthful of his beer.

'Hannah's spent years helping me look after Ma while you've been off enjoying yourself cruising. I wouldn't blame her if she resented you, but she doesn't.'

'It's obvious that she does.'

'It's not obvious to me. When she came home yesterday and told me she invited you for dinner, I told her she didn't need to do that.'

'Yeah, she caught me by surprise too.' Lizzie went to the kitchen, grabbed two more beers, and handed one to Tommy.

'You know what your problem is Lizzie, you're always ready to think the worst of people, always suspicious. Hannah told me that she thinks you are doing a great job with Ma, that she knows how difficult she can be.'

'I only see what people show me. And you know what, I think your behavior has been a little on the extreme side lately.'

'What do you mean?'

'Joe Moretti told me you threatened Tina Chandler and that he let you off with a verbal caution. 'Why would you do that Tommy? It was just a photograph in the newspaper.'

'It was a photograph of my family, my children. They are not newsworthy; I was protecting them.' His face in a tight grimace, he folded his arms. 'I don't want my girls growing up with the shit we did. I've worked hard to build a good life for my family, one I'm proud of.'

'I don't get it Tom, why do you feel so threatened by this court case?'

'I saw and heard more than you did, I got a lot of abuse at school. Kids said terrible things about Paddy to me, called him all kinds of disgusting names. You've had it easy.

'I wouldn't call it easy. I never fitted in anywhere, not at home, not at school. You act like I've been on vacation for a decade.' She could feel her blood pressure rising. 'I worked my ass off. I started in housekeeping on a ship at eighteen. You have no idea what that was like. But you know what, at least I had good preparation at home, cleaning, doing laundry, making all the beds from the age of eight. The family domestic doormat.'

'Stop exaggerating Lizzie.'

'Fuck you Tom, you ran off to college and did your utmost to avoid coming back. So, yeah, I might not have dealt with what you did at school, but it was hell at home.' She was fed up with his self-righteousness. 'Ma holed up in her bedroom and Dad working all the hours possible in the day, coming home and numbing himself with whisky.' She drew a breath before letting a decade of resentment tumble out. 'Then he dropped dead, and I was the one who found him, I was the one who called Father Larkin and the police, I was the one who dealt with the funeral arrangements.

Where were you, eh?

'Lizzie…'

'No don't Lizzie me, you got all the opportunities, education, support from Dad, Christ you even inherited his business.' She could tell from the look on his face that he knew she was right. 'I got nothing, no one took an interest in me, nobody checked to see I did my homework, to see if I was okay. I was lucky to even graduate. The only thing that kept me going was the hope that one day I could escape.'

'Stop…'

'No, you need to hear me out for once. Like you, I'm proud of the career I've built, but I did it on my own, nobody handed me a business on a plate.' The lump in her throat was choking her. Do not cry, she told herself. 'Get me another beer.'

'I think you both have had enough.' Hannah had been standing there listening to her tirade.

'I don't know what to say, I'm sorry.' Tommy sat slumped on the sofa, eyes puffy like he'd gone a few rounds with Mike Tyson. 'It's just I want it to be over, so we can get on with our lives. Paddy took away so much from us, I can't bear it all being dragged up again.'

'You might not want it, but it is going to happen. You didn't even have the decency to tell me how Paddy died, I had to find out from the newspaper.' She had the upper hand now and wasn't going to let go. 'I took Ma to court, she needed to see for herself. She wants Paddy's story to be told and I'm not going to stop her. I came home today to find that journalist sitting in the kitchen interviewing her, photos of Paddy everywhere.'

'How could you let that happen? You're supposed to be protecting her.'

'I can't control everything. Ma is an adult. And only a few moments ago you were telling me that Hannah said I was doing a great job with Ma.' Lizzie stared at Hannah. 'I'm wondering if the person you're really wanting to protect is yourself, Tom?' She gulped back the last of her beer. 'I'd like to go home now. Whatever it is you wanted to talk about can wait.'

'I'll drive you, he's in no fit state,' Hannah grabbed her keys and opened the front door. 'C'mon, Lizzie. Let's get you home.'

'Thanks for the pizza.' Lizzie grabbed her coat and followed Hannah out.

*

The drive home alone with Hannah filled her with dread. She closed her eyes and rested her head on the window.

'I guess you both got a raw deal,' Hannah said.

'Yup.'

'No wonder you were such a loner in high school. Helluva lot to deal with.' She looked across to Lizzie. 'You know I want you and Tommy to be close. I want the girls to know their aunt.'

'Doesn't feel like that.'

'You're their only auntie, I'm an only child. I don't have any family. After my mom died my dad moved south. He's only really interested in fishing.' Hannah pulled into Maura's driveway and put the car into park. 'Can we start over?'

'Sure.'

'I'm sorry that Easter dinner went wrong. I was oblivious to Ma not having read the paper because she always reads the paper. All the conversation I ever have with her is about what she reads in the paper.'

Lizzie's face softened. 'It's okay. Let's start fresh.' She gave Hannah a hug. 'Thanks for the ride.' Lizzie shut the door and walked toward the house. A fresh start, that's what she had tried to give herself by leaving. She was a different person now, a professional, well liked, and respected.

*

Maura was stretched out on her recliner still awake when Lizzie walked into the living room. She went straight to the kitchen and poured herself a proper drink. The Chinese takeout sat unopened on the kitchen table.

'You didn't eat your dinner, Ma.' An act of defiance, but it wouldn't last, she liked her food too much.

'I wasn't hungry, and that food is too salty.' She turned the volume down. 'I was looking through all the photographs and was so sad. I don't ever want people to forget him.' She sniffled. 'Help me upstairs to bed.' She guided her mother up the stairs and went to enter the room, but Maura blocked her. 'I can do the rest myself, goodnight.' Her mother shut the door.

'This is bullshit,' Lizzie said. She didn't deserve this petulant behavior. Looking at the photographs lining the staircase as she descended, she noticed there were none of her. She wandered around the hallway and living room looking at all the photos, pulling down the frames from the fireplace mantle. There were her father's Purple Heart and Bronze Star in separate frames with photos of Paddy, Tommy and Hannah, and her grandchildren. Her brother was the one who died, but she was the one who had been erased and forgotten.

Chapter 8

Paddy managed to ruin what had started out as quite a pleasant dream. She had been lying on the ground covered by snow, reaching out to touch a single snowflake falling, at peace. Then he appeared holding his face, droplets of blood soiling the pure white blanket. She grabbed her chest, sat up and panted. How could these nightmares have come back with such vengeance? He was terrifying. She was ill, her head fuzzy, it was her own fault. She knew she needed to rein herself in, but the circumstances in which she was living made that a challenge. Ma's bedroom door was open, bed vacated. She went down to the kitchen where her mother was sitting crunching on a piece of toast.

'I called for you, but you didn't come, so I came downstairs by myself.'

'Well, I guess you can do more than you think.' Lizzie was in no mood to deal with a sulky child, she was tiring of her mother's selective helplessness.

'It's nearly ten o'clock, I wanted you to take me to the novena group this morning. It starts at half past.'

'Alright. I'll go get dressed.'

'And brush your teeth, you reek of booze. I don't want people thinking you're an alcoholic.'

'There are worse things I could be.'

*

Lizzie dropped her mother off at church and made her way to the coffee shop. The queasiness had persisted, a muffin and black coffee might settle her stomach. Sugar and caffeine, a miracle cure. She grabbed the newspaper as she sat down, relieved to see the Bruins on the front page, rather than the O'Donnell family. The bakery made the best blueberry muffins, light, and bursting with fresh berries. She took a bite and looked up. Joe was standing over her smiling.

'You mind if I sit with you?' Lizzie wasn't in the frame of mind for deep conversation, but couldn't bring herself to say no. 'You alright? You look kinda pale.'

'I'm fine, just a bit of a stomach bug I think.' She wasn't lying to herself, only to Joe. 'I've been meaning to ask you, is it possible for me to get a copy of the coroner's report on Paddy?'

'The coroner's report is normally given to the next of kin, but I'm not sure about other family members. I can find out for you. Is there something specific you're looking for?'

'No, I feel like I'm in the dark about a lot of things. I'd just like to see it.'

'I'll make some enquiries and get back to you. You'll probably have to fill in a form.'

'Thanks, Joe. I'm sorry, I'm not well. I've gotta go.'

Lizzie jumped up and ran for the restroom. She needed to stop drinking.

*

She picked up a bottle of ginger ale from the package store, avoiding making direct eye contact with the bottle of Jack Daniels on the shelf, like an embarrassed lover. Blue sky, sun shining, she decided to drive out past the lake for a walk to clear her head. Only a few days earlier it had been snowing, yet today it was a balmy seventy degrees. There had been many parties on the lakeshore when she was a teenager and she had attended all of them, though the memories had become hazy. She had been reckless, she remembered that much, and suffered the consequences for this carelessness, ending up pregnant at sixteen. Her only friend, Jeannie, had driven her to the Planned Parenthood clinic in Denton for a termination. She never told anyone else, not even Joe. Joe wanting her to keep it would have been unbearable, she hadn't needed another person to look after.

A row of tiny brown clapboard cottages lined the lakeshore, almost blending into the woods behind them. Several had been converted to year-round houses, though most were still for seasonal use. A "For Sale" sign hung on the front post of the cottage at the end of the row. Lizzie wandered up to the front porch and peered through the window. The place looked unloved, abandoned but with lots of potential that resonated with her. She tapped the realtor's details into her phone curious to find out who the seller was, then realized that she had cut it fine to collect her mother.

*

Maura was standing outside the church hall when she arrived having an animated conversation with two women Lizzie didn't recognize. She carried on talking despite seeing Lizzie sitting there. Lizzie knew intimately her mother's ways of showing her displeasure, she was going to keep her waiting. Eventually, she hugged the ladies and got into the car.

'I didn't recognize those two women. Who are they?

'Just some friends from the novena group. The grey haired one was Joe Moretti's mother, Angela.' Lizzie was surprised to hear Ma describe them as friends, she didn't recall her mother ever having had friends.

'I didn't recognize her, she had black hair the last time I saw her.'

'A lot changes in ten years, Lizzie.' Maura fastened her seatbelt and checked herself in the mirror. 'Angela is desperate for Joe to settle down and have children. I told her there was no chance of that happening with you, you're not the marrying type.' Her mother knew where to stick the knife in to inflict the most pain.

'True, I'll be back at sea soon, so you won't have to suffer me for too much longer. I'll be out of your hair in eight weeks, and you can have the house to yourself again.' Lizzie looked straight ahead while driving.

'I didn't mean it that way. I like you being here.' Maura put her hand on Lizzie's shoulder.

'Whatever.' Lizzie rolled her eyes. 'Your radiation therapy starts on Monday, is there anything we need to buy over the weekend?'

'I don't know, I'll have to read the pamphlet they gave me. I wish you hadn't reminded me.'

They drove in silence the rest of the way home and spoke little for the rest of the day. Maura sat glued to the tv watching mindless shows, dozing off from time to time. Lizzie prepared some creamy chicken and rice, but her mother said she wasn't hungry. She had no idea how long this cold war would continue but hoped her mother would wake up in a better mindset in the morning. She said she didn't need any help getting to bed and left Lizzie alone downstairs. As much as she resented her mother's lack of affection, she couldn't bear the loneliness. The dreariness of her mother's life was draining her of her own life force. Pouring herself a cocktail, she put on some music and daydreamed about her colleagues cruising the Caribbean, longing for the sea air and all that she was missing.

Chapter 9

The waiting room was painted a pale green, perhaps with the intent to calm and soothe the cancer patients, but Lizzie was queasy. It had been a heavy weekend celebrating the Bruins winning the first-round playoffs with Joe on Saturday night, then most of Sunday night in front of the tv with a bag of Cheetos and her favorite drink.

'It says here Ma that you're not supposed to have sexual intercourse during radiation therapy.' Lizzie glanced at Maura hoping for a smile, but she sat stone faced. 'You know, not many seventy-year-old women get tattoos. You're going to be very trendy.'

'Can we just sit quietly, Lizzie. I'm nervous and you aren't helping.'

The therapist called them into the treatment room. 'Mrs. O'Donnell, can I call you Maura?' Not waiting for an answer, she continued. 'Today we're going to do some preparatory scans and several tattoos on your abdomen, they're just tiny dots like a freckle but they are permanent. Your treatments will start tomorrow and continue every day for four weeks, except weekends. Do you have any questions so far, Maura?'

Ma said no, but Lizzie piped up. 'Is she likely to have

any side effects?'

'It varies from patient to patient. I'll get you a leaflet that talks about radiation side effects for uterine cancer and how to manage them. Most commonly patients get diarrhea, sometimes bladder discomfort and tiredness. It's important to eat well and drink plenty of fluids during treatment. Shall we go through for your scan, Maura?'

Lizzie stood up to follow her into the next room.

'You wait here, I want to go by myself,' Maura said. The rejection burned in Lizzie's chest.

*

Lizzie had just settled Maura back at home when Tommy arrived bearing gifts. Danish pastries, and fresh brewed coffee. She had left him a message to visit their mother, Ma'd been asking for him and Lizzie hadn't seen him in the week since Hannah had invited her over. She was worried about her mom, the pamphlet said that side effects weren't usually experienced until the second week of treatment, but Maura seemed more tired than usual, and it had only been a few days. Lizzie was cooking healthy meals, determined to get it right, but her mother's anxiety level was rising, she wasn't sure if it was the treatment or the fact that her interview had yet to appear in the paper. Her mother had asked repeatedly if Tina Chandler had left a message on the landline.

Tommy leaned over and kissed Maura on the forehead and handed her an apricot Danish, his way of worming out of not having visited sooner.

'How's our patient doing?' He didn't wait for an answer, he wasn't interested. 'Listen, I've got great news. Hannah is pregnant, I'm gonna be a dad again.' He seemed delighted; Lizzie couldn't quite believe it. He already had three children, why did he need another? Or was he hoping for a son, maybe that was it – he wanted a boy.

'Oh Tommy, that's wonderful news.' Maura wrapped her arms around her son. 'When is the baby due?'

'He's due in mid-September, Hannah's already twenty weeks, we had the scan yesterday.' His face beamed.

'But that's five months already, how could you not have told me? She was prickly, 'Are you saying it's a boy?'

'Yes, it's a boy. You're going to have a grandson, Ma. Hannah has struggled these last few months and you weren't well, so we wanted to wait to tell you.'

'Great news, Tom.' He would be thrilled to have a son to carry on the family name. The patriarchy lives on; she detested these outdated concepts. 'Guess we're going to have to make a trip to the yarn store Ma, you'll want to get knitting.'

'I've got to get to work but will stop by again soon.' Lizzie followed Tommy out to his car. 'This was what I wanted to tell you the night you came over Lizzie. Part of the reason I asked you to come look after Ma was because Hannah was having terrible morning sickness and couldn't cope with looking after her.

'Part of the reason? You told me Ma said she needed me.'

'Yeah, well…'

'So, you just made that up?'

'Keep your voice down. She does need you.'

'She never asked for me, did she? You lied to me. You really are a prick.' He had played her; he knew that she still craved Ma's approval. Even after all these years she could still be hooked.

'You're here now and doing a great job.' He was trying flattery, she wasn't stupid. 'We were hoping that you might stay on longer, until the baby is born. I can help you out with money if that's a problem.'

'Seriously Tom?' Lizzie was flabbergasted by his audacity. 'There's no way I can live with her until September. Our relationship is already strained at the best of times. I'm happy for you, but I have my own life to get back to and I already signed a contract for July.'

'You're so damn selfish Lizzie. What are we supposed to do then?'

'You've got some nerve.' It wasn't her fault that his wife

was pregnant. That was a choice they had made. 'I don't know, wait and see. She seems to be doing some things for herself, maybe she won't need much help. We could always bring in a care giver for her.'

'A stranger? No way, family is supposed to look after family.'

'Well, if you feel that strongly, that's your answer. You look after her.' Lizzie headed back to the house. He had some nerve and she wasn't going to be guilted into staying longer with her mom. She already felt trapped.

*

The news of another grandchild on the way seemed to have lifted her mother's spirits and she was almost pleasant to Lizzie as they drove to the hospital for her radiation appointment the next day.

'After the appointment, will you drive me to the craft store please? I'd like to start knitting a blanket and Tommy really has not given me much notice. I don't know why they kept the news from me.'

'He told you why, Ma.'

'My cancer shouldn't have been an excuse; it would have cheered me up when I was so unwell.'

'I think you're missing the point. Hannah wasn't well and she wasn't ready.'

'Well, I still think Tommy should've told me. I would

have kept it a secret.'

'I'm going out this evening, so let me know what you'd like for dinner, and I'll get it prepared early.'

'Don't bother. Just make me a sandwich and I'll have a can of tomato soup. Where are you going?'

'Out with Joe and a couple of his friends. We're just going to watch the game and get a bite to eat.'

'You seem to be spending a lot of time with him. I hope you aren't leading him on.' Lizzie's fists clenched the steering wheel. Did her mother really think that little of her?

*

The team at the Denton Memorial Hospital cancer center ran the place like a conveyor belt, ushering patients in one door and out another. Lizzie had marveled at their ability to show compassion while at the same time maintaining the highest level of efficiency. In some ways it was no different to her role managing customer experience on board. Each morning she'd put on her bright, happy face to deal with the myriad of customer queries and complaints, from sea sickness to lack of sunbeds on deck. She was good at sorting out problems, making customers feel valued, and they showed their appreciation. Appreciation, however, was not a concept Ma was familiar with.

'Maura, we're ready for you now. Come on through,' the radiation therapist said.

She got up and made her way toward the treatment room, then turned around. 'Well, are you coming Lizzie?' Ma's fluctuation between emotional aloofness and sudden neediness left Lizzie not knowing whether she was coming or going. It had always been like this, she remembered. Was she stupid? Why would this time be any different? She would have to ride the wave, letting her mother take the lead. It was better than the silent treatment.

'How have you been this week, Maura?' the radiation therapist asked.

'I've noticed she's been very tired.' Lizzie said.

'No other changes?'

'No, I'm fine. Let's get on with it.' Maura was on the cusp of rudeness again.

'Fatigue is common, so you'll want to get plenty of rest and not push yourself too hard, Maura. It may get worse in the coming weeks. But we'll do some blood tests to check your levels.' Get worse, not push herself, Lizzie could see that all the progress she had made with Ma being reversed. 'You'll need to wait outside, Miss O'Donnell.' The technician pointed to the row of chairs in the hallway.

Lizzie took a seat, closed her eyes, and drifted off, waking when she heard the technician's voice. 'That's it. You're done for today, Maura. We'll see you on Monday, have a good weekend.'

As they walked back through the parking lot Ma stopped in her tracks. 'You know I can speak for myself, Lizzie.'

'I was only giving my observation.'

'Well, next time don't. I'll be the one to decide what I tell the therapist.' She started walking toward the car. 'And all this Maura business, she must have said my name a dozen times. I'm Mrs. O'Donnell, not Maura.'

'I'll leave you to tell the therapist how you'd like to be addressed then.'

*

Ride each wave as it comes. Lizzie imagined herself on a surfboard in Maui as she parked up at the craft store. A much more pleasant visual.

'Do you need me to come in with you?' she said.

'Suit yourself.' Ma opened the car door.

'Alright, I'll stay in the car.' Lizzie waited until her mother was in the store before making her way over to Dunkin Donuts. The jelly doughnut covered in powdered sugar in the window had her name written on it. Taylor Swift belted out her latest hit on the radio as she devoured the doughnut back in the car. The lyrics resonated with her, she had had her share of ex-lovers just like the girl in the song, but always ended it before it got too far. She wasn't leading Joe on, no matter what Ma said. They were friends, maybe more than friends and like Taylor, she had a blank space to fill on the friend front.

Maura shouted for Lizzie to open the trunk of the car so she could put her shopping bags in. 'Jesus, how much did you buy? You said you were just getting a little yarn to make a blanket.'

'There were some nice baby patterns and I want to knit the baby some sweaters and things for winter. They won't have any boy clothes and we can't have him wearing the girls' hand me downs.' Maura was a talented knitter when she put her mind to it. Lizzie still had a scarf from childhood, fluorescent pink with a matching hat, though she'd no idea where the hat had gone.

By the time they returned home, Maura was exhausted and settled down into her recliner for a nap. Lizzie took herself upstairs to what had been her childhood bedroom and lay down on the single bed, closed her eyes and tried to remember how the room used to be. A white four poster bed with brightly colored quilt and matching rug, the walls painted a pale pink and decorated with stenciled flowers. It had been such a shock when she first arrived, expecting to see it unchanged. She opened her eyes and looked around the empty room. More like a nun's convent cell than the colorful room of her childhood, the walls bare and shelves empty. She got up and rummaged around in the closet. Her mother seemed to have thrown out most of her belongings, her whole childhood reduced to one small cardboard box stuffed in the closet containing few memories. She pulled out the pink scarf, wrapped it around her neck and buried her nose into it inhaling deeply. Warm tears streamed down her face as she lay back down on the bed and sobbed quietly.

*

The day had dragged on, one monotonous routine. The only thing that kept her going was looking forward to this evening's outing with Joe. She couldn't wait to get out of the house and was already sitting on the front steps as he pulled up.

'Bad day?' Joe asked.

'Could've been worse.' Lizzie laughed. 'Do you mind if we skip the game tonight? I've been thinking about pizza all day, is Romero's still open in Denton?

'Still the best pizza in the area. I don't mind missing the game. We're leading three games to two, but Montreal's a stronger team, they're gonna take the series.'

'I can't believe you said that, Joe. Where's your loyalty? That's heresy from a diehard Bruins fan.'

'Well, it's true. The Canadiens are a stronger team.'

'Don't let your pals hear you talking like that, they'll crucify you.'

Smoke was billowing from the chimney at Romero's as they pulled into the parking lot. Serving authentic Italian wood-fired pizza, Romero's had been in the same family since 1948. Johnny Romero, grandson of founder Livio, now ran the place but the menu had not changed, nor had the interior. There was something comforting about the red vinyl upholstered booths, Formica tables and the daily specials scrawled on paper plates taped to the walls. Romero's was old school. Lizzie's mouth watered as she read through the menu.

'I don't know why you still look at the menu after all these years. You always order the same thing in the end,' Joe's laughing eyes sparkled.

'I used to, but I haven't been here for a decade, maybe my palate is more sophisticated now.' Part of her was defiant and wanted to order something out of the ordinary, but she had been nostalgic all day and the calzone reminded her of some of the happier times she had spent there with Joe in high school. After tutoring her for hours, he would drive her here as a treat. 'I'll have the ricotta and spinach calzone, please.' She had often wondered if she'd been born into the wrong family. Surely, she was meant to be an Italian? Their cuisine was infinitely better than Irish food.

'With the marinara sauce on the side.' Joe added.

'You so love being right, Joe. I bet you'll order a pie topped with Italian sausage, peppers, and onions?'

'Correct, but I don't even pretend to look at the menu.'

The waitress delivered two bottles of Peroni and frosty glasses to the table, along with fresh parmesan and dried chili flakes. 'You've almost got everything you need now.' Joe gazed at her. She found the intimacy of his eye contact uncomfortable and looked away, changing the subject.

'You said something about the coroner's report on the phone. Did you get it for me?'

Joe took out a document from his breast pocket. 'You'll need to get your mom to complete this form and sign it. The next of kin must make the request and authorize you to access the report. Once that's done, I can sit down and go over it with you at the station.'

'What? You mean I need permission from my mother? That's ridiculous. God, you cops really make life difficult.' She took the paper and put it in her handbag. 'I'll talk to Ma about it when I get home and then drop it by the station.' The news left her deflated. She loathed bureaucracy. Another hurdle to jump to get her mother's agreement.

Steam was rising from inside the calzone as the waitress placed it in front of Lizzie. She put her nose close to it and breathed in. 'Smells fantastic, just like I remember.' She shook the parmesan, like snowflakes over the calzone until it was covered in a dusting of cheese and sliced into it, dipping each piece into the marinara sauce. 'How's your pie?'

'Excellent.' The cheese slipped off and a string was hanging from Joe's chin. 'How's your mom doing with her treatment?'

'It's going okay, she seems tired and low, but I'm not convinced it's the therapy that's causing it. I don't think I told you, she contacted the reporter from the Denton Times and decided to give her an exclusive interview.'

'Holy shit, I'm not sure how wise that was, Lizzie.'

'Yup, I know. But she's obsessed with keeping Paddy's memory alive and not thinking about other possible consequences.'

'Do you know what she told the reporter?'

'Nope, she won't say and at this point I'm not going to force the issue. She's done what she's done and will have to live with the fallout.'

'The thing is, this is no longer a local story Lizzie, the AP has picked it up and there is national interest. It's rare that a cold case is solved twenty-one years on, and people are captivated. I think your mom needs to be careful.'

'You try telling her that. She might listen to you. Anyway, I think she is nervous because Tina Chandler hasn't been in touch yet to tell her when the interview will be published. It's been nearly two weeks. I'm wondering if she's had second thoughts. Something seems to be bothering her anyway.'

'I'll talk to my boss, Officer Kominsky about it. The States Attorney won't want your mom saying anything that might jeopardize the case. Did she get paid for the interview?'

'Oh, god, I hope not. That didn't even cross my mind. I better get back and see how she is. I can't wait to get my own life back.'

Joe was frowning.

'I can only deal with one depressed person at a time, Joe. Cheer up.'

*

By the time Lizzie got home, Ma was asleep in her recliner, a half-eaten sandwich and empty bowl of soup on her side table. The television was at full volume, she didn't understand how her mom could sleep through it. The neighbors could hear it half-way down the street. She opened the front of her father's old walnut secretary desk in the corner and took the document Joe had given her from her pocket. There was no point in talking to her mother about it, she wouldn't want to see the coroner's report if it didn't fit with her take on events and would object to Lizzie getting a copy. She took a seat and practiced Ma's signature multiple times on a blank sheet until it was just about perfect, then filled out the form and signed it. Looking over her shoulder at her mother sleeping in her chair she regretted having got rid of the hospital bed. It was too late to attempt to get her into bed and Lizzie didn't want an argument. Taking the path of least resistance, she got the comforter and pillow from her mother's bed and tucked her in, listening to the hum of the La-Z boy as she pressed the button to full recline mode.

*

'Why didn't you wake me last night? Maura said. She was fully dressed and hovering over Lizzie who had been fast asleep.

'It was late Ma, you looked comfortable enough where you were. I didn't want to disturb you.' She couldn't be bothered if Ma wanted to hear the whole truth. This role reversal was exhausting. For years she had tried everything to please and bring her mother back but to no avail. Why was she wasting her time again?

'Well, I wasn't comfortable at all, didn't sleep a wink and now I have to go off for my treatment exhausted.'

Lizzie didn't believe her. If she hadn't slept, it was because all she did all day was sleep, sleep, sleep. Even being in her presence was soporific, her own eyes often drifted shut, head dropping. She was turning into her mother. The less she did, the less she wanted to do.

'You shouldn't have got rid of my hospital bed, I wasn't

ready. Get up, I don't want to be late for my appointment.'

'What do you want for breakfast?'

'I've already eaten, just get yourself ready.'

The irony of this situation was not lost on Lizzie. Her mother loomed over her, fully clothed and competent, having prepared her own breakfast, while complaining about a god-damn hospital bed. Lizzie was ready to blow a gasket.

Chapter 10

The entrance to Newham police station was on the side of the white clapboard town hall building built in 1789. Pretty much every municipal office was located there – a one stop shop for the community. Lizzie's hands shook as she walked in, her oily Catholic guilt rising to the surface. Like most people she was guilty of doing something wrong, somewhere, at some point in her life. A young lad in a blue starched uniform grinned at her, he seemed to know her.

'Hi, I'm here to speak to Officer Moretti. My name's…,' she said through the glass window.

'Lizzie O'Donnell, I've seen you in the paper. And well, Joe has mentioned you too.' he said. It was disconcerting to be recognized by strangers. She imagined it would only get worse when Ma's interview was published. 'Go on through, Joe's in the office, second door on the right.'

Joe was sitting behind a desk looking very official. 'Filing reports,' he said.

'Must be interesting, you get to know all the town gossip,' she said.

'Nope, dead boring, but yes, I do know all the hot gossip, somebody's been tipping cows again on the Darcy farm. A Few school kids caught shoplifting from the candy store.

And an elderly driver ran a stop sign and crashed into a big yellow school bus. Small town dramas.'

She wanted to tell him that his talents were wasted here but smiled instead.

'You've had a more interesting day than I'm having. Here's the consent form for the coroner's report.'

'Oh, good, your mom was fine with it then?'

'Yes, all fine. She doesn't want to see it though, so it will be me on my own.' Lying and forgery, that's why she was nervous. A minor peccadillo, she kept telling herself. 'When do you think I'll be able to see the report?'

'We have to run it by the States Attorney first, Ms. O'Donnell,'

Lizzie turned to see where the voice had come from.

'I'm Pete Kominsky, the Resident State Trooper. Joe ran your request by me,' he said, standing in the doorway. An imposing figure in a beige uniform, gun holster on his hip, he looked like he might even be old enough to have been on the original case. 'We'll call you when we have it, but it might take a few weeks.'

'I hope you don't mind me asking, but were you on the case back in 1993?'

'Not directly, but I was aware of it. Joe mentioned to me that your mother has been interviewed by the Denton Times. I wish she had cleared it with us first.'

'I'm sorry. I would have stopped her if she'd told me.'

'I've asked Joe to have a chat with her about it and I'll be contacting the reporter. Your mother sounds vulnerable, easy prey for journalists. I want to keep her safe.'

'That would be helpful,' Lizzie said.

'Also, the pre-trial hearing has been scheduled. It's going to be held in the judge's chambers, so it won't be open to the public,' Kominsky said. What a relief, the last thing she wanted was to be sitting in a court room with Ma in her current fragile condition, the side effects of the radiation making her need the toilet frequently. 'We'll let you know the outcome.'

'Is your mother up for a visit today?' Joe asked.

'I'll call you.'

The Denton Times

Keeping the community informed with independent local reporting

GRIEVING MOTHER PAYS TRIBUTE TO MURDERED SON
By Tina Chandler
May 14, 2014

Twenty-one years after the murder of her son, Paddy, Maura O'Donnell speaks for the first time, paying tribute to him, opening up about the gap left in her family's life and her shock at the arrest of a suspect so many years later. 'It's been twenty-one years but sometimes I still can't believe Paddy's gone. I'll walk into the kitchen and expect to find him standing in front of the fridge, door wide open, saying "What's there to eat, Ma?" He had an amazing ability to make me laugh and teased me mercilessly but was never mean spirited. Paddy was, well, he was just perfect. I couldn't have asked for a more loving son.'
Sitting with Maura at her kitchen table her grey eyes reveal a deep sorrow. A native of Boston, she and her husband Jim relocated to Newham when she was pregnant with Paddy in 1977. Her younger son, Thomas, took over the family's construction business when Jim died suddenly of a heart attack

and he and his family live locally. 'It's been over ten years since Jim died. Paddy's murder left him heartbroken, he blamed himself for not realizing that Paddy hadn't come home. It was tough on him, the police pulled him in for questioning like he was a suspect. I don't know how anyone could have thought Jim would have harmed his son, he was a gentle person. In the end, his heart just couldn't take it.'

Surrounded by photos of Paddy, there is a sense of how adored he was by his family. 'Paddy was only sixteen when he was taken from us, his life was just beginning. He was a talented athlete, a champion wrestler and hoped to gain a scholarship to college. He was so strong, it was devastating to see him lying in a casket, so still.' We take a pause and Maura shows me Paddy's room which she has kept as a shrine - a tribute to him and a place where she can continue to mourn privately. 'This is my way of keeping Paddy near me.' The walls are dotted with photos of a curly red head in Newham high school's wrestling uniform holding various trophies, alongside photos of him dressed in a cassock. 'He was a committed Catholic and had a strong faith which was unusual for a boy of his age. He served as head altar boy at Our Lady of Lourdes, Father Larkin relied on him heavily and was a true mentor to Paddy.'

A handsome young man, I was surprised not to see photos of him with a girlfriend and asked Maura. 'Spending so much time at the church and with his studies and wrestling, he didn't seem interested in finding a girlfriend. Maybe he was still a little immature and not ready for a relationship.' I mention to Maura that people may wonder what Paddy was doing out in the middle of a blizzard. *'He was a teenager, and quite independent. He had gone to meet some friends at the arcade in Denton. It was snowing when he left but the storm had not really hit yet. Things are different now with cell phones, back then we just assumed he was where he said he was and that he'd come home. We thought he was safe; we thought our community was safe.*

'I thought his funeral would be the most difficult thing I had ever done. But living life without him has been far more difficult.' I ask how she has coped all these years, and she says her faith has kept her going. *'Paddy was my greatest blessing.'*

Clearly a strong and courageous woman, Maura, while still recovering from surgery for cancer, attended the arraignment hearing of the suspect in her son's murder. *'It was a shock when the police turned up at the door to tell me they had arrested someone for Paddy's murder and the hearing was an emotional day for me, but I needed to bear witness for Paddy and see the man who took his life. But I have to admit, he looked very ordinary, small, and weak. I was surprised he could overcome Paddy; Paddy was so strong.'* When asked about the future, Maura said her focus will be on making sure no one ever forgets Paddy. *'People talk about getting closure and peace. I don't know that I'll ever find those, I won't ever be at peace. I'm broken forever. No mother should ever have to bury their son. But I do want justice for Paddy, that's all I can hope for now.*

Two weeks had passed by the time the interview was finally published. Maura had been unwell during the last phase of her treatment and had put off meeting with the police until today. As Lizzie read the interview, she wasn't sure what to think, except that she didn't matter. Not even a mention of her in the article, it was like she didn't exist. Even the priest got a mention. But Maura would be delighted with the article even if the police and States Attorney might not be. What had she been thinking, to comment on Jason Edwards looking weak, and not understanding how he could have overcome Paddy? Lizzie hadn't known that her father had been a person of interest and interviewed about Paddy's death. Her mother had a knack for misrepresenting situations, making it sound like dad had been the one trapped in grief, not functioning. It was a complete projection. The poor man suffered and went to an early grave, but it was her mother's fault, not Paddy's.

She carried the tray with tea and toast, newspaper on top, up the stairs to Ma's bedroom. Her mother had taken to her bed the previous day and it was going to take a herculean effort on Lizzie's part to get her up. Appealing to her vanity might be the only way to rouse her. Maura looked attractive, handsome, in the photo that accompanied the interview. Such a waste of her life to have been locked in grief for two decades. Lizzie wished she could tell her mother that she needed to move forward without Paddy but that wasn't a conversation that Maura would entertain.

'You're on the front page, Ma.'

Maura sat bolt upright and reached for the paper. 'But Tina didn't call me? She said she would, she said she'd call to let me know when it was finished. I wanted to read it first.'

'Well, that's what hacks are like, it's all about the story. Once you open your door and open your mouth, you can't take it back.'

'It's a good photo of me though, isn't it, Lizzie?'

'Yeah, Ma.' She was not right in the head, that's the only excuse Lizzie could make for her. This fixation on how she looked to the outside world seemed more important to her than what she said in the interview. She wanted to be a celebrity for all the wrong reasons. Lizzie was skeptical. Was it all about keeping Paddy's memory alive? 'The police are not happy about you having given an interview without consulting them first.'

'But I didn't say anything bad.' She folded her arms across her chest and frowned.

'That's not the point, you're being naïve. Joe will be

around today to talk to you about it. Tomorrow is the pre-trial hearing.'

'I want to be there.'

'You can't, it's a closed hearing. Joe will let us know the outcome. Read your article and bask in your fame, it's what you wanted.'

'Lizzie, I…'

'Don't, Ma. I'm going to get dressed, we need to get to your appointment.' She was not in a frame of mind to listen to her mother make excuses, or play poor, poor, pitiful me, you don't understand what it's like to lose a child. She wasn't in the frame of mind to deal with her, full stop.

*

Lizzie, accustomed to the hospital routine, came prepared with her own reading material. With her nose in a book, people tended not to try to speak to her. She didn't want to know the ins and outs of strangers' cancers, treatment plans or side effects. And she did not want to hear about their prognoses. Her book was her armor, even her mother let her be when she was reading. This morning the only friends she wanted to welcome were the silent, pale green walls of the waiting room. Soothing, comforting, they held her together in a way her mother never had. She told Maura to go in for her treatment alone, it saved her from her mother's game – I need you, I don't want you, I love you, I resent you. Maybe she didn't love Tommy either, but at least she showed him respect. Either way, Lizzie needed to keep herself in a good place, limit the damage her mother could do to her. It was a matter of going through the motions, thinking of her as a seventy-year-old stranger whom she had been called to look after. Detachment, emotional detachment, that was what was required for her to survive the rest of this stay.

Maura slept most afternoons after her treatment but would rally in the evenings in time to watch some re-run or other on television and eat a meal. Their conversation had become limited to what happened in the latest episode and whether her mother had enjoyed the meal. Lizzie had taken to asking her to rate the recipes and was keeping score. If she got above a six out of ten, she knew it was worth cooking again. This was her only way of getting a performance review and job satisfaction. After twelve weeks of cooking, she might end up with enough recipes for a cookbook, some tangible output from this period of incarceration.

*

'Ma?' Tommy's voice boomed in the hall.

'Keep it down. She's resting still, Tom. We can talk in the kitchen.'

'How long is this gonna take? He tapped his finger on the table and looked up at the clock.

'No idea.' She looked down at her phone and finished her text message to Joe.

'Is there anything we need to ask Moretti? I mean, has Ma done any harm to the case with this interview?'

Lizzie shrugged her shoulders, 'There were a few lines that were strange. What was all that business about Paddy not having a girlfriend? It was like the reporter was fishing for something.'

'How am I supposed to know?' Tommy always got defensive when she asked him anything about Paddy.

'I think she was trying to figure out if Paddy was gay and Ma wasn't taking the bait.'

'Maybe.' Tommy was pacing back and forth in the kitchen.

'Well? Was he?' She leaned against the counter and watched him closely.

'Was he what? Tommy popped a piece of Nicorette in his mouth and chewed frantically.

'Gay.' Lizzie shook her head. 'You aren't listening.'

'No. He wasn't gay.' Tommy stopped pacing for a moment and stared out the kitchen window. 'He had multiple girlfriends. He just never told Ma about them.'

'Did you know they took Dad in for questioning after Paddy's body was found?'

'I think that was all routine stuff. They didn't arrest him

or anything. Ma was exaggerating.' The doorbell went. 'That must be Joe, you better get Ma up.'

'I'll get her in a minute.' She wasn't going to be bossed around by her twitchy brother who seemed to suddenly want to take charge after having shown little interest for weeks.

Tommy shook Joe and Officer Kominsky's hands and showed them into the living

room. 'Wasn't expecting to see you, Pete,' he said.

'Thought it might help if I spoke to your mother too. Might reinforce the importance of not speaking to the press. I had quite a heated phone call from the Assistant States Attorney, he wasn't happy,' said Kominsky.

'I'll get our mother,' Lizzie said. The men looked at her and continued talking.

*

Lizzie held Maura's arm to steady her as she sat down in her recliner. A deep furrow appeared across her brow. But the scars of her emotional wounds ran much deeper. Lizzie wasn't sure if it was having the whole of Newham's police department in her living room or if her mother was afraid of being held accountable.

'Mrs. O'Donnell, I wanted to talk with you about the interview you gave the Denton Times and let you know the outcome of the pre-trial hearing,' Kominsky said. 'I thought…'

Maura talked over him. 'Well, I called Tina Chandler and told her I wanted Paddy to have a voice, that I wanted people to know about him. I'm his mother.' Her voice clipped and strained as she attempted to get the upper hand.

'Yes, I understand that, but I want to be clear about the protocol around speaking to the press. In the future, call Joe if you wish to speak to the press and run through what you would like to say.'

She shook her head and turned away. 'I don't need Joe to help me with what I want to say. He was only a child when Paddy was killed, he wouldn't remember.'

'I appreciate that Mrs. O'Donnell…'

'I think what Pete is trying to say Ma, is that you need to clear what you are going to say with the police before giving any more interviews,' said Tommy.

'The problem Ma is that once you start talking the reporter can twist what you say. They're looking for an angle, a story to sell newspapers,' said Lizzie.

'Your daughter's right. Victims or surviving family members are easy prey for journalists. They can sound very sympathetic and make you all sorts of promises that they don't follow through on,' Officer Kominsky said. Maura's cheeks flushed. 'Did Tina Chandler pay you for the story?'

'What kind of person do you think I am?' Maura was

agitated, her voice rising in pitch. 'I didn't take a cent from that woman, she promised she would put some money in a memorial fund for Paddy. I just want to keep his memory alive.' Lizzie counted three, two, one and waited for her mom to turn on the waterworks. 'I didn't say anything wrong, you read the article.'

'You commented on the case Mrs. O'Donnell and that is what we need to avoid happening. I understand your motivation and that you didn't mean to jeopardize the case, but that is what can happen when you speak to the press. The last thing we want is for Edwards' case to be thrown out because he can't get a fair trial.'

'But I didn't say anything bad about him.'

'No, you didn't this time, but you said something that could potentially undermine the prosecution's case. You raised doubt over how Edwards could have physically overcome Paddy, that Paddy was much stronger. This is a line of inquiry the defense attorney might decide to follow.'

'I didn't know, I'm…' Maura put her head in her hands, her shoulders began to shake. The pressure was rising. Lizzie hoped Kominsky could defuse the situation before her mother exploded.

'I just want everything to be clear to you, Mrs. O'Donnell. I know you want justice for Paddy and the best thing you can do is to not speak to the press anymore. The national press has taken an interest in the story too and we don't want to feed them any information that might jeopardize the trial. We have no idea who might come out of the woodwork, there are all kinds of cranks out there.'

'Yes, I understand' Maura pulled a hankie from her sleeve and wiped her nose. Lizzie wasn't sure how much her mother really understood, no doubt she would be taking her indiscretion to Father Larkin for absolution. 'But what about the hearing?'

'The trial date has been set for November 15th. Edwards will be held on remand pending outcome of the trial.'

*

Lizzie opened her laptop and downloaded the digital version of the Denton Times. After Kominsky's visit she wanted to re-read the article but didn't want to ask her mother for the hard copy. Scrolling down the page until she reached the end, she clicked on the icon and up popped the comments, forty-seven so far and it had only been day one. The first few were sympathetic, clearly written by committed Christians sending her mother healing prayers and encouraging her to live a life of Christian joy. These were followed by opportunists touting their services, grief counsellors offering confidential sessions at a discounted rate, a psychic healer and medium purporting to be able to reach Paddy in the netherworld, and a few gentlemen seeking female companionship, commenting on Ma's beauty. Next came the abusive messages, what a lousy mother she must have been, how crazy she must be to have made his room into a shrine. It wasn't pleasant reading. Although she had to admit, they had a point. The worst was to come, a series of comments about Paddy saying he was a crack head, a pervert. This type of troll was deranged, but the wilder their allegations, the more comments they attracted. Among all these comments, one stood out, someone called Tedx claiming to have known Paddy saying things aren't always what they seem. She closed the laptop, it was overwhelming even for her.

SUMMER 2014

Chapter 11

By the time June arrived Lizzie was at breaking point, firefighting on multiple fronts. There had been renewed interest in Paddy's case by the press following the publication of her mother's interview. The phone rang incessantly with requests for comments or interviews to the point where she unplugged the landline. The comments box on Tina Chandler's interview with her mother had been inundated with so many vile messages that the newspaper had closed it. The comments, though disturbing, led the police to follow up on potential new witnesses, according to Joe. He had kept quiet of late, closed lipped even when she probed. Was something up with the case? Or was he having second thoughts about their relationship?

But the icing on the cake was her mother. Although Maura had completed her radiation therapy and got the all clear, she continued to be in a state of perpetual suffering and had taken to her bed yet again. Lizzie had wondered what was up until she found a printout of the digital version of the interview, including pages and pages of comments, on the kitchen table.

'Where did this come from?' Lizzie had asked as she flipped through the pages. Her mother didn't have a printer and barely knew how to use the computer.

'I asked Hannah to print me off a copy of the interview. She dropped it off.' Her mother crushed some oyster crackers into her bowl of clam chowder, swished them around, then slurped a spoonful. 'Why?'

'I don't think it's a good idea for you to read all of this. It might upset you, there are some nasty people online.'

'I'll be the judge of what is a good idea for me to read. I know you're just looking out for me, but I'll be fine.' She finished the last of her soup, wiped her mouth and took the printout from the table. 'I'll read it upstairs.' She patted Lizzie on the shoulder and left the room.

And that was the last time she had been downstairs. Lizzie could hear her sobs but her knocks on the door went unanswered. Déjà vu. After a couple of days Lizzie had grown impatient and drove over to see Hannah.

'Lizzie, what brings you by?' Hannah's face was pale with a washed-out greenish tinge.

'What did you think you were doing giving Ma a printout of her interview with all those comments? Lizzie's voice shook. She gave Hannah a cold, hard glare.

'She asked me for it. I was trying to help.' Hannah stepped back from the doorway.

'Help? Did you read the comments?'

'Well, no. I just printed it and dropped it off.' She

scraped her hand through her hair and tucked it behind her ear. 'Maura was insistent. I was in a hurry with the girls. I didn't…' She was talking rapidly, stumbling over an apology.

'You really are stupid.' Lizzie shook her head and walked back to her car. There was no point in continuing the conversation. Did she think somehow her mother-in-law would enjoy reading about her life as a celebrity no matter how vile? There was no point in trying to talk to Tommy about it. He had a blind spot when it came to his wife. As a result of Hannah's idiocy Lizzie was now in full damage limitation mode, trying to figure out how to get her mother back on her feet. It didn't help that everywhere they went people would whisper. Everyone knew the sordid details. It was only a matter of time before some unscrupulous local would take payment for providing 'the dirt', however old or invented, on their family.

*

A few days later, when her mother was still holed up in her bedroom Lizzie became increasingly concerned. She pulled up in front of the rectory at Our Lady of Lourdes, got out of the car and rang the doorbell. Last resort – Father Larkin.

'Lizzie!' The priest's eyes widened. 'Is everything okay?' He looked at her eyes welling up and she burst into tears. 'Come in, come in.'

'I'm so sorry, I didn't know what to do…' she sniffled. 'It's been days, she's not coming out of her room.' She wiped her eyes with her sleeve. 'It's just like I'm a kid again. I can't do this…' She was blubbering, stumbling over her words.

Father Larkin handed her a glass of water and sat down next to her on the sofa, stroking her head, his voice soothing and calming. 'It's alright, just let it all out.' She felt safe in his embrace, like she used to feel with her dad. The shaking in her body slowed and she took some short deep breaths until the sobs subsided. She remembered sitting on this same sofa being consoled by Father Larkin the day her father had died. The shock of finding him on the floor of the garage, eyes bulging, and face contorted, had tipped her over the edge. She ran and hitched a ride into town, too afraid to go back. The priest had rescued her and taken charge that day. She needed him to rescue her again.

'Can you come over and talk to my mother? She's been like this since she read the comments on her interview. I'm afraid.' She sat up and composed herself. 'I'm afraid she might hurt herself; she's not eating. Maybe you can help her understand, put things in perspective?' She took a sip of water and let out a deep sigh. She felt sick. 'Tommy's no help and I don't want her to end up on the psych ward.' She put her hand over her mouth, ran to the kitchen and spewed into the sink, then turned on the faucet and rinsed it down.

Father Larkin's hand was on her back.

'This really has got you churned up.' He smiled and handed her a towel. 'I'll follow you home and talk with Maura.'

'Don't tell her I sent you.' Lizzie hugged him tight, inhaling the familiar scent of his Barbasol shaving foam. She closed her eyes and pictured the red, white, and blue striped can sitting on the vanity in the family bathroom, her head poking through the open door spying on her dad while he lathered the white foam on to his face. Spotting her, he'd turn and wipe the foam on her nose and laugh. She missed him. Father Larkin was kind, but he wasn't a replacement. She let go. Father Larkin held her hands and looked directly at her.

'It'll be okay, Lizzie.' The authority in his voice had always reassured her. He was supposed to have a direct line to God after all. But in her experience things had rarely turned out okay.

*

Father Larkin never disclosed what he had said to Maura and Lizzie didn't dare ask, but it had worked. He had winked at her when he came down after two hours and asked for a tray of sandwiches and tea to take back upstairs. An hour later she heard the front door open, and he slipped out without a goodbye. That evening Lizzie heard the familiar sound of the steps creaking and her mother appeared at the table, still in a robe and slippers, but she had emerged from the darkness.

'Can I have some toast please, Lizzie? With butter and honey.' She put her hand on Lizzie's and looked up at her, holding her gaze. 'Thank you.'

Lizzie's face flushed as she popped two slices of bread into the toaster. Father Larkin was nothing short of a miracle worker. Maura went into the living room and sat down in her recliner with Lizzie following closely behind carrying the tray. She sat down next to her mother. 'What do you want to watch this evening, Ma?

'Hand me the clicker and I'll look through tonight's programming.' She took a bite from her toast and pointed the remote at the television with her other hand.

Lizzie smiled, her mother was the only person she knew who used the word clicker and pronounced it, 'clicka'. Her Boston accent was still strong. They sat watching back-to-back episodes of LA Law in silence until Lizzie noticed her mother's eyes closing and she chivvied her up to bed. Lizzie sat back down in the recliner and stretched out. Things were looking up.

*

The following day, the morning of her thirtieth birthday, Lizzie woke and made a bee line to the bathroom, spewing the contents of her stomach into the porcelain bowl. She popped a couple of Alka Seltzer into a glass of water hoping this might settle her stomach and made her way downstairs.

With her mother still asleep, the house was quiet allowing her some mental space. She had just sat down on the toilet when her cell phone rang. She always felt weird answering the phone while on the toilet but could see it was Joe. Holding the phone under her chin, she ripped open the plastic packet and pulled out the white stick. It had been in her bag for almost two weeks, but she couldn't ignore it any longer.

'Hey Joe. What's up?'

'Sorry to bother you so early but I need you to come down to the station.'

'What? Right now?'

'Yes, it's Tommy. He's been arrested. I'll fill you in when you get here.'

She put down the phone and felt the warm stream on her fingers and held the stick under it. Wiping the stick dry she stared at it, waiting, watching, until a second blue line appeared. 'Shit.' She sat back, stunned. By her calculations she was about ten weeks pregnant, the first trimester almost gone, and she hadn't even realized. How could she have been so careless, she was thirty, not sixteen again? She put the pregnancy test back in the packet. She'd have to find somewhere to dispose of it where her mother wouldn't find it.

She threw on her clothes and made her way to the station, the day was going from bad to worse. It was not how she had anticipated spending her birthday. What the hell had Tommy done? She was grateful the station was empty this early in the morning, the last thing they needed was to be the subject of further town gossip. Joe was standing behind the glass talking to Officer Kominsky, he waved for her to come to the door and buzzed her in.

'Tommy got into a fight late last night at the Town Tavern and has spent the night in the cell. I tried calling Hannah, but her phone was switched off. I didn't want to drive over knowing she was alone with the three little ones.'

'Do you know what happened?'

'We've taken statements from the few guys who were left in the bar. It sounds like the victim…'

'Hold on, victim?' She felt a new wave of nausea come over her and sat down. 'Can I have some water? What had Tommy done? Her heart was racing along with her thoughts. 'Please don't tell me he killed someone?'

Joe handed her a glass of water. 'He didn't kill anyone, but he attacked a man and landed him in the hospital. According to the witnesses, the guy was goading Tommy, but he really lost it and beat him badly, broke his nose and cheekbone.'

'Has Tommy revealed what this guy said to him?'

'Not really, he's been quiet. The witnesses said the victim was taunting him about Paddy, making sordid comments about your family. Tommy apparently tried to ignore it at first, but then snapped. Made some offensive comment about his ethnicity. The guy's a Nipmuc.'

'Had he been drinking?'

'They'd all been drinking, including the victim. The other guy actually threw the first punch, but probably regrets that now.'

'Oh, so Tommy was just defending himself?'

'Possibly, but I'm concerned that after he hit back once, he didn't stop, even when the guy was on the ground. His friends had to pull him off. We're going to release him, but I can't guarantee he won't have to appear in court.'

'Great, just what we need, another court case.'

*

The drive back to Tommy's house seemed to go on forever. Tommy looked terrible, his eye was a dark shade of purple and swollen shut. Lizzie glanced across at him and for an instant saw Paddy's face, that same purple swelling. Blinking and shaking her head, she tried to delete it from her mind, but couldn't.

'What were you thinking, Tom?' Each time she looked

over at him she saw Paddy. Her body was shaking. She couldn't look at him again. 'Seriously, don't you think we have enough shit to deal with?'

'Enough, Lizzie,' he snapped. 'He got under my skin. You know what that feels like, don't you? He stared ahead.

'You need to get your act together, get some help, some counselling or something. You can't go beating people up just because they're making fun of your family.' She feared what he would be like when the trial took place, and they were under more scrutiny.

'I know. I don't need a lecture. I'll deal with the consequences. Just drive me home, alright?'

'What's Hannah going to say when she sees the state you're in?' Lizzie turned into Tommy's driveway.

'I'll deal with that. Go home. Oh, and happy birthday.' Tommy shut the door and walked towards the house. She considered going after him but decided against it, he could deal with his mess. She had her own to take care of.

Chapter 12

The Planned Parenthood clinic had not changed in the fourteen years since Lizzie had last visited, the waiting room painted the same pale green as the cancer center. She surveyed the faces in the waiting room. A teenage girl sobbed. Her boyfriend with his arm around her shoulder tried to console her. An older woman, heavily pregnant, stared blankly at the wall while her three children chased each other around the room. And Lizzie. All of them carrying a similar level of angst, in need of calm surroundings after having been accosted by "pro-lifers" brandishing posters of aborted fetuses outside the clinic. There was nothing pro-life about any of these fanatics. The receptionist took Lizzie's details and gave her a questionnaire to complete. She ticked No to most of the boxes, then ticked Yes, to having had a previous termination. It was so long ago, she'd put it out of her mind, but a flood of memories rushed her and suddenly she was sixteen again. The dry mouth, clutching her bag tightly to her chest, not knowing if she was doing the right thing. With hindsight, her decision to terminate her pregnancy at sixteen was the right one, but she couldn't help but wonder what might have been. Had she gone through with it, her child would have been fourteen. Would their parents have forced them to marry? And if they had, would they still be together raising their teenage daughter? Her life would have been over, she would never have escaped. Or might they have forced her to have had the baby adopted? They would have convened a meeting with Father Larkin and made all the arrangements, not taking into consideration her wishes. Sent her away on a fictious school 'exchange' program only to return nine months later having given birth, empty handed. No, she had made the right decision.

The nurse called her name and Lizzie followed her through to the examination room. She dreaded what would be coming next, legs in stirrups and a full pelvic examination.

'It says here that you think you are about ten weeks along in your pregnancy. Is that right?'

'Yes, I'm pretty certain of the date. I had a one-night stand and had sex with another partner a few days later. But the second one used a condom. I feel embarrassed saying this, I'm thirty years old and should've known better.'

'Not to worry, Liz. Sometimes things happen that we aren't prepared for. We all make mistakes.' The staff had been compassionate the last time she came. It must take a special person to be so non-judgmental. 'So, I'm going to do an ultrasound to take some measurements to confirm the dates and the doctor will come in to examine you. Would you like to see the screen and have me talk you through what I am looking at or would you prefer not to know?'

'I'd rather not look if you don't mind. I haven't really got it all figured out yet.' She tried to fight back the tears welling up. She was a mess.

The nurse squirted the cold gel on Lizzie's stomach and pressed the probe around her belly. 'It's okay, Liz. You don't have to have it all figured out, whatever you decide will be what's right for you. This is your life and your decision.' She put her hand on Lizzie's shoulder and squeezed it. 'All done.'

'I had some certainty in my life. Everything's turned upside down.'

The doctor joined them in the room, washed her hands and put on a pair of gloves. 'I'm just going to warm my hands up.' She palpated Lizzie's stomach and did an internal examination. 'This might feel a little uncomfortable. Just shout if you want me to stop.' Lizzie closed her eyes and felt her jaw tense. She felt so violated.

The doctor pulled off her gloves and tossed them into the bin. 'I know you haven't decided about whether to continue with this pregnancy and there is no need for you to decide today. We can arrange some counselling for you if you think that might help. The doctor smiled at Lizzie and waited for a response. The last thing she wanted was to discuss her unplanned pregnancy with a counsellor. 'If you decide to terminate, it's best we do it as soon as possible. You're beyond ten weeks, so it would have to be a surgical termination. Ideally, it's best to do carry out the procedure before twelve weeks.' Her voice was measured, flat. This was routine for her.

'How soon can I get an appointment once I've decided?'

'We can usually schedule patients in with a couple of days' notice. That would give you about ten days to think it over. Would you like me to schedule you an appointment with one of our counsellors?'

'No, I think I've made my mind up, but I'll take a few days to think it over.'

'That's fine. If you change your mind, you can give us a call.'

On the drive home she berated herself for her stupidity and tried to recall the night at the Town Tavern, what the stranger she had sex with looked like, but drew a blank. She couldn't even remember his eye color or voice. He must have been ordinary looking, otherwise she would have remembered. Then she wondered, might it be Joe's? They'd used protection, but condoms weren't fool proof. How could she have a baby if she didn't even know who its father was? And she would be alone this time, no friend like Jeannie to hold her hand and help her home.

*

She called out to Maura and went upstairs to check in on her. Confronted with an empty bed, she had a sudden and overwhelming sensation of dread. Panic. She ran downstairs calling out again. No response. She went down the hall to Paddy's room and shook the doorknob. The door was locked. Pounding on the door, she called out and put her ear to the door. Silence. Her heart raced as she headed out the back door and down the steps to the garage. She lifted the overhead door and had a flashback of her father's body on the cold cement floor. The garage was empty. Maura had to be somewhere. She walked around the side of the house near the watermill, still and dry, the stream long since dried up, expecting to find her mother slumped over, dead. Her mind was racing. The thought of losing her mother without ever getting her back was too much to bear. She went back inside to look for her phone then noticed a note on the kitchen counter. Maura's ornate script saying she had gone to lunch with Hannah and the girls and would be back by dinner.

Lizzie slumped down on the kitchen chair and rested her head on the table. The fear of losing her mother had made her hysterical. It must be hormones. She went to the sink and poured herself a glass of water and took a large gulp, then remembered it was her birthday. How could her mother not have invited her to lunch on her birthday? No card, nothing, her own mother had forgotten her birthday. She lifted the glass, threw it, and listened to it shatter watching the drips of water run down the wall. She sat down on the floor and cried. Not receiving a card shouldn't have come as a complete surprise; it had happened many times before. But she had hoped this year might be different, what with all the care she had been giving her mother and the fact that she was physically present on the actual day. She picked herself up, got the dustpan and broom from the closet and swept up the broken glass.

Telling herself it didn't matter, there was an upside to her mother being out. She had some time to herself and had been meaning to stop by the realtor in town to get the details of the cottage she had seen by the lake.

*

Franklin Real Estate was located on the village green next to the flagpole. Lizzie's dad had been friends with the owner Matt and Matt's daughter, Tara, had been in the year above Lizzie at school. She was caught off guard when she entered the office, hearing a woman's voice call out. 'Can I help you?' She had expected to see Mr. Franklin, but instead it was Tara.

'Lizzie O'Donnell, you have not changed one bit.' Tara said.

'Tara! I had no idea you worked for your dad. I was expecting to see him here.'

'He retired a couple of years ago and I took over the business, it's mine now. Is there something I can help you with?'

'I was out by the lake the other week and noticed there was a cottage for sale, can you give me the details?'

'Sure, that's the Mattison's old place. Mrs. Mattison passed away last year, and her kids all live out of state, none of them have used the place in years.' She swiveled around on her chair to the filing cabinet and pulled a hard copy of the details from a plastic sleeve. 'The drawback is that it's a summer house. There's a wood burner, but most buyers are looking for a fully winterized place.'

'But it's plumbed and wired right?'

'Oh, yeah, it's in surprisingly good condition, no structural problems, just a bit tired. Are you looking for yourself?'

'Yes, I work away but I'm thinking it's time I had a proper base somewhere. What's it selling for?'

'Let me look.' Tara flicked through her folder. 'It's on for one hundred and seventy-five thousand, it's one bedroom but you could go up into the attic space. Would you like to take a look? I'm happy to show you around.'

'That would be great. Any scope for negotiating the price? I'm keen to buy a place and get it rented before I go away again in July.'

'Might be tight to complete in less than six weeks, but I'll do my best. To be honest, there has been zero interest in the place, and I imagine the family would like a quick sale. Everyone wants enormous houses these days with multiple bathrooms, cinema rooms, high ceilings. These little places are hard to move.'

'When can we arrange a viewing?'

'I can take you now if you've got time.' Tara stood up and pulled her fitted skirt down. 'Just let me grab the keys.'

'Perfect.'

'I meant to say, I'm so sorry for what your family is going through. Must be hard.'

'Thanks. It is.' Lizzie strained a smile. 'Most people around here just stare.'

*

By the time Lizzie got back to the house she had not only made an offer on the lake cottage, but also had it accepted. One of the benefits of being known in a small town was that local people were eager to help and happy to have one of their own buying properties keeping the city folk out. Tara was nothing if not efficient and told the seller it was a local family buying knowing that people had funny emotional attachments to properties. She had beaten them down on the price, telling them they were unlikely to get a better offer and got Lizzie an appointment with the mortgage advisor at the savings bank. Lizzie reckoned she could install a wood burner and rent the place out year-round, it would be a good investment. Pleased with her purchase, she had mixed herself a drink to celebrate and was about to take a sip, when Tommy walked through the door.

'Got a message from Hannah to pick you up and take you to our place. Something going on with Ma, that's all she said.'

'Christ, alright let's go.' Trust Ma to spoil her good vibe. 'What did Hannah say about your arrest?'

'She's not really speaking to me. Told me I needed to get a grip, that we have a son on the way and what kind of role model am I going to be if I'm locked up?'

'You had it coming, Tom. What are you going to tell Ma about your black eye?'

'I walked into a two by four on a construction site.'

The tension eased from her shoulders, it was good to laugh.

*

'Right, take a deep breath Lizzie, God knows what we're walking into.'

Lizzie prepared herself for the worst as Tommy opened the door and thrust her forward. 'You coward,' she said. She could hear children's whispers. 'Hannah, Ma?' she called out as she walked into the kitchen.

'Surprise! Happy birthday Aunt Lizzie,' the girls cried out as they began to sing Happy Birthday. They pushed her forward toward a rainbow confetti cake and helped her blow out the candles. 'We made it ourselves and we made you dinner too. We're having a fiesta.'

'Wow, you have well and truly surprised me. I didn't think anyone remembered it was my birthday today. Thanks Ma.'

'Don't thank me, it was Hannah who remembered. It had completely slipped my mind, what with me being so ill.'

'Well, guess it's expecting too much from you, hey Ma.' Lizzie wished her mother could have at least pretended she had remembered. The girls pulled her over toward a piñata and gave her a stick to hit it with. She swung and missed, then passed it on to the children. 'You girls are probably better at this.' Tommy handed her a beer. 'Thanks, Tom but my stomach hasn't been great, think I'll just have a coke.'

'Well, that's a first,' Tommy said. She knew he was teasing but it hit home. She couldn't remember the last time she had turned down a drink.

As they took their places at the table, Joe walked through to the dining room carrying a bunch of pink roses. 'Sorry I'm late, got called out to a domestic,' he said.

'No problem, Joe, take a seat next to Lizzie,' Hannah carried through a giant tower of nachos topped with jalapenos to accompany the bowls of salsa and guacamole already on the table, then returned with a huge tray of enchiladas.

'Looks fantastic.' It did look great, but the aroma made Lizzie feel queasy. She grabbed some plain tortilla chips and took a sip of her coke. The girls didn't hold back, they dove in like vultures until only a few scraps remained. 'I have some good news to share. I got myself a birthday present today, I bought the old Mattison cottage on the lake.'

'What? You bought a house? Just like that?' Tommy said.

'Yup, I decided it's time I got a property and it's a good investment. I'm going to rent it out.'

'Why didn't you run it past me, I could have found you a place? Those cottages don't even have central heating.' Tommy shook his head in disbelief.

'The place found me. I love it and the seller wants a quick sale, so hopefully it will all be sorted out before I leave in July. If you give me a competitive quote, I might let you do the renovations, Tom.'

'Why buy a place that you have no intention of living in?' Ma blew on the forkful of steaming food before putting it into her mouth. 'Once you leave in July you won't be back,' Ma said. For once couldn't Ma let her shine?

'She already said, she's gonna rent it out, Ma,' Hannah smiled at Lizzie then wiped the cheese sauce running down Siobhan's chin.

'I think it's great news, Lizzie,' said Joe. 'I know Ed Mattison well, he'll be delighted that you're buying the place. I guess you can use it yourself when you're on leave?'

'That's the plan.'

'It would be great to have Aunt Lizzie around more wouldn't it, girls?' Hannah said.

The children were tucking into bowls of ice cream and cake, their faces covered in frosting and rainbow sprinkles. They lifted their heads and nodded in unison. She couldn't remember the last time her family had celebrated her birthday.

'You really shouldn't let the children pour so many of those rainbow jimmies on their cake and ice cream,' Ma said.

'It's a party, Ma.' Lizzie grabbed the canister and shook the sprinkles over her ice cream. She wasn't going to let her mother spoil things. It was good to see Tommy's children enjoying being with her. Maybe the novelty would wear off when they got to know her better, but she was enjoying sitting around the table with them all.

'Are you coming to the town meeting next week?' Tommy said.

'Yeah, I'll be there on duty,' Joe said.

'What meeting?' Lizzie asked.

'I've got a planning application in to build a small shopping plaza just beyond the intersection on the road to the lake. There's been some opposition and they've called for a town meeting.'

'Will you come, Lizzie? I need as many votes as I can get.'

'Sure, but what's the objection?'

'Oh, you know, people around here don't like change much,' Joe said.

'Dad had the same problem when he put in the application for the supermarket,' Tommy said.

By the time Hannah brought a pot of coffee to the table Ma had fallen asleep and was snoring, Lizzie's cue that it was time to go home.

'Hannah, thank you for going to so much trouble. I appreciate it.' She felt a bit guilty about having called Hannah stupid the other day, but not enough to apologize.

'The least I could do after the way your day started.' Hannah looked over to Tommy and shook her head in disgust. She didn't appear to be in a forgiving mood, Tommy's punishment no doubt would drag on. At least she had a backbone, Lizzie admired that.

'I can drive your mother and Lizzie home. No need for you to go out of your way,' Joe said.

*

Joe waited until Lizzie got Maura into the house. 'That was a nice evening, Happy birthday again. I didn't want to say in front of your mother, but I've got the coroner's report for you finally.'

'Thanks. Can I come by tomorrow?' An anxious anticipation came over her.

'We can't do it until Friday morning. That okay?

She nodded yes, but the thought of waiting four more days would eat away at her. Was it wrong to feel both excited and uneasy about what she might discover?

Chapter 13

Lizzie's copy of the coroner's report shook as she held it, she hoped no one noticed. She hadn't expected there to be other people in attendance, thought it would be just Joe and her, until Pete Kominsky entered the room with a dark-haired woman she didn't recognize.

'Lizzie, this is Karen Chu, she's a forensic pathologist with the coroner's office. It's great she can be here to answer any technical questions you might have.' The pathologist smiled and reached out to shake Lizzie's hand.

'Pleased to meet you Miss O'Donnell…'

'Liz is fine.'

'Thanks Liz, I've only been recently appointed so wasn't part of the team that conducted the autopsy on your brother.' That was obvious from her face, like Lizzie she had probably still been a small child in 1993. 'But I've reviewed the file and hope I can answer any questions you might have.' A relaxed smile crossed her face as she leaned forward. She seemed keen to please. 'Shall I take the three of you through the report section by section?'

'That would be helpful, Karen.' Pete said. Lizzie and Joe both nodded in agreement.

'Each body tells a story. Our job as medical examiners is

to try to piece together that story.' She spoke like a professional, detached from the fact that the body was in fact, Lizzie's dead brother. 'We start with an external examination of the body, then do an internal examination and take blood and other tissue samples and report on those results. Then the coroner gives an opinion on cause of death.'

Lizzie's eyes were drawn to her father's name - James O'Donnell, father of the deceased, had identified the body. It must have been so hard for her dad, but why hadn't her mother gone? Perhaps she had been there but broke down and couldn't cope with seeing Paddy's body in a black bag. Lizzie could see Karen's mouth moving but she felt like she was caught up in a thick fog. Still thinking about her dad standing there looking at Paddy's body. His son. A corpse. A cold, heavy feeling came over her. The weight of the grief her father must have felt that she was now experiencing.

'A gold chain and crucifix…' Karen was listing the clothes and accessories Paddy had been wearing.

'I remember that jacket.' Lizzie interrupted Karen's flow. 'My dad bought him that when he won the state wrestling championship.' The smell of stale cigarettes wafted in the air making her dizzy. She looked around the room, no one else seemed to notice. Joe's eyebrows drew together as he looked over at Lizzie and mouthed, 'You okay?' She nodded and took a deep breath.

'The body was found by a passer-by, a neighbor walking his dog, who saw the red and black checked jacket.' That was the thing about dog walkers, they always took notice of their surroundings, particularly in their neighborhood. She wondered which neighbor it had been. 'Part of his body was still covered in snow which made it difficult to establish his date and time of death.'

Lizzie closed her eyes and inhaled. What an awful way to die, she wouldn't wish this on anyone. Discarded, like garbage.

'You mean a body covered in snow doesn't decompose normally?' Lizzie asked.

'That's right, if the body is frozen the normal insects and bacteria that would assist decomposition aren't present, so it's kept artificially fresh.' She looked over at Lizzie to check that she was okay to continue. 'It's the signs of maggots, insects, etc. that help us establish how long a corpse has been laying around.' Worms crawling in, worms crawling out was all Lizzie could think of.

The report was full of technical jargon, like a foreign language. 'What does lividity mean?' she asked.

'It's the unnatural color of the skin after death. Typically, post-mortem lividity is bluish purple, but in your brother's case the skin was bright pink which is typical of a body subjected to extreme cold at time of death.'

'So, he froze to death?' Lizzie imagined Paddy's face lying dead in the snow. Gruesome. She shuddered.

'Not exactly, he died from other injuries, and then the body was frozen in the snow. The coroner's opinion was that he died from compression asphyxiation. He was found lying prostrate, so it is likely that his attacker got on top of him and held his face down, smothering him. The x-ray showed a few cracked ribs which most likely happened when his attacker jumped on him.'

Lizzie's mind moved back to Jason Edwards standing in court. Would he have been big enough or heavy enough to have broken Paddy's ribs?

'But there were other injuries as well?' Joe added.

'Yes, he appears to have been struck several times in the face, there was swelling and bruising to his eye and cheekbone and a laceration on his face, probably from an instrument with a sharp edge. And he was sexually assaulted, his injuries are consistent with what we normally see in rape cases.'

Lizzie saw the cold hard words in print, rectal lacerations. The coroner had been putting it delicately to her, sparing her the details. 'Are you saying the samples they took from Paddy over twenty years ago still had Jason Edwards' DNA on them?' Lizzie asked. It was hard to believe that DNA could be kept that long.

Joe jumped in, 'That's why we arrested him. His DNA matched with the sample from the crime scene.'

'I was asking Karen, Joe.' It was a lot to take in. She didn't need Joe jumping ahead, confusing her.

'Yes, that's right. Jason Edwards DNA was found in samples taken from Paddy's rectum.'

'But what about blood? Did you find blood? I mean if he had hit Paddy, maybe Paddy hit him back.' It didn't make sense.

'Sometimes, however, in this case there was no blood, but there was semen. I understand this might be distressing for you Liz.'

'It's…I'm okay, what about all the toxicology results?' The image of 'semen' made her want to heave.

'Your brother appears to have been well over the limit in terms of alcohol in his bloodstream. That alone would have made him wobbly and vulnerable, but there was also evidence that he had used cannabis and heroin shortly before his death. He wouldn't have been very lucid, likely easy prey.'

Vulnerable? Easy prey? He had pushed her back on the bed and clasped his hands around her neck, squeezing until she released the candy she had taken from her fist. Coughing and spluttering, she ran from the room crying.

Lizzie's pulse raced. She rubbed her hand on her neck remembering the sadistic grin on his face.

'The next section of the report lists all the evidence collected and then the final section of the summary report gives the coroner's opinion on cause of death.'

Lizzie scanned the list of evidence, it read like a shopping list, then stopped at number six, samples of blood A+. 'Whose blood sample is this, where it says blood (A+)?' she asked.

'That's Patrick's blood.'

'It can't be…' This was confusing. The room was closing in on her. She shifted her weight on the seat and cleared her throat. 'Sorry, could you pour me a glass of water, Joe?

'Why do you say it can't be? Kominsky asked.

'It's just that I'm O+ and both our parents were too. I must have it wrong.'

Lizzie watched Karen's lips move as she explained the coroner's opinion, only taking in the occasional phrase here and there.

'The main headline is that the coroner's opinion was that Paddy's manner of death was consistent with homicide. I would agree with his findings. Paddy was drunk, high on drugs and therefore vulnerable to attack and probably unable to fight back. He was beaten, raped, and suffocated to death. A very disturbing attack.'

'How did they establish the estimated date of death then if the body was frozen?' Kominsky asked.

'By the stomach contents. The long report suggests that the stomach sample contained partially digested meat, cheese, and vegetable matter such as peas. Mrs. O'Donnell appears to have confirmed to the coroner that she had prepared a meatloaf for dinner the night of Paddy's disappearance.' Lizzie heard the words 'meatloaf' and was transported back to her childhood. She had loved her mom's meatloaf with a large squirt of ketchup on the side. Back to a time when food was love. When Ma looked after her, when she was important. Before the role reversal, before Paddy ruined everything.

'Lizzie?' Joe said. She looked startled.

'What…?'

'Karen asked if you had any further questions.'

'Oh, sorry, no. That was helpful. Can I take this copy home with me?'

'Yes, that's your copy. If you find you have any more questions, please feel free to call me.' She handed Lizzie her card.

'Thanks.' Lizzie looked at her phone, she was going to be late to collect her mother from church again. 'I'm sorry, I have to pick up my mother and I'm late.' She rushed back to her car and put her hand to her chest. Her heart pounded like a bass drum vibrating through her body. The tightening in her chest made it impossible to breathe. Beads of sweat ran down her face as she released her clammy hands from the steering wheel and wiped them on her shirt. Terrified she was going to die, she put down the window and tried to call out to Joe. A numbness crept down her body and she became detached from herself.

'Lizzie, Lizzie!' Joe's voice called. She threw back her head, coughed and pushed his hand away. The intense smell of ammonia burned her nostrils. She shook her head and took a deep breath.

'You fainted. I saw you slumped in the car as I was pulling out.' He wrapped his arms around her and she began to sob. 'I think I should take you to the emergency room to get checked out.'

'No, no.' She shook her head. 'I had a panic attack, that's all.' She hadn't expected it to be so overwhelming, for it to have brought back so much to her. 'It took me by surprise is all. Hand me that bottle of water from the back seat please.'

Joe covered his mouth with his hand and rubbed his lips in thought. 'I really think I should take you to the hospital.' He lifted her chin, so their eyes met.

'I said I'm okay. I'll just sit here for a few more minutes. You go.' She didn't want him fussing over her any longer than necessary. 'I'll call you later to let you know how I am.'

'Promise?' Joe raised his eyebrows and smiled.

'Promise.'

Chapter 14

The church parking lot was empty by the time Lizzie arrived except for Father Larkin's car parked in front of the rectory. Maura was nowhere to be seen. Lizzie looked at her phone, she was a half an hour late, perhaps Ma was still inside the church hall knitting prayer shawls. The door to the main entrance was unlocked. Lizzie entered the church, the red votive candles lit the way like a landing strip. She stopped and stared at the dozens of little flickering lights, the prayers of the lost, the grieving, their hopes that even the smallest light could drive back the darkness. She headed down the side aisle, stopping when she heard some noise, voices appearing to come from the confessional. She didn't think they heard confessions in the old confessional booths anymore. These days it was all face to face – transparency. What more could Ma have to confess; she barely left the house? Lizzie took a seat in a pew a few rows back. The last thing she wanted was for her mother to accuse her of eavesdropping. The confessional booth curtain rustled, and a man rushed out. He pulled at something on his neck, looked at her and darted out of the church. A moment later Father Larkin emerged calling, 'Dylan, son, come back.' He turned and Lizzie caught his eye.

'Mary-Elizabeth, what are you doing here?' His voice cracked, face red and flustered.

'Looking for my mother, she wasn't out front. I didn't realize you did confessions at this time of day, Father.'

'She's in the rectory, just go ring the bell.' He hurried off toward the sacristy. As she slid out of the pew, she noticed a chain and crucifix on the floor, picked it up and put it in her pocket.

Lizzie rang the rectory doorbell and heard a voice shout, 'Come through!'. She didn't recall ever having been in the rectory. It was surprisingly beautifully decorated for a priest who was supposed to live modestly. She walked through to the kitchen and found Maura wearing an apron standing over the stove, stirring a pot.

'What are you doing, Ma? I've been looking for you. You said you'd be out front of the church.'

'I lost track of the time. I…'

'You said you were knitting prayer shawls with your group?'

'We were, that finished earlier. I told Father Larkin I'd make him some stew. He seems a bit thin and sad.'

'He didn't look sad to me. I just saw him in the church.'

'Well, you don't know him like I do, Lizzie. He always has a lot to deal with.'

'Right, well, are you ready to go?'

'Just give me a minute, I don't know why you're in such a hurry. It's not like you have a job to get to.'

'I did have a job; I gave it up to come look after you.'

'I didn't ask you to come,' Ma said.

'Well, if you're capable of looking after the priest now, I guess my work is done here. I'll wait for you in the car.'

*

Lizzie turned on the radio and searched for some decent music. Her mind wandered back to the coroner's report, she didn't understand how Paddy could have been A+, when she was certain both her parents were O+.

She startled as her mother got in the car clutching a sheet of paper in her hand.

'What's the paper, Ma?

'Oh, it's a list of some things for Father Larkin. I said I'd pick them up.'

'Why doesn't he do it himself? Bit much asking one of his parishioners, especially one recovering from cancer.'

'He's busy and it's no bother. Just drive me to Wegmans.'

'Fine.'

'What are you making for dinner tonight?'

'I was planning on making chicken parm, why?'

'Can you make three portions?

'Are you inviting someone over?'

'No, I wanted to get some food containers so when you cook you can put the third portion in a container, and I can freeze it.'

'You mean to give to Father Larkin? You want me to do his cooking too?'

She looked surprised at having been caught out.

'What's wrong with that?'

'Everything. You're the one who said you'd like to cook for him, so you do it.'

'Really, Mary-Elizabeth, you are so uncharitable.'

'And you're so manipulative.'

Ma got out of the car, huffing, and puffing as she grabbed the shopping cart.

'I'll be back for you in an hour.'

*

Lizzie decided to use this interlude to stop by the realtor's office to get an update from Tara on the house purchase. She was in a hurry and had decisions to make. Tara shoved her hand in Lizzie's face, sporting what looked to be a large solitaire diamond engagement ring, her face glowing.

'What do you think, Lizzie? Brett and I got engaged yesterday.'

'Congratulations, that's great news.' Lizzie knew the pressure Tara must have been under, thirty and still single. She had been dating Brett since high school. What had taken Brett so long? 'Have you set a date?'

'Not yet, but I want a big white wedding with lots of bridesmaids.'

'That's great, Tara, I'm happy for you both.' She meant it, she was happy for Tara, but she'd rather gouge her eyes out than have a big fancy wedding. Lizzie was not the marrying type, her mother had been at pains to remind her.

'So, the Mattison cottage. All coming along well. Fastest and smoothest sale I've ever had. We'll be ready to close before the end of the month.'

'That's not long. I need to get organized, furniture to buy, etc.'

'I think the Mattisons are happy to leave the furniture if you want it. Too much of a hassle for them to clear the place with them all living in different parts of the country.'

'That would suit me fine, one less thing to worry about. But just the furniture, I want to buy my own soft furnishings and other bits.'

'When will you be leaving Newham?'

'My new contract starts on the sixth of July. I'll have a couple of days training and prep, then we set sail on the ninth, a big tour of the Caribbean.' It sounded fabulous because it was. She was missing her colleagues, her life.

Tara's eyes lit up. 'That's what I want to do for my honeymoon.' She sounded like she had been planning this wedding her whole life. Lizzie hoped she wouldn't be disappointed or end up being one of those bridezillas she'd seen on some reality show Ma liked to watch. 'I'll keep you posted on the closing, but let's make sure the bank transfer is set up and ready to go.'

*

Outside Wegmans, engine running, Lizzie waited for her mother. The reality of becoming a homeowner had not yet sunk in. She had never considered buying a house, let alone one in Newham, until that morning when she came across the cottage. It seemed right somehow. From the car she watched Ma do battle with the shopping cart, the wheels determined to pull her in the opposite direction, but they underestimated their opponent. Regaining control, she stood tall, pushed the cart laden with grocery bags the last few yards across the lot, then feigned a struggle when she caught Lizzie's eye. Lizzie wasn't playing this game, not jumping to attention. She stayed in the car, popped open the trunk and waited until her mother was at the car.

'Damn cart, didn't you see me struggling?' Maura was flustered.

'Sorry, Ma. I was listening to the radio. But you've managed on your own, isn't that great.'

'Help me load the bags then.'

'You said Father Larkin only needed you to pick up a

few things. Looks like you've bought half the store.'

'I'm going to do some cooking and needed some things of my own. Swing by the rectory again on the way home and you can give him his two bags.'

Chapter 15

Lizzie pressed the rectory doorbell and waited for what seemed an eternity. She was about to turn around and go back to the car when a disheveled looking Father Larkin appeared at the door, opening it just enough to see who was there. She apologized for the disturbance and handed him the two bags, realizing he was doing his utmost to avoid eye contact. Odd. She had never seen him behave like this before.

She headed home contemplating how to broach a discussion about Paddy's autopsy report with her mother. How could she get the truth while avoiding confrontation and being stonewalled?

'You go inside and put your feet up, Ma. I'll bring the groceries in and get us some lunch.'

'I'd like a sandwich, not too much mayonnaise.'

'Sure. Where do you want all this food to go?'

'Put all the meat in the freezer and the rest in the fridge and pantry.'

Lizzie unpacked the bags trying to figure out what meals her mother had planned based on the ingredients. Looked like there might be a beef stew, chicken pot pie and a fish pie. Her mother had been a good cook once, that much she did remember from childhood. Ma cooking was a good thing, even if it was for the priest, and called her to the table for lunch.

'It's chicken salad, not too much mayo.'

'Looks good. Can you pour me a glass of iced tea?'

'You know, Ma, I've been thinking about the interview you gave to Tina Chandler…'

'I don't…' A deep line appeared across Ma's brow.

'And I've realized how important it is, you know, um, for you to be able to talk about Paddy.'

'Yes.' Ma's face softened.

'I don't really remember Paddy very well and I'd like to know more about him. Maybe you could show me some of the photos you shared with the reporter?'

'After I finish eating, if you go upstairs to my closet, there's a shoebox on the top right shelf. Bring it down.'

Lizzie went up to Ma's bedroom and looked around. Pictures hung on all four walls, family photographs taken at the annual parish photo day each year up until Paddy's death. She stared at the wide grin on her face in each photo. She had been a happy child. Paddy and Tommy stood next to each other in the final photo, both sullen faced and Tommy the same height as Paddy, though four years younger. Opening the closet doors she admired her mother's wardrobe, an amazing collection of clothing for someone who rarely went out. She pulled the brown cardboard box down from the shelf and carried it back downstairs to the kitchen.

'Here's the box, Ma.'

Maura opened the lid and poured the contents on the table, photos, a baby bracelet, lock of hair and a locket. Lizzie picked up the locket and examined it. Her mother reached to grab it from her, but Lizzie pulled her arm away and read out the engraving.

'To Maura with love PR.' She opened it to find a tiny photo of a young red headed man. 'Who is he, Ma?

'Patrick Reynolds, he was my fiancé.'

'You were engaged before you met Dad?'

'Yes, he died. But I already knew your father. He was Patrick's best friend.'

'What happened to him?'

'An accident on a construction site in Boston. Wasn't wearing his safety harness.'

Lizzie watched her mother's eyes start to well up. It was hard to imagine her with a life before her dad.

'Oh, Ma. That's so sad.' She wasn't used to pitying her mom. 'You must've been devastated.' She listened to Ma's sniffles. 'But wait, then you married Dad, his best friend?'

'Don't be so judgmental. It wasn't really like that, Lizzie, I...' Ma's face flushed.

'You were pregnant, weren't you?'

'Why do you say that?'

'Because he looks just like Paddy, and I know from the coroner's report that Paddy had blood type A+ and the rest of us are O+.'

'How...'

'I needed to know what happened to Paddy, in the same way that you need to keep his memory alive.'

'You went behind my back?' Maura sat frozen, her mouth open.

'It's not like you were forthcoming with information, Ma.'

'But you had no right...'

'I'm not judging you. I just want the truth. Did Paddy know?'

Her mother startled in silence, then spoke in a quiet voice. 'He found out when he was about fourteen, he asked your father and I separately about our blood types for some homework he was doing and figured it out.' What a way to find out, it was like something out of a soap opera.

'Why didn't you just tell him when he was old enough to understand?'

'We had said we would, but it never seemed the right time. Then when he found out he was so angry.' Maura stood and walked to the sink. She turned on the faucet, filled her glass with water and stared out the window. 'I'd never imagined there could be such rage in him'.

'What do you mean?'

'He changed, started challenging your father, saying he wasn't his dad, he couldn't tell him what to do.' She sat down at the table and wiped her eyes with a napkin.

'That's not surprising, didn't you try…'

'I tried to sit him down and tell him about his father, he had been the love of my life. We were engaged before he and your father were drafted for Vietnam. I wanted to get married right away but Patrick said to wait until he returned. And I waited, I did.'

Lizzie pulled a copper bracelet from the box. 'What's this?'

It's Patrick's POW bracelet. We all wore these for the soldiers taken as prisoners of war and missing in action. I didn't take it off until he came home in 1973. I waited five long years.' She held the bracelet in her hand and rubbed her fingers over the inscription. 'He wasn't the same. He was in Walter Reed Hospital for almost a year before coming home to Boston.'

'What do you mean?'

'I mean, some people are irreparably damaged. I could see it in him. He still loved me but kept putting off the wedding saying he wanted to save up more money. It was your dad who got him a job on the construction site. They had been in the POW camp together.'

Lizzie lifted two medals from the box and handed them to her mother. 'Dad's medals are on the mantlepiece. Are these Patrick's?'

'Yes. He saved your father's life before they were captured.' Maura placed them gently back in the box and wiped her nose. 'That's why your dad married me. He felt he owed it to Patrick to look after me.' Maura put the lid back on her memory box. 'I wanted your brother to know how grateful I was to have him as a reminder of Patrick. He was just so angry.'

'What about Dad?

'Your father tried his best to explain, but Paddy didn't want to know. He said he could never forgive us for lying to him.' She wiped her eyes. 'He called me a whore.'

'Does anybody know?'

'Just Father Larkin as my confessor.'

'Jesus, Ma.'

'We only did what we thought was best. Your father was a good man, and I did grow to love him.' Maura was sobbing uncontrollably. 'I don't want to talk about this. I need to lie down.' Lizzie tried to take her mother's hands in hers, but she pulled away. She went upstairs to her room and shut the door leaving Lizzie alone in the kitchen.

Lizzie sat back in her chair and looked through the photos. It was like some tragic love story, with tragic consequences. Oh, the guilt and shame, the loss her mother must carry. And the respect she had for her dad, marrying his best buddy's pregnant girlfriend, rescuing her from the shame of being an unwed mother. But they should have told Paddy. No wonder he was so screwed up. Lizzie picked up her car keys and stormed out to the construction yard.

*

As she pulled into the yard, she spotted Tommy, his head under the hood of a green dump truck. He had been keeping a low profile since his arrest and was still waiting to hear whether charges were to be pressed. He stood up and glanced at her as he ran a cloth over the oil dipstick and placed it back in the engine.

'What's up, Lizzie? I'm working.'

'What's up is that I just found out that Paddy was only our half-brother. Did you know this?'

'Where did you hear that?'

'Ma told me.'

'Well, she never told me.' He lifted a spark plug from the engine and blew on it. 'I did once hear Paddy arguing with Dad shouting, "You're not my father".'

'And you didn't think to tell me?'

'Look, you can't just storm in here like this. I'm working.'

'Why didn't you tell me?' She insisted.

'You were only a little kid. And he was always so mouthy. What's it matter?'

'It explains why Paddy went off the rails. You should've told me.'

Tommy shrugged his shoulders. 'He's dead, it's over. And it's not like you've been around much over the last ten years.' She didn't understand how he could be so dismissive.

'Why do you always come back to me not being around?'

'How did you find out?' he said, ignoring her comment.

'I requested a copy of the coroner's report and went over it at the station. I saw Paddy's blood type was different to ours.'

'You should leave well enough alone Lizzie. I can't see how digging this all up is helping.'

'I want to know the truth, Tom.'

'Yeah, be careful what you wish for. I expect you've gone and upset Ma.'

'If Ma had told him maybe he wouldn't have been all screwed up.'

'He was born wrong.'

'Tommy…'

'I gotta get back to work.' Tommy disappeared into the belly of the truck tinkering with the engine.

She stood for a moment in disbelief. How dare he dismiss

her like that, like this revelation was somehow trivial. 'What's it matter? He's dead.' This was their family. How could they all have kept this secret and God knows how many others from her? She deserved to know the truth.

Chapter 16

The display case in the foyer at Newham High was filled with shiny gold trophies and cups. A celebration of the town's sporting achievements. Lizzie stared at the huge trophy with Paddy's name engraved on it, wrestling State Champion 1992/93. A framed photo of him in a crouched menacing pose in full wrestling gear stood next to it. She put her nose up to the display case to get a closer look at his face and felt a chill down her spine. She'd seen that expression before. Her flashes of memory didn't seem to align with her mother's description of her eldest brother, which confused her. A hand pressed on her shoulder and startled her.

'Sorry, Lizzie. Didn't meant to make you jump,' Joe said as he reached for her hand. 'You not going into the meeting?' She pulled her hand away and looked around the foyer. 'Relax, nobody's around,' he laughed.

'Just waiting for my mom. She needed the restroom.' She brushed her hand against his. 'Go on in, I'll see you in the hall.' She didn't want to attend the town meeting, but her mother had insisted they show a unified front for Tommy's sake. He needed the votes. Lizzie had been avoiding Tommy since their last conversation at the construction yard a week earlier. She didn't much care if he got planning permission for his shopping center even if it was meant to be a legacy to their father who had purchased the land decades before.

'I'm ready,' Ma said clutching Lizzie's hand. 'How do I look?'

'Great, Ma. That's a nice color lipstick on you.' Her mother had covered the bed with outfits trying to decide what to wear to the meeting. 'It's important we make the right impression,' she had said. In the end, she settled on a floral summer dress and pale blue cardigan.

Lizzie held her mother's hand and headed down the hallway to the school auditorium. It had been twelve years since she had last entered the building and she expected memories to come flooding back, but none did. Her high school years were mostly a blur; she had walked the halls in a haze most of the four years she had been a student there. Not that anyone took much notice. She had been inconsequential. The janitor was carrying extra folding chairs and held the door open for them. He unfolded two chairs at the back of the hall and motioned for them to take a seat.

'This is no good. I can't see anything back here,' Maura said. She stood up and looked around the room until she spotted two empty seats toward the front of the room. 'C'mon, Lizzie. I'm going to the front.'

'I'm good. You go ahead.' She was happy to remain in the background unseen watching her mother walk down the aisle. The skirt of Maura's dress swished as her substantial hips swayed. Lizzie had always wanted to be curvy but had ended up with a straight up and down figure devoid of waist or hips, rather than her mother's hourglass figure. Heads turned and Maura was under the spotlight as the whole row stood to allow her to squeeze past to the empty seat in the middle of the row. Lizzie shook her head incredulously. Her mother knew how to get the attention she wanted. She scanned the room and counted heads. There must've been about four hundred people in attendance. A big turnout. The room was equally divided between white haired retirees and middle-aged couples with children. It would be a close vote.

'Good evening, folks. I'm Jean Sharp and I'll…' A gross screeching sound filled the auditorium causing the townspeople to cover their ears until a technician came on stage and adjusted the microphone. 'Guess I've got your attention now,' she cackled as she looked at the audience over a pair of reading glasses that sat halfway down the bridge of her nose. She cleared her throat then continued. 'I'll be the moderator for tonight's special town meeting which has been called following the submission of a petition signed by two hundred residents.' The town meeting had a long history in Massachusetts going back to the original settlers and was lauded as the most democratic form of governance. Something they took great pride in. Perhaps it was democracy in its purist form, but it seemed a highly inefficient way to do town business. 'Tonight, you are asked to consider the planning application submitted by Thomas O'Donnell of O'Donnell & Sons Construction to build a shopping plaza consisting of eight retail units and a community center.' She rifled through her papers, pulled out a single sheet and held it up. 'I refer you to the meeting protocol which will be strictly adhered to. If you wish to speak you must raise your hand and wait until I recognize you.' Her voice was taut, like a snappy school mistress. 'Please note that the zoning and planning board has already recommended approval of this application. We will hear first from the applicant, Thomas O'Donnell.' She pointed to Tommy in the audience and motioned for him to join her on the stage, then stepped away.

Tommy put his fist to his mouth and coughed. 'Evening everyone. Many of you know me. I'm Tom O'Donnell a born and bred son of Newham.' He rubbed the back of his neck and grinned at the silent audience. 'Twenty-five years ago, my father, Jim, bought the tract of land on which I propose to build a small shopping plaza. Our little town is growing, and we need more local amenities. People are tired of having to drive all the way to Denton for everything.' Heads bobbed up and down in agreement on the right-hand side of the room. 'The plan includes a community center which will be subsidized by rents from the retail units. The town, particularly our teenagers, needs a space to gather safely. I hope you will support the project. I'm happy to take questions.' He wiped his brow and stood back from the microphone.

Lizzie admired his self-assurance. He made it sound like such an altruistic venture. Surely, he was going to make a buck out of it? She looked at the sea of raised hands. They'd be here all night if all these people were allowed to speak. It seemed a perfectly reasonable development to her. What could be so objectionable?

'We don't want a strip mall!' a croaky voice shouted. 'You ruined Denton with all your strip malls.'

'This isn't a strip mall, Sir…' Tommy began before being interrupted by another heckler.

'But you built all those other ones, didn't you?'

'I did, but if you look at the plans, this small plaza is in keeping with our local architecture and heritage regulations.'

'It all starts with one strip mall,' another angry voice shouted. 'There'll be undesirables hanging out in the parking lot.'

'Why can't teenagers just use the high school as a gathering place? We don't want city folk and drug dealers hanging around a youth center. It'll be like that damn arcade in Denton. All sorts of goings on there.'

The moderator had lost control of the meeting. Her face beet red, she approached the microphone and appealed for silence, but the torrent of complaints kept coming. She clenched and unclenched her fists and repeated over and over, 'Silence, please' to no avail. Lizzie chuckled to herself, democracy at work. It was pandemonium until Father Larkin hobbled up on stage and took the microphone. The room fell silent.

'This isn't how we conduct ourselves in this town' His eyes narrowed as he stared out at the audience, most of whom were members of his congregation. 'Miss Sharp has asked for silence. Can we show her some respect?' He spoke calmly and turned to the moderator. 'Before I step down, I'd like to say that this project has my full support. The O'Donnell family has always done good for our community. Jim built many of your homes and a supermarket that we needed and his son, I am sure, will carry on in the same vein.'

The moderator stepped forward and took the microphone from Father Larkin. 'Now can we hear from some of our younger residents please?' She pointed at a fortyish woman whose hand was raised. Lizzie was losing interest. The meeting dragged on, the toing and froing, those for, those against rehashing the same issues over and over. People liked to hear the sound of their own voices. After more than two hours, the moderator called for a vote, but not before a tall Nipmuc named Eddie Cisco took the stage and grabbed the microphone from her.

'This application should be rejected, you can't build on stolen land! The land is part of the reservation and was sold without the authorization of the Nipmuc nation.' Eddie Cisco had been agitating for reclamation of Nipmuc lands for twenty years without much success. His voice was drowned out by a chorus of 'Vote, vote, vote' coming from the crowd and he was escorted off stage by the state trooper.

'May I see a show of hands for those in favor of approving this planning application?' The moderator surveyed the room. 'Can we have a full count, please?' Her assistant clambered up on stage and handed her a sheet of paper. 'And a show of hands for those opposed to the approval of this planning application?' The white-haired contingent raised their hands in unison. A few minutes later a second piece of paper was passed to the moderator. Miss Sharp stood straight backed and announced the results. Those in favor, two hundred and twenty-eight. Those against, two hundred and sixteen. The ayes have it. The application is approved.' A low-pitched grumble came from the left-hand side of the auditorium. The pensioners were displeased.

Lizzie yawned as she walked out into the foyer. It was as if all the air had been sucked from the room. She scratched at an insect bite on her arm until it bled.

'Don't scratch,' Joe said. 'How was that for excitement?'

'Scintillating. Shouldn't you be directing the traffic out of the parking lot?' She linked her finger with his. 'I better go get my mother.' Maura was standing on the other side of the foyer with her arms wrapped around Tommy.

Joe gestured with his thumb near his ear and his pinky pointed at his mouth, 'Call me,' then walked off.

'You okay, Lizzie?' Father Larkin approached and placed his hand on her shoulder. 'Heck of a meeting.'

'A lot of small minded people. That's for sure.'

'Folks need reminding of their sense of common humanity from time to time is all,' he said before being called away by some disgruntled parishioners.

Lizzie crossed the room and joined her mother and Tommy. 'Congratulations,' she said.

'I never doubted it would pass.' His chest puffed up, he gloated.

'Guess it helped that Father Larkin gave you a rousing endorsement.' Lizzie stared at Tommy.

'I didn't need his support.'

'Whatever.'

'Let's go, Lizzie. I'm tired.' Maura held Tommy's face in her hands and kissed him on the forehead then grabbed Lizzie's arm and walked toward the exit. 'Didn't Tommy do great?'

'Yeah, Ma. He got exactly what he wanted.' Funny, he had a knack of always getting just that.

Chapter 17

Lizzie crawled slowly past the shopping plaza site and looked up at the giant O'Donnell and Sons sign that had been erected. Tommy had wasted no time in getting his crew on site to begin clearing the land. She sped up and turned on to the road toward Denton. A white envelope stamped with a red double 'C' Carson Cruises logo slid off the dashboard as she turned. She had pulled it from the mailbox the previous week but had put off opening it avoiding its contents. She had had an unblemished record in her ten years with the company, but the night Tommy had called her begging her to come home, suggesting their mother was terminally ill had pushed her over the edge. Her stomach was in knots by the time she pulled into the Planned Parenthood parking lot. She lifted the envelope from the black floormat. Day of reckoning. Her avoidance strategy had run its course. She slid her nail through the back of the envelope and pulled out the letter feeling a huge lump in her throat as she read.

Following the incident on board during your last tour…

We are cancelling your contract which was due to begin on 6th July…

The occupational health team has recommended substance misuse counselling…

I know you will be disappointed at this news…

The health and safety of passengers and crew is paramount at sea….

We look forward to welcoming you back when you have been declared fit for service…

Please contact James Macintosh, HR Manager to discuss further…

Lizzie's tears smudged the ink on the letter as she slumped back in the driver's seat. How could she have let this happen? Getting fired hadn't been part of her life plan for 2014. But neither had coming back to Newham, buying a house, or having a baby. Her chest felt like it was in a vice. She had left this to the last possible moment. She took a deep breath, exhaled through her mouth, and got out of the car trying to ignore the lone earnest protester brandishing his placard saying, Jesus loves the little children, with a photograph of an aborted fetus below it. She was trying to be pragmatic, not allowing her inner turmoil to take over, but she was a hot mess.

'I…might I speak to someone? She bit the outside of her lip and could taste the blood. 'I was here a few weeks ago but can't remember the name of the nurse who saw me. My name's Liz, Liz O'Donnell.'

'Do you have an appointment?' the receptionist asked staring at the dark circles under her eyes as Lizzie shook her head. 'Let me see what I can do, just take a seat.' The pale green walls were little comfort to her today. Her head was spinning, and she was nauseous. She was more at sea on dry land than she had ever been on the high waters. She took a seat in the waiting area her body in knots.

'Liz, would you like to come through?' The nurse smiled and Lizzie's body relaxed slightly, recognizing a familiar face.

'I know I've left this…' She burst into tears as the nurse led her into a side room.

The nurse handed her the box of tissues and sat quietly.

'I was certain, but now I'm confused.' She wiped her eyes and sniffled. 'I keep trying to think of a good reason to have this baby.'

'And what have you come up with?'

'I think about what it would be like to have someone to love, who loves me back.'

'Is that not a good enough reason?'

'Is it enough, though?'

'What do you mean?'

'I mean, shouldn't there be something more?'

'Liz, people have babies for all sorts of good reasons, some conscious, some unconscious.'

'It's just that I've considered all the reasons not to have a termination.' She reeled off her tick list in between sniffles. 'I mean, I'm thirty, financially stable, in good health. I'm single, but that doesn't matter these days. But I hadn't really focused on good reasons to have a baby, if you know what I mean?'

'Is wanting someone to love who will love you back not a good thing?'

'I guess so.' It was like a foreign concept to her, life experience hadn't reinforced it as a truth.

'And is it enough for you?'

'For me?'

'Yes, for you.'

'Yes, I think so.' Lizzie nodded her head.

'Then you've got your answer.' The nurse smiled and held Lizzie with her warm hands. 'I'll refer you to the women's health clinic and they'll take charge of your pre-natal care and delivery and be in touch to book your first appointment.'

Lizzie stood and gave the nurse a hug. Caught up in the wave of her own emotion, she had let her guard down. If only this stranger could have been her mother.

*

In her car in the parking lot she played mental gymnastics with herself, debating about whether to make the call, then finally dialed.

'Carson Cruises, if you know the extension number of the staff member or department you wish to be connected to, please enter it now,' the recorded message said.

Her hands shaking, she made three attempts to tap the number in before getting it right. In the decade she had been with Carson Cruises, she'd never let the team down, not even a sick day. She was embarrassed about what had happened on board, terrified of what her boss would think of her.

'James McIntosh,' his voice boomed the other end of the line, a Scottish brogue still discernible even after thirty years in New York.

'James, it's Liz O'Donnell.'

'Ah, Liz, I've been waiting for your call,' he said then went silent. 'How are you, hen?' The concern in his voice was a relief to Lizzie. She had been terrified of disappointing him, letting the team down.

'I'm sorry James, I'm sorry about everything.' She sniffled. 'I'll get myself sorted out.'

'Slow down, Liz. I know you will. Just take this time to be with your mother and get the help you need. You keep in touch and let me know when you're ready to start.

Perhaps the Christmas cruise?'

'Hopefully,' she said knowing full well her life was about to change radically. She pulled out of the Planned Parenthood parking lot. How much longer could she keep her pregnancy a secret?

Chapter 18

Tommy walked into the coffee shop and was greeted by a dozen people before making his way over to the table where Lizzie sat reading the Denton Times. She had texted him after returning from the clinic the previous night.

'Geez, Tom, you're a local celebrity,' she said. No one greeted her that way.

'What's so urgent that you needed to meet early in the morning? I've got a lot of work on today. I don't want to rehash our last conversation.'

'Well, you'll be pleased then. You know you asked me to stay on until after Hannah has the baby?'

'Yeah, you said no.'

'I've changed my mind. I'll stay on until after the trial's over on one condition.'

'Oh yeah, what's that?' Tommy raised his eyebrows.

'You do the repairs on my cottage. I'll stay and look after Ma, but there's no way I can go on living with her. There's not that much that needs doing, mostly decorating.'

'Since when are you an expert on house repairs?'

'I had a full survey done. Don't want it updated, I like the faded mid-century feel. And what's not to like about a baby blue bathroom suite?'

'What about Ma?'

'I'll check in on her every day and chauffeur her around, but honestly, I think she needs to get back to doing things for herself. My moving out will encourage that.'

'I wouldn't be so sure.'

'Well, those are my terms. You in?'

'Sounds like I don't have a choice.'

'I'm closing on the cottage on Friday. You can meet me there in the afternoon and we'll figure it out. Family discount and all.' Lizzie picked up her bag of bagels. 'Gotta run, Ma needs her breakfast.'

*

Lizzie picked a bunch of day lilies from the front border of the house and put them in a mason jar on the kitchen table. The splash of yellow brightened the room. While the bacon was frying, she cut the bagels in half and put them in the toaster. Lightly done, that's how her mother liked it. Apart from attending the town meeting, her mother had barely ventured out of her room in the weeks since the revelation about Paddy's parentage. Lizzie hoped the aroma of bacon and fresh coffee might coax her back downstairs.

'You coming down, Ma? I got fresh bagels from the bakery this morning. I made you a bacon bagel.' Lizzie waited, about to give up and return to the kitchen when she heard floorboards creaking on the staircase.

Maura sat at the table, poured a coffee, and took a sip, her whole being oozing anger. Rigid, silent. Lizzie placed the bacon bagel on a china plate in front of her and gave her a napkin.

'Listen, there's something I wanted to tell you, Ma.'

Her mother stared at her blankly, then tore into the bagel. She had never seen her mother devour food like that but was relieved that it was the bagel being ripped apart rather than her.

'I've decided to stay in Newham until after the trial.' She waited for a response watching her mother dab her mouth with her napkin. Maura's face softened.

'Are you pleased?'

'Of course, I'm pleased. I'm your mother.' She took a sip from her mug. 'You shouldn't have gone behind my back.'

'But you wouldn't have agreed. I needed to know what happened.'

'Your brother was murdered, that's what happened. You got what you needed.' She took the last bite of her bagel and got up from the table. 'You can drop me at the rectory in fifteen minutes. And take these bags to the car for me.'

*

Lizzie lugged the grocery bags into the rectory and dropped them on the kitchen counter.

'You can go now. Pick me up at five o'clock.'

'Five? You're going to be here the whole day?'

'Yes, I'm working. It'll give you plenty of time to go home and clean the house.'

Lizzie caught a glimpse of Father Larkin in his study, head bowed, stringy wisps of grey hair combed over to one side and greased down. She slipped by without him noticing her.

'Go home and clean the house….' How dare she! That's all Lizzie had been doing for months. At least her mother was out of the way for the day, giving her some time for herself. She was about to turn the key in the ignition when her phone vibrated, a text message from the women's health center confirming an appointment at eleven o'clock. She started the car and headed back to Denton.

Maura must have been only a couple of years older than Lizzie when she found herself pregnant with Patrick Reynolds' son. She wished she could ask her more, but her mother was in full armor mode. She'd already shut it down, that was her modus operandus. Now they had something in common, but Lizzie was certain Maura wouldn't see it that way. No, she would wait to tell her about the baby.

Chapter 19

The waiting room at the morning prenatal clinic was a hive of activity. Women with all sizes of baby bump chatted, swapping stories, children playing on the floor, the cheerful yellow walls adorned with posters celebrating pregnancy and childbirth. Lizzie took the only empty seat under a poster warning about the dangers of alcohol use during pregnancy. The universe sending her a message. With no visible bump she was a fraud. It still didn't feel real. She heard her name called and made her way towards the reception desk but stopped in her tracks. A tall blonde woman with her back to Lizzie was booking her next appointment. She turned when she heard Lizzie's name called for the second time.

'Lizzie?' Hannah said.

Oh shit, Hannah, the supermom, was the last woman she wanted to run into. 'Please don't say anything. I haven't told anyone yet.' Lizzie's voice cracked as she choked back tears. She was shaking. 'Sorry, I'm a little nervous. Don't know what to expect.'

'I can come in with you if you want. The girls are at summer camp. I've got time.'

'Would you?' She wasn't sure about Hannah as an ally

but didn't want to be alone.

Hannah put her arm around Lizzie's shoulder as she walked toward the nurse.

'We're going to do an ultrasound first, then the doctor will see you and we'll do some blood tests,' the nurse said.

The gel was cold on Lizzie's belly. The sonographer pressed the probe on her abdomen and moved it around until she found the heartbeat. She turned the screen toward Lizzie and showed her the baby's outline.

'You can see the heart beating, nice steady rate.'

Lizzie looked over at Hannah and smiled, tears streaming down both of their faces.

'Looks like from these measurements that you're about twelve weeks pregnant. Is that what you expected?'

'Yes, I think that's right,' Lizzie said.

The sonographer printed out the images and wiped the gel from Lizzie's belly.

'That's my work done. If you just stay put the doctor will be in shortly,' she said and left the room.

'When are you going to tell Joe?' Hannah asked.

'It's not Joe's.' Lizzie watched Hannah's mouth drop. 'At least I don't think it is. You weren't expecting that, were you?'

'Ah, no,' Hannah laughed awkwardly.

Lizzie raised her eyebrow.

'But I want this baby, so I'm gonna go it alone.'

'People will talk, Lizzie. You know what they're like around here.'

'We're already news.' Lizzie put her hand on her belly. It was too late to let the doubt seep in, she'd deal with whatever was thrown her way. 'I've got a few weeks before anyone will notice. Please don't say anything to Tommy or Ma. I want to tell them myself.'

'Your secret is safe with me.' Hannah pulled her in close and held her tight.

'Great.' Lizzie was unconvinced. Hannah didn't have a great track record on the secret keeping front, but she was going to have to trust her.

*

Joe was hunched over, his arm resting on the roof of the state police car talking to Kominsky when Lizzie pulled up beside him in front of the town hall. They hadn't spoken since the town meeting and Lizzie suspected Joe might be avoiding her. He patted the roof of the car sending Kominsky on his way and turned toward Lizzie's car.

'Haven't heard from you for a while,' Lizzie said.

'There's been a lot going on at work.'

'Have you been avoiding me?'

'Why would I do that?' He lowered his chin and pulled back on his neck.

'I don't know, maybe us being friends might be a problem for you, with work and all.'

'No, honestly, I've just been busy.' He cleared his throat and stood rigidly.

'You want to meet up tomorrow? I'm closing on the cottage and picking up the keys. We can have a little celebration out there.'

'Sure, sounds good.' He glanced down at his phone, then looked away. 'My shift finishes at six, I'll come by after.'

*

Maura was standing in front of the rectory talking to Father Larkin when Lizzie pulled up. At least she wasn't late. Lizzie nodded at him and leaned over to open the passenger side door.

'You'll need to get out and help me with these bags, Mary Elizabeth.'

'Sure, Ma.' Lizzie wasn't bothered, it was all for show. She needed Father Larkin to see her authority over her daughter.

'Mary Elizabeth, your mother has worked tirelessly today preparing my meals for the week. I hope you'll look after her this evening,' Father Larkin raised a spindly finger and replaced the strand of hair that had fallen in his face. It was a bad comb over.

'Maybe it's too soon for her to be working so hard?'

Lizzie replied.

'Don't be ridiculous Mary Elizabeth, I'm fine.' She didn't seem to be in a better mood. 'I don't know why you say these things in front of Father Larkin like that, it's embarrassing.'

'Maybe it's too much for you, too soon. It's not like you've worked in years.'

'I'm quite capable, I've run a home for almost fifty years.'

Her life through rose tinted glasses. Lizzie opened her mouth, then closed it. There was a limit to how much energy she had for giving her mother a reality check. She started the engine and reversed out.

'Did you get the cleaning done?'

'No, I've been busy, it can wait until tomorrow.'

'Busy with what, exactly?' She opened her handbag and pulled out a tissue then blew hard.

'Just some of my own errands. I'm closing on the Mattison cottage tomorrow.'

'I still don't understand why you've bought that place, you'll be gone soon,' she said matter of factly while shoving a Vicks inhaler up her nose.

'It's an investment, Ma, for the future.' She put her hand on her belly then looked over at her mother. 'You getting a cold?'

'It's nothing, probably just hay fever.'

They pulled into the driveway and Maura slid out of the passenger seat.

'Bring the bags in Lizzie, I'm going to put my feet up.'

'Yup.'

And I'll have my dinner on a tray in front of the television, I want to catch up on General Hospital.'

Lizzie smiled to herself, order had returned.

Chapter 20

Lizzie pushed the pile of bridal magazines to the other side of the desk as Tara placed two champagne flutes down, then pulled a miniature bottle of Brut from the drink's fridge behind her desk. She popped open the bottle and poured two glasses despite it being ten o'clock in the morning.

'We've got to celebrate, Lizzie,' Tara clasped a pink rabbit foot keychain in her left hand while pouring the champagne with her right. She handed both to Lizzie and poured herself a glass of champagne. 'Let's toast. I know you'll be off soon, but hope you'll have many years of happiness in your home.' Lizzie raised her glass, then took a sip. It had a strange metallic taste against her teeth.

'I'm going to be hanging around for a while, at least until the court case is over. Can't leave my mom.'

'That's fantastic news. You'll be here for my bridal shower, you have to come!'

Lizzie nodded, took another sip from the glass hoping it would taste better second time around, but the metallic taste was still there. She put the glass down.

'I really appreciate all you've done for me. It's all gone so smoothly. I can see why your dad entrusted you with the business.'

'He didn't really have much choice, my brother's in rehab.' They both burst out laughing.

'I'd forgotten about Ted, is he doing okay?'

'Hard to say, he's been battling addiction for years. Comes out, goes back. Father Larkin has tried to help him multiple times, but he keeps relapsing. My dad says this is the last time he'll foot the bill.'

'I'm so sorry. That's tough for you all. Listen, I've got to be going, Tommy is waiting for me out at the lake. I've got him doing the redecorating for me.'

'I had a terrible crush on that brother of yours, shame Hannah snagged him first.' They both laughed. She'd have made a fun sister-in-law but that would have been with the old Tommy, not this one. Lizzie would settle for having Tara just as a friend, a novelty in itself.

The late morning sun lit up the trees in vibrant shades of green as Lizzie made her way to the cottage winding around the perimeter of the lake. The pink key chain was swinging from the rear-view mirror. Tommy's Cadillac sparkled on the drive, but he was out of sight. He must devote a lot of time to keeping his status symbol spotless. She grabbed the keychain from the mirror and headed down toward the dock. Tommy was sitting, jeans rolled up, legs dangling in the water.

'You'll need a new dock,' he said.

'Well, hello to you too, Brother.' She dangled the keychain in his face. 'Shall we go inside?'

'What the hell kind of keychain is that? Don't see many bunnies that color.'

'Tara, guess she remembered I used to like fluorescent pink at school and wanted to bring me some luck. God knows I need it.'

Tommy reached for the key and Lizzie pulled away.

'Before we go in, I want to remind you that I am not looking for perfection. I want it freshened up. That's all.'

'Yes, yes, just let me do my job now, please.' Tommy grabbed the key and opened the front door. 'This lock will need changing.' He took a notebook out of his jeans pocket, grabbed the pen from behind his ear and started to jot down notes. 'Leave me to it. I'll call you when I'm ready to go over the list.'

'Right, well I'll get out of your way then.'

Lizzie found two old cedar Adirondack chairs in the basement and dragged one down the lawn to the water's edge. She closed her eyes and let the sun warm her face imagining herself in the water, her baby squealing with delight as they splashed together. A good decision, she could feel it in her bones. They'd be happy here, the two of them. Adrift in her daydream she jumped when she heard him.

'I hate to admit it, but you were right. There's not a lot wrong with this place. Kinda wish I'd bought it myself.'

'I'll take that as high praise.'

'Come up and I'll walk you through.' Tommy led the way and held open the door to the screened in porch for her. 'This'll be nice in the summer, keeps the mosquitoes out, but no use in the winter. I could close it all in for you and winterize it?'

'Nah, I like it how it is. It's got charm.' The Mattison's had left a rattan sofa with faded blue and white striped cushions and an old maple Hitchcock rocker. She lifted the matching blue and white striped cushion to reveal the rush seat. 'Do you think this is a real Hitchcock chair?'

Tommy flipped the chair over and examined it carefully. 'Look here.' He pointed at a signature. L. Hitchcock, Hitchcocks-ville, Conn. Warranted. 'The real deal. Lucky you.'

Lizzie sat on the chair and enjoyed the motion as she rocked back and forth and imagined a baby in her arms. Her baby. Tommy opened the door from the porch to the living room.

'If I blow foam insulation into the walls and install an electric radiator in the bedroom, the wood burner alone should keep the place warm.' He chewed on his fingernail, yellowed from years of smoking, and spat out the hangnail.

'That's disgusting,' Lizzie frowned. 'Go on.'

'This knotty pine is beautiful. You've got the same in the bedroom. I think the wood will come up nice if we sugar soap it.' He walked through the living room and opened the door to the bedroom. 'See, it won't be so dark once it's washed.' The bedroom was large enough for a double bed and she could put the crib against the wall. Tommy opened the door opposite the bedroom revealing a tiny pale blue bathroom suite. 'Not what I would choose, but it's all in great condition, even the tiling.'

'How long will it take you to do the work?'

'It's just cosmetic. The bathroom and kitchen need painting, but they're small. I reckon I can get it ready in a week. Have you told Ma you're moving out yet?'

'No, I'm working towards that. She still thinks I'm renting it out.'

'I've gotta get to another job. I'll message you the quantities and type of paints needed. You choose the colors, buy it all and drop it off here.' He was smiling.

'What's got you smiling, Tom?'

'I was just thinking about your tiny house compared to my big house. How much space do people really need?'

'You need more than one bedroom with a wife, three kids and another on the way.'

'But I could be happy in a house like this. You've got a

great spot here.'

'You can always come around on your own and fish off the dock if you need some solitude. Or bring the girls for a swim.'

'You won't get rid of them once they see this place.'

Chapter 21

Yummy Tummy, the sign alone brought a smile to Lizzie's face. The local takeout joint was famous for its dumplings and General Tso's chicken. She examined the menu and placed her order. The morning sickness seemed to have disappeared overnight, her appetite returning with a vengeance. There was no such thing as over ordering with Chinese food. You were always hungry again a few hours later. She stopped at the package store and picked up a six pack for Joe and a large bottle of Coke and went back to the lake.

She dragged two chairs and a small side table on to the dock. It didn't feel rickety, no immediate danger of sinking. Tommy had probably been exaggerating, though if he wanted to build her a new one, she wouldn't object. She laid out the plates and chopsticks on the table and took the white cartons from the bag. Hearing Joe call out her name she looked up and motioned for him to come down to the water.

'Perfect timing, I've got everything here, come down while it's hot.' Lizzie opened the lid, the sweet aroma of the deep-fried chicken filled the air.

'General Tso is making my mouth water.' Joe leaned over and gave Lizzie a peck on the cheek. 'I so need this after the day I've had.'

She grabbed the bottle opener, flicked off the cap and passed Joe the ice-cold bottle of Bud.

'Chug this back, you'll feel better.'

'You not having one?'

'I've already got a drink. What's got you riled today then?'

'Don't laugh, it's the planning for next week's Fourth of July parade.' Aside from the switching on of the Christmas lights, it was Newham's biggest community event. 'I've had to do a risk assessment for a terrorist attack.'

Lizzie spat her coke as she burst out laughing.

'Seriously? How likely is it that terrorists will target the Newham parade?'

'It's one of those low risk, high impact scenarios. People are still shaky after the Boston marathon bombing.' The bombing had scarred Boston and all the surrounding communities. Everyone seemed to know someone who knew someone who had been killed or injured. 'I spent all day working on it and I'm not done yet.'

'At least if something happens all the emergency services will be there marching in the parade.'

'True.' Joe helped himself to a second portion of chicken and rice. 'You gonna show me the house?'

'The tour won't take long. Leave everything here, we can

come back down and have a fire.' Lizzie opened the screened in porch door and showed Joe into the house. 'It's tiny, I know, but perfect for me. Tommy's going to give it a lick of paint and do a few minor repairs over the next week so I can move in.'

'Move in?'

'I've decided to stay until after the court case, but I can't go on living with Ma.'

Joe's face lit up.

'That's great news. I can give you a hand when you're ready to move in.'

'C'mon, let's go make a fire.' Lizzie grabbed a few logs from the wood pile. 'Scout around for some tinder and kindling, will you?'

'Sure.' Joe poked around the yard then dumped a pile of bark, dried leaves and sticks next to the logs.

Lizzie pulled a Denton Times from her bag and began ripping strips of newspaper. 'At least this rag is useful for something.' It had been some weeks since the O'Donnell family had last appeared on the front page, which was a welcome relief. But it would be the quiet before the storm, once the trial started, they would surely be headline news again. She was determined to enjoy the quiet while it lasted. She built a tepee of sticks and logs, crumpled the paper between them and lit it. Her lungs became a pair of bellows breathing life into the fire until the flames began to dance.

'You must have got the campfire badge in Girl Scouts.'

'Some things you never forget. Here, have a fortune cookie.' Lizzie cracked her cookie in half and pulled out the thin white strip revealing the fortune. 'What's yours say?

'Avoid taking unnecessary risks. Lucky numbers: 11,16,23,29,38,' Joe said.

'Pretty much fits with your day then.' They both laughed.

'How 'bout yours?

'If you look back, you'll soon be going that way.' Lizzie threw the paper into the fire. 'These are always a load of nonsense.' She had been spending a lot of time looking back lately but with a baby on the way it was time to look forward.

'I don't know about that. I sometimes get the one that says, you will be hungry again in one hour and it's usually true. Where's the box with the leftover chicken?'

They sat in front of the fire gazing at the moon rising over the lake, its reflection rippling across the water.

'It's good you're staying Lizzie.'

'Yeah, I hope so.' She felt so comfortable with Joe. He was like her favorite oversized old sweater. She could wrap herself up in him. But how would she tell him about the baby? She could pass it off as his, but it wouldn't be right.

Chapter 22

The Fourth of July parade was Newham's annual salute to America, the locals up early lining the roads with their chairs to reserve the best spaces along the route. An honor guard of stars and stripes lined both sides of Main Street - red, white, and blue the compulsory colors of the day. Uncle Sam on stilts policed the main street, encouraging the crowd like a cheerleader while the ice cream van did a roaring business in patriotic snow cones. Groups of children seated on the curb licking the icy sweet, red, white, and blue treat waved their little American flags and showed off their blue stained tongues.

Lizzie had been given strict instructions by her nieces about the placement of chairs. She could feel people's eyes on them as they passed by, the glances, the whispers. She should have been used to it by now, but it still raised her blood pressure. Ma stood fanning herself while Lizzie nabbed a spot under the oak tree opposite the VIP viewing podium and unfolded the chairs.

'It's far too hot for me to be here.' Maura plonked herself down on one of the chairs, the plastic sagged under the weight of her bottom. 'I feel faint.'

'What do you want me to do about it? I told you how hot

it was going to be today.'

'I know, I know.'

'Do you want me to take you home?'

'No. I'll stay, I want to see the girls. Go get me a cold drink.'

She could feel the heat rising inside her. Deep breaths. It was far too hot to get worked up.

'Right, I'll go to Jefferson's. What do you want?'

'Anything as long as it's cold. And get me something to munch on too.'

Lizzie walked down Main Street until she reached Jefferson's country store. It was amazing that the family run business had survived the arrival of Wegman's supermarket in town. They wouldn't be able to compete with the big chain forever. Jefferson's would have a similar fate to the old stores on Main St that went bust when the shopping mall opened in Denton. Shame, it had such character. She grabbed a couple of cokes and two bags of chips and took her place in line at the checkout.

'Where's the party?' Joe stood shoulder to shoulder with Lizzie holding a bottle of water.

Lizzie jumped.

'You startled me, Joe. Shouldn't you be out looking for terrorists?'

'Don't be so flippant, that's exactly what I'm doing.' Joe

leaned in and whispered, 'Wanted to tell you the police have decided not to charge Tommy.'

'Hannah will be relieved, last thing she needed with another baby on the way.' Lizzie handed the cashier a twenty-dollar bill and waited for her change. 'Have you told Tommy yet?' She picked up the bag of groceries and headed toward the exit.

'Only found out yesterday evening and didn't have time to stop by. You know, parade duties. I'll tell him today. Where are you sitting?'

'Just opposite the viewing podium. Want to get a good view of the local celebrities.'

'I'll be walking the crowd.'

'Be vigilant, Joe,' she said straight-faced as she walked off into the sea of red, white, and blue.

*

Lizzie returned to find Ma had been joined by Hannah, the pair both seated in the shade fanning themselves. Hannah's sundress exposed her long thin frame distorted by the size of her baby bump.

'Sorry, did I take your seat, Lizzie?' Hannah said.

'It's fine. I can sit on the blanket.' She sat down and was confronted with Hannah's ankles. 'Jesus Hannah, your ankles are huge.'

'I know, it's the heat. I still have twelve weeks to go.

Hope this heatwave doesn't continue all summer.' She put her hand on her stomach and rubbed it. 'This little guy is so active. This'll be you soon…'

'What will be soon?' Ma asked.

'Nothing, Ma. Hannah said the baby will be here soon.' Lizzie sat tight lipped, why couldn't Hannah keep her big trap shut? She was simply incapable of keeping a secret.

'Sorry.' Hannah mouthed and shrugged her shoulders looking embarrassed. 'You wanna feel?' Hannah asked. Lizzie placed her hand on Hannah's stomach and felt a ripple move across her abdomen, then a sudden jab and pulled her hand away. 'He's got a good right hook.' Hannah laughed. 'It's like there's a bar-room brawl going on in there sometimes.'

Lizzie stopped herself from making a comment about Tommy and bar room brawls. She'd leave the delivery of that news to Joe.

'Who's marching with which groups?' Lizzie asked.

'Tommy's leading the little league baseball group. Claire's with the Brownies and Siobhán and Katy are marching with 4H.'

'I can't wait to hear the bagpipes,' Ma interjected.

Lizzie heard the familiar sound of snare drums as the crowd began to clap, the parade marshal announcing the arrival of the Newham fife and drum corps leading the festivities for the fiftieth year in a row to the tune of Yankee Doodle.

'Our Paddy could have been the lead drummer,' Maura said wiping her eyes.

Ignoring her mother, Lizzie heard someone shouting her name. She looked across to the viewing podium and saw Tara dressed as Lady Liberty, waving at her. Her sash advertised Franklin Real Estate. She managed to stop herself from laughing and waved back, then noticed a woman taking her photo. It was Tina Chandler. She wanted to cross over and rip the camera from the journalist's hands. Could she not leave them in peace?

'Paddy didn't play the snare drum, Ma. That was Tommy.'

'Oh, was it… well, I'm sure Paddy could've played too.' Lizzie looked at Hannah and rolled her eyes. It wasn't worth continuing this line of conversation.

They sat watching an endless stream of community groups march by waving to the crowds until finally Tommy's float appeared. He had transformed the flatbed truck from the building yard into a baseball stadium, complete with AstroTurf and a giant papier mâché baseball and bat. The boys in their little league uniforms sang along to a recording of Take Me Out to the Ballgame, while playing catch atop the truck and throwing candy into the crowd to huge cheers.

Hannah beamed. 'Tommy has to win a prize this year.'

'Where did he find the time to build that float?' Lizzie asked.

'He's been working on it late at night when he can't sleep, which is most nights.'

'Impressive. You've got one talented husband there, Hannah.' Joe sneaked up and crouched down next to her chair. 'And I've got some good news for you. No charges will be filed against Tommy. You're good.'

Hannah gave Joe a hug, her eyes welled up.

'What's going on?' Ma asked.

'Nothing, Ma. Hannah's hormones just got the better of her.' Lizzie smiled at Hannah. 'Right, Han?' She noticed a man across the street in a navy polo shirt, an American flag bandana wrapped around his head, holding a little girl's hand. She'd seen him somewhere before. 'Joe, who's that guy across the street holding hands with a little girl?' She caught his eye as she pointed him out. He looked on edge.

'That's Dylan Jones,' Joe said and gave him a wave. 'Why do you ask?'

'Oh. I've seen him somewhere before.' His face was etched in her memory, he was the man Father Larkin was calling after, the one who had rushed out of the church confessional the day she had been looking for Ma. 'Never mind.'

Joe dipped his chin and spoke into his walkie talkie. 'Roger that. Sorry, I've gotta move on now.

Lizzie waited until a column of vintage cars crept past, then crossed the street. The great and good of Newham town council were streaming public service announcements over a loudspeaker. She made eye contact and approached Dylan Jones, smiling she reached into her handbag and pulled out her fist.

'I think this is yours,' she said putting out her hand.

He looked around the crowd quickly and grabbed the chain from her palm. 'How did you know this was mine?

'I was in the church when you dropped it.' She stared at him intently. 'I tried to give it back, but you ran off.'

'Thanks,' he said and turned away.

'Hold on, I'm Liz, Liz O'Donnell.'

'I know who you are.' He grabbed his daughter's hand and walked off.

She shook her head as she waited to cross back over to the other side of the street. Such a strange encounter. A small child stepped out into the road and was snatched up quickly by Joe, the father shook Joe's hand and patted him on the back. Lizzie could see he took this job seriously and enjoyed being part of the community. You could be cocooned here, meet your wife, have kids, and never leave. All so safe, a bucolic bliss.

'Here they come,' Maura shouted and took to her feet.

Lizzie wasn't sure who Ma was talking about, all she could see was a group of middle-aged men in white polo shirts carrying a banner that read, Knights of Columbus Celebrates Marriage & Family. Behind them Father Larkin, in full dog collar, pulled a child's wagon filled with candy and tossed it out to the onlookers. Lizzie shuddered. She was about to become an unwed single mother in this god-fearing town.

'Over here, Father Larkin!' Maura waved her arms and shouted to get his attention. He made his way toward her, sweat dripping down his face. 'You poor man, here, have this cold drink.' She handed him Lizzie's coke.

'Thank you, Maura.' He took a long swig, then put it on the ground, taking Maura's hands in his. 'And thank you for the delicious meals.' He smiled at her then re-joined his fellow Knights of Columbus.

'That was my drink, Ma.'

'Here, you can have it back.'

'No thanks.' The thought of drinking his backwash made her nauseous. Her mother's fascination with him was perplexing. She wondered if something more was going on between the two of them, then dismissed the thought and shook her head. That would be too weird.

A shrill wail filled the air as the bagpipers approached dressed in their tan kilts complete with sporran and playing God Bless America. The loudest cheers saved for them as they marched by with a strong sense of pride and honor embodying the strength and freedom their instruments represented. Lizzie glanced over at her mother, a few tears streamed down her face, and handed her a tissue. Maura always cried when she heard bagpipes playing. Lizzie had assumed that it reminded Ma of Paddy's funeral, but given recent revelations, perhaps Patrick Reynolds had been a piper and it was he who she mourned.

'Here come the girls finally.' Hannah stood up as the 4H float passed by, her two daughters trying to wave while stroking rabbits.

'I loved 4H when I was a kid. All those animals. I remember wanting to be a vet or a farmer,' Lizzie said thinking aloud.

'You weren't in 4H,' Maura said.

'I was until Paddy died, then you wouldn't take me anymore.'

'That's not true.' Maura folded her arms and looked away.

'Look, there's Claire.' Lizzie changed the subject, watching her niece carrying the American flag in a holster.

'The Brownie uniforms certainly have changed.' Claire's head turned to the right, focused on her color guard duties as they passed the podium, while the troop of little girls trailing behind in brown vests, white polo shirts and blue scarves giggled and marched out of step to the beat. 'She looks very professional, Hannah.'

'In her element, she likes being in charge.' Hannah folded the chair. 'I'm not going to stay for the muskets and cannon being fired. Are you going to come by for the fireworks tonight?'

'Let me get Ma home and settled and I'll see.' She was warming to Hannah, even though she nearly dropped her in it again. Maybe it was hormones, but it was good to be included.

*

Lizzie loaded the chairs and blanket into the trunk, got back into the car and turned the air-conditioning to max.

'I'm exhausted, will you please get me home now.'

'I'm trying Ma, there's a huge line of traffic. You'll just have to be patient.'

'People were staring at us today. I could feel it.' Maura said looking out the window.

'It's no surprise, is it?' Lizzie was struggling with the heat and losing patience.

The line of traffic began to inch forward as they

gradually approached the intersection. The traffic light was out and Joe, whistle in his mouth, was directing the cars in all four directions like an orchestra conductor. Lizzie indicated left and put down her window as he waved her forward.

'You going over to Tommy's later?'

'Not sure yet, gotta see how Ma is.'

'Hannah invited me so I can pick you up if you want.' He put the whistle back in his mouth.

'I'll message you.' Lizzie closed the window, turned left, and drove away from the center of town.

'You're spending a lot of time with him.'

'We're friends, Ma.'

'Like you were in high school?'

'What's that supposed to mean?'

'You led him on.'

'What would you know about it? You were locked away in your bedroom.'

'Angela told me you broke his heart.'

'You shouldn't listen to gossip.' Lizzie pulled the car into the garage and helped her mother up the stairs to the kitchen.

'Get me a glass of water and a couple of Tylenol. I need to lie down.' She made her way to the living room, sat down in her chair, and put it in full recline mode. 'It's hard to keep a secret in this town, Lizzie.'

'You'd know better than me.' Lizzie handed her the glass of water and pills. 'Would you like me to share your secret with them all? How would that be?' Her anger made her cruel. She wanted to hurt her mother, give her a dose of her own medicine.

'Stop it,' Maura sobbed.

'Or maybe you'd like to tell them my secret?'

'What's that then?'

'I'm pregnant.'

Lizzie stood silently waiting for a response. She could see Ma chewing over her words, the blood draining from her face.

'Have you told Joe?'

'It's not his.'

'Jesus, Mary and Joseph! Well, whose is it then?'

'I don't know.'

'How could you… how could you be so loose? Have you no shame?'

'Go ahead, Ma. Cast the first stone. That's rich coming from a woman who got pregnant out of wedlock.'

'How dare you!' The indignation in her voice fueled Lizzie's anger.

'We're more alike than you think, both unmarried and pregnant, except that I'm not going to marry another man and pretend to the world my child is his.'

'Maybe you should. I'm sure Joe would raise your child; he'd be a good father.'

'This isn't the 1970s. I can raise my child on my own.'

'Not in this town you can't. And how am I going to face everyone at church?'

'Thanks for your support. You know what, I think it's time I moved out.' Lizzie went upstairs and pulled her suitcase out from under the bed. The cottage had only just been painted, but she could camp out there. Anything would be better than staying another night with her. She packed her bag and made her way downstairs. 'There are some leftovers in the fridge. I'm going.'

'But what about me, what about church in the morning?'

'I'll be by to collect you at ten o'clock.' Lizzie grabbed the bottle of Jack Daniels, walked out the door and breathed freely for the first time in months.

Chapter 23

The smell of fresh paint left Lizzie lightheaded. She opened all the windows, turned on the ceiling fan and watched the blades whip around the hot sticky air. She should have bought an air conditioner, it had been naive to think there would always be a breeze off the lake. Tommy's crew had done a nice job on the place, the pale blue walls in the kitchen gave a cool freshness to the room and matched the cushions on the porch. She turned on the faucet, put her mouth under and sipped the cold water. Walking through to the bedroom she stopped to admire the warm honey color of the pine walls, threw her bags on to the bed, laid down and stared at a pair of knots on the ceiling that resembled an owl.

She felt unburdened, free from Ma's shackles. Perhaps she had been a bit rash, melodramatic in her departure. No regrets, but in her haste, she had left without any bedding or toothbrush. Rifling through the suitcase she pulled out her bikini. She slipped off her shorts and t-shirt, put on the navy bottoms and massaged her belly. A swelling, imperceptible to the outside world, but she could feel it. Her breasts were another matter, anyone seeing her bursting out of her bikini top would think she had had breast augmentation. This strange fullness, her body changing, was not as unpleasant as she had feared.

The instant her body hit the water she was cool and cleansed, absolved of life's myriad of sins and indiscretions, she floated on the surface of the water staring up at the sky. The chatter and distractions of life, her mother, drowned out by the hum of the lake. She began to flutter her feet, her arms executing alternating movements – one arm sweeping underwater as the other arm rose, propelling her into the deeper water. Stopping to take in the view, she tread water, then dove down to see if she could touch the bottom unintentionally entering a dense underwater jungle.

Her body became entangled in the slippery lake weed and she began to panic, unable to see a way out in the murky water, her torso and legs wrapped tight. The fear of suffocation, of drowning, came flooding back to her as she struggled to hold her breath. At least this time she had control of her arms; she wasn't entombed in snow. Pulling at the weed around her legs, she released herself and floated to the surface gasping for breath. Those who describe drowning as being peaceful had clearly never experienced it, it was a terrifying struggle. She flipped on to her stomach, pulling her knees in, then thrust her legs and swept her arms backwards gliding toward the ladder. Holding it with both hands she hoisted herself up on to the dock and grabbed her towel.

She caught her breath, let out a long sob from somewhere deep inside and sat with her emptiness. As she stood, her stomach began growling. With no food in the house, she would have to make her way over to Tommy's. She slipped off her bikini, hung it on the railing and went into the house. Her phone pinged as she tried to pull her underwear over her damp skin. A message from Joe, should he pick her up. She tapped into her screen, Will meet you there.

*

Lizzie stood at the front door, bottle of Jack Daniels in hand, and rang the doorbell. She had already poured a couple of shots. Call it dutch courage. She wasn't really in a party mood, but hunger overrode everything.

'Weren't you bringing Ma?' Tommy asked.

'Nice to see you too, Tom.' Lizzie handed him the bottle. 'How about you fix me a drink? Ma's not coming.'

'But the girls…'

'We had a fight, I've moved out.'

'What the hell, Lizzie.' Tommy poured a shot, filled the glass with ice and topped it up with Coke. 'Here.' He handed it to her.

'Lizzie, you shouldn't…' Hannah said.

Hannah glared at her as she took a large gulp.

'It's fine, Hannah.'

'Have I missed something here?' Tommy asked.

'No, Ma was just being her vile old self. I've moved into the cottage, it looks great by the way.'

'But it's not ready yet.'

'Near enough, I'll stay out of the guys' way during the day. I just need a place to sleep. Can you lend me some bedding and towels?'

'Come with me and I'll get you some,' Hannah headed down the hallway to the closet. She grabbed a woven beach bag and filled it with a set of sheets, blanket, and towels. 'You really shouldn't be drinking, Lizzie. It's bad for the baby.'

'One drink won't hurt. You have no idea what I just went through with Ma. She wasn't exactly supportive of my pregnancy. More concerned about her reputation than my well-being. Same old bullshit…'

'I'm sure she was just in shock.'

'She called me loose! My own mother.'

'Oh, I don't know what to say.'

'Nothing to say. I don't want to tell Tommy yet, so please don't say anything.' Lizzie placing the bag by the front door. 'I'm starving, literally hungry all the time.'

'You'll get used to it. Come out back and I'll get you a burger.'

'You go ahead, I just need the bathroom.' Lizzie waited until Hannah was out of sight, went into the kitchen, took two long swigs from the liquor bottle, wiped her mouth with her hand, and topped up her glass. Then she made her grand entry to the backyard party surrounded by the best of Newham. She surveyed the crowd, Tommy's little league team and parents, his crew from O'Donnell & Sons and a couple of local politicians. He had everything, all the trappings of the good life. It was a patriotic crowd all decked out in red, white, and blue. She spotted her nieces standing with their mother by the barbecue and joined them.

'Where's that burger you promised?'

'Aunt Lizzie,' the girls screeched.

'You all were excellent in the parade.' Lizzie grabbed a plate and waited for Tommy to flip her burger. 'I'll have cheese on mine please, Tom.'

'Daddy won the big prize for his float,' Siobhan said. 'Look!' Claire struggled as she carried the trophy over to show Lizzie.'

'That's some prize,' Joe said holding an empty glass.

'Looks like you need a top up. I'll get you another.' Lizzie put her empty plate down and went back into the kitchen, grabbed Joe a cold Bud and topped up her own glass. She was losing control. She knew it, but somehow didn't care as the warm buzz hit her. All that tension dissipating, her body relaxing, she recalled why she enjoyed alcohol so much. She swayed as she walked out into the yard and handed Joe his Bud. 'Happy Fourth of July!' She tapped her glass against his beer bottle. 'What happened to that burger of mine, Tom? Everyone was looking over at her.

'It's just here, come get it.'

She danced her way over to the buffet table, filled her plate with macaroni salad, coleslaw and a scoop of baked beans and presented her empty burger bun to her brother. Her nieces followed behind her like she was the pied piper.

'How much have you had to drink? You're loaded,' Tom said.

'Relax, I'm just celebrating.'

'Don't embarrass yourself or me in front of our guests.' His eyes narrowed.

'You're just like Ma, always worried about what other people will think, ashamed of me, admit it.'

Hannah grabbed Lizzie's plate as it slipped from her hand.

'Come inside with me, it's hard to eat standing up. We can sit at the table.' Hannah walked behind Lizzie as she staggered back into the house. 'What are you thinking? You haven't had just one drink.'

Lizzie shoveled the food into her mouth. 'I haven't eaten all day. The drink went straight to my head, I guess.'

Hannah brought the half empty bottle of Jack Daniels over to the table.

'This was almost full when you arrived. You can lie to yourself, Lizzie, but you can't fool me. You're hurting your baby. I don't know why you're having it if you're going to be so irresponsible. You should've had an abortion like you did in high school.'

'How did you know about that?' Lizzie put down her burger and wiped her mouth.

'Everyone knew, Jeannie told us all.'

Joe stood in the doorway listening. Lizzie looked over at him, heat rose up her neck. The look on his face left no doubt that he had heard it all.

'You can never keep your mouth shut, can you Hannah? I don't feel well, I'm going home.' She watched Hannah pour the bottle of Jack Daniels down the sink. 'Bitch.'

'You're not driving in the state you're in.' Hannah grabbed the keys. 'I'll call you a taxi.'

'I'll take her home,' Joe said, helping Lizzie up from the table.

'I need my bag of linens. It's by the door.'

Fireworks, like man-made shooting stars, lit up the sky over the lake as Joe drove Lizzie back to her cottage. The heavy silence made the journey feel like an eternity. Lizzie's head was spinning, she was already regretting her indulgence. Alcohol might make her feel good, but it blunted her judgement. She had been so good since she discovered she was pregnant, had not had a drop of alcohol. Her problem was that she was an all or nothing girl and when she wanted it all, there were usually dire consequences. That night on her last cruise and tonight, being just two examples.

Joe opened the passenger door and helped her out of the car. She rummaged through her bag and handed him the front door key.

'Interesting choice of keychain,' he said.

'A gift from Tara.' The outside world began to spin, and she spewed vomit across the driveway, whole bits of macaroni landing on her shoes. 'I need to lie down.'

Joe helped her into the bedroom, left her and returned with a glass of water and two Tylenol.

'Is what Hannah said, true?'

'Which bit?'

'Both.' His voice cracked as his eyes welled up. *Was it mine? Is it mine?*

'Yes and no, but…'

'No buts, Lizzie. You should've told me.' He picked up her empty water glass and hurled it across the room, the sound of glass shattering made her jump. Joe stood over her furious tears running down his face. 'You just didn't care about me.'

'I didn't care about anything, or anyone, especially myself.'

'Well, I'm done caring about you.' He stormed out leaving her in a crumpled mess behind.

Lizzie curled up in the fetal position holding her belly and let out a deep moan. What had she done?

Chapter 24

The morning light streamed into the room, almost blinding Lizzie as she reached for her phone. She was fuzzy, fuzzy headed, fuzzy mouthed, fuzzy about the previous evening's events. It hadn't gone well, she remembered that much. The shrill of her mother's voice sent a shooting pain directly to her brain.

'Mary-Elizabeth, where are you? You were supposed to pick me up fifteen minutes ago?'

'I'm on my way, running a few minutes late is all.'

'Well, now you've made me late. Hurry up.'

Lizzie dragged herself out of bed and made for the bathroom. She leaned over the toilet and spat into the bowl, there was nothing left to purge. Looking into the bathroom mirror, she didn't like the person looking back at her. This was not who she had worked so hard to become. Lizzie the cruise director wouldn't unravel like this, she would be cool, calm, collected. She kept her drinking in line, except for the one mishap. What was she doing here? She squirted toothpaste on her finger and brushed her teeth, then splashed some cold water over her face. Still dressed in yesterday's clothes, she grabbed her keys and got into her car hoping she was not over the limit.

Maura was standing by the mailbox as Lizzie pulled up to the house. 'Where did you stay last night? You didn't come home.'

'At the lake, like I told you.'

'You smell terrible,' Maura said giving her the once over. 'And you look a mess. I don't want people at church seeing you in this state, so stay in the car.'

'I'll just drop you around the back and go. That way there's no danger of any of your pious pals seeing me.'

'You need to change your attitude.'

'Sure, Ma, whatever you say.' She pulled into the back of the church and parked. 'If you're that ashamed to be seen with me, then maybe it's time you started driving yourself again.'

Her mother had not driven in over twenty years and there was no way she would have the guts to get behind the wheel again at her age. 'Pick me up at twelve.' She slammed the door and walked off.

*

Famished, Lizzie headed to the diner on the road to Denton and ordered a bacon and egg bagel with melted cheese and took a seat by the window. Her well-ordered life was unravelling. If you look back, you'll soon be going that way. The Chinese fortune cookie was right, she should never have come back. At work she knew who she was, she had order, structure, respect. In Newham, she would never escape her past, she would forever be the girl whose brother was murdered, the girl who had an abortion, the girl with the strange mother, the girl whose father drank himself to death, the girl who didn't belong – a misfit, an 'other'. She undid the button on her jeans, she wouldn't be able to wear these for much longer and reached around to her pocket to answer the vibrating phone, hoping it was Joe. It was Tommy.

'Yeah, Tom?'

'Where are you?'

'I'm getting breakfast at the diner.'

'I need to see you.'

'Look, if you're just going to give me an earful about last night…'

'Hannah told me your…news. I just want to talk.'

'Meet me at my cottage in fifteen minutes. Haven't got long, I've gotta get Ma at twelve.'

As the waitress walked by, Lizzie asked her to wrap her breakfast bagel to go, paid at the counter and headed back out. In the car she unwrapped the bagel, grabbed one half, took a large bite and reversed out of the parking lot. A blob of cheese landed on her lap. She scraped it off and licked her finger clean. The saltiness of the bacon made her thirsty but she'd nothing to wash it down with.

*

Pulling into the driveway, she saw Tommy sitting on the step by the screen door smoking a Marlboro.

'Smoking kills,' she said. 'Don't worry, I won't tell Hannah. Unlike her, I can keep a secret,' she sniped, unable to hide her disdain for her sister-in-law.

'Don't blame Hannah, she was just concerned about you, and it seems with good reason.'

'Always take her side. I asked her not to say anything, she just can't keep her big mouth shut.'

'That's not fair, Lizzie. I could see you were drunk. It was embarrassing.'

'Now, you sound like Ma, more worried about how things look than what I might be going through.'

'Why didn't you just tell me? I'm happy for you if this is what you want.'

'Really? You know it's not Joe's?' She waited for his reaction, expecting him to ask whose it was.

'Han told me. If this is what you want…'

'I don't know what I want anymore. I feel lost.' She wiped her nose and eyes with the back of her hand. 'I stupidly hoped Ma might be supportive for once, but she just thinks I'm a slut.'

'Forget about what Ma thinks, you need to focus on yourself and the baby.'

'I don't need a lecture, Tom. Last night was a one off, I honestly had not had a drink since I found out I was pregnant. Ma set me off.'

'Yeah, I know the feeling. Sometimes you just need to check out, be numb, feel nothing.'

There was a softness in his voice that reminded her of their childhood, to a time when he had always had her back.

'Unlike you, I have to deal with Ma every day, so it's hard to forget about what she thinks when she's shoving her warped morality in my face.'

'Give her time, she'll come around to the idea.' He reached over and put his arm around her. 'Do we need to re-think the renovations? I can create a second bedroom in the attic space.'

'Not just yet.' Lizzie looked at her phone. 'Sorry, I've got to go get Ma soon.'

'Hannah wants you to come for dinner tonight.'

'Not tonight. Tell her to come by if she wants to apologize.' She picked up his cigarette butt from the ground and handed it to him. 'I need to have a shower.'

Chapter 25

The novena group was assembled outside the front of the church as Lizzie pulled up. July was the month they dedicated to the precious blood of Jesus. This devotion to his body parts was a peculiar Catholic practice that struck Lizzie as downright bizarre, but Maura believed in its redemptive capacity, despite the lack of tangible evidence. Had she been praying for Lizzie's redemption or her own? She surveyed the group, but her mom was nowhere in sight. Rolling down the window to ask Maura's whereabouts, she caught Angela Moretti's eye. Joe's mom strained a smile, turned away and walked toward her car. A woman in a seersucker dress pointed in the direction of the rectory and went back to chatting with the group.

The rectory door was held open with a brick, a large fan stood guard in the hallway circulating the humid air. Lizzie waited in the hall and called out several times before walking through to the kitchen where Father Larkin stood next to Maura who was supervising his cookery lesson.

'I'll wait for you in the car, Ma.'

Father Larkin jumped as the wooden spoon slipped from his hand. Red sauce splattered across the floor like a crime scene.

'You shouldn't sneak up on people like that,' Maura said.

'I called through several times; you must've been deep in conversation.' She looked at Father Larkin's flushed face and was disgusted. She knew the type. It made no difference that he was a man of the cloth. To think that she had thought so highly of him. He was using her mother - she just couldn't see it. 'I'll be in the car.'

Lizzie put on the air conditioning and reclined her seat singing along to Iggy Azalea's, Fancy. How this song could have been number one for so many weeks puzzled her, maybe she was getting old. Drifting off, she recalled how fancy her old life was, not quite LA or Tokyo, but it was glamorous compared to where she currently found herself. She was sitting on the beach in Cancun, margarita in hand laughing. Enjoying herself, proper belly laughing, watching the jet skis go by, checking out the talent on the beach. How could she have let guilt drag her back here? She didn't owe anybody anything, certainly not her mother. It was that hook, that hope that just maybe this time, she might get her mother back. That things would be different.

Maura slid into the passenger seat. 'I need to get some shopping done in Denton, then stop at Wegman's on the way home,' She put the sun visor down, slid open the mirror and looked at herself, then brushed a few stray hairs back. 'What are you waiting for?'

Lizzie started the engine and pulled out of the parking lot. 'Which stores do you want to go to in Denton then?'

'I need to go to Bed Bath & Beyond.'

'Fine, I need to go there too.' Lizzie glanced over at Maura, she appeared to be smiling about something. 'All seemed very cozy in the kitchen with Father Larkin.'

'I don't know what you mean. I was teaching him how to cook.' She was indignant, Lizzie had hit a nerve. 'Father Larkin says there are a lot of young couples looking to adopt babies, he could help you, you know, go away, then come back after the baby is born.'

'And why would I want to do that? If I didn't want my baby, I would have aborted it.'

'Mary-Elizabeth!'

'Do you really think I am that incapable of raising my own child?'

'I was thinking more of the baby growing up without a father…'

'I grew up without a mother.' It slipped out, she hadn't meant to say it. 'I didn't…'

'You haven't the first idea about being a parent.' Ma frowned revealing a deep crease between her brows.

'You're right, I haven't, but I'm going to learn. You'll just have to get over the shame of having a bastard grandchild.' Lizzie got out of the car and grabbed two carts.

'We don't need two carts, I'm only getting a couple of things,' Maura said.

'But I need to furnish my house. You can wait for me at the checkout.' She turned right toward the bedding section, the buzz of a new homeowner shopping spree came over her. At thirty she was buying pots and pans, cups and saucers, a kettle and toaster – making a home for the first time in her life. Nesting. Her mother was not going to spoil this for her.

Maura was sitting by the windowsill drinking a bottle of Nestea when Lizzie finished at the checkout. A teenage boy walked next to her carrying a large cardboard box that he loaded into the trunk of the car.

'What is all this?' Maura asked.

'All the stuff for my house, I'm starting from scratch.'

'You aren't seriously going to live there? I thought…'

'You thought what exactly? That I was just having a tantrum, that I'd come back and live with you? Lizzie stared at her. 'Yes, Ma. I'm seriously going to live there. Now let's go to Wegman's.'

*

They went their separate ways around the supermarket. Lizzie managed to fill her cart to the brim even though she was shopping for one. She lugged the groceries out to the car and went back in to find her mother. An intense craving for Klondike ice cream bars had come over her in the supermarket and she didn't want the two boxes to melt in the heat. She found Maura standing in line waiting to buy a lottery ticket from the customer service counter.

'We need to go, Ma. I don't want my frozen food to thaw.'

'I'll only be a minute, it's the Powerball draw tonight.'

'Meet me in the parking lot.' Lizzie took Ma's shopping cart out to the car and unloaded it.

By the time they got back to the house it was well past lunchtime. Lizzie was famished, she seemed to be in a perpetual state of hunger. She put away the groceries while Maura took her place in her recliner.

'It's awfully hot, Lizzie. Turn on the A/C, will you?'

Lizzie came through with a ham and cheese sandwich, chips, and an iced tea for and switched on the A/C.

'Aren't you going to sit and eat with me?'

'No, I've gotta go. I'll pick you up in the morning.'

'I've got the hairdresser at nine o'clock. Don't be late.'

Chapter 26

Lizzie dug through the shopping bag and grabbed the first thing she could find, a container of potato salad. Flicking the lid off, she dipped three fingers in, scooped out a silky white clump and dropped it into her mouth, crunching on little bits of celery. She had nearly polished off the container when she heard voices outside and went to investigate. The three nieces clad in matching unicorn swimsuits peered around the corner, giggling.

'There must be chipmunks out here,' she said loudly and put her head around the corner. 'Aha, I knew there were rodents.'

'We're not chipmunks, Aunt Lizzie, we're unicorns,' Claire said. 'Can we go swimming now?'

'I have a job for you to do first and if you're good, no fighting, I've got Klondike bars. Come help me unload my car.' Lizzie walked toward her car and came face to face with Hannah, tears running down her face. She wasn't in a forgiving mood and uncertain that the tears were genuine; she didn't like being ambushed or emotionally manipulated. Hannah was clever bringing the children along with her, no way Lizzie could kick off.

'I'm so sorry, Lizzie. I didn't mean for Joe to hear…'

'You're sorry Joe heard? Or you're sorry for what you said to me?'

'Both. I know you want this baby. I was just worried about your drinking, what you might do to yourself and the baby.'

'I haven't drunk since I found out I was pregnant. It was a one off, won't happen again.'

Hannah leaned in and hugged Lizzie. 'Do you want me to talk to Joe?'

'I think you've done enough already.' Hannah had a point but Lizzie wasn't ready to let her off the hook just yet. 'If you want to be helpful, carry some of these bags in. There's a lot of unpacking to do.'

They emptied the bags and began to set up house. Lizzie went back out to the car and lifted the heavy cardboard box, carrying it into the bedroom. She slid the air conditioner into the open window and turned it on to maximum. The cool air blew on to her face. The clatter of silverware and kitchen utensils being put away in the kitchen distracted her. Little girls playing house. They were in their element.

'Come see, Lizzie, we've made your house beautiful. Can we go swimming now?' The three girls bounced up and down like Mexican jumping beans.

'Wow, you've done a fantastic job. I should've hired you girls sooner. Let me find your mommy and we can all go down to the dock together.' Lizzie walked through to the bedroom where Hannah was folding her old set of sheets. 'You didn't need to make my bed for me, Han.'

'I needed something to do. I really am sorry.'

'C'mon, the girls are itching to get in the water. Your ankles look hideous, would do you good to get them in some cool water.'

'Last one in is a rotten egg.' Lizzie raced down the lawn to the dock and jumped in. 'The temperature's perfect, jump in girls.' She tread water waiting while each girl mustered up the courage to jump in, giving each one a big clap. 'Right, you all stay in this shallow end. I'm going to keep your mommy company in the sunshine.' She climbed up the ladder and spread her towel out on the dock next to Hannah.

'You were right, the water feels good. I think the swelling is going down already.'

'I hope mine don't end up like that.' Lizzie looked at Hannah's belly extending over her bikini like a giant beer gut. 'Doesn't seem possible that my belly will look like yours in a few months.' She put her hand on her stomach. 'Am I showing yet?'

'I can see a tiny bump, but I already know you're pregnant. I doubt strangers would notice yet.'

'Did Jeannie really tell everyone that I had an abortion?'

'I might have exaggerated a bit, but she did tell a few of us in the locker room at school. Not in a gossipy malicious way, she was just upset as I recall.'

'Why was she upset? I was the one who was pregnant.'

'I think she felt guilty, you know, that she had helped kill your baby.' Hannah looked down at her feet in the water and fluttered them.

'Oh. She was supportive at the time but then she distanced herself from me. I was more alone than ever, and Tommy was at college.' Lizzie waved to the girls splashing in the water. 'How about doing some handstands for us?'

'We're happy for you Lizzie. I know you're kind of unconventional and sure, people here will talk, but we're here for you. Your Ma will come around eventually, give her time.'

'I'm more worried about Joe than Ma. I don't know what to say to him.'

'Can we have Klondike bars now? The girls stood shivering on the dock while Hannah handed them towels.

'Sure, go get them from the freezer and bring one down for each of us.' Lizzie looked at Hannah. 'Do you think Joe will ever forgive me?

'You were sixteen, I might've done the same. If he doesn't forgive you then the friendship's not worth much.' Hannah smiled at the girls walking down the lawn, hands and faces already covered in melting ice cream. 'They're going to need to go back in the water to wash their faces.'

Lizzie unwrapped the silver foil and took a bite into the crunchy chocolate coating until the cold vanilla ice cream gave her a brain freeze. A few more bites and she had devoured the whole bar.

'I'm hungry all the time. Is this how it's going to be from now on?'

'Pretty much, except the last few weeks when there's no more room and every time you eat you get terrible heartburn.' Hannah called to the girls that it was time to leave. 'Come say goodbye and thank you to Lizzie.'

'Can't we stay, maybe we could have a sleepover?' Claire asked.

'Aunt Lizzie has only just moved in so let's leave her to get settled. You're welcome to come eat at our house tonight if you want.'

'Thanks, but I'm tired, think I'll have a quiet night in.' Lizzie smiled at the unicorns dancing up the lawn to their car, as they turned and waved. She had thought she wanted a boy, but these girls had changed her mind. She'd wait for the surprise.

Wandering back up to the house, she took off her swimsuit, towel dried her hair and crawled under the covers of the freshly made bed. She wasn't used to napping during the day. At work she would have been on high alert, no time for tiredness. The crisp sheets were cool against her skin, she gave into her fatigue and let her body relax, drifting off to sleep, finding herself alone, floating in a rowboat through dense fog. Disoriented, her heart was racing. Panicking in the silence, she called out, only to hear the echo of her own voice. Where was she? It was somehow familiar to her. She reached for the oars and began rowing, the sound of the water lapped around her. She saw the hands on the oar and froze. The weight of him pulling himself up tipped the boat and plunged her into the dark water. He climbed in and laughed. 'I'm not going down for this,' he said. She looked up at Jason Edwards' face as she fell into the depths. Lizzie sat bolt upright in bed gasping, holding her chest. It's just a dream, it's just a dream.

*

The sound of the dawn fishing boats heading out for an early morning bass competition woke her. In the morning mist they moved like an invisible swarm of locusts, engines screeching and echoing as they charged across the lake. She grabbed her phone and realized she had slept through the night. Despite her nightmare, it had been her longest sleep for weeks. Had it not been for a sudden urge to pee, she would have stayed in bed, but since she had risen, she took in the sunrise. Holding her mug, she looked out at the lake.

There was no rowboat. Jason Edwards must have been occupying a space in her subconscious despite there having been no press coverage recently. She could only imagine what it must be like to sit in prison for months awaiting trial having protested your innocence.

A crow cawed from a tree in the cottage next door. The row of identical tiny cottages had been unoccupied over the holiday period which surprised her, especially in this heatwave. She had meant to ask Tara for the neighbors' details, in a friendly way, to introduce herself, but otherwise was happy to be left alone. She would stop by Franklin Realty after collecting Ma.

Pangs from her stomach sent her to the kitchen. She pulled the box of batter mix from the shelf and poured it into the bowl, added some oil, an egg and water, then stirred. Scooping the batter, she poured it into the pan and watched the air bubbles rise and pop on the pancakes as they cooked before flipping them, aiming to get the perfect golden finish. The intensity of her hunger made her wonder if something was wrong with her, until she remembered that she had slept through dinner the previous day. She slid the stack on to the plate, spreading a layer of butter between each pancake before drowning them in maple syrup. Pancakes were harder to cook than people imagined. Two batches had already gone into the garbage blackened from distraction - too much nonsense inside her head. She went out to the screened in porch and cut into the fluffy white cakes, swirling the forkful around to mop up extra syrup before putting it into her mouth. With the boats gone, the lake was still except for the occasional ripple on the surface, the remnants of rings left by fish jumping for air. Having finished the last bite, she looked around like a guilty child then licked the plate to get the last of the syrup. There was no one around to tell her off, in any case, this was her house, and she made the rules.

Heading over to her mother's she had almost put Joe out of her mind until she saw his squad car parked in the spot usually occupied by his Jeep outside the police station. She was relieved he was nowhere to be seen. The guilt was there for a reason, a reminder that she had done something wrong. Not the abortion, she didn't regret that, but yes, she should have told Joe. It was all so long ago for her, but a fresh wound for him, that much she did understand. He would need time and sorry wasn't going to fix it.

The Denton Times

Keeping the community informed with independent local reporting

COLD CASE MURDER SUSPECT CHARGE DROPPED FOLLOWING 'NEW EVIDENCE'

By Tina Chandler
July 6, 2014

Denton, MA. – A Harewood county prosecutor has dropped one of the charges against a man accused of two counts of sexual assault and second-degree murder after new evidence was submitted. Jason Edwards no longer faces a sexual assault charge relating to an incident that took place in Denton in March 2014.

Edwards, 39, was arrested and charged with sexual assault following a night out at the Promises Nightclub in Denton. He pleaded not guilty at his pre-trial hearing and has maintained his innocence since his arrest.

Prosecutor, Matthew Brooks stated, 'We have a duty to keep cases under continuing review and following new evidence that emerged which contradicted the alleged victim's version of events, the charge was dropped. Dylan Jones, 37, of Newham, falsely claimed that he was raped in the parking lot of Promises Nightclub after having stopped to assist a motorist in need.

An informant familiar with the case told the Denton Times that Jones, a married man and father of two, fabricated the assault story to hide his homosexual double life from his wife. The county prosecutor's office refused to comment further on the case.

Mr. Edwards' defense attorney, Eileen Murphy stated, 'While Mr. Edwards is relieved that this charge has been dropped, this false accusation has ruined his life. He vehemently maintains his innocence of the remaining charges and I look forward to defending him in court. In the meantime, I will be asking Judge Baxter to review his decision to withhold bail.'

Edwards remains on remand in Harewood County Prison pending trial for the sexual assault and second-degree murder of Patrick O'Donnell in March 1993. A trial date has been set for November 15, 2014.

Mr. Jones could not be reached for comment.

Chapter 27

Lizzie sat on the wooden bench on the front porch reading the article. The headline was misleading, not surprising as it was written by Tina Chandler, the woman was prone to exaggeration and sensationalism. She breathed a sigh of relief, the charges relating to Paddy's death stood but how unlucky for Jason Edwards. The impact that one unfortunate event can have. Had he not been falsely accused he would have got away with murder and Lizzie would have been back at sea, enjoying life. She wouldn't have minded never knowing who killed Paddy, her mother was the only person it mattered to. How one lie can change the course of someone's life. No way to rewind. That went for Dylan Jones too. What a shocker. Had he been confessing his sins to Father Larkin the day she saw him rush out of the confessional?

'Morning Ma.' She threw the paper on the kitchen table and called again from the bottom of the stairs.

'You're early.'

'You told me not to be late.' She scrunched up her face then tried to relax it trying to maintain her cool.

'Fix me a coffee, I'm just coming.'

Lizzie did as she was told then sat down at the kitchen

table. She wasn't sure if she should alert her mother to the paper's headline or just leave it on the table for her to find. Either way there would be drama to deal with.

'Did you get my paper?' Maura called as she came down the stairs. She looked pale as she sat down at the table.

'You alright, Ma? You don't look good.'

'I'm not sleeping very well these last few nights. All this business with you and Joe, it's very upsetting.' She sipped her coffee and reached for the paper.

'There's an article about Jason Edwards. They've dropped one of the charges.'

'Oh, lord.'

'It's not the charges relating to Paddy's death, it's the recent charge, the one that got him arrested in the first place.' Lizzie watched Ma's hands shake as she read the paper.

'This Dylan Jones, I think your father was in the Lions Club with his father.'

'I think I remember him, he had an electrical company, didn't he?

'Yes. That's it. His poor mother and his poor wife to find out he was a homosexual, a deviant like that.'

At least there was someone for the town to gossip about other than the O'Donnell's for once. And surely being an unwed mother was less shameful than being caught cruising in a parking lot.

'What about being falsely accused?' That seemed a great injustice.

'He killed Paddy, that's what's unjust – robbing me of my son, Paddy never growing old.' Ma wiped her nose with her tissue. 'Why didn't Joe come tell us this news? Call him and find out what's happened.'

'I'll do that later, we need to get you to the hairdresser.'

*

Lizzie pressed the entry bell and was buzzed into the police station by a young constable. He seemed so cheerful, too cheerful given the seriousness of his job.

'I'll get Officer Kominsky for you. Take a seat.' He dashed off before Lizzie could say that it was Joe she was looking for. As she sat waiting, the young officer kept looking over at her. His attention was unsettling. She was about to ask him if there was some sort of problem when Officer Kominsky called her through to his office.

'I'm sorry to keep you waiting, Miss O'Donnell. A bit short staffed today.'

'I was actually looking for Joe, I don't mean to take up your time.'

'Officer Moretti is on vacation, two weeks in the Cape I believe.'

'Oh… he never said.'

'Last minute decision, he needed to use his days or lose them. But what can I do for you?'

'We saw the article about one of the charges against Jason Edwards being dropped. My mother is distraught and wants to know why the police didn't tell us in advance. She thought that was Joe's job as family liaison officer.'

'Had Joe been here I'm sure he would've informed you in person, but he left two days ago. I'm afraid this is my fault, I should've stopped by to break the news to your mother. I know how fragile she is.'

'Is the article true though?'

'It's true that the charge has been dropped. I can't comment on the rest.'

He wasn't giving much away, but neither had Joe when she came to think of it. She'd asked him about Dylan Jones and had received an equally vague response. Was there some kind of connection between him and Paddy? And the crucifix, she was certain Paddy had had one similar. Dark grey with two loaves and fish engraved on it. It was unusual.

'What are the chances that he'll be released on bail?'

'I honestly can't say. That's down to Judge Baxter. His lawyer has requested a new bail hearing. Don't think it's been scheduled yet, but I'll let you know when I have any news.'

'And will the bail hearing be public?'

'Should be unless the judge decides to deal with it in his chambers.'

'Like I said, I'll let you know when I have news.'

The young officer grinned at Lizzie as he buzzed her out of the station. It was as if he knew something that she didn't. Joe had left without a word. She had made such a mess of things again and couldn't see a way forward.

'Well, what did Joe say?' Ma slid into the passenger seat checking her hair in the mirror.

'Your hair looks lovely. She did a nice job on the color.'

'I don't know what you mean, this is my own color. I'm blessed not to have grey hair.'

Had she not been around for months and watched the roots change from chestnut to grey, Lizzie would almost have believed her.

'Joe's on vacation. Officer Kominsky confirmed that the one charge has been dropped and that Edwards has applied for a new bail hearing.'

'They're not going to let that monster out, are they?'

'That's for the judge to decide. Officer Kominsky said he'll let us know when he has any news.'

'Why didn't Joe tell you he was going away?'

'I don't know, Ma.' Lizzie shrugged her shoulders, if she had a different mother, a supportive one, she might have confided in her. But hers was incapable of suspending judgement or extending any empathy where Lizzie was concerned. For many years Lizzie believed there was something wrong with her. Her mother blamed her; she had always known that. Growing up she hadn't appreciated just how abnormal their 'normal' was. She had adapted, managed, like kids do. The best strategy for dealing with her was the one Lizzie had adopted – put an ocean between them.

'I'll ask Angela when I next see her at church.'

'Whatever Ma. Anywhere you need me to take you?'

'Just home. I don't want to miss my soap.'

Lizzie pulled the car up in front of the house and unclipped her seatbelt.

'You don't need to come in, I'm fine. Just pick me up at ten o'clock tomorrow.' Ma walked up the path, lifted her arm and waved with her back to Lizzie then let herself into the house. This was how it was going to be – no mention of the baby Lizzie was carrying.

Chapter 28

Early August ushered in a new heatwave, the air so thick with humidity, it was like she had just stepped out of a hot shower. Even the refrigerator door was sweating. Floating in the water was the only way to stay cool, though the lake was rapidly approaching bath water temperature. She was stretched out like a starfish, gazing down at the tiny swell of her belly when she felt it for the first time. At first, she dismissed it as gas, but the nervous little twitches persisted like a tumbling motion inside her. Butterflies, quickening, her baby was moving. A wave of emotion welled up inside her. She rolled over and dove down to the cooler water to wash the hot sticky tears from her face. Sitting with conflicting feelings was more difficult than she had imagined. The elation of her baby moving for the first time alongside the profound sadness of having no one with whom to share it. She climbed up the ladder on to the dock, grabbed her bottle of water and glugged back. It was one of those days when she could drink constantly, but her thirst never satisfied.

The faint sound of a phone ringing came from the house. She sprinted up the lawn hoping it might be Joe. She knew he had returned from his vacation two weeks earlier, but she hadn't had the courage to call him. The screen lit up, missed call from Hannah. She tried not to feel disappointed as she dialed.

'Hi Han. Sorry, I missed your call. I was trying to stay cool in the water.'

'It's pretty oppressive out there. Our A/C is out, the girls are driving me crazy, and my ankles are like two beach balls. I was wondering if we could come by for a swim?'

'Yeah, that's fine. I'm not going anywhere, you can hang out as long as you'd like.'

'Great, I'll bring a picnic. Anything you want me to pick up from the grocery store?'

'I'm good. Just come over when you're ready.' Lizzie opened the door to her bedroom, the rush of cool air enveloped her, and she collapsed on her bed. The fatigue was debilitating some days. She couldn't imagine holding down a job at the moment and had no idea how Hannah was managing to run after three children while heavily pregnant.

The sound from a glass shattering was followed by a cacophony of 'Shsshs's'. The nieces had arrived. Lizzie laid in bed staring at the ceiling, the wood knot owls staring back at her. She wished they could speak, she needed some of their wisdom. The whispers outside the door grew louder until there was a tentative knock and the door cracked open enough to reveal three sets of grey eyes.

'Girls, come away from the door.' Hannah's voice sounded sharp, the heat must have been taking its toll on her. Lizzie stood up and stretched in her damp bikini. She had no idea how long she'd been asleep but was better for it. Hannah's voice was raised again; she needed rescuing. Lizzie practiced her best auntie smile in the mirror in preparation for her grand entrance.

'Well, well. What have you all been up to out here? I heard mice scrambling around.'

'We brought a picnic, but mommy says it's too hot to sit outside and eat.' Claire protested while the other two nodded in agreement.

'How about I steal your mom away since she's no fun and we'll have our own picnic?' Lizzie took Hannah by the arm, led her into the bedroom and ordered her to lie down on the bed. The girls slipped off her sandals and placed a pillow under her feet. 'Go get your mom a cold washcloth from the bathroom.' Lizzie turned up the aircon. 'You rest here. I'll take care of them.' Lizzie looked at Hannah's poor ankles and tried not to laugh, then placed the cool cloth on her forehead. 'C'mon girls, let's get some lunch. I think we'll be alright if we spread the blanket under the tree in the shade.'

A new bead of sweat ran down Lizzie's face as she dropped a dollop of macaroni salad on each of the plates. She sliced the Portuguese rolls in half and spread mayonnaise on each side then instructed the girls to choose their filling – ham, chicken, or cheese. Three little sets of hands delved into the tortilla chip bag pulling out great handfuls and sprinkling them on to their plates. 'You girls go get settled on the blanket and I'll bring the lemonade and cups down.' She took the pitcher from the fridge, added a load of ice, grabbed the paper cups and her plate of food, balancing it all as she made her way down to the picnic area. Lizzie listened to the girls chatting about their friends and who they wanted to invite to their respective birthday parties while they ate lunch. The friendship politics of young girls was exhausting; she hoped she might be spared this with her own child. She lay on her back and looked up at the leaves rustling on the branches above. The wind was picking up.

'Your tummy is looking fat, Aunt Lizzie, you ate too much lunch,' Siobhán said.

'Yes, it is a bit fat.' She didn't want to tell them she was pregnant without their mother around, there might be questions about mechanics that she didn't want to answer. 'How about we cool off in the water? Go grab your life vests and we can have a nice float.' She gathered up the plates, swatting the flies away from the half-eaten sandwiches, and carried them up to the house. From the window she watched the girls struggling to blow up an inflatable unicorn, each taking it in turn to pant into the nozzle. White caps appeared on the lake as the wind rushed across. A severe weather warning had been issued for late afternoon with scattered thunderstorms and flash flooding. It was hard to predict which direction the storm would take.

'I think this might help.' Lizzie handed them the foot pump and watched as they took turns jumping up and down on it until the unicorn came to life. 'I think we should put a rope around the unicorn's neck, so she doesn't fly away in the breeze.' She tied the lead around its neck and carried it down to the water. The girls jockeyed for position on the float, elbowing one another until the smallest fell in. She resurfaced, giggled and with great determination pulled herself back on to the float. Lizzie pulled them around as they took turns feigning falling in, then jumping back on, amazed by their stamina. She tied her end of the rope on to the dock and climbed out of the water. The dark clouds in the distance were moving quickly, bringing with them rumbles of thunder.

'Time to get out girls, storm's coming.' She gathered up the towels from the dock while the girls continued to splash each other in the water, ignoring her request. 'Out, now!'

She was starting to sound like a mother with her shouting. The girls hopped out and wrapped themselves up in the towels as Lizzie walked up to the house.

'What about our unicorn?' Claire shouted.

'It's tied up, it'll be fine.' Lizzie waved popsicles around in the air and the girls came running. She was also getting the knack of bribery. They climbed up on the kitchen stools slurping their frozen treats and watched the storm draw nearer, the trees writhing and flailing in the wind as the sky darkened. It was hard to imagine this was the same lake that earlier that morning had been serene, its surface still like a sheet of glass. Lizzie looked in Hannah's beach bag and pulled out a pad of paper and box of crayons. 'How about we draw the storm?' She tore off a sheet of paper for each girl and spread the crayons out on the kitchen table.

'You too, Lizzie, you need to draw with us.' Claire pointed toward the dock. 'Look, our unicorn is flying.' The wind had lifted the inflatable toy and it was hovering above the angry white caps, its white body and rainbow mane standing out against the blackened sky. A clap of thunder made them all jump and huddle up against Lizzie. 'One, one thousand, two one thousand…' Claire counted. A bolt of lightning flashed across the lake. 'It's getting nearer.' Then the rain came, torrential sheets of water running down the windows rendering the lake invisible.

'Isn't it amazing to watch girls? Be grateful that we are on dry land. When we get storms at sea the whole ship rocks and passengers get sick everywhere.'

'Yuck. Do you have to clean it up?'

'Not me personally, but yes, the staff has to clean it up.' Lizzie put the finishing touches on her flying unicorn.

'Gross. Are you going to go back to work on ships again?'

'Maybe one day, but not anytime soon. I'm going to be around for a while.'

'That's good. You're more fun than Grandma.'

'Siobhan!' Claire said.

'What? It's true,' Siobhán rolled her eyes and kept on coloring.

Lizzie's phone lit up; it was Tommy.

'Hey Lizzie, you okay out there, you got power?' he said.

'Yeah, we're fine. I've got Hannah and the girls here with me.'

'Good, cos a bunch of trees have come down bringing the power lines down with them. The power's out in town. Ma called me in a panic. Is it okay if I bring her over?'

'If you have to.'

'Power's out at our place too so I'll stop and pick up a bucket of fried chicken from the deli for dinner. And… uh, well maybe Ma should stay with you tonight.'

'Seriously, Tom?'

'You've got power.'

'Great, thanks. Stop at your house and get an air mattress, cos I'm not sharing a bed with her.' Lizzie put the phone down. 'Looks like we're going to have a party here tonight girls.' The shrieks of approval pierced her eardrums.

*

The storm passed, blowing in an area of high pressure with cooler, drier weather. By the time Tommy arrived with Ma, the skies were blue again and the children were on the dock fishing.

'They shouldn't be down there by themselves.' Ma's first words as she entered the house.

'They're wearing life vests and I've been watching them.' Lizzie passed a bowl of chips to Tommy. 'Why don't you go down and give these to your daughters. I only came up to the house to get them a snack.'

'Where's Hannah?' Tommy put the bucket of chicken on the counter.

'Asleep in my bedroom for the last four hours. Leave her. I'll wake her in a minute.' Lizzie emptied the bucket of chicken out on a baking tray, put it in the oven to keep it warm then set about making a salad while Maura sat staring at her. 'Why don't you give me a hand Ma?'

'I'm very tired. Can you pour me a glass of wine?'

'I don't have any alcohol in the house, just lemonade or

iced tea. Which will it be?' Lizzie tapped her fingernail on the counter waiting for a response.

'Can't you…' Ma started, but then stopped. 'Never mind.'

Lizzie handed her mother a chopping board, knife, cucumber, and tomatoes. Maura looked up at her then eventually picked up the knife and began to chop the vegetables. She could hear the girls shrieking as Tommy threw them one by one into the water.

'Have you been looking after them all this time?' Ma tossed the vegetables into the salad bowl, then grabbed the head of lettuce and began to tear the leaves. 'I'm surprised Hannah was comfortable leaving them with you for so long. You have no experience looking after children.'

'Hannah was struggling with the heat and her ankles, she needed a rest.'

'Only another few weeks to go and I'll have a grandson. I finished the baby blanket.'

'That's nice.' Lizzie went into her bedroom to wake Hannah and emerged in a striped bikini.

'Good Lord, put some clothes on. That's obscene. Have you no shame?'

'You might be ashamed of my pregnancy, but I'm not. Hannah will be out in a minute. I'm going swimming.' She turned her back on her mother and headed down to the water, managing to let go of her rage as she jumped on the floating unicorn and joined in the fun.

*

By the time the children, Tommy and Lizzie came up to the house Hannah was sitting at the table with Maura, the table set and ready to eat. Hannah had disengaged written all over her face, the look Lizzie often got when Ma had been bending her ear for too long, that gone away to a distant planet look. Hannah leapt up from the table when Lizzie came into the kitchen, making a quick escape.

'I've got everything ready. Just need to get the chicken out of the oven.' Hannah seemed so eager to please. 'Thanks for letting me sleep for so long. I couldn't believe I slept for four hours, I didn't even hear the storm.'

'The storm was amazing, you can ask the girls. Now let me see those ankles.' Lizzie looked down at Hannah's legs relieved to see the swelling had gone.

'Back to normal.' Hannah opened the oven and pulled out the tray.

'I'll do that, you go get the girls seated and catch up with Tommy.'

Lizzie carried the platter of chicken over to the table and took a seat on a folding chair. She was about to reach for a chicken drumstick, caught her mother glaring at her, and put her arm down.

'Bless us oh Lord and these our gifts which we are about to receive from thy bounty through Christ our Lord, Amen.' Maura had to play the matriarch wherever she went.

'Girls, can you believe your mommy slept through the storm, all that thunder and rain? 'Lizzie refused to let Ma take control in her own home. 'You should show her the pictures we all drew.'

'The unicorn flew, Mommy. So high, it almost flew away,' Siobhán said.

'And Martha jumped into Aunt Lizzie's lap when the thunder crashed,' Claire said.

'To be fair, I think we all jumped when that hit.' Lizzie bit into the chicken drumstick. 'Nice crunchy coating, Tom.'

'I think Jefferson's deli counter does the best fried chicken, Wegman's can't compete.' Tommy glanced over at Ma. 'Don't you think, Ma?'

'I suppose. I saw Angela Moretti today.' Maura scooped up a forkful of macaroni salad and slid it into her mouth. 'She says Joe is back.'

'Yeah, I saw him outside the police station yesterday.' Tommy reached forward and grabbed a chicken wing from the platter. 'Didn't have time to stop and talk.'

'Daddy, you're being greedy.' Claire giggled and took another piece for herself.

'She's got a point, Tom. You've had four pieces of chicken already. Me and Lizzie are the ones who are supposed to be eating for two?' The words came out of Hannah's mouth before she had engaged her brain.'

'Why does Aunt Lizzie need to eat for two? Claire asked.

'Because I'm having a baby too. You're all going to have a new cousin in January.'

'You shouldn't be telling…,' Maura interrupted, her face reddening.

'And before you ask, I don't have a husband like your mom.'

'Does that mean you're a lesbian?' Claire chomped on a carrot stick. 'Because we know there are all different kinds of families, right Mommy?'

'Yes, Claire. That's right. There are,' Hannah said.

'But no, I'm not a lesbian. The baby's daddy just isn't around anymore.' Lizzie looked over at Tommy for some assistance.

'Aunt Lizzie's baby is lucky because it will have all of us as its family.' Tommy squirmed uncomfortably in his seat.

'I can't believe the nonsense children are being taught these days.' Ma said stone faced. 'Angela said that everyone in town will think that Lizzie's baby is Joe's. She's upset about it.' She wiped her eyes with her napkin. 'I can't believe you are putting me through this.'

'Girls, why don't you go outside and collect some sticks for the campfire, it's starting to get dark.' Tommy was trying his best to deflect and not to subject his daughters to their grandmother's tirade.

'I'll bring the bag of marshmallows down when we've finished clearing up.' Lizzie's whole body was raging, but her voice was calm. She was not going to allow Maura to do this to her.

'I'd like you to take me home, Tommy.' Maura stood and made her way towards the door.

'But there's no…' Tommy looked at Lizzie and rolled his eyes.

'I have an oil lamp and flashlight. I'll be fine.'

'I don't think…'

'Don't argue with her, Tom. Take her home if that's what she wants.' Lizzie stacked the plates, carried them over to the sink and started washing up. 'Hannah, grab yourself a chair down by the firepit. I'll be down as soon as I finish.'

'I can give you a hand, Lizzie.' Hannah put her arm around Lizzie and gave her a squeeze and whispered, 'I'm so sorry, you didn't deserve that.'

'Go on Tommy, get Ma home. The girls will be wanting their fire soon.' Lizzie walked to the door. 'I'll pick you up at ten for your hospital appointment, Ma.'

*

Lizzie and Hannah sat by the firepit looking out at the water, the lake had returned to its calm state, if only she could do the same.

'You shouldn't let Ma get to you like that.' Tommy had somehow managed to make a roaring fire despite most of the kindling being damp. 'She's set in her ways, we can't expect her to change.'

'I think Lizzie has every right to feel upset. Your mother was vile.' Hannah slid a marshmallow on a stick and thrust it into the flames. 'You don't understand, she doesn't do it to you.'

'She's a misogynist.' Lizzie peeled the charred outer crust from her marshmallow and sucked back the gooey inside. 'And a hypocrite.'

'What do you mean?' Hannah asked.

'You didn't tell her, Tom?' Lizzie shook her head in disbelief. 'Ma got pregnant before she was married, but her fiancé died. Our dad, his best friend, married her and raised Paddy as his own.'

'Oh my god, she's kept that a secret all these years?'

'She'll change her tune once you have the baby.' Tommy stoked the fire, the logs were nearly out. 'Pass me that newspaper, I need to get this going again.'

Lizzie picked up the paper and noticed a photo of Dylan Jones on the front page. It was dated fifth of August. Jones was coming out of the courthouse handcuffed.

'Did you see this? Dylan Jones has been arrested on obstruction of justice charges.' She passed the paper to Tommy. 'Do you think he knew Paddy?'

'Dunno.' His brow furrowed. 'Yeah, they were altar boys together. Think they might've both wrestled.' Tommy shredded the paper into strips and placed it under the logs. 'Are the girls okay, Han?'

'They're fast asleep on Lizzie's bed. They had such a great time with you today.' Hannah reached out for Lizzie's hand. 'You're going to be a great mom, Lizzie.'

'With everything that happened today I forgot to tell you that I felt the baby move for the first time.' She put her hands on her belly and smiled.

'It's a weird but amazing sensation, isn't it? Listen, Tommy meant what he said, you've got all of us to support you. Right, Tom?'

'Yup. It's getting late. We should be going.'

'I'm gonna stay here by the fire for a little longer. You guys okay to see yourselves out?' Lizzie wrapped an oversized sweater around her and moved her chair closer to the fire. She couldn't get the photo of Dylan Jones out of her mind.

Chapter 29

Lizzie stepped out of the car and undid the button on her shorts. She was nearing the point at which maternity clothes with elastic panels would be required. The coffee shop was almost empty, save a table of elderly women chatting about someone or other's hysterectomy. She bought a coffee and cinnamon bun and sat down on the sofa by the window. It was too early to pick up her mother and she wanted to limit her exposure to the negativity that undoubtedly would be thrown her way. She broke the bun in half releasing the most divine aroma and popped a piece in her mouth.

'They're the best, aren't they?' Tara was standing by the counter. Lizzie had forgotten how tall she was. 'Do you mind if I join you?'

'Not at all. I've got to go pick up my mom in ten minutes. Hospital appointment.' Lizzie took a sip of her coffee and pulled another piece from the sticky bun. 'Sit down.'

'I haven't seen you since you closed on the house, except a quick wave at the parade.' Tara fidgeted with her engagement ring nervously. 'I heard a rumor…but didn't want to ask, is it true you're…'

'Pregnant?' Lizzie could see how uncomfortable Tara was, better to put her out of her misery. 'Yes, Tara. I'm pregnant and no, Joe is not the father.'

'I didn't mean… I'm sorry. It's just that word seems to have spread.'

'It's okay, I'm not with the father and I'm really happy about the pregnancy. You did a great thing for me getting me the cottage.'

'Oh, I'm so happy for you.' Tara's face relaxed. 'We'll need to throw you a baby shower.'

'I'm not sure that's a good idea, but I appreciate the offer.' She could see the disappointment on Tara's face. 'You have plenty to do with your wedding coming up. If you need help choosing a cruise for your honeymoon, I'm happy to help.'

'Would you? That would be fantastic.' Tara reverted to her bubbly self.

'I meant to ask, was your brother friends with Dylan Jones?'

'Oh, now that is a scandal. Ted knew him from Our Lady of Lourdes, they were altar boys together.' Tara leaned forward to whisper. 'You know they've arrested him.'

'Yeah, I saw it in the paper. What's Ted said about it?'

'I talked to him on the phone, his voice was very shaky. He seemed upset but didn't want to talk about it. Hard to say, he's up and down a lot of the time in rehab. But something's not right.'

Lizzie looked down at her phone. 'Shit, lost track of time, I better get going. Can't have Maura late for her appointment.'

*

Lizzie had grown accustomed to the silent journeys. Conversation limited to collection and drop off times, with the odd errand or shopping list added in for good measure. It was almost a relief to not have to put up the pretense. Maura glanced over at the speedometer, then looked away.

'Something wrong, Ma?'

'You're speeding.' She was itching to pick a fight for some reason.

'I'm going forty.'

'More like fifty.'

Lizzie took her foot off the accelerator and watched the speedometer fall to thirty-five.

'I think it's time you bought your own car.'

'Fine.'

'Tommy says he'll take me out practice driving, so I'll need my car back.'

'Fine.' Lizzie pulled up in front of the hospital main entrance. 'I'll drop you here and go park.'

'No need. I'll go in by myself. Pick me up at two o'clock.' She got out of the car, adjusted the belt on her checked seersucker dress and headed toward the revolving door.

*

Lizzie had three hours to kill and made her way back to her mother's house. The key was still in the glass bowl. She opened the door, the hairs on the back of her neck lifted. It was the smell, Maura had been burning incense and candles in the room. A set of rosary beads lay on the desk next to a small bottle of what appeared to be holy water and a crucifix and chain. She took the crucifix in her hand and examined it. It had the same engravings as the one she had returned to Dylan Jones. What strange ritual had Maura been conducting? Probably something recommended by Father Larkin. Rummaging through his closet, she found what she was looking for, Paddy's 1992 Newham High School Yearbook. Careful to leave everything else in place, she grabbed the book and locked the room, returning the key to its rightful position in the bowl. A strong scent of lilies in the air, she followed it to the living room where a bouquet of flowers sat on the coffee table. A plastic stick with a card attached was lodged in between the flower stems. 'Maura, thank you for all you are doing for me, Peter.' A bit too familiar for Lizzie's liking. It had made her wonder if her mother's brief had extended beyond cooking.

She wrapped the yearbook in a plastic bag and locked it in the trunk. There would be plenty of time in the evening to look through it. On the way back to Denton she pulled into the parking lot of the public library, hoping they would have an archive of The Denton Times. It had been years since she had set foot in a library and hadn't a clue how to search for anything on the computer system.

'I'm looking for some newspaper articles from the Denton Times,' She found it impossible not to stare at the multiple piercings on the receptionist's face. He couldn't have been more than eighteen but had fully embraced the gothic look.

'What year?' He was reading and barely looked up at her. She focused on the yellow and red cover, Zodiac, the shocking true story of the nation's most bizarre mass murderer.

'1993.'

'What dates you looking for?'

'Mid-March to about September, I think.'

He pulled out a box of rolls and handed it to her.

'What's this?'

'What you asked for.' He stared at her with a look of dumb insolence. 'They're on microfiche. The reader's over there.' He pointed to a carrel in the back corner of the reading room. 'You know how to use it?'

'I'll manage.' She didn't need the humiliation of this surly youth giving her a demonstration.

'I need to see some ID and sign here.' He sat back down at the desk and resumed reading. Lizzie handed him her driver's license, he yawned and looked at her. 'I've seen you in the paper, haven't I?'

She signed the form, turned away and carried the rolls over toward the carrel.

'Hey, wait. You'll need this.' He handed her a box. 'It's the lens for the microfiche reader. Just slide it into the slot and turn the dial to focus.' He stood staring at her. 'It's sick how they found the guy who killed your brother after all this time.'

It was unsettling to have strangers recognize her let alone an apparent true crime devotee. She feared he might ask for her autograph next. Perfect stalker material. He was back at his desk but had taken his phone out. Shit, was he taking a photo of her? She didn't have the energy to confront him and sat down in front of the reader, realizing that she should have paid more attention in school when they did their library visits.

The ON button was in clear view at least. She powered up the machine and opened the glass plate, then inserted the reel of film on to the spindle and thread it under the rollers and plate through to the right-hand side on to the empty spool. So far, so good. She found the fast forward knob, turned, and listened to the whirring noise it made, but the screen looked empty until she realized, she had not put the lens in. As she twisted the dial on the lens an image came into focus. She fast forwarded to the thirteenth March 1993 headline, Storm of The Century to hit East Coast, not realizing that the storm had been so widespread closing every airport from Halifax, Nova Scotia to Tampa. Turning the dial slowly, she moved forward a few days and stopped when she saw the headline.

The Denton Times

Keeping the community informed with independent local reporting

LOCAL TEEN REPORTED MISSING IN STORM OF THE CENTURY

By Tina Chandler
March 17, 1993

Denton, MA. – Police are asking for help locating a 16-year-old boy who went missing earlier this week.

Newham Police Lt. Chris Field told the Denton Times that Patrick O'Donnell has been missing since the 13th of March and police are continuing to look for him. His parents informed police that they last saw Patrick on the evening of 13th March, the day the storm hit. However, they failed to report him missing until three days later. The family denies there was any altercation or argument but has put out an appeal which reads: 'Paddy, we are all terribly worried about you, please come home or at least make contact and let us know you are safe.'

If you have seen Patrick or have any information about his whereabouts contact Newham Police Department at 413-743-1045.

The O'Donnell family could not be reached for comment.

Lizzie saw the name, Tina Chandler, and her heart sank. She had no idea that Chandler covered the original story of Paddy's disappearance. No wonder she was like a dog with a bone. How often is it that a journalist gets the chance to cover and get closure on one of their old stories? She must have been straight out of journalism school, yet her style remained the same – factual coverage with a hint of suspicion. And this article left the reader doubting the parents. What sort of parents wait three days to report their son missing? She pressed the print button and waited for the machine to spit out a hard copy.

Scrolling forward she found the article about the discovery of Paddy's body, an article about her dad being taken in for questioning and coverage of the funeral. All written by Tina Chandler, each article looking for a new angle. Without warning, she became breathless at the sight of the image of her family on the steps of the church, her mother slumped over the onyx coffin. Her heart was racing. There she was, a tiny girl in a black wool coat with velvet collar and cuffs, white ankle socks and black patent Mary Janes, holding her father's hand. She adjusted the focus to zoom in on her eight-year-old face. Blank, she looked like a mannequin in a department store void of emotion, frozen. Her hand trembled, as she pressed the print button.

'Look, lady. I already told you. The box you want is checked out, being used by another library patron.' The library assistant's voice was raised, Lizzie couldn't help but overhear.

'But I called ahead and asked for it to be reserved for me,' the woman insisted.

'I don't know who you talked to, but it wasn't me and nobody left me a note. You'll just have to wait.'

Don't mess with a goth. She was gathering up her things when she sensed someone standing behind her.

'I pre-booked this box, how much longer are you going to be?' Tina Chandler stood over her. Lizzie turned and took some pleasure in seeing all the blood drain from her face when she realized who Lizzie was. The library assistant came running over.

'Is this lady bothering you, Miss O'Donnell? I told her she had to wait.'

'No, it's okay. I'm finished for today.' Lizzie took her printouts and stood up. 'I didn't realize you covered the story of my brother's disappearance.' She saw Tina Chandler staring at her swollen belly. Before the journalist could get a word in, Lizzie added, 'Your journalistic style hasn't developed much in twenty years. Guess that's why you never moved on.' She picked up the box and carried it back to the reception counter, retrieving her ID. 'I'll come back another day. Thanks for your help.' She saw the relief on the youth's face as she turned, shot Tina Chandler a death stare and walked out. In the parking lot she heaved into a garbage can, hoping no one saw her and got into her car, her hands still shaking.

*

On the drive back from the hospital Lizzie's heart rate settled. Maura had taken herself into the living room as per usual while Lizzie prepared lunch. She couldn't get the image of herself as a small girl out of her head. Paddy's death had turned their lives upside down, inside out and spat them out, empty. Her mother was a shell of the person she once was. She longed for that mother, the one who had brushed her hair before bed, read with her and let her cuddle in her lap. In the photo slumped over Paddy's coffin, it looked as if she would have climbed in there with him if she could have.

She was carrying the lunch tray through to the living room when the doorbell rang. Putting it down on the coffee table, she went to the front door.

'Joe…come in.' She tried to make eye contact, but he turned away.

'I just need a quick word with your mother.' He didn't wait to be invited in and eased past Lizzie into the living room. 'Mrs. O'Donnell, I'm sorry to interrupt your lunch.'

'Joe, come join us. Where have you been hiding? Barely see you these days.'

'Thank you, but I've got to get back to the station in a minute.' He took off his hat and ran his hand through his thick hair, placing the hat under his armpit. 'I came by to tell you that Jason Edwards' bail hearing has been set for the eleventh of August. It's open, so you can attend if you'd like.'

'They aren't going to let that monster out, are they, Joe?'

'We'll have to wait and see what the judge decides.' He avoided looking over at Lizzie and put his hat back on. 'I'll be there on the day if you decide you want to attend.' He walked back to the front door. 'Bye, Lizzie.'

'Joe…can we…' A rush of emotion came over her, her eyes filled with tears.

'Not now.' Joe headed back down the front path to his car. She missed him and he couldn't even look at her. She sat down in the living room and took a sip of water.

'Look what you've done to that boy, Lizzie,' said Maura chewing on her ham and cheese baguette. 'You should be ashamed of yourself.'

Lizzie sat looking at her, the tears rolled down her face. This time her mother was right, she was ashamed of herself. She picked up her keys and left without saying another word.

Chapter 30

The unopened bottle stood on the kitchen counter, the warm amber liquid silently seducing her. She had intended to pour it down the drain weeks earlier but told herself that it would be a waste to dispose of it and if she had guests, they might drink it. This was the last bottle, she rationalized, as she poured a shot into the tumbler and listened to the crackling sound of the liquid meeting the ice. She filled the glass with Coke and carried it out to the screened in porch. It would be cooler outside, but she seemed to have become a magnet for mosquitoes which she put down to pregnancy hormones; she had developed 'sweet meat' as her dad used to say.

She stretched out on the chaise-longue and stared at the wolf on the book's cover then took a sip and felt the warmth slide down her throat. A great fuss had always been made of yearbooks, teenagers spending hours working on their entries, voting for class superlatives – 'most likely to succeed' -whatever success was-, 'best dressed', 'best looking', 'most individual', the list went on. Had there been a category for 'most likely to die first', Paddy would have had it in the bag, he didn't even make it to senior year. Lizzie flipped through the pages scanning the staff pages and stopped to admire the

Vice Principal with whom she had become acquainted, having spent many a day in the suspension room for truancy. He had tried to figure out what was going on with her, she knew that. 'You're a bright girl, Lizzie. I just don't understand it, if you would just come to school…,' he had preached, shaking his head in frustration. Her response had always been to shrug her shoulders and say she didn't know, she just couldn't concentrate. It was easier to say that than to admit that people treated her like a freak, that she had no friends and couldn't see how her life would amount to anything beyond cooking and cleaning and looking after her mother. She didn't need a high school diploma for that. In any case, she had lived in the shadow of Paddy and Tommy for years, nobody noticed her. How could she have told him that what everyone considered aloofness was in fact extreme loneliness?

The individual profiles of the senior class made for amusing reading, young people's aspirations – the serious Ivy league bound seeking wealth and power, the jocks wanting to become professional football or baseball players and the burnouts simply looking to have a good time. Lizzie turned the page and spotted a photo of Dylan Jones. His profile read: Dylan Edward Jones, Nickname: 'Jonesy boy', Activities: Wrestling (Captain), MA State Champion; Curly in Musical Theatre production, Oklahoma! Youth

Committee Our Lady of Lourdes, Altar Server. Ambition: College, become an Accountant and get married. A model citizen. Being arrested for obstruction of justice had not been a burning ambition of his back then. Clearly, college, accountancy, marriage to Cindy and the two children produced by this union had not been enough for him. He was the year above Paddy at school, but they shared common interests – both wrestling and both altar boys. They must have known one another. Lizzie flicked through to the sports section and scanned through the wrestling photos. There was Paddy standing tall, arm around Dylan Jones in the team photo, grinning, the other side Ted Franklin. All three with matching crucifixes around their necks. The cocky grin on Paddy's face made her shudder. She'd seen it before.

She closed the book and took the last gulp of her drink. The entry for her own yearbook had been blank aside from her photo and name. She hadn't seen the point in writing anything, not having participated in any activities and without any ambition beyond running away. Getting out of Newham, she had managed that and more. In fact, she had far exceeded anyone's expectations of what she might achieve given she had only scraped through by the skin of her teeth. It was only Joe's kindness and brain power that had got her through. His patience, refusal to give up and last-ditch attempt to teach her trigonometry, resulted in her passing the course with a D, thereby enabling her to graduate at a ceremony she declined to attend. She knew now how important a high school diploma was, but back then she didn't care. Joe had saved her ass more than once and each time instead of showing gratitude, she had treated him badly, pushed him away. He had been the only person she had dared to get close to, a closeness that had left her more vulnerable than ever. She was a slow learner and he had been a glutton for punishment. The truth was she had found it hard to connect with anybody, emotionally shut off, that's what she had become. But the day she left Newham she was liberated, free to reinvent herself.

Another drink, she craved the numbness. But a little flutter in her belly sent her a much-needed reminder that she was responsible for more than herself. She put the thought out of her mind. It was so much easier to be numb than sit with shame, guilt, and regret. If only there were an easy fix.

*

A blue heron took flight from the dock, she admired the expanse of its wings, gliding just above the water's surface in search of its next meal, then was reminded of her own hunger. Rummaging through the fridge she scraped together a smorgasbord of cold fried chicken, left over potato salad, hummus, and carrot sticks, sat down at the kitchen table, and began reading through the articles she had printed out at the library. Her father's face stared back at her from the page. She hardly recognized him; he had been a handsome man, well-built and hardworking, but the photo of him leaving Newham police station made him look like he had been dragged under a bus. He had been arrested in connection with Paddy's death following an anonymous tip-off, questioned for hours, held overnight in a cell, then eventually released without charge. According to the article, neighbors had heard shouting coming from the O'Donnell home on the evening of the blizzard. A witness said they had seen Paddy storm out of the house and walk down the street in the snow. What had they been arguing about? They could have been describing any household with a teenager in Newham, nothing out of the ordinary. Another sterling piece of investigative journalism by Tina Chandler.

It didn't make sense that her dad had denied any argument. The account he had given police was that he had sent his workers home early due to the storm, gone for a quick Friday afternoon drink at the Town Tavern, then come home to a family dinner of meatloaf and spent the evening watching television until he was forced to drive to the hospital following Lizzie's accident. But they were always arguing, though she had never understood quite why until recently. She looked at the photo of Paddy alongside her father's. They bore no resemblance to one another, like two random strangers. She was surprised that no one had picked up on this, not even Tina Chandler.

As it turned out, Jim O'Donnell had been the only person ever questioned in connection with Paddy's death, but his release without charge had not put him beyond suspicion. Tina Chandler's follow up articles all focused on little details, like why would parents allow their son to go out on foot in the middle of a blizzard. She was looking to blame them despite the lack of evidence. When that failed, she had turned to the more sordid details of Paddy's final movements, interviewing witnesses at the arcade who said Paddy had turned up drunk and high at six o'clock sporting a large bruise to his cheek, eye swollen shut. He'd been obnoxious goading the other kids there, before disappearing around eight o'clock. The headlines did not make for pretty reading, even after twenty years. By the time July 1993 had come around, the articles were few and far between and by September it seemed the case had been all but forgotten. Order had been restored to the little community of Newham.

The months of intense scrutiny must have taken their toll on her parents, the family still grieving the loss of a son. Lizzie had hoped that reading the newspaper coverage would shift something in her, open some memories, but all it had done was raise more questions for her. Her dad had lied, but why?

Chapter 31

They made their way through security into the courthouse and found Joe waiting at the bottom of the staircase. He directed them up the stairs to courtroom two and said he would join them. They must not have been expecting much of a crowd given the size of the wood paneled room. Lizzie and her mother took a seat in the front row of the public gallery. She took a bottle of water from her bag and gulped it back, then offered it to Maura. An unexpected thump in her belly caught her off guard and she jumped.

'Stop fidgeting, Lizzie.'

'I'm not fidgeting, the baby kicked, it took me by surprise is all.'

'It's only going to get worse as the months go on, so you better get used to it.' Maura stared ahead, her face a blank canvas.

Lizzie jumped at the sound of the door slamming and watched as a couple in their seventies took seats at the end of the row. Did they have some connection to Jason Edwards or were they simply retired members of the community having nothing better to do with their time? The court officer requested all those present to rise, the Honorable William H. Baxter was presiding again. As everyone rose, the door slammed again. Lizzie turned and stared at Tina Chandler, who was perfectly coiffed. She smiled at Lizzie and took a seat in the row behind.

'This is a bail review hearing in the case of the Commonwealth vs Edwards, requested by the defense.' Judge Baxter cleared his throat and looked to the prosecutor. 'In the normal course of events bail reviews are called because the defendant has been in breach of conditions of bail, so this case is highly unusual. Mr. Cranston, given recent developments, is the Commonwealth now recommending bail?'

'No, your honor. The defendant has been charged with second degree murder, a violent crime and major felony. Irrespective of the recent sexual assault charge which has been dropped, the Commonwealth maintains that there is strong evidence connecting the defendant to the murder of Patrick O'Donnell and that he continues to pose a danger to society.' Matthew Cranston sounded confident, perhaps it was his three-piece Brooks Brothers suit that gave him the air of superiority. Lizzie marveled at his ability to smooth over the fact that Edwards had been falsely accused by Dylan Jones.

'Miss Murphy, let the court hear your argument for bail.'

'Your honor, there is a presumption in the Commonwealth of Massachusetts that individuals charged with crimes other than first degree murder should be released on bail providing they do not pose a flight risk.' Eileen Murphy seemed more prepared for court this time, her hair brushed, wearing a black polyester trouser suit and blouse. 'My client has already been incarcerated for four months, deprived of his liberty despite being presumed innocent. Had he not been falsely accused of sexual assault, we would not be standing here today.'

'I am aware of this Miss Murphy, get to the point please.'

'Your Honor, Jason Edwards poses no flight risk, nor any danger to society. Until his arrest he was employed full-time, he owns his condominium and has strong ties to the community having been born and raised in Denton. He has no history of violence and no criminal record.' The public defender was getting into her stride, her voice strong and steady, she turned and stared at the prosecutor. 'My client has suffered a major injustice having been falsely accused. His parents are here in court and are willing and able to post cash bail. Mr. Edwards is willing to submit to pre-trial services.' She adjusted her cuffs and sat down.

Had this been a television courtroom drama, Lizzie would have been rooting for the public defender. Divided loyalties, this was the man accused of her brother's brutal murder after all, but she couldn't help but feel the deck had been stacked against him. He sat head bowed looking more skeletal than his appearance four months earlier, prison life obviously not agreeing with him.

'Having listened to arguments, I am going to release Mr. Edwards on fifty thousand dollars cash bail.' The judge did not go as far as to say an injustice had been done to the accused, but his stern tone of voice indicated he was not pleased with the prosecutor. Lizzie looked over at her mother who was now sobbing.

'But this monster killed my boy,' Maura shouted. Lizzie pulled on her mother's arm for her to sit down. 'No! I won't be silent.'

'Please, Ma. This is not the time or place for this. Sit down and be quiet.' Lizzie whispered. She could hear the rumblings in the courtroom and caught the judge's disapproving eye. She put her arm around her mother and tried to comfort her.

'Mr. Edwards, you must surrender your passport, wear an electronic tag and will be subject to a curfew between nine o'clock pm until six o'clock am, seven days a week. A trial date has already been set for 15 November and I expect to see you here in court.' As Judge Baxter rose and made his way out of the chamber, Maura left the courtroom sobbing hysterically. Lizzie was too drained to run after her. She would calm down in her own time.

The elderly couple at the end of the row made their way

down to the front of the courtroom and embraced Jason Edwards. Lizzie tried to imagine what it must be like to receive that kind of parental love even when accused of murder. His parents had probably re-mortgaged their house to post bail. She turned and found Tina Chandler behind her.

'Can I have a word with you?' The journalist addressed Lizzie in a taut but shaky voice, she couldn't decide if Tina Chandler was nervous or angry. 'Look, I'm sorry about what happened in the library the other day. I'm not the enemy here.'

'You could've fooled me.' Lizzie didn't have the time or energy to play games with Tina Chandler. 'I've read every article you wrote about my family and this case.'

'And I expect you have a lot of unanswered questions.' Tina Chandler's voice was suddenly honeyed, and her face softened. 'I know you don't trust me, but we have more in common than you think.'

'I find that hard to believe.' Lizzie knew it was unwise to get involved with her, but she had tweaked her curiosity. 'Fine. Go on then…'

'We both want the truth.' She was staring at Lizzie. 'I think I can help you, if you'd agree to meet me, totally off the record, time and place of your choice.'

'I need to think about it.' Lizzie took the card from Tina

Chandler's hand and pocketed it. 'I'll be in touch.' She walked toward the exit and saw Joe standing by the courtroom door.

'What did she want?' Joe asked.

'Nothing really.'

'Best if you steer clear of her.' Joe's voice was flat to the point that Lizzie couldn't tell if he was looking out for her or telling her off. 'Your mom is in a terrible state out in the corridor, I think you need to get her home.' He walked off and left her alone to deal with her burden. So much for family liaison support.

*

The encounter with Tina Chandler the previous day had been on Lizzie's mind the whole drive to the clinic. What was her agenda? She was still thinking about her when the sonographer squirted a blob of cold gel on her belly making her shiver and bringing her abruptly back into the room. She moved the probe around until they both heard the regular thumping of a heartbeat. 'One hundred and forty beats per minute. Regular and strong,' the sonographer said. She pressed the button to take a photo. 'Would you like to know the baby's sex?'

'I… Can you tell for sure?'

'Let's have a look.' She pressed down on the probe and slid it to the left making the baby turn. 'Just trying to get the right position. Now's the time to say if you want to know.'

Lizzie hesitated, not sure what she was afraid of. There were enough surprises in life, maybe if she knew this at least she could prepare. 'Yes, go on then. Is it a boy or a girl?'

'It's a girl.'

'Are you sure?'

'Yes, look.' She enlarged the image on the screen. 'Definitely a girl.' The sonographer handed Lizzie a piece of tissue.

'That's great. Thank you.' She wiped the gel from her belly and pulled up her shorts. A daughter, it hadn't quite sunk in.

'We'll see you in another four weeks. Look after yourself and make sure you drink plenty of fluids in this heat.'

She sat in the car looking at the photo of her baby - a girl, a daughter, she was going to have a daughter of her own. She was determined to be a good mother, a better mother than her own had been. Reversing out of the parking space she decided to keep this news to herself, no one would be interested anyway. A bulletin came on the radio as she pulled out.

'Breaking news. The actor, Robin Williams, is dead at the age of 63 from an apparent suicide. His representative said he had been battling depression of late. His wife stated, 'This morning I lost my husband and best friend while the world lost one of its most beloved artists and beautiful human beings. I am utterly heartbroken…'

Tears streamed down her face as she pulled over into the McDonalds parking lot. The memory of her dad dropping her and Tommy off at the cinema on a snowy January day to see the matinee of Mrs. Doubtfire came rushing back. A rare moment of normality. It had been a couple of months before the first anniversary of Paddy's death and their mother was holed up in his bedroom most of the time. She had prayed for her dad to hire Mrs. Doubtfire to come fix their family. Tommy had given her a false sense of hope telling her not to worry, that their family would soon get back to normal. It seemed ridiculous her being so upset about the death of someone she had never met, but she had seen virtually every film he had made. She put it down to hormones, wiped her eyes with the back of her hand and drove on.

Chapter 32

The faithful of Our Lady of Lourdes filed into mass prepared for their holy day of obligation, the Feast of the Assumption, fanning themselves with their hymnals. Lizzie had managed to avoid mass since Easter, but the heat was sweltering, the church air conditioned and she could embarrass her mother with her pregnancy showing. She knew Maura couldn't bring herself to tell her not to attend mass. Her hypocrisy had some limits. But she was displeased that Lizzie had turned up in a form fitting dress that accentuated her baby bump. 'Can't you wear something looser? It's like you're showing off,' she had said.

They sat down next to Tommy and the girls. 'Where's Hannah?' Lizzie asked.

'She's not well. Heat's got to her and her legs have swelled up again.'

The congregation stood as the organist began to play. 'Hail Holy Queen enthroned above, oh Maria… Lizzie remembered this hymn and joined in singing at the top of her voice. Her mother nudged her. 'Stop drawing attention to yourself.' She ignored Maura and kept singing. As a child she had not understood what the feast was about, she imagined the Virgin Mary being beamed up to heaven like

Captain Kirk in Star Trek. Unfathomable. Even as an adult she couldn't get her head around it. She scanned the congregation for familiar faces as Father Larkin droned on and spotted Tara Franklin sitting next to a man she assumed was her fiancé.

'Today we celebrate the triumph of the Mother, Daughter and Spouse of God. Like all good mothers Mary loves us, watches over us, and protects us. She is the mother with whom we can share every joy and sorrow.' Father Larkin preached to his congregation. Lizzie had drawn the short straw on the mother front. She was more likely to share her joys and sorrows with Mary than her own Ma who wept into her handkerchief as Father Larkin continued his sermon about the great sacrifice of a mother losing her son, and the humility that Mary had shown carrying this great burden. It dawned on her that her mother probably thought she had a special affinity with Mary, both having lost their cherished sons. She'd heard enough, the wooden pew was too uncomfortable, she needed to get out. Leaning across she whispered to Tommy to take Ma home, got up and walked down the center aisle, her baby bump on show for all to see.

She drove over to Tommy's house to see Hannah, rang the doorbell, and waited. A smug satisfaction had come over her as she walked down the church aisle, her head held high.

Maura would be livid. She rang the doorbell again, then opened the door and called out for Hannah with no response. The house was eerily quiet without the girls running around. She made her way upstairs, knocked on the bedroom door and opened it expecting to find Hannah sound asleep on the bed. The bedroom was the size of Lizzie's whole cottage, light and airy, with a Scandinavian feel to it. Hannah might be loose lipped, but she had good taste. She was about to walk out when she heard a faint groan coming from the bathroom. Hannah was on all fours on the marble floor.

'My water broke, Lizzie,' said Hannah, panting with each contraction. She was pale and sweating. 'It's too soon.'

'I'm calling an ambulance!' She dialed 911, then called Tommy but his phone must have still been on silent. She was totally ill-equipped to deal with this. 'I'm going to text Tommy. They're all still at church but I'll tell them to meet us at the hospital.' She grabbed a face cloth and ran it under some cold water, wrung it out and wiped Hannah's face with it. 'Is there anything I can do?'

'Just don't leave me.' Hannah groaned as a wave of contractions came. This would be her in a few months. Terrifying. The scene in front of her was a far cry from the water birth with gentle moody lighting she'd been imagining. Lizzie rubbed Hannah's back as each contraction arrived over the following fifteen minutes until she could hear the ambulance siren in the distance.

'Ambulance is nearly here, Han. I'm going downstairs to let the paramedics in.' The ambulance with flashing lights was climbing the drive followed by Joe's police car. Lizzie stood waiting at the front door. 'She's upstairs having contractions in the bathroom, but it's four weeks early.' Lizzie stared wide eyed as the paramedics grabbed their kit and entered the house.

'She'll be alright, Lizzie.' Joe stood next to her.

'How can you possibly know that?' Lizzie barked at Joe releasing some of her pent-up anger. Why had she wasted so much time feeling guilty about Joe? He had frozen her out, when all she wanted was to talk, to explain. She wasn't the same person she had been at sixteen.

'I've seen a few deliveries, thirty-six weeks is far enough along. Trust me.' Joe's eyes were focused on Lizzie's belly. She put her hand on her abdomen and looked up at him.

'I'm going to ride in the ambulance with Hannah. Can you find Tommy and take him to the hospital?'

Hannah emerged from the house, paramedics either side supporting her into the ambulance. 'Her blood pressure is elevated, we need to get her to the hospital.' The paramedic helped Lizzie into the vehicle and slammed the door as it sped off. Lizzie held Hannah's hand and wiped her brow.

'It's all going to be fine, trust me.' She needed to believe that for both of them.

Chapter 33

Thomas James O'Donnell Jr. came into the world at twelve thirty-eight in the afternoon, weighing in at five pounds and four ounces. They had been in the delivery room but fifteen minutes when he emerged with a fierce cry, his skin covered in a white, cheesy layer of vernix and a head of soft ebony hair. His whiteness matched Lizzie's face, drained of all color, as the obstetrician handed her the pair of scissors and instructed her to cut the umbilical cord. This should have been Tommy's job, but he had yet to arrive. She looked up at an exhausted but smiling Hannah who was nodding, encouraging her to go ahead. She had never been so terrified yet thrilled. The midwife handed her the swaddled bundle to hold while the medical team turned its attention to Hannah. Her blood pressure had been dangerously high by the time they arrived at the hospital that Lizzie's whole body was tensed with worry she could barely open her jaw. It was a blessing that Tommy Jr. had been in a hurry to be born, rescuing his mother from danger. Still the team wanted Hannah hospitalized and monitored for a few days.

Lizzie gazed at baby Tommy's blue eyes and pursed lips. He was making sucking noises and turning his head in the direction of Hannah's voice when Lizzie passed him over to her. 'He knows his mom's voice, Han.'

'Sorry, I kinda threw you in at the deep end then. I'm so grateful you turned up when you did.' Hannah unwrapped his swaddling and laid him on her chest skin to skin.

Tommy burst into the room with pupils like saucers. 'Oh, thank God. I'm so sorry, Han. I shouldn't have left you alone.' He was sobbing in a way Lizzie had never witnessed before.

'We're both fine. You can thank your sister for that.'

'Actually, you can thank Father Larkin for the hard pews and dull sermon.' Lizzie laughed. 'I couldn't tolerate sitting there listening to him drone on.' Lizzie moved toward the door. 'I think you three need some time alone.'

Joe was pacing in the corridor as Lizzie came out of the delivery room. 'How's…?'

'They're both fine. Where's Ma and the girls?'

'Your mother drove them home.'

'She what?'

'She said she'd take them home.'

'Jesus, Joe. Ma hasn't driven in over twenty years. I better go check on them.'

'You haven't got a car. I'll take you.' He walked down the corridor toward the main entrance with Lizzie following behind. She was buzzing, the adrenaline still rushing through her body. Joe opened the rear passenger side door for her. 'Sorry, it's against regulations for you to sit in the front seat.' They rode in silence until the police radio chatter started. 'I'm going to have to drop you and run, Lizzie. There's been an incident at the lake.'

Lizzie stood in the driveway, head spinning, as the flashing lights and siren faded into the distance. Her niece tugged on her shirt. She turned and saw her mom standing at the front door with the two younger girls.

'Is Mommy okay?' Claire was sobbing.

'Your mommy's going to be fine. You have a new baby brother.' Lizzie took her hand and walked into the house. 'Let's get some lemonade.'

'Have they named him?' Ma fussed about the kitchen, agitated.

'Thomas James O'Donnell Jr.' Lizzie cut the lemons in half and pressed them down on the juicer.

'Oh, I hoped they might call him Patrick.'

'I'm sure you did.'

'I might have a word with Tommy.'

'We're calling him TJ, Grandma. We already decided.' Claire piped up. 'When can we see him?'

'You'll have to wait for your dad to come home.' Lizzie stirred the pitcher and poured the lemonade into four tumblers and handed one to Ma.

'None for me, I'm going home.' Ma was jingling the car

keys in her hand.

'You want me to drive you?'

'No, I can drive myself. You need to sort out your own car, Lizzie. I can't keep lending you mine.' Maura picked up her handbag, kissed the girls on the forehead and headed out.

*

It was late by the time Tommy walked through the door, the girls were curled up on the sofa, cuddling their teddies and sound asleep. They were adamant that they wanted to stay up to see their father. Lizzie had been left stranded with them, but the girls clearly adored her, and she had enjoyed making pizzas with them.

'You look wiped.' Tommy was beaming as he cracked open a beer. 'I don't know how to thank you!'

'How about lending me a car? Ma drove hers off into the sunset.'

'God help the other cars on the road. Take Han's car. She won't be driving for a couple of weeks.' He picked the cheese off a slice and put it in his mouth. 'Do you know what's happening by the lake? There were fire and rescue trucks there and the whole area was cordoned off.'

'Joe said there was an incident, that's all I know.' Lizzie took the car keys. 'Congratulations, Bro. TJ's just gorgeous.' She hugged him tight, then laughed. 'You need a shower.'

The Denton Times

Keeping the community informed with independent local reporting

CORONER'S REPORT: DEATH BY SUICIDE ON LAKE WUNNUMWAONK

By Tina Chandler
26 August 2014

Denton, MA. – The Harewood County coroner's office determined that a man whose body was found on Lake Wunnumwaonk died by suicide.

Dylan Jones's cause of death was ruled a suicide by drowning on Monday. His body was recovered by Newham search and rescue crew on the afternoon of 15 August in Massasoit Cove, a popular bass fishing spot, after his abandoned boat was discovered by two teenage fishermen.

Newham search and rescue team divers recovered the body after a short search. A car battery had been tied to Mr. Jones' ankles with an extension cord. The toxicology report revealed evidence of sedatives in his blood stream and a blood alcohol level twice the legal driving limit.

Mr. Jones was last seen at the Lake Wunnumwaonk boat launch around noon on 15 August. He was known locally as a keen fisherman. Staff at the boat launch said he seemed in good humor as he took his Crestliner Bass Hawk boat out for an afternoon's fishing.

Jones had been released on his own recognizance on an obstruction of justice charge relating to a false accusation of sexual assault he made in Spring 2014. He was due to appear in court on 28 August.

In March 2014, Jones alleged Jason Edwards sexually assaulted him after an encounter outside a Denton nightclub. Edwards was charged with sexual assault and in a routine DNA database search, his DNA matched with DNA from the historic Patrick O'Donnell murder case which had remained unsolved since 1993. Edwards was recently released on bail and is awaiting trial for second degree murder. The sexual assault charge against him was dropped after new evidence came to light.

Jones, a married man, and father of two, had been living apart from his family since his arrest. Police revealed at the inquest that he had mailed a suicide note to his wife the day before his drowning. According to a family friend, Jones was depressed and struggling to live with the shame and harm done to his family by his actions.

The Jones family could not be reached for comment.

Chapter 34

Call her morose, but Lizzie became fixated on how long it took for Dylan Jones to drown after he jumped. He had clearly been serious about killing himself, a car battery tied to his ankles. But what if he had changed his mind after jumping? Would he have struggled? It didn't bear thinking about. There was no worse way of dying and she was grateful that she had no memory of her own near-death suffocation as a child.

'His poor family.' Lizzie said as she rocked Tommy Jr. in the chair, the baby sound asleep in her arms. 'Do you know his wife, Han?'

'Not all that well. Their daughter is in Claire's class at school. She's kinda quiet, but sweet.' Hannah stood at the kitchen island chopping vegetables. 'The funeral is next Tuesday at Our Lady of Lourdes.'

'You gonna go?

'I think so. Tommy wants to go. You know he built their house?' She placed the vegetables in the salad bowl, along with some chopped hard-boiled egg, sliced ham, and cheese. 'Let's eat this and then I'll take you to pick up your new car.'

Lizzie laid Tommy Jr. down in his wooden cradle and

took a seat at the breakfast bar. 'Sounds like a plan.' She heaped a load of the salad on to her plate and crunched on the lettuce. 'I'm pretty sure Dylan Jones was friends with Paddy. They wrestled together in high school.'

'Tommy's never mentioned that, but he never talks about Paddy. Your Ma says she's going to the funeral. She's been visiting his wife and taking food over.' Hannah sat opposite Lizzie, pulled the salad bowl in front of her and began eating directly from the bowl. 'No point in dirtying another plate. I'm famished. Tommy Jr. is sucking the life from me.'

'Ma loves to play the good Samaritan. She just wants something to gossip about with her novena ladies.' Lizzie heard a little cry and jumped up to check on the baby. He wasn't hers but she felt like she had developed a special bond with him having been there when he came into the world. She hadn't spoken to her mother since the afternoon of his birth when she had driven off with the car leaving Lizzie stranded. 'I might go along with you to the funeral if you don't mind.' She was curious. 'Shall we go get this so-called new car of mine? I'm looking forward to being the proud owner of a 1993 blue Ford Escort.'

'I wish you would let us help you get something newer.'

'It just needs to get me around town. It's not like I've got any long road trips planned.' She rubbed her belly and laughed. 'I'll be lucky to get beyond Denton once this little girl is born. Anyway, Tommy checked it over, said it seemed fine.'

AUTUMN 2014

Chapter 35

A north-eastern Atlantic air brought cooler temperatures mid-September. The cold hitting the warm water's surface created an impenetrable morning mist over the lake. Lizzie waded into the warm water unable to see more than a few feet ahead and took a leap of faith diving in, then turned and floated on her back. She had so enjoyed her morning swims and would miss them as the autumn drew nearer. Floating in the deeper water she was enveloped by a heavy silence, not a boat in earshot, not even the crows were cawing. The busy summer season was over. She embraced the stillness and studied the movements of her belly, sensing every flutter and enjoying a sense of well-being in that moment before her thoughts took her elsewhere.

Her eyes closed, she ruminated over the language in the letter that had appeared in her mailbox, an invitation from the state police to attend a voluntary interview at the Newham police station on September 16th at 10:00 am. Her assistance was requested as part of a review of evidence in preparation for the upcoming trial of Jason Edwards and new information that had come to light. She couldn't imagine what insight she could possibly provide. Her whole body shook. Could she refuse to attend? Should she contact a lawyer? If she did, would they think she had something to hide? She needed to know if Tommy and Ma had received similar letters. It had been three weeks since she had last spoken to Ma and she was dreading seeing her at the funeral, but at least the letter gave her an excuse to speak to her.

She pulled herself up on to the dock shivering in the chilly air, wrapped a striped beach towel around her shoulders and made her way back up to the house. Her bed was strewn with funeral outfits, she couldn't decide which one to wear. On this occasion she needed to blend in, not stand out and settled on a pair of black linen pants and matching tunic. Her curls, the gift of a hot, humid summer, had disappeared overnight leaving her with damp straight hair for the first time in months. She debated whether to blow dry it but decided it would be just fine by the time she got to the church. Grabbing a cardigan and her keys, she hurried out the front door anxious to stop at the coffee shop before heading to the church.

*

Lizzie paid for her coffee and cinnamon bun and sat down at a table in the corner giving her a view of the whole room. Looking down at her hands, she tried to twirl her ring to no avail, her fingers increasingly resembled sausages as the weeks had gone by. If this was what was referred to as 'glowing' during pregnancy, she could do without it. She unraveled the outer layer of the bun and pulled off a piece. It was still warm. She popped it into her mouth and savored the taste of cinnamon mixing with the sweet sticky icing. Heaven. A shrill voice from a table across the room pierced her eardrums. She turned her head to see whose it was but didn't recognize the woman sitting with Angela Moretti and a few of Maura's cronies.

'Well, I heard he was one of those…you know,' the shrill voice said.

'But his poor wife…'

'Never mind that, she's better off without him. She's young and pretty, she can start again.'

'What did the note say, Angela?'

'How should I know?'

'Your son's a cop, surely he tells you things.'

'He's not saying much at the moment,' Angela said.

'He's not still torn up about that O'Donnell girl?'

'Even her own mother wants nothing to do with her,' the shrill voice said.

Lizzie had heard enough. She threw her napkin down, walked past their table and stopped. 'Morning Mrs. Moretti.' The chatter stopped, Lizzie glared at them and said, 'You all have a good day now.' She took some small pleasure in calling out the gossiping witches.

*

The muffler on her Ford Escort rattled as she pulled up beside her mother's car in the church parking lot. Maura's back was turned as Lizzie approached her.

'Morning Ma.'

'Where did you come from?'

'I just got out of my car.' Lizzie pointed to the Ford Escort.

'Looks like a piece of junk.'

'All I could afford, and I needed a car quickly since you left me stranded.'

'Why are you here? You didn't even know the family.'

'Trying to be a supportive member of the local community.' She pulled the letter from the state police from her backpack. 'Did you get one of these?'

Maura took the letter than handed it back to her, waving her hand. 'I haven't got my glasses, just read it to me.'

'The state police have asked me to come in tomorrow for a voluntary interview in preparation for the upcoming trial, part of a review of evidence and new information. I thought maybe you and Tommy had received letters too.'

'No, I haven't. She looked down at Lizzie's swollen belly and sighed. 'You shouldn't be here. I'm in a hurry, Cindy and her children need me.'

Lizzie stood by the car watching Maura walk off and

choked back tears. Her mother's sudden need to be needed sat in stark contrast with Lizzie's experience of her mother's absence - where had Ma been all the times when she had needed her? She was angry at herself for hanging on to that little hope that her mom might change. It would never happen.

Lizzie entered the church and scanned the congregation until she saw Hannah and Tommy sitting towards the back. She slid into the pew next to Tommy and handed him the letter.

'What's this?' he whispered.

'Just read it.' Lizzie watched as the color drained from Tommy's face. 'Did you get one too?'

'No, I don't understand. You were only a little kid back then.' Tommy wiped his brow with his sleeve. 'What could you possibly tell them? Have you asked Joe?'

'Joe and I haven't spoken since the day TJ was born. I can't ask him.'

'I can't imagine it will be anything important. Just go along and see what they say.' He folded the letter and handed it back to Lizzie as the entrance hymn began. It was meant to be a song of hope and consolation. The last time Lizzie had heard it was at her father's funeral. She had chosen it specially, in fact, she had organized the whole service. She missed him. Ma had been in no fit state to do much of anything other than pray. Lizzie watched as the pall bearers carried the pine coffin down the aisle followed by Dylan Jones's wife. Her hand was firmly clasped to Maura's and Maura's arm was around her shoulder. Maura had found her calling - professional griever. It made sense, she had dedicated her life to grief. It was the only thing that she truly understood. Two small girls trailed behind holding hands occasionally looking back to an elderly woman for reassurance. It was hard to imagine these small girls not being afraid, even if the hymn told them so.

Lizzie surveyed the packed church trying to identify which members of the congregation came to offer support and who was there to gawp and gossip. Tina Chandler stood at the back of the church scanning the crowd in much the same way as Lizzie. Their eyes met, both nodding to acknowledge one another. She still had the card Tina had given her at Jason Edwards' bail hearing and had been tempted to call her out of curiosity to see what information she might share but had decided against it, hearing Tommy's voice in her head. 'Leave well enough alone, Lizzie.'

Father Larkin swung a gold thurible suspended from a chain over the coffin and recited a prayer. The scent of incense wafted through the church making Lizzie's eyes water. She hated the smell. She wasn't alone, a chorus of coughs echoed around the church. The priest handed the smoking dispenser to one of the altar servers and took to the pulpit.

'I am the resurrection and the Life. Those who believe in me, even though they die, yet shall they live, and everyone who lives and believes in me will never die,' Father Larkin bellowed, his arms raised, clearly a fire lit in his belly. Like Ma, he seemed to be in his element. 'Resurrection means that even if we forsake our life, God does not forsake us. In our grief we must acknowledge that suicide is unexplainable. Our brother Dylan, in his darkness, forsake his life, but God is with him, and God will be with his wife and children through their grief.'

A sudden thump to the right side of her belly made Lizzie jump. She rubbed her side and lifted her right buttock trying to ease the sciatica induced by the hard wooden pew. She wasn't sure she could sit through the rest of the service.

'In this hour of darkness, we look to the Scriptures to reassure us. As is written in Isaiah, with everlasting kindness I will have compassion on you. Though the mountains be shaken, and the hills be removed, yet my unfailing love for you will not be shaken. Let us show our compassion and understanding to the Jones family in their hour of need.' Father Larkin stepped down from the pulpit and crossed the altar. 'Let us pray…'

An electric shock ran from Lizzie's lower back down her leg. She whispered to Tommy that she couldn't sit anymore. As the congregation rose to recite The Lord's Prayer, she ducked out of the church.

A cool breeze rustled the leaves on the maple trees, a few on the verge of turning yellow. She limped around the green in front of the church for a half an hour bending from the waist repeatedly and trying to stretch her lower back and legs. A pair of women's loafers came into her view as she rolled back up to standing.

'I hear you're helping the police with their enquiries on your brother's murder case.' Tina Chandler stood with an air of confidence. In her mid-forties, but she still seemed to have the hunger of a young journalist. There was a softness about her hazel eyes that Lizzie had not noticed before, her smile revealing matching crows' feet.

'Who told you that?'

'It's impossible to keep anything a secret in this town for long. Too many loose lips, too much gossip.'

'You can say that again. Nobody can mind their own business here.'

'When are you due?'

'Beginning of January but wouldn't mind if it were earlier. I didn't realize how uncomfortable pregnancy can be.'

'I was sick throughout my whole pregnancy, walked around with a drip attached to me. Vowed I'd never go through it again. Minute after my son was born, I was craving fried chicken.'

'Did you send your husband out to KFC?' Lizzie laughed.

'No husband, his father wasn't interested. I've raised him on my own.'

'I'm going it alone too.' Lizzie glanced back at the church. The undertaker was opening the back of the hearse. 'Looks like the service is finishing.'

'If you want to talk, you've got my number.'

'Yeah.' Lizzie nodded.

Heading back to her car she spotted Joe and Pete Kominsky having what looked like an argument, Joe's arms flailing in the air while Kominsky stood with arms folded across his chest. He looked displeased at Joe's outburst. She walked on and met Hannah coming out of the church.

'You okay, Lizzie?'

'Yeah, just a bit of sciatica.'

'Go home and lie down. You can come to our house for dinner later. I'm sure the girls would love to spoil you and I could do with the company, Tommy's going out.'

Chapter 36

The sound of the kettle whistling snapped Lizzie out of her reverie. She had been watching her blue heron take flight, wishing she too could fly off. The police interview was looming and making her anxious, more so now that she knew neither Ma nor Tommy had been summoned. She couldn't understand what she might offer the police that could be of any use. Tina Chandler's business card stared at her from the kitchen counter. Maybe it was time to hear what the old hack had to say for herself. She tapped a message into her phone, If you're still interested, meet me at Chip's Diner in Denton on Wednesday at 10. What did she have to lose? She poured herself a cup of chamomile tea, laid down on her bed and opened her book. Only three pages in, her eyes heavy, she drifted off to sleep.

She awoke to the sound of her phone pinging. The sun was already low in the sky, she picked up her phone, it was Hannah asking whether she was coming for dinner. She didn't really feel up to it but didn't have the heart to say no. Hannah had been going the extra mile to make up for the trouble she had caused, and she could do with help with the baby. Lizzie had assumed that Maura would take every opportunity to hold her new grandson, but according to

Hannah, she had barely been over. She was sending them a message, she was displeased with their choice of name, that's all it could be. Lizzie grabbed her cardigan and stepped out into the cool early evening air, picked up a damp yellow leaf from the ground, smelled it, then twirled the stem through her fingers.

*

Lizzie held the blue swaddled bundle, rocking back and forth while her nieces were completing a jigsaw on the coffee table.

'I feel like I should be helping you in the kitchen, Hannah.'

'You are helping, you've got TJ off to sleep. He's been crying all afternoon.'

'Do you have him on some kind a schedule?'

'Schedule?' Hannah laughed. 'You've got so much to learn, Lizzie.' Hannah crunched on a carrot stick while stirring the pot on the stove. 'Girls, time for bed'

'Shall I take them up?'

'No, no, you stay with TJ. Rule number one – never wake a sleeping baby.' Hannah gathered up the trio and led them upstairs, the disgruntled children attempting to negotiate more time to no avail.

Lizzie stared at TJ sleeping, his heart shaped lips pursed and making little sucking movements. The dark hair he had been born with had fallen out and replaced by a downy white fuzz. Maybe Hannah would finally get the blonde-haired child she had craved. The smell of chili con carne filled the room, Lizzie was about to get up and stir the pot when Hannah re-emerged.

'Here, let me take TJ and put him in the Moses basket. Dinner's ready.' Hannah lifted the bundle liberating Lizzie.

'Smells good.' Lizzie ladled out a portion of chili into her bowl, topping it with grated cheese and a dollop of sour cream. 'Where's Tommy at tonight?'

'Oh, he's out at a meeting.' Hannah's voice sounded wobbly. 'Can you serve me up some chili too please?'

'What kind of meeting?' Lizzie wouldn't normally have pressed Hannah but sensed something was up. She dipped a tortilla chip into her chili and crunched on it. 'Did I ask something inappropriate?'

'He's at an Alcoholics Anonymous meeting. Don't tell him I told you.'

'What? AA?' Lizzie couldn't believe what she was hearing. 'How long has he been going to AA meetings?'

'Since just after Claire was born. He started drinking quite heavily and decided to get help.'

'But he's been drinking the whole time I've been here.'

'Exactly. He'd been sober for six years. Then all this stuff with Paddy, it's been hard.' Hannah was choking back the tears. 'He promised me when TJ was born that he wouldn't drink again. He's been back at meetings each week ever since.'

'I had no idea.'

'That's why we have no hard liquor in this house. I warned him after that bar room brawl that I wouldn't go through it all again.'

'Did he say why he started drinking, was it to do with Paddy?'

'He doesn't like to talk about it. Paddy is never mentioned in this house. But look, your dad was a drinker and it's not like you don't like a tipple yourself.'

'True. I'm just shocked, that's all. I won't say anything.'

A small cry came from the Moses basket. 'I need to give him a feed.' Hannah sat down on the sofa and lifted the baby to her breast. 'I'm terrible with secrets. But you already know that.'

Chapter 37

Lizzie pressed the entry phone, stated her name, and was buzzed into the station lobby. The young officer greeted her with his usual disconcerting enthusiasm and told her to take a seat in the waiting area. She had slept fitfully the previous night, too much on her mind. Tommy, an alcoholic. How could she have known; she had been at sea for the last decade. It wasn't as if she had seen him regularly. Sitting in the waiting room she tapped her foot repeatedly, overcome with a sudden urge to run, her heart was pounding. She put her head down and took some deep breaths.

'Are you okay, Miss O'Donnell?' Kominsky asked.

She looked up. 'Sorry, yes, just a bit of indigestion.' She patted her belly and stood up.

'We'll be in the main conference room if you'd like to follow me.'

The young officer grinned at her as she walked past the window and down the hall. It was a sterile place, no walls painted soothing colors to be found. The starkness was deliberate, to make people feel ill at ease. Kominsky pressed the switch, and the fluorescent lights began to flicker and dance before emitting a harsh white light. The long conference table was covered in plastic bags, contents unknown.

'Have a seat here, Miss O'Donnell. My colleague Detective Field will be joining us shortly.'

'I don't really understand why…'

'Just hold that thought until Detective Field joins us, then we'll explain everything.'

Lizzie knew this wasn't going to be a cozy informal chat with the authorities. 'Will Joe be joining us?'

'No, Officer Moretti is not part of the investigating team in your brother Paddy's case.' Kominsky lifted the pitcher of water, filled three glasses, and passed one to Lizzie.

'Thank you. Should I have contacted a lawyer for this?' Her mouth was parched, she gulped back the water. 'I'm just confused…'

'Nothing to worry about Miss O'Donnell.' Kominsky looked out the window into the corridor and motioned to his colleague to come into the room. 'This is Detective Field, he will be assisting me with your interview today. He was part of the original team that investigated your brother's death.'

'I don't understand how I can help with your enquiries exactly?' Lizzie fidgeted with her hands under the table. 'I was only eight when my brother died.'

'Let me explain.' Kominsky pressed the record button and spoke into the machine. September 16th, 2014,

Voluntary interview with Elizabeth O'Donnell.

'It's Mary Elizabeth,' Lizzie interrupted.

'Voluntary interview with Mary Elizabeth O'Donnell. Resident State Trooper Peter Kominsky and Detective Chris Field in attendance.' Kominsky took a pen from his pocket and wrote the date and time down on a yellow pad. 'We have asked you in today for a voluntary interview, you are not under arrest or even under caution. In preparation for this case to go to trial both the prosecution and defense have requested a review of evidence. As part of that review, some new information has come to light that we think you may be able to assist with.'

'Uh huh.' Lizzie stared blankly.

'It was brought to our attention that you were the only member of your family not interviewed after your brother's death.'

'Yes, that's right. I have almost no memory of that time.'

'Except that we know that you were out playing in the snow the night of the blizzard.'

'That's right. My brother Tommy and I were making a fort and digging tunnels.'

'And can you confirm where it was you were playing?'

'At the end of our street, Maiden Lane, it's a cul-de-sac. The snow plows piled up all the snow at the end creating a mountain. Must've been about twenty feet high.' Lizzie put her hand on her leg to stop it from shaking, she needed the bathroom but didn't dare ask. 'I don't understand why this is relevant.'

'Your brother, Paddy, his body was found at the cul-de-sac. It was the murder site.'

'Oh.' She was flushed and reached for her glass of water. 'I…I didn't know that.'

'I imagine your parents kept most of the details from you so as not to upset you.' Detective Field added as he filled her empty glass. 'Can you tell us what you do remember from that night?'

'Tommy and I were digging.' She took a deep breath, her heart was racing. 'The snow was coming down hard.' She swallowed and looked up at the officers staring at her. 'I guess the snow gave way and I got buried. The rest of what I know is just what I was told happened. I have no memory of it all.' She sat back in her chair and wiped the corner of her eye. 'The doctors said it was my brain's way of protecting me from the trauma of having been buried.'

'And what were you told?'

She rattled off by rote, devoid of emotion, like it had happened to someone else. She wanted it over. 'Tommy went back to the house to get a new flashlight so that we had better light for digging. I stayed behind. When he came back, he said all he could see was my hat sticking out of the snow. He dug me out not knowing how long I'd been buried for and carried me home.' She clasped her palms under the table. 'My parents drove us to the hospital in the middle of the storm and I woke up a week later. They said I had developed pneumonia after dry drowning.'

'And you never saw Paddy there?'

'No.' Lizzie was lightheaded. 'I'm sorry, can we take a bathroom break?'

'Yes, of course.'

Lizzie followed Kominsky out of the conference room and down the hall to the restrooms. She sat down in the stall and took deep breaths. Her head was spinning. She flushed the toilet and washed her hands in the basin, splashing cold water on her face. Her face looked blotchy in the mirror, what a mess. How could Tommy not have told her that Paddy died in the same spot where they had been playing? She made her way back to the conference room and sat down. A cup of tea and chocolate chip cookie were on the table in front of her.

'That was most helpful, Miss O'Donnell. Now we'd like to show you all the evidence that was found at the murder site. Bear in mind it includes everything that the plows picked up as they cleared the street over the whole winter. We'd like you to see if there is anything you recognize.'

Lizzie stared at the mass of bags on the table. Where to

start? It seemed like a pointless exercise to her. What might an empty coke can mean or a cigarette box? She sifted through the bags, until she came to a bag containing a red Bic lighter and stopped.

'Is that something you recognize?'

'No, but Paddy did smoke. I remember that.' She continued in the same vein then looked up at the clock on the wall. She'd been at it for over an hour. A flash of pink caught her eye and she reached for the bag, opened it and gasped. 'That's my hat.' The dizziness took her by surprise, she needed to sit down. 'I was wearing it along with the scarf my mother knitted for me. Pink was my favorite color.'

'We'd like to take a DNA sample from you if you don't mind.' Detective Field pulled out a kit and put on latex gloves.'

'Yes, I guess…I mean if you have to.' She stuck out her tongue as he swabbed her mouth. 'What are the brown specks on the hat?'

'Blood spatter.'

'I didn't know I got cut.'

'The paperwork says it's Paddy's blood.'

'I don't understand.' She waited for a response, but there was an awkward silence. 'How could Paddy's blood be on my hat?' Her body trembled. 'I'm tired, I don't think I can do anymore today. Can I go?'

'Just one more thing, can you look at this?' Detective Field pulled the red and black checked jacket out of its bag.

Lizzie stood staring at the jacket and was overcome again with the smell of stale cigarettes and beer. Her legs crumbled beneath her. When she came to, she was lying on the floor in the conference room, a blanket folded under her head.

'I'm sorry, I don't know what happened.' She tried to sit up.

'Take it slow, Miss O'Donnell, you fainted.'

'Must be my blood pressure, it's been low lately.'

The two officers helped her up to sitting and gave her a can of Coke. 'The sugar will help.' They told her to rest and left the room, returning twenty minutes later. 'How are you doing?'

'Better, thanks. Can I go now?'

'Yes, we'll be in touch if we need to speak to you again.' Detective Field opened the door to escort her out.

Outside in the parking lot she leaned against her car and closed her eyes. She heard her name being called and turned.

'Lizzie, I'm sorry. I had to tell them.' Joe was frantic.

'Tell them what?'

'That you were there, you know…where Paddy's body was found.'

Her body went rigid. 'All those nights out…we were friends. You were just pumping me for information?'

'I…'

'You even slept with me. Was that all in the line of duty too?' She pulled her keys from her bag, opened the car door, and turned back looking Joe squarely in the eyes. 'Did you think I was somehow involved? Like I killed my brother?'

'Lizzie! I never said that.' Joe's voice was breaking.

'Or is this how you get your revenge for me not telling you I was pregnant all those years ago?' She got into her car and drove off.

Chapter 38

Lizzie poured a shot of bourbon and tossed it back, swishing it around her mouth before swallowing, then poured two shots into the tall glass and filled it with Coke. She wandered down to the lake and sat on the edge of the dock dangling her legs in the water. Even the bourbon couldn't mask the smell of him, she couldn't get away from it. It was as if Detective Field had unleashed a genie from its bottle when he opened the bag, releasing Paddy into her consciousness. She could see him, smell him. He was haunting her, standing beside her staring. His silence menacing. She couldn't escape him. Could she have been there when he died? She was beginning to think this was a possibility. He had been there, he had to have been, but Tommy had never mentioned it. Was he protecting her from the truth, that she was a murderer? She stretched out on the dock and looked up at the night sky, her finger tracing the outline of the Big Dipper until she had counted all seven stars. She closed her eyes and saw her pink hat. Happier times, the excitement at unwrapping the hat and scarf Christmas morning and wearing them around the house all day. Her mom had been so proud of the complex cable pattern and pompom. Warm tears ran into her ears, she opened her eyes only to see the blood-spattered hat. She closed her eyes again, shaking her head, but the image remained. Each happy memory overridden with the shadow of Paddy's death.

*

The sound of someone banging on the door woke her. She had no recollection of coming back into the house the previous evening but must have spent the night on the sofa. As she rose to get the door she tripped over the almost empty bottle. Her cheeks were burning.

'Lizzie, let me in.' Tommy continued to pound on the door.

'I'm coming.' She took the chain off the door and opened it a crack. 'I'm not well, Tom. Whatever it is, it can it wait?'

'No, it can't. Just let me in.' He handed her the newspaper as he walked into the room. 'Jesus, Lizzie, you look a mess?' Walking over to the kitchen he put on a pot of coffee. 'You need to stop drinking, you're not going to find any answers in the bottom of that bottle.'

'You'd know all about that.' She lashed out at him, the truth was hard to hear. 'You have no idea what I went through yesterday at the police station.'

'No, I don't, but that journalist seems to think she does.'

'What do you mean?'

'Take a look at the front page.'

The Denton Times

Keeping the community informed with independent local reporting

SISTER OF MURDERED TEENAGER QUESTIONED IN COLD CASE MURDER INVESTIGATION

By Tina Chandler
16 September 2014

Newham, MA. - The thirty-year-old sister of a teenage boy murdered in 1993 has been questioned by state police in connection with his death. Mary-Elizabeth O'Donnell was seen leaving Newham police station on 16th September after a two-hour interrogation. Resident State Trooper Peter Kominsky refused to confirm or deny that Miss O'Donnell has been assisting the police with their enquiries.

The trial of Jason Edwards, arrested for the murder of Patrick O'Donnell, is scheduled to begin on 17th November.

The pregnant Miss O'Donnell looked visibly distressed as she leaned against her car after the extended interview.

Miss O'Donnell could not be reached for comment.

The photo made Lizzie look like she was nine months pregnant. How could the paper publish this non-story? She threw it into the garbage can.

'Exactly where it belongs.' She rested her arms on the counter and sighed. 'Somebody in the police department is leaking information to Tina Chandler.'

'What makes you think that?' Tommy asked.

'She mentioned me helping the police with their enquiries when I spoke to her at the funeral. Somebody had to have told her.'

'Maybe you should make a complaint, tell Joe.'

'Don't see much point in that. Joe's the one who dumped me in it in the first place.'

'What do you mean?'

'Joe told Kominsky that I had been digging at the end of the cul de sac, where Paddy's body was found.' Lizzie's voice was shaking. 'Why didn't you tell me that Paddy died right where we had been playing?'

Tommy opened his mouth as if to speak, then closed it again.

'Did I kill Paddy?' She was relieved at having asked the question. 'Is that it? You've been trying to protect me.'

'Don't be ridiculous, Lizzie. You did not kill Paddy.' Tommy ran his hand through his hair and laughed awkwardly. 'You were tiny, only eight years old. What makes you think you killed Paddy?'

'The police have my hat, there's blood spattered on it.'

'Your hat must've fallen off when I dug you out of the snow and been left behind.'

'But how did Paddy's blood get on it?'

'I don't know. Maybe Jason Edwards hit him, and the blood landed on the hat. I really don't think you should be worrying about this.'

'But I am. You don't understand what it's like to not remember.'

'Maybe it's better not remembering. I've spent my life trying to forget.' Tommy put his arm around her shoulder. 'Once the trial is over, we can finally put this to rest and move on. You've got so much to look forward to with the baby coming.'

'I wish she could have taken a more flattering photo of me.' Lizzie smiled through her hangover. She didn't want to talk about it anymore. 'I need a shower, have to get to my pre-natal appointment at the clinic.'

Tommy picked up the bottle and poured it down the drain. 'If you need help, next time you call me.'

She waited until she heard his car engine start, then pulled the newspaper out of the garbage and re-read the article. Tina Chandler had a clever way of saying nothing yet insinuating the worst. It was what was left unsaid that was damaging. She had done this to Lizzie's father, but Lizzie hadn't anticipated that she would come under Tina's scrutiny herself. She was in two minds about cancelling the meeting she had arranged with the journalist for the following morning, but decided it was an opportunity to at least vent her anger.

Chapter 39

The stainless-steel siding on Chip's diner gleamed in the morning sun. The original Chip, a Denton legend, had died of a heart attack around the same time as Lizzie's dad. His two sons took over the business and under their direction the diner had continued to be a popular local gathering spot, even at two o'clock in the morning. Tina Chandler was already sitting in a booth when Lizzie arrived. The turquoise vinyl seat squeaked as Lizzie slid in.

'I thought you might not come.' Tina said in an almost apologetic tone, sipping her coffee.

'On the contrary, I've been very much looking forward to this conversation.' Lizzie caught the waitress's eye. 'I'll have a large stack of buttermilk pancakes with bacon, extra crispy, please.' She looked at Tina, waiting for her to order. 'You not eating?'

'Just a re-fill, please.' Tina ripped open three sachets of sugar and poured them into the steaming mug.

'Adding sugar won't make you any sweeter.' Lizzie could feel the venom rising in her. She wanted to be spiteful. 'Do you really not care what damage you do to people?'

'I'm just doing a job. Covering an important local story.'

'You can't even take a decent photo.'

'There's nothing wrong with the photo, that's how you looked – tired, distressed.'

'I didn't realize pregnancy related fatigue and hormonal stress were so newsworthy.'

'Ok, Liz. I can see you want to vent. That's fine, I'm used to it. Go on…' She sat back in the booth, hands up, ready to be fired upon. 'This is entirely off the record, no recording, no notebook.'

'Everyone…' Tears were welling up in her eyes. She wasn't doing rage very well. It was hard to shoot someone who had already surrendered. 'They…' She didn't seem able to spit the words out. 'Do you think I killed my brother?'

The journalist burst out laughing, her mouth in a broad grin. 'Short answer. No.'

'Then, why…'

'Look, Liz. I'm just trying to figure out where this story is going. The police are being so tight lipped and with the trial eight weeks off, well, I'm just being provocative.'

The waitress placed the plate of steaming pancakes in front of Lizzie. She slapped on a load of butter and drowned the fluffy cakes in an unhealthy portion of maple syrup. Tina watched as she picked up a piece of bacon, dipped it into the syrup and crunched on it.

'I want the truth, just like you.' Tina's face screwed up

watching Lizzie attack her breakfast. 'When was the last time you ate?'

'The truth?' Lizzie stuffed a forkful of pancakes into her mouth and chewed. 'I'm listening.' She put down her fork, her cheeks reddened.

'I covered your brother's story from the time he was reported missing, but you know that already. It bothered me when the leads dried up and the police lost interest.' She gulped the last of her coffee and called the waitress for a refill. 'When they arrested Jason Edwards I said, yes, here's my opportunity to tell the story – to find the truth.'

'And what is this truth then?'

'I'm not sure. But given you took the time to go through all the old articles I think we're both searching for the same thing.'

Lizzie sat silently for a few moments. She wanted to trust Tina, perhaps having her onside might help her and she didn't trust the police anymore. 'Do you know what happened to me the night my brother went missing?'

'I know you were only eight years old.'

And with that, Lizzie spilled her guts to a woman she had intensely disliked and mistrusted up until a moment before. Something shifted when Tina had uttered the word truth that made Lizzie want to take the risk. What more did she have to lose? She shared her fractured memories, the flashbacks, nightmares and what she'd been told. None of it made sense but Tina sat there riveted.

Chapter 40

Lizzie stood on the dock admiring the scarlet, gold, purple and orange display. The fall blaze of the hillside was mirrored in the still water. Each October crowds came from all over the world to see this natural autumnal pyrotechnic display. It was her favorite time of year too. The quiet roads between Newham and Lenox were clogged up with leaf peepers making the grand tour. It was a double-edged sword, local businesses benefitted from leaf tourism, but locals looked on the largely geriatric leaf peepers with disdain. They drove so slowly it was impossible to get anywhere.

She looked down at her abdomen, incredulous that it could have grown so large that her belly button popped out, and she still had just over two months to go. Her last check-up had gone well but her anxiety was running high, fueled by the summons delivered that morning to her mailbox. Witness for the defense? Imagining taking the stand made her nauseous. Could she refuse? She dialed Tommy's number, but it was busy. Not having anyone to turn to was not unfamiliar, she'd managed most of her life on her own. People were unreliable. They let you down, leave you vulnerable. And trusting Tina Chandler with her story left her feeling even more naked. Chandler said she was on her side, time would tell. She took her keys from her pocket and walked up to the car.

The traffic in the center of town had come to a standstill outside the police station. Strangely her mother and Father Larkin were having an animated conversation with Joe. Maura's arms flailed in the air. From Lizzie's end it didn't look good. Father Larkin had his arm around Ma consoling her while Joe looked on. The traffic inched forward enough for Lizzie to pull into the parking lot. By the time she got out of the car and across the street, Maura and Father Larkin had driven off and Joe sat in his car staring, in a daze. Lizzie tapped on his window and took some pleasure out of seeing him startled.

'You were away with the pixies.'

'Got a lot on my mind. What can I do for you?'

'What's going on with my mother? I saw her with Father Larkin talking to you. She looked upset.'

'She's been called as a prosecution witness and is nervous. I was trying to reassure her.'

'Looks like we're on opposite teams.'

'What do you mean?'

'I assumed you knew. I've been called as a witness for the defense.'

'Shit.'

'Can't imagine I'll make a very credible witness. Miss O'Donnell, is this your hat? Yes. Can you explain how your brother's blood got on it? No. I don't remember anything from that night.'

'I'm sorry.'

'Yeah right, me too. I'm sorry I ever came back to this town.'

'Don't say that I…' his voice trailed off as she turned and walked away.

Lizzie crossed the street and went into the coffee shop. Father Larkin was standing in line paying for two coffees and an apricot Danish.

'Morning Father,' she said. He flinched. 'Bit jumpy today?' She was amused by her ability to make everyone jump.

'No, no, hadn't realized you were behind me is all. Your mother's over at the table in the corner. Why don't you join us?'

Lizzie followed the priest over to the table and sat down. 'Don't look so surprised, Ma. Father Larkin asked me to join you.'

'I really don't need your…'

'Maura is a bit shaken up. She's been called to testify for the prosecution at the trial.'

'I've been summoned to testify too. Got a letter this

morning.'

'Why would the prosecution want you as a witness, you were a child?' Maura had stopped sobbing and was tucking into her apricot Danish, her appetite unaffected.

'They don't. I've been summoned by the defense.'

Maura dropped her pastry on to the paper plate. 'You can't do that.'

'I don't have a choice.'

'But we're family, we're on the same side.'

'It's not about sides, Ma.' Lizzie's chair scraped the floor as she slid back. She couldn't remember the last time her mom had been on her side. 'It's about finding the truth. I've gotta go.'

*

The goth library assistant put down his book and managed to smile when Lizzie appeared at the reception desk. She stared down at his latest book jacket, the big bold red letters – BIZARRE CRIMES, YOU COULDN'T MAKE IT UP, Incredible Real-Life Criminal Cases.

'Any good?'

'Just started it, but yeah.' He looked pleased that Lizzie had taken an interest. 'Your friend is waiting for you in the study room you booked.'

Lizzie made her way to the room, pushing the door open with her shoulder so as not to spill the tray of coffees. She set it down and pushed a white paper bag across the table. 'I got you a blueberry muffin.'

'Let's get to work.' Tina unrolled a long sheet of paper across the table. 'This is where we left off last week…'

'Hold on.' Lizzie choked up. 'I've got some news.' She pulled out the letter from her backpack and handed it to Tina. 'Take a look.'

'Oh, right. Shit. Wasn't expecting that.'

'Neither was I.'

'Well, all you can do is say what you know for sure.'

'Just makes me feel even more anxious. My nightmares have worsened since we've been going over everything.' She pulled her hair back and tied it in a scrunchy. 'Paddy is haunting me even more.'

'You said you wanted to know what happened, you want to remember.'

'I do, but…'

'Nobody said it was going to be painless.' Tina took a bite of her muffin. 'It's good. Thanks. Can we get to work now?'

Over the four weeks since the pair had joined forces, they had constructed a timeline of Paddy's movements from their pooled resources. The long sheet had some obvious gaps that neither could fill in.

'I think we should look at Dylan Jones,' Lizzie said. She

pulled out Paddy's high school yearbook and opened to the sports section. 'You see this, Dylan and Paddy were teammates – they look pretty friendly in this picture.'

'And Jason Edwards is the link between the three of them.' Tina looked up at Lizzie. 'Can you find a way to talk to Jones's widow?'

Lizzie scratched her scalp. 'There might be a way. Leave it with me.'

*

Lizzie was about to get back in her car, her hand sore from knocking, when Hannah finally answered the door wearing a grubby pair of sweatpants, her eyes hollowed.

'Hey, you look terrible.' Lizzie barged past her into the house and put a brown paper bag on the kitchen counter. 'I brought you some lunch,' she said. The baby's angry wailing echoed through the hall. Lizzie followed Hannah upstairs.

'He's been so unsettled, cried all night. I'm losing my mind.' A tear rolled down Hannah's face. 'All this demand feeding is killing me. I can't manage with the girls as well.'

'You got a bottle?'

'Yeah, but I was saving my frozen breast milk for an emergency.'

'I think this classifies as an emergency.' Lizzie went into the bathroom and filled the bath. 'Have a good soak, relax.

I've got TJ.' She took the screaming baby downstairs, placed him in the baby bouncer and switched it on. The calming vibrations soothed him while she hunted around the kitchen for a bottle and pulled a bag of breast milk from the freezer. She hadn't expected it to be so yellow. It was overwhelming to think of all the equipment she would need to buy, now she could add vibrating baby bouncer to the list. There was no way she could afford all this gear; she'd have to pare it down to the essentials.

She lifted TJ from the chair and sat down on the sofa. He nuzzled his face in towards her chest, rooting for milk until he found the latex nipple and began to suck. She was getting the knack of this mothering business and held out some hope that she might be able to cope with her own baby when the time came. By the time Hannah appeared, he was sound asleep in Lizzie's arms. Hannah lifted him and placed him in the Moses basket.

'I feel human again.' She stretched out on the L shaped sofa and wrapped herself in a fleece blanket. 'You have impeccable timing, Lizzie. Rescued me again.'

Lizzie stood over the stove and stirred the pot.

'Smells good.'

'It's chicken and dumpling soup from the deli.' She ladled the soup into a bowl and placed it on a tray along with a chunk of farmhouse bread and butter. 'Here you go.

Eat up.'

'This is just what I needed. Thank you.'

The gratitude seemed genuine and in a strange way she was enjoying looking out for Hannah.

'Has Ma not been around at all?'

'Not really, she stopped by the other day but rushed off. Said she needed to help Cindy Jones.'

'Can you help me out with something?'

'Sure, anything.'

'I want to speak to Cindy Jones. Do you think you could arrange a play date for Claire with her daughter?'

'Oh, I don't…' Hannah stopped slurping her soup and put her spoon on the tray, her eyes widened.

'If it's too much to ask, I…' Lizzie tried a different approach – emotional blackmail.

'No, no. I guess I can arrange it.'

'It's just that I want to talk to her without Ma around. It's important, I wouldn't ask otherwise.'

'I'll see what I can do.' Hannah gave a faint and uncertain smile.

'Can we keep this between the two of us? Tommy doesn't need to be bothered with it,' Lizzie said.

Chapter 41

The smell of eucalyptus overpowered Lizzie as she entered the church, each pew adorned with a floral display. Tara had spared no expense for her big day. She took a seat towards the back of the church not wanting to stand out. Tara had been so grateful to her for helping to organize their dream cruise and insisted Lizzie attend the wedding. Though she felt like a beached whale and unable to sit through a ceremony, it had proved impossible to say no to Tara. She watched the guests' reactions as they filtered into the church, bowled over by the sheer extravagance of it all, and smiled.

The congregation stood as the sound of Pachelbel's Canon filled the church and the bridesmaids sauntered down the aisle in burgundy satin gowns. November was a tricky month for a wedding, the trees having already shed most of their leaves, but not quite winter, it could feel drab. Tara came into view, her arm through her father's, wearing a long-sleeved ivory lace gown and carrying a bouquet of dark lavender roses, purple dianthus, and thistle. Elegant. She winked at Lizzie as she passed by, mouthing thanks. Lizzie looked down at her ever-expanding belly, like a beached whale, there was nothing elegant about being seven months pregnant. She drifted off as Father Larkin's voice echoed around the church. He was droning on about the sanctity of marriage and the family again. She was the anti-Christ sitting there, a representation of everything he preached against.

She was relieved that Tara had opted not to have a full wedding mass, it would have been torture to have sat for much longer. Tara and her new husband beamed as they made their way out of the church to applause. Lizzie stood and waited for the guests to leave, row by row in an orderly manner, until it was her turn. She cradled her bump protectively as she tried to squeeze out of the pew.

'Bit of a tight squeeze.' Joe extended his arm. 'Can I give you a hand?'

'I'm okay, but thanks.' She smiled at the brunette attached to Joe's other arm. 'You not going to introduce me?'

'Right, uh… this is Antonia. Antonia, this is Lizzie.' Joe wiped a little bead of sweat from his brow. 'Nice service.'

'Yes, Tara looked so happy,' Lizzie said. Antonia, a nice Italian girl, Joe's mom would be thrilled. Lizzie not so much, but she had no claim to Joe.

'You going to the reception?'

'No, I'm not really up to it.'

'Shame.' Antonia smiled and put her arm around Joe's

waist.

'Joe, I think you have a mole at the station,' Lizzie said.

'What do you mean? This really isn't the time…'

'Just what I said, somebody in your department is leaking information to the press. You need to get on top of it with the trial starting on Monday.'

'You sure you're not being paranoid?'

'Don't be an asshole, just look into it.' Lizzie joined the receiving line and kissed Tara on both cheeks. 'You look stunning, and such a beautiful service.' She smiled, hoping that was what she was supposed to say. 'I'm not well enough to make the reception.' She pointed to her swollen ankles. 'My colleague, Martin, will meet you at the first-class lounge at Boston Harbor. Everything's taken care of. Have a wonderful honeymoon.'

She walked back to her car fuming. 'Shame', she couldn't get that catty voice out of her head, nor the look on Antonia's face as she gave Lizzie and her sack dress the once over. Who was she in her slinky silk dress anyway? Her legs buckled, she was about to hit the ground but was caught by a pair of arms.

'Close call,' he smiled and took a drag from his cigarette which he had somehow avoided burning her with.

'Thank you.' She took a deep breath resting her hand on the hood of the car. 'Nice tux. Guess you're in the wedding party?'

'I'm Ted, Tara's brother.'

'Sorry, I'm a bit shaken.' She fumbled with her keys. 'I'm Liz.'

'Let me give you a hand.'

'Tara told me you've been having a hard time. I'm sorry.'

'I got out of rehab a few weeks ago. So far, so good,' he laughed.

'Is Father Larkin helping you out?' she asked.

The color drained from Ted's face. 'Steering well clear of him.' He looked over his shoulder. 'I gotta go.'

Lizzie grabbed his wrist. 'Wait, you were friends with my brother, Paddy, weren't you?'

'Yeah, kind of.' He opened the car door for her, avoiding making eye contact.

'I need your help. Would you be willing to talk to a friend of mine?' She looked up at him. 'I know you've had a tough time, but I think we can help each other.'

'I dunno.' He took a last drag and flicked the butt into the churchyard.

'Please, Ted. It's important.' She wrote her number on a piece of paper and handed it to him. 'Call me.'

*

The craving for bourbon was at its worst in the evening when she was alone at home. With no alcohol in the house, food had become her crutch, her Saturday nights reduced to lying on the sofa gorging on junk in front of the television. She was turning into her mother. The return of NHL ice hockey to NBC had been a welcome distraction. The Bruins were up against the Edmonton Oilers, the game tied at the end of the first period. Despite wearing her Bruins jersey, watching at home lacked atmosphere. She missed the buzz of the bar, the roar of the crowd as the puck hit the back of the net. The second period had been so slow, no goals scored, that she almost turned the game off. She decided to give the Bruins another chance and was glad she had so. Four goals scored in the final period gave her team a five to two victory, but it was a lonely celebration for Lizzie. She turned out the lights in the living room and got ready for bed. It was becoming increasingly difficult to find a comfortable sleeping position and she knew that the minute she closed her eyes he'd be back again, looming over her like a silent stalker. She wished he would speak, give her some indication of what he wanted from her. Maybe he could fill in the gaps. She closed her eyes and hoped for the best.

The smell of urine and cigarettes filled her nostrils and woke her. Damp sheets, she cursed herself, a thirty-year-old bedwetter. The midwife had advised her to set an alarm every few hours to avoid this embarrassing inconvenience, but she'd taken no notice. What little sleep she was getting was precious, there was no way she was going to wake herself up deliberately and it would be over in a couple of months. But the smell of stale cigarettes remained a mystery. So strong she could almost taste it in her mouth. Pregnancy was doing strange things to her senses.

She turned on the faucet, filled her glass and stared out the window. A camouflaged jon boat moved across the water, a black and white pointer riding in its bow, on the lookout for waterfowl. She had grown accustomed to the sound of gunshot over the last couple of weeks and seeing the hunters return with duck, coot, and mergansers. She remembered ducks hanging from the rafters in the garage, her father sitting next to Tommy teaching him how to pluck the bird. Tommy had yet to answer her texts about whether he would accompany their mother to court. She took the lack of response as a negative. The courthouse would be a zoo. Would Maura cope on her own? She would have told Joe, but he'd already called her paranoid, and, in any case, she was no longer responsible for her mother. There was nothing for her to feel guilty about. She kept telling herself this hoping she would eventually believe it.

The Denton Times

Keeping the community informed with independent local reporting

COLD CASE ACCUSED OPTS FOR JURY TRIAL IN MURDER CASE

By Tina Chandler
21 November 2014

Denton, MA. - The latest on the trial of Jason Edwards charged with the murder of the teenager Patrick O'Donnell in 1993. Edwards decided to stick with a jury trial rather than have a judge decide his fate. Judge William H. Baxter had given Edwards until Monday to decide whether he wanted to switch to a bench trial. Mr. Edwards' attorney, Eileen Murphy, had claimed that her client would not get a fair trial in Denton due to intense media coverage of the case.

The vetting and selection of the twelve jurors and five alternates proved contentious, with both sides using their peremptory challenges to excuse potential jurors without cause. Further intense questioning of potential jurors led to the dismissal of multiple jurors, to the point that an additional pool had to be called. The jury selection process took four days in a trial that was originally scheduled to only last five days.

Judge Baxter swore in the jury and alternates late Thursday evening. Opening statements are expected to begin on Friday.

Chapter 42

Tina Chandler had been remarkably restrained in her coverage of the jury selection. It was a circus, the courtroom baking, and benches hard. Lizzie would struggle to sit through the rest of it. If jury selection took four days, how long might the case drag on for? The arrogance of the prosecutor, Matthew Cranston, in his polished wing tips and double- breasted designer suit, had been astounding. He took one look at potential jurors, waved his hand, and dismissed them. Lizzie was certain he was both homophobic and sexist. He seemed to want to stack the jury with older women and straight young men, though Eileen Murphy wasn't going to let him get away with it and rose to the challenge, arguing back fiercely.

Tommy had refused outright to attend any of the trial so far, claiming he had more important things to do. The construction of his shopping plaza had come to an abrupt halt when the diggers came across the remains of a Nipmuc burial ground. He had tried to keep it hidden but word got out and Eddie Cisco and gang had been staging daily protests. Tommy claimed it would bankrupt him if it went on much longer. Still Lizzie shouldn't have been the only one to keep an eye on their mother. She had been calm up to now, but with opening statements due to start, Lizzie was preparing herself for the worst. She pulled the wool turtleneck dress over her head and smoothed it around her belly, then sat down and tugged on the zipper of her suede boots until it eased past the fattest part of her calf.

*

A rafter of wild turkeys was crossing the road as Lizzie pulled up in front of Maura's house. Thanksgiving was only a week away and she was yet to get an invitation anywhere. She rang the doorbell and got a shock when Father Larkin opened the door and greeted her.

'I'm accompanying your mother to the courthouse.' He offered, as if she might think he had ungentlemanly reasons for being in the house alone with her mother.

'Right, I'll just go upstairs and see if she needs anything.' As Lizzie walked toward the staircase, Father Larkin grabbed her arm.

'That won't be necessary.' He took his hand off her. 'She's not up there.'

'Where is she then?' Lizzie was about to walk into the kitchen when she heard sobbing. 'You shouldn't let her do this, it's not healthy.' She stood outside Paddy's room.

'She's saying the rosary, it's fine.'

'It's far from fine.' Lizzie was incensed. She had a distinct feeling that this priest had been manipulating her mother for years. 'I'll see you at the courthouse.'

*

A huge crowd had formed on the courthouse steps making it difficult for Lizzie to weave her way to the door. Her bump had come in handy as she pushed past people saying, 'heavily pregnant woman coming through'. She knew people were staring at her, not her belly, recognizing her face from the papers. She tried not to think about it and stared at the screen looking for the courtroom, Commonwealth of Massachusetts v. Edwards.

'It's courtroom three,' Joe said on his own, in uniform, no Antonia hanging all over him. 'They've moved it to the largest courtroom.'

'Thanks.' Lizzie started to walk up the steps, then stopped to catch her breath.

'You okay?' Joe asked.

'Not really. Could do without all this.' She winced at the stitch in her side. 'Still, only another six weeks and my body will be mine again.' She turned and continued up the staircase.

'Lizzie…'

She pretended not to hear him calling, she couldn't let him see her face flushed, choked up with tears.

The courtroom was already half full, she recognized some faces, a few of her mother's cronies and people she had seen around town. She found a place toward the front of the public gallery, pulled a cushion out of her bag, and sat down on it. Her phone pinged. 'You okay?' She scanned the room, spotted Tina Chandler sitting at the other end of the courtroom and tapped into her screen. 'Just about.'

'Move down, Lizzie.' Maura was flustered, out of breath, her face red and blotchy. 'Father Larkin and I need some space.'

'You two aren't supposed to be in here until after you testify. Who let you in?'

Her mother shrugged her shoulders. She was wearing the same navy outfit Lizzie had chosen for her months earlier, aware that it flattered her figure. Lizzie could see Tina Chandler, phone in hand, arm raised, photographing her mother - her headline photo for the next day's edition of the Denton Times. Maura knew she would be the center of attention and lapped it up. If the photo was a flattering one, she would have no complaint. In contrast, the last thing Lizzie wanted was to be photographed in her state of advanced pregnancy, and Tina had promised not to photograph her again, a pact made as part of their unorthodox alliance.

'How come you can be here?' Maura asked.

'The defense withdrew me from the list of witnesses.' She had been deemed unreliable, therefore unhelpful.

Lizzie squeezed past her mother, her belly almost touching her face.

'Where are you going?' Maura asked.

'Nowhere, I just need to stretch my legs. I'm uncomfortable.'

'You've gained too much weight is what the problem is,' Maura sniped. 'In my day, they were strict about weight gain in pregnancy.'

'Thank you for the belated interest in my well-being.' Lizzie slid past Father Larkin, avoiding contact with him, and walked to the back of the courtroom. She needed air.

The packed courtroom, all those people breathing, had depleted the room of oxygen. She found the court security officer and explained that her mother and the priest needed to be removed from the gallery until after their testimony. She sat down on the bench in the corridor for a moment, waiting until she'd seen her mother and the priest escorted out, then pulled a bottle of water from her bag and returned to the courtroom as the clerk was ushering in the jury.

'All rise! The court is now in session. The Honorable Judge William H. Baxter presiding. All those having business before this honorable court are admonished to draw near, give their attention, and they shall be heard,' the Clerk announced.

Judge Baxter took his place at the bench, poured himself

a glass of water and adjusted the neck of his black robe. The blue shield of the state seal of Massachusetts dominated the paneled wall behind him, the gold native American at its center holding a bow and arrow standing proud in the center. He cleared his throat and banged his gavel. 'The Defendant, Jason Edwards, has been charged with the sexual assault and second-degree murder of Patrick O'Donnell, aged 16, on or about the 12th of March 1993, charges to which he has pleaded not guilty. I now call on the prosecution to deliver its opening statement.'

Matthew Cranston rose and approached the jury, somehow managing to smile yet look serious. 'May it please the court, counsel, members of the jury. This is a case of brutal sexual assault and murder. You are here because on or about the 12th of March 1993, this man, Jason Edwards, violently raped, physically assaulted and intentionally suffocated a sixteen-year- old boy, Patrick O'Donnell.' The prosecutor already seemed to be enjoying the theatre of the courtroom, turning, and pointing to the defendant for emphasis, like he was in an episode of Law and Order. 'It is the burden of the prosecution to prove to you beyond reasonable doubt that Jason Edwards is guilty, and I am confident that the evidence I present to you during the trial will confirm the defendant's guilt.' He leaned on the rail and focused on making eye contact with the female jurors.

Smarmy, on the wrong side of awareness of his good looks, he clearly thought a lot of himself. Lizzie was already turned off, but maybe this kind of behavior appealed to older women. No doubt her mother would fawn over him. He continued his monologue, summarizing Paddy's last known movements and the discovery of his body, characterizing Jason Edwards as a depraved deviant.

'Members of the jury, the Commonwealth will call multiple witnesses in this trial who will confirm Patrick's last sighting and present irrefutable DNA evidence that directly implicates the defendant.' He paused and drew a breath, then pointed toward Lizzie in the public gallery. All eyes were upon them. 'The family of Patrick O'Donnell has waited twenty-one years for answers and justice for Patrick, a son and brother brutally taken from them, his life only just beginning. At the conclusion of this case, and after you have heard all the evidence, I am confident that you will return a verdict of guilty and deliver justice for Paddy.' He smiled at the jury, a few heads nodded in agreement with him, and stood in silence as if waiting for applause.

Lizzie stood up to stretch her legs, her toes numb, she was glad of the short recess and a chance to stand in the foyer.

'You okay?'

'Yeah, fine, Joe.' She tossed the empty bottle into the

garbage can. 'I need the bathroom before the trial resumes.' She started walking down the corridor. He ran to catch up, putting out his hand.

'Lizzie… I'm sorry.'

'Sorry for what?'

'Everything.' His eyes welled up.

'Yeah, me too.' She put her hand on his shoulder. 'Maybe we can get a bite to eat when this is over?'

'I'd like that.'

*

Eileen Murphy had really upped her game. Standing before the jury in a fitted pantsuit and just the right amount of makeup, she looked earnest and trustworthy as she delivered her opening statement.

'In a criminal case, as Mr. Cranston has already stated, the prosecution has the burden of proof. I ask that each of you wait until you have heard the evidence from all the witnesses before deciding what really happened. We do not contest the fact that Jason Edwards had sexual intercourse with Patrick O'Donnell on the 12th of March 1993. We agree that this happened and there is of course, DNA evidence that confirms it.' She was succinct, straight talking, no drama, no nonsense.

'However, this is all that can be proven, there is no other forensic evidence linking my client to the crime as he did not kill Patrick O'Donnell, someone else did. Patrick O'Donnell was a confused and damaged young man, who had sadly fallen into drug addiction. His need to feed his addiction led him to engage in risky behaviors that put him into contact with undesirable and dangerous drug dealers.'

Awkward murmurs echoed in the courtroom forcing Judge Baxter to bang his gavel and ask for order to be restored.

The defense attorney, unflustered by the commotion, paused before continuing. 'Please remember that it's the prosecution that must prove beyond a reasonable doubt, that Jason Edwards did anything more than engage in sexual intercourse with his friend, Patrick O'Donnell.'

Lizzie shuddered each time the defense attorney uttered the words sexual intercourse. The defense attorney's portrayal of her brother, 'the cherished son', was like an alternate reality to the angelic description touted by her mother.

'My client has nothing to prove, he is innocent until proven guilty. There are simply too many unknowns, twenty-one years after the event. I ask you to weigh all the evidence, and return the only possible verdict, a verdict of not guilty.'

The Denton Times

Keeping the community informed with independent local reporting

GRIEF STRICKEN MOTHER BREAKS DOWN IN COLD CASE MURDER TRIAL

By Tina Chandler
25 November 2014

Denton, MA. – It was standing room only at Superior Court on Monday as Assistant States Attorney, Matthew Cranston, presented the prosecution's case and the court heard compelling witness testimony from Maura O'Donnell (the mother of the deceased), Father John Larkin, Detective Chris Field, and a forensic pathologist.

The mother of Patrick O'Donnell, clearly very distressed and requiring several breaks to compose herself, testified that the family had enjoyed a meal together at home before Patrick went out to meet friends. 'It was an ordinary happy family meal,' she said.

Father John Larkin added to Patrick's final movements with his testimony. According to Larkin, he came upon Patrick *walking along Route 29 in the snow and gave him a lift to the arcade in Denton around 6.00pm.*

Detective Field, who was an investigator on the original case, testified that multiple witness statements confirmed Edwards presence at the arcade that evening and that he was seen with the victim. Graphic images of Patrick's injuries were shown by the forensic pathologist, who confirmed that semen on the body belonged to Jason Edwards.

The trial continues Wednesday with cross examination of the forensic pathologist by the defense. The accused, Jason Edwards, is expected to take the stand when the defense presents its case.

Chapter 43

Maura's photograph could have been described as handsome had it not been next to the headline – Grief-stricken Mother Breaks Down at Cold Case Trial. The headline set the tone, there was no need to read the rest of the article. Tina had needed to jazz up what had been an otherwise long and boring day in court, Lizzie understood that. She had let out a sigh of relief when Judge Baxter announced the trial was to be adjourned early, to enable him to hear an emergency case. It was all more exhausting than she had anticipated. She spent the rest of the day under a blanket, the fireplace roaring, enjoying the solitude. In a few short weeks she would no longer be living alone. She unpacked the two boxes of clothing that Hannah had dropped by, sorting the outfits by size. Holding up a newborn onesie, she found it hard to imagine a baby being that tiny. Hannah had given her a list of everything she needed for a layette, essential items highlighted in yellow. She was grateful for the hand me downs, knowing that money would be tight, her savings mostly depleted. She would have to find some sort of work once the baby was born. Tara had given her a five-star review of her honeymoon cruise, perhaps there was a market for bespoke cruise consultancy.

She woke up early Wednesday morning in a cold sweat. The sun rising over the lake revealed a hillside of dark bare trees, their skeletons exposed. She was relieved not to take the stand. Tommy had not even checked in to ask about how the trial was going. His disinterest in the case was abnormal.

*

The parking lot at the courthouse was already full when Lizzie pulled in. She drove around twice before giving up and parking in the municipal lot a short walk down the street. The female security guard took one look at her belly as she waddled into the foyer and fast tracked her to the front of the line. By the time she climbed the stairs to courtroom three, she was out of breath and desperate to sit down. The courtroom was already full, but a steward motioned to her that there was a seat at the end of a row half-way back. She struggled to lift herself when the clerk called for all present to rise, only half rising before plopping herself back down on her cushion.

Eileen Murphy looked at Judge Baxter and smiled, then called the forensic pathologist to the stand for cross examination.

'You testified that the semen recovered from Patrick O'Donnell's rectum was that of my client. Is that correct?'

'Yes, ma'am.'

'And the semen that was recovered from Patrick O'Donnell's oral cavity?'

'That wasn't a match with Jason Edwards. It didn't match with anyone on the DNA database.'

'So, a second man had sexual relations with Patrick O'Donnell that night?'

'That's correct, but there is no way of knowing whether it was before or after he was with Jason Edwards.'

'But it's possible that this second man inflicted these injuries on Patrick O'Donnell.' Eileen Murphy clicked on the remote and an image of Paddy's bruised and swollen face appeared on the screen.

Lizzie gasped. It was suddenly hot. Her heart was racing, the room began to spin. It was the face that had been tormenting her most nights.

'Yes, it's possible.'

'Then this is the man the police should be looking for as my client has denied inflicting any of these injuries.'

*

Lizzie was grateful for the short recess after having listened to a long-winded Matthew Cranston finally rest the prosecution's case. The tightness in her chest and reflux was unbearable. She needed some air. The image of Paddy's face shook her to her core. She saw it everywhere. As she stood in the parking lot it dawned on her, the face in her nightmare was real – a memory, distorted, fragmented, but a memory just the same. She was certain of it. The taste of acid in her mouth was foul. She dug through her bag and found a packet of Tums and made her way back to the courtroom.

*

Eileen Murphy approached the jury and smiled. 'You must all be exhausted from listening to the testimony and evidence presented by the prosecution over the last two days.' The jurors' heads bobbed in agreement like nodding toys. 'The defense calls Jason Edwards to the stand.' Jason Edwards stood in the dock, wearing an ill-fitting dark suit and tie, and looking more emaciated than at his bail hearing. He raised his right hand and was sworn in. With the forensic evidence tying him to Paddy's death, Lizzie was surprised that the defense attorney would even put him on the stand.

'Mr. Edwards. You said in your statement to the police that Patrick O'Donnell got into a dark car, maybe a Buick, driven by an older man and left the arcade and that was the last you saw of him.'

'Yes…that's right.'

'And at the time were you able to identify the older man?'

'No, ma'am. I wasn't.'

'And can you identify him now?'

'Yes, he's here in the courtroom.'

'Can you point him out?'

The jury members' eyes flickered over the silent courtroom until he pointed towards Maura and Father Larkin.

'It's him, the priest, Father Larkin. When he took the stand yesterday, I recognized him. He'd been in the arcade parking lot before, the last time I saw Paddy, and he took him after. I didn't know he was a priest.'

A collective gasp filled the courtroom, all eyes on the priest. Lizzie looked at her mother, her hand across her mouth, stunned in disbelief.

'No, that can't be,' Ma whispered and turned to face Father Larkin.

'It's okay, Maura,' he said taking her hand. 'I can explain.'

Maura pulled her hand away and turned to look at Lizzie as Judge Baxter banged his gavel trying to restore some sort of order to the courtroom. 'This case will be adjourned until after the Thanksgiving holiday. I'd like to see both attorneys in my chambers.' The judge rose and left the courtroom, a sense of unreality palpable among the gallery, the enormity of Jason Edwards' revelation having not yet sunk in.

Father Larkin put his arm around Maura's shoulder and ushered her out of the courtroom, his head bowed avoiding eye contact with the gallery. A stunned Lizzie sat frozen in her seat. Could this be?

'Talk about drama,' Tina said, sitting down next to Lizzie. 'Looks like you were right.'

'I can't believe my mother just walked out with him.' She stumbled on the steps and Tina caught her.

'Are you okay?'

'Yeah, just got something I need to do.'

'Thanks for arranging things with Cindy and Ted. They've been very cooperative and put me in touch with a couple of other people.'

'Good. Let me know when the story's ready.' Her hands still shaking, she fumbled for her keys and headed to the parking lot.

Chapter 44

The house was in darkness when she pulled into the driveway. It was late, too late to be stopping by Tommy's, but her rage was gnawing away at her. Ruminating over everything for hours since the judge called for a recess had only fueled her rage and she needed answers. She rang the doorbell, waited, then pressed the bell four times in quick succession and stepped back to see if any lights came on. Nothing. She banged on the lion shaped iron door knocker and held her finger on the doorbell until the hall light came on.

'What the hell, Lizzie?' Tommy rubbed his eyes.

'Paddy was there with us that night, wasn't he?' Her eyes wide and heart pounding, she knew she probably looked crazed.

'You woke me up for this? Jesus Christ, have you been drinking again?' He shook his head in disbelief. 'This has really got to you. I told you not to go to the trial.'

'I know you're lying to me. All this time, my nightmares, seeing Paddy's swollen, bruised face…'

'I don't know what you're talking about.'

'They showed a photograph of the injuries to Paddy's face at the trial.'

'And?'

'That photograph, it's a memory, not a nightmare. It was the same.' Her heart raced and she felt flushed. The rain had changed over to snow earlier in the day and it was too cold to be standing outside. 'Let me in, I'm not leaving until you tell me the truth.'

Tommy ushered her into the kitchen, his index finger over his mouth a signal for her to be quiet. 'Look, I don't know what you think you remember.' His voice was calm and measured. 'But yeah, Paddy was there.'

'How could you…'

'Wait…he came by to taunt us and left.'

'How did he get those injuries then?

'You don't remember?' He raised his eyebrows and shook his head in disbelief. 'You see, you don't remember anything, Lizzie.' He was gaslighting her, her own brother.

'Go on then, tell me what happened.'

'At dinner that evening, Paddy and dad had a terrible argument and dad whacked him across the face. Told him he was out of control, and he was having no more of it.' Tommy poured himself a glass of water. 'He was a waste of space, Lizzie, causing Ma and Dad so much heartache. I took you out of the house to get us away from a bad situation.'

'And what happened after?'

'I don't know, you and I went to tunnel. He was taking the shortcut to the main road and saw us. Gave us his usual abuse and went on his way.'

'You and Ma have known this all these years and never said anything to the police?' Her pulse was racing. She couldn't believe his nonchalance. 'I just listened to Ma and Father Larkin both give sworn testimony about Paddy's final movements. They both lied under oath.'

'She didn't want dad to get into any more trouble. He had nothing to do with Paddy's death.'

'And neither did Jason Edwards, I suspect.' She stormed out of the kitchen. Tommy followed her and grabbed her arm from behind as she opened the front door.

'Let go of me!' She stared at him and for the first time saw fear in his eyes.

'What are you gonna do?' He let go, his hand shook.

She stood outside the front door, snowflakes fell on to her eyelashes and mouth as she spoke. 'I really don't know.'

*

Tears streamed down her face as she drove along the darkened road back towards the lake, the car's wipers struggling to move the heavy snow as it hit the windshield. She had no idea what she should do. All this time, they had lied to her, to the police. Ma so hell bent on justice for Paddy that she was willing to lie under oath, hell, even the priest was lying. Lizzie changed the channel on the radio looking for some music.

As she came around the bend a deer appeared out of nowhere in her headlights. She slammed on the brakes and the car started to spin on the icy surface. Instinctively trying to steer out of it, she realized too late that this was the opposite of what she should have done. The car gained momentum as it slid, spinning downhill until it took out the wooden guard rails and landed in a ditch. Lizzie's neck snapped back, the seatbelt jerked and caused a sharp pain in her abdomen. She sat stunned for a moment, then undid her seatbelt and opened the door, falling out on the snow-covered ground. Reaching into her pocket for her phone, she dialed 911, laid back on the ground, the pain in her belly growing in intensity.

The sight of blood on her hand from between her legs, spilling on to the snow triggered something in her head, the fragmented memories swirled. She heard his voice like he was right there with her.

*

Paddy said, 'What are you doing out here, you little shit?'. The acrid smell of alcohol from his breath and pores wafted toward her before his face came into view. He struggled to keep his footing as he stumbled closer. Short and stocky, he loomed over her like the Hulk during one of his episodes.

Eyes red and watery, pupils like pinholes. A nasty purplish black swelling extended from his cheekbone to his brow. 'I said, what are you doing out here, runt?' Paddy raised his fist. 'Answer me!' He spat a large wad of blood-stained gob into the snow.

'Leave her alone, Paddy.' Tommy emerged from the backside of Everest holding his shovel. Paddy laughed, unzipped his jeans, and sprayed a fountain of dark yellow piss across them like a fire hose, steam rising as it hit the snow. The stench of his urine on her clothes was overpowering.

'What big man, are you her protector now? Let's see what you've got Tommy c'mon bring it on.' He stumbled backward and his red Bic lighter fell deep into the tunnel. 'Look what you made me do.' Paddy grabbed Lizzie's hair and dragged her toward the tunnel, pushing her down on to all fours. 'Go get it, Lizzie,' he said.

She jumped three feet down into the snow bunker foyer, then slid into the tunnel, chest heaving and icy tears streaming down her face, her hand searched around in the darkness for the lighter. Heart racing, shallow breaths, it was suffocating. A warm stream came through her snowsuit as she lay there sobbing. There was a tug, her legs being dragged out of the tunnel. It was Tommy pulling her up by the armpits.

'Deep breaths, Lizzie, slow, deep breaths. You're okay,' Tommy said. He climbed out of the bunker and stood atop Everest, eye to eye with Paddy. Though four years younger, he matched Paddy in height. Lifting the shovel, he swung it toward Paddy's face, the blade gashing his already bruised cheekbone, sending a shower of blood across the snow. Paddy grabbed his face but was too unstable to strike back. 'You prick. If you want that lighter, go get it yourself. Or are you too much of a sissy that you gotta send your eight-year-old sister?' Tommy said.

'Fuck off Tommy. I was digging tunnels long before you little shits.' Paddy jumped down into the bunker and dropped down on his belly moving combat style toward the back of the tunnel until he was out of sight.

Before she had time to climb up and out of the bunker, Lizzie's legs buckled as the snow tumbled down all around her. She heard a muffled cry from deep within the tunnel, as the summit of Everest collapsed on them. Then silence. Upright but entombed in snow, she inhaled icy droplets that settled in her chest until there was no air left, just freezing cold. As she drifted in and out of consciousness, she could hear a voice calling her name and the sound of a rodent-like scratching. The scratching became louder and closer until she let out a faint cough. Tommy had cleared the snow from her face and was digging frantically to release the rest of her body. Lifting her from the snow, he slid down the snowbank with her on his back. An icy chill came over her head, her hat had disappeared. With her chin resting on his shoulder her body began to shiver. Tommy's voice soothed her.

'It's okay Lizzie, Paddy can't hurt us anymore.'

*

She recognized the voice that soothed her, but it was no longer Tommy's.

'You're gonna be okay, Lizzie. The ambulance is here.' Joe took off his coat, covered her and sat down next to her. 'Stay with me, Lizzie. You're gonna be okay,' he repeated, his voice cracked.

'Joe, I remember what happened.' She said through the mask being put over her face. She winced, a sharp pain in her belly, but too weak to cry out as they lifted her on to the stretcher into the ambulance.

Chapter 45

The familiar pale green walls of the hospital were the first thing Lizzie noticed when she woke disoriented, the side effect of the sedative she had been given after delivery. As the room came into focus, she saw Joe asleep in a chair in the corner.

'I want my daughter,' she said in a quiet voice and pressed the call button.

A nurse poked her head around the door. 'Ah, you're awake, Miss O'Donnell.'

'Where's my baby? Where's Grace? I want to see her now.'

Joe sat up, bleary eyed. It had been a long night in the chair. 'Are you sure you're up to it, Lizzie, there's no hurry? You need to rest. The nurses have her.'

'I need to see her now.' Lizzie cried, her breasts tingled.

'I'll get her for you.' The nurse smiled and left the room.

'I left a message for your mother and Tommy,' Joe said. 'They should be here soon.'

'I don't want to see anyone. I just want to be alone with Grace.'

The nurse came back into the room holding a tiny pink swaddled bundle and placed it gently into Lizzie's arms.

'Here's your Grace.' She sat down next to Lizzie and poured her a glass of water.

'She's so tiny, so perfect.' Lizzie held her close to her chest. Deep primal groans, her grief, filled the room. The nurse sat next to her stroking her shoulder, comforting her until the sobbing subsided. 'This was my fault.' Lizzie said between sobs.

'It most certainly was not your fault. It was the accident, you lost so much blood. She was just too tiny.'

'I didn't want her enough.'

'Nonsense, that's grief talking.' The nurse shook her head looking at the bundle. 'There's something we should talk about before your family arrives. I know this may sound strange to you, but we have a specialist photographer here at the hospital who can take photos of you and Grace if you'd like. Many parents find it helpful to hold on to the memory.'

Lizzie looked over at Joe. 'Yes, I'd like that, but I don't want my family here for it. Is the photographer here now?'

'She is. I'll make the arrangements.'

*

The commotion in the hallway made it impossible for Lizzie to rest. Her mother's voice bellowed. Lizzie heard the whole exchange.

'But I'm her mother,' Maura shouted. 'I want to see her.'

'I'm afraid you're going to have to be patient. She's not ready to see you.' Joe's attempt at diplomacy a complete failure. 'She only wants to see Hannah.'

'Hannah? Why Hannah?' Maura said.

'I'll stay with her, Ma,' Hannah said. 'You go back with Tommy and help him with the turkey.'

'Some Thanksgiving this is turning out to be,' Maura said as her voice trailed away.

Lizzie managed a smile amidst her tears as Hannah drew near her bedside, her daughter still in her arms.

'I can't let her go yet,' Lizzie sobbed.

'You don't have to.' Hannah climbed into the bed next to Lizzie, stroked her hair and began to sing softly, a lullaby.

Chapter 46

Lizzie crunched along the freshly shoveled path, holding on to Hannah for support. When they reached the front door, she grabbed the railing with one hand while holding her abdomen with the other, the scar still fresh in more ways than one, while Hannah searched for the key. In the days following Grace's death she thought the ache of her grief would be permanent. Her whole body burdened like she was carrying around one of those weighted anxiety blankets.

Hannah unlocked the door and they entered. The flames from the fireplace made the room glow. 'Tommy came by earlier and got the fire going. I changed your bed and stocked the fridge.' Hannah waited for a reply from Lizzie, but she just stared out the window at the lake. 'There are some Thanksgiving leftovers in there too. I know you like turkey.'

'It all looks so peaceful when it's white.' Lizzie turned towards Hannah. Her face was sallow, and posture hunched over like she was in pain. 'Thanks for everything.'

'I'm not sure about you being here on your own. Are you sure you won't reconsider and come stay with us?'

'I'm fine. I need to be alone and rest.' She hesitated, then continued. 'But tell Tommy to come by tomorrow morning,

I need to talk to him.'

'Sure, don't hesitate to call me if you need anything.'

Hannah had been so supportive; it didn't sit comfortably with her that she was about to turn Hannah's world upside down.

*

Lizzie slipped on her flannel pajamas and bathrobe, wrapping herself in a fleece blanket on the sofa and gazed at the fire. The shower had done her good, she had been unprepared for the postpartum mess, adding insult to injury. She looked at her phone. Four missed calls from Tina Chandler. She couldn't deal with her yet; it was Tommy who was on her mind. Between the waves of grief that swamped her, he was all she could think about. How could he have lied to her all these years? All this time standing by, allowing her mother to blame her. He owed her an explanation. Though it was true he had saved her, his account of events had a colossal omission – he had left his dead brother behind, crushed under the weight of the collapsed tunnel. Not only had he left him behind, but he also didn't tell anyone that Paddy was dead. He let his parents agonize over Paddy's whereabouts until his body was found. What kind of person did that?

She opened the fridge, pulled out the foil wrapped parcel and Tupperware boxes and placed two slices of white bread on a plate. Opening the jar of mayonnaise, she dipped the knife in and spread a large dollop, then placed the roasted turkey breast on top. The aroma of stuffing warming in the microwave filled the kitchen, sausage, apple, onion, and raisins. She scooped it on the sandwich, then cut it in half and took a bite. Other than the sandwich, there wasn't much to feel thankful for. Sitting at the counter she looked out at the fresh white snow. Pure, clean. She wanted to be cleansed, rid of the sordid mess in her life, a mess not of her making. The O'Donnell mess that she had tried to escape. But most of all, she wanted Grace back, her whole body ached for her.

*

From the window Lizzie watched Tommy take a long drag from his cigarette and flick the butt into the snow. Before he had a chance to knock, she opened the door.

'You wanna pick that up?' She was doing her utmost to be calm but wanted him to know she was no pushover.

He handed her the coffee cup and paper bag before bending down. 'Hannah said you wanted to see me. I'm so sorry.'

'Sorry about what exactly?'

'About the baby, of course.'

'But not about lying to me?'

'I thought we cleared that up the night you came by?'

'Thing is, Tom. At the worst moment of my life, lying in the snow, my baby dying inside me, it all came flooding back. Everything, like I was there again.' She went on and recounted in detail what happened the night of the snowfall, watching the blood drain from Tommy's astonished face. 'How could you, all these years…?'

'I…I don't know what to say.' Tommy sat down on the sofa, his head in hands. 'I don't want lies to run my life anymore. That night, I saw how Paddy turned on you, how abusive he was…' He spoke haltingly. 'I thought he would start to take it out on you like he had on me for years.'

'What are you saying?' She stared at Tommy's sullen face, his eyes cast down. 'You mean you were…'

'He handed me over like fresh meat to that priest.' Tommy wiped his face with his sleeve. 'Or do you not want to believe me? He was like his acolyte.'

'Why didn't you tell anyone?'

'Father Larkin was our parents' close friend. They trusted him, had him stay with us when they went out. And Paddy said I would be sent away if I told. He took a deep breath in and exhaled. 'I just wanted to forget. If I didn't say anything, it never happened.' His voice cracking, he looked up at Lizzie. 'And it didn't matter anymore. Paddy was dead. I thought I could move on. But I was wrong.' Tears rolled down his face as he tried to talk through his sobs. 'Ma kept him everywhere.'

'Haunting us.' Lizzie said.

'I thought I was hiding it, but Hannah knew all along something bad had happened to me. Even at the bottom of the bottle I couldn't get rid of the shame.' He sat back on the sofa and took a deep breath. 'I just wanted a normal life. I'd managed that until all this happened with the arrest.'

'I'm sorry this happened to you.' She was sorry for him; how difficult it must have been. 'Even more sorry that you carried it all these years.' She held his hand. 'But why didn't you tell Ma and Dad that Paddy was buried under the collapsed tunnel?'

'I was focused on you, getting you out. I knew he was probably already dead, suffocated, there was nothing I could do for him. He got what he deserved.' His hands clenched, he looked right through her. 'As the days went on it became more and more difficult. Ma would have blamed me. You know Ma, her golden boy could do no wrong. She wouldn't have believed me if I'd told her what had happened, she was always making excuses for him, protecting him.'

'And then you protected yourself at my expense.' She could feel the vibration of her voice shouting, anger flooding back in. 'I got the blame.'

'I was only twelve, Lizzie. If I'd known what was going

to happen to Ma, to our family, I would have told the truth.'

'But now you're thirty-four and still you didn't come forward. You were happy for an innocent man to be tried for a murder that never happened.'

'I was afraid.'

'Afraid? More like worried about your reputation. You and Ma really aren't that different.'

'That's not it. Really, Lizzie. I didn't want people to see me as a victim, my children. I worked hard to build a good life, a life I was proud of.'

Lizzie wanted to believe that deep in his heart, Tommy was a different man. She was torn.

'What are you gonna do?'

'I don't know.' She rubbed her forehead. It was exhausting. 'I think you should go. I need to rest.'

*

It was dark when she woke from a long undisturbed sleep. For the first time in months, Paddy was gone. She stoked the embers on the fire and added a new log, then picked up her phone and dialed.

'Joe, can you and Pete Kominsky come over first thing in the morning? I want to make a statement.'

# The Denton Times

Keeping the community informed with independent local reporting

CHARGES DROPPED, COLD CASE COLLAPSES

By Tina Chandler
3 December 2014

Denton, MA. – In an unexpected twist of events, Jason Edwards walked free from Superior Court on Tuesday as all charges against him were dropped following dramatic testimony from the sister of the deceased, Patrick O'Donnell.

Mary-Elizabeth O'Donnell, (age 30), was only eight years old when her brother went missing. She testified that on the night of the Storm of the Century, she had been tunnelling at the end of their road (the site where the body was discovered) with her brother, Thomas. Thomas had returned to the family home to fetch a flashlight when Patrick turned up, drunk and high, his face bruised. He lurched toward her and cut his face on her shovel, dropping his lighter down into the tunnel. When he crawled into the tunnel to try to retrieve the lighter, the tunnel collapsed, crushing him, and killing him almost instantly.

Miss O'Donnell was also buried in the snow and rescued by her brother Thomas upon his return, unaware that Patrick had also been buried. Miss O'Donnell had spent a week in the hospital following the accident and never regained her memory of the traumatic events. Recent focus on the case and a tragic car accident that resulted in the loss of her unborn child, triggered her memories of the fateful night. States Attorney, Matthew Cranston, praised Miss O'Donnell for coming forward with the truth, averting a potential miscarriage of justice.

Eileen Murphy, attorney for the defendant, expressed her client's relief that there was no case to answer. 'Mr. Edwards' life has been ruined by what turned out to be a tragic accident. He has lost his job, reputation and was wrongly incarcerated. We will be seeking compensation from the court.'

The O'Donnell family was not available for comment.

Chapter 47

Lizzie let herself into her mother's house and called out to no response. Since the collapse of the trial two weeks earlier and Father Larkin's subsequent arrest, Maura had gone underground, unable to show her face in town. The town, traumatized by the revelations, was divided. It had shocked the Newham community to its core. The old guard had become very vocal, determined to see order restored, refusing to believe that a man of the cloth who had been at the heart of their community for over thirty years could have committed such heinous crimes. But DNA doesn't lie. The cat was out of the bag. They resented being back in the spotlight for all the wrong reasons. A sexual abuse scandal wasn't what they wanted the good name of Newham to be forever associated with. They didn't want to be another Columbine or Sandy Hook, with a Wikipedia page a permanent reminder of tragedy.

A more skeptical younger generation demonstrated support for the victims: questioning how Father Larkin could have gotten away with it for so many years. People had to have had their suspicions. He had made himself out to be a trusted family friend to so many, and parents sent their children to him for guidance. He knew their secrets.

Lizzie had considered leaving without saying goodbye, like she'd done at eighteen, but she was an adult now and needed closure. The sound of her mother's familiar sobs filled the hall to Paddy's room. Candles lit, she was on her knees praying.

'I hope you're asking for forgiveness.' Lizzie stood over her. 'I'm leaving tomorrow, came to say goodbye.'

'Oh, Lizzie. It's so awful. This town, the church, was my whole world. I'm finished here.'

'Is that all you can think about? Yourself?'

'What do you mean? I've lost everything. I lost my Paddy…and now you're leaving me again like you did before.'

'Well, we have that in common now, we both know what it's like to lose a child.'

'Don't be ridiculous, it's not the same thing. You didn't even know your baby.'

'At least I didn't hand my child over as a sacrificial lamb to a pervert.'

'But I didn't know.' Maura sobbed.

Lizzie's body stiffened.

'You can't tell me you didn't have any inkling of something being wrong. You turned a blind eye, colluded just like a lot of people in this community.'

Maura dropped to her knees. 'You're leaving me again,

just like before. Tommy's not speaking to me. I'll be all alone for Christmas.'

'I know you're miserable, Ma, but it's not my job to entertain you until you die.' So that was her crime – having left her mother. She was done here. 'You'll have to find a way to live with your guilt and shame. If only you had told Paddy the truth.' She walked down the hallway toward the front door.

'Wait, Mary-Elizabeth.' Maura unclasped her necklace and placed it in Lizzie's hand. 'I want you to have this.'

Lizzie stared at the St. Christopher's medal, put it in her pocket and left.

*

Joe carried her suitcases out to his car while she took one final look at the lake, a thin sheet of ice covering it. The cottage would be here waiting for her when she was ready to come back.

'Don't worry, I'll take good care of the place. I really appreciate you renting it to me.'

'You can't go on living with your mother forever.' Lizzie laughed. 'I know you'll look after it. I trust you, Joe.' She couldn't have asked for a better friend. He had been there for her at the worst moment of her life, despite everything.

'You have good instincts, Lizzie.' His face serious. 'You were right about a lot of things.'

'What do you mean?'

'Terry, our desk constable, for one. He was fired this morning. He'd been leaking information to the press.'

'It was that smug look on his face, I knew he was too keen.'

'You oughta be a cop.'

'I'll think about it. Can you pull into Franklin's for a minute?'

'No problem.' He parked the car outside under the flagpole.

Tara jumped up from her desk when she saw Lizzie at the door.

'I just wanted to say goodbye. I'll be back for summer.'

Tara wrapped her arms around Lizzie. 'I don't know how to thank you. Ted's doing so well now, he's finally found his voice.' Tears streamed down Tara's cheeks as she held the door and waved goodbye.

Joe started the engine and handed Lizzie the paper. 'You might want to read this on the way to the airport. Your friend Tina's done great work.'

The Denton Times

Keeping the community informed with independent local reporting

LOCAL PRIEST CHARGED WITH TEN COUNTS OF HISTORIC SEXUAL ABUSE

By Tina Chandler
18 December 2014

Denton, MA. – The small-town community of Newham was left reeling when Father John Larkin, pastor at Our Lady of Lourdes in Newham for thirty years, appeared in court on Wednesday, charged with ten counts of historic sexual abuse dating from 1988.

Among his victims were Patrick O'Donnell, who died in 1993 at age 16 and Dylan Jones (39), who took his own life earlier this year. Father Larkin is accused of molesting altar boys as part of 'religious training' and during spiritual counselling sessions. Larkin spent years building trusting relationships with his victims and their families. According to one of his surviving victims, Ted Franklin, Larkin would ply them with drugs and alcohol before sexually assaulting them. 'He told me this was what God wanted for me.'

Larkin, age 80, wore an orange prison jumpsuit and handcuffed, spoke only briefly to enter a not guilty plea. A request for bail was denied by Judge William H. Baxter. He will remain on remand until the pre-trial hearing scheduled for 25 January 2015.

Resident State Trooper, Pete Kominsky, has appealed to members of the public who may have further information regarding this case to contact them.

Father Gerard Dunn, spokesperson for the diocese, offered prayers for the victims and the diocese's full cooperation with the investigation.

The departure lounge was heaving with Christmas travelers. Lizzie found a seat and took the newspaper from her bag. The truth was all she had wanted, they owed that much to his deceased victims - Paddy and Dylan. She pulled her vibrating phone from her coat pocket.

'You didn't say goodbye,' Hannah said.

Lizzie could hear the distress in her voice.

'I just couldn't. Tell the girls I'll see them in the summer.'

'Tommy told me the whole truth… what you did for him. I'm so sorry, Lizzie. Thank you for sparing him, for giving us a new life.'

'Tell him, we're even,' her voice was cracked. 'Gotta go, we're boarding.' She didn't want Hannah to hear her distress.

WINTER 2014

Chapter 48

The view from the officers' area on A deck was breathtaking. Her arm outstretched, she looked up and traced the five stars of the Southern Cross dominating the night sky and exhaled. She had forgotten how relentless the seven-day work week could be and was relieved when the schedule showed her working the day shift on New Year's Eve.

She'd found a last-minute cruise contract. Someone had pulled out. No questions asked. They were just relieved to find an experienced cruise director. A one-hundred and sixty-day in-depth Southern Hemisphere cruise was not an opportunity to be missed and she needed to get away, find her sea legs again. She knew grief was like a monster. That it might sneak up on her when she least expected it. A smell. The sound of a baby crying. But grief wasn't going to ruin her, eat her alive and spit her out like an empty shell as it had done to her mother. And she didn't want to be one of those people who stayed even though they should go. Not belonging anywhere could be liberating.

She stirred the ice in the tumbler with her finger and took a sip. Pulling the photo from her blazer pocket, she stared at it. The gift of Grace. Her daughter had restored her memory. How one so little, having never taken a breath, could have had such an impact. If ever a life had had meaning, Grace's had. Grief and gratitude could coexist. She knew she would go to the place of - if only, of regret, of what might have been but never was. But her life wasn't going to stop. The grief wasn't going to shrink. She needed to grow her life around it while never forgetting the subtle sweet scent of her newborn daughter's head.

She took another sip tasting the sweet warmth in her mouth and throat as she swallowed. Her phone vibrated. A message from Tina.

Hope you're okay. Just wanted to wish you a Happy New Year, new beginning. Have been headhunted by the Boston Globe. Who'd have thought it? Thank you. T x

The sound of thumping music and drunken revelers singing in the staff bar filled the air as the door opened.

'Another drink, Liz?' he asked.

She looked at her empty glass. 'No, I'm good, thanks.'

Acknowledgements

I wrote the first line of *After The Snowfall* in the autumn of 2016 when I enrolled on a short story writing course at Goldsmith's taught by Giovanna Iozzi. Thank you, Giovanna, for introducing me to the world of fiction writing and whetting my appetite to learn more. A huge thank you to my friend Rachel Dobson who gave me the push I needed to join Giovanna's course!

I owe particular thanks to my Faber Academy novel writing tutor, Shelley Weiner, and to my Faber writing group. Thank you Alexandra, Barbs, Geraldine, Helen, Jenny, Kathryn, Michelle, Naomi, Sophia and Tara for your encouragement and continued support. Thank you to Sarah Lawton for editing advice.

At a low point during the pandemic, Neil and Jenny Bailey walked into my life and offered to read my manuscript. Your enthusiasm for my story took me by surprise and I am deeply grateful to you for nudging me along and guiding me through the publishing process.

I am grateful to my many beta readers on both sides of the Atlantic. Thank you to Maureen Stapleton, Tiffany Flynn, Ann Cummings, Kate Brian, Julia Dodd, Tina Pugh and Jane Walker for reading early drafts. Deepest thanks to my

American based readers, Tina Allegrezza, Ellie Campbell, Sharon Lom, Robin Wolf, Joscelyn Silsby and Mark Caicedo. You have all given me the most incredible support, feedback and encouragement.

A special thank you to Gillian Burrows who followed the development of this book on our Friday walks in Greenwich Park and painted its beautiful cover illustration.

To my children Jess, Ellie and Ned who are all following their own paths and have encouraged me to follow mine.

Lastly, to Alan for being my trusted first reader and best first husband.

About the Author

Angela Sweeney was raised in New Fairfield, Connecticut but now calls SE London home. *After The Snowfall* is her first novel.

Printed in Great Britain
by Amazon